D0035421

FATAL DIAGNOSIS

"How do you know the war went on
for some time?"

Wharton turned to face Barrett. "A close
examination reveals secondary plant growth
and attempts to repair the damage at Terra
Nova, Mr. Barrett. It was probably destroyed
early in the conflict. In the city of Durbanville, on
the other hand, human remains are visible and
the vegetation apparently had no time to grow
back after the blast. The logical conclusion is
that Durbanville was destroyed shortly
before the wavefront from the
Antares supernova arrived."

"What do you suppose started the war?" Alicia
Delevan asked from her seat opposite Wharton.

Wharton shrugged. "I have no idea, dear lady.
I'm afraid we'll have to go down and
dig through the ruins to find the answer
to that question."

Also by Michael McCollum
Published by Ballantine Books:

A GREATER INFINITY

LIFE PROBE

PROCYON'S PROMISE

ANTARES DAWN

Michael McCollum

A Del Rey Book

BALLANTINE BOOKS • NEW YORK

A Del Rey Book
Published by Ballantine Books

Library of Congress Catalog Card Number: 86-90860

ISBN 0-345-32313-0

Manufactured in the United States of America

First Edition: August 1986

Cover Art by Don Dixon

To Robert, Michael, and Elizabeth

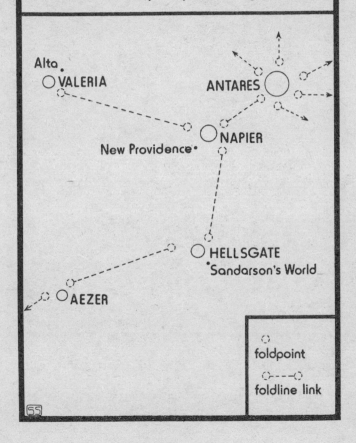

FOLDSPACE CHART

ANTARES CLUSTER/NAPIER SECTOR

(structure of foldspace prior to august, 2512)

Alta •
◯ VALERIA

ANTARES ◯

◯ NAPIER

New Providence •

◯ HELLSGATE
• Sandarson's World

◯ AEZER

◌
foldpoint

◌----◌
foldline link

65

CHAPTER 1

The landing boat fell in a nose-high/belly-down attitude toward the blue-white orb of the planet below. Outside the hull, the first whispery breaths of the hypersonic wind tugged at the boat's wings and control surfaces, causing them to be bathed in a nearly invisible envelope of plasma glow. Inside the hull, the keening of the wind was more sensed than heard, and the first gentle tugs of deceleration were but a foretaste of the pressure soon to come.

Captain Lieutenant Richard Drake, commanding officer of the Altan Space Navy Cruiser *Discovery*, the landing boat's sole passenger, lay strapped into an acceleration couch and gazed out the viewport next to him. Drake was of medium height, with a slender build, black hair, and the faded tan of an outdoorsman who has spent the last eight months in space. He was thirty-five, but looked younger. His hair, which he wore in the close-cropped style of a military spacer, showed a touch of gray around the edges. His eyes were green, and widely spaced above a broad nose and high cheekbones. A whitish scar ran diagonally across his left eyebrow—the result of a collision during a secondary school athletic contest.

Drake's expression was pensive as he gazed at the plasma flow building up on the leading edge of the landing boat's wing. In his pocket was a message flimsy that ordered him to report to the Admiralty Building in the

Altan capital of Homeport without delay. The message was stamped MOST SECRET and signed by First Admiral Dardan himself.

"What have we done to deserve this high honor?" Commander Bela Marston, Drake's second in command, had asked when Drake showed him the order aboard *Discovery*.

"You don't suppose he's found out about those extra field coils we requisitioned the last time we were undergoing maintenance at Felicity Base, do you?" Drake had asked, only half in jest.

Marston had shaken his head. "No, those old coils should have been junked ten years ago."

"That won't save us if Dardan thinks he's going to have to go back to Parliament for a supplemental appropriation this year."

"Good point, Skipper" Marston had said. "Shall I have your yeoman lay out your armor-plated underwear?"

Drake had nodded, laughing. "Not a bad idea. I might need them."

The landing boat touched down at Homeport forty minutes after it encountered the first wisps of Alta's atmosphere. As soon as the craft had parked at the passenger terminal, Drake unstrapped and made his way to the starboard airlock where a nervous crew chief watched intently as a cantilevered loading bridge maneuvered slowly over the boat's glowing wing surfaces.

"What's the matter, Chief?" Drake asked. "Don't you trust the port handlers?"

"Trust them fumble-fingered goons with *Molly* here, Cap'n? No, sir. Not as far as I can spit under triple gravs."

The landing boat had touched down well past local sunset, but the million-candlepower beams of the spaceport's polyarcs had no trouble turning night into day. Drake watched as the loading bridge sealed itself against the hull. When the chief signaled that all was secure, he stepped onto the spidery trusswork and crossed to the terminal beyond.

Inside, he found Commodore Douglas Wilson waiting for him. Over the years, Drake had served three tours of duty under the older man's command. He had long since learned to sense Wilson's every mood. Drake could tell that the Commodore was excited and trying mightily to hide the fact.

"Good to see you again, Richard," Wilson said. "How was your trip?"

"Rough enough, sir. I haven't had to suffer through a maximum-performance reentry since my days at the academy. What's up?"

"The admiral will brief you," Wilson said noncommittally. "Come on, I've a car waiting."

Drake followed as Wilson led the way to an Admiralty limousine. An enlisted driver helped him with his hand luggage, then slid behind the control panel while the two officers arrayed themselves in the backseat for the ten-kilometer drive to the Admiralty.

"How is that young lady of yours?" Wilson asked as the driver maneuvered the car into the heavy traffic headed for Homeport.

"Cynthia? She's fine, sir." Drake gestured at the overnight bag. "I was hoping for a chance to see her this trip."

Some unidentifiable emotion flashed across Wilson's features. "Sorry, Captain, but you won't be on the ground that long."

"Oh?" Drake accompanied his question with raised eyebrows, but the commodore refused to rise to the bait. Instead, he leaned back in his seat and gazed out the window at the shadowy trees zipping past at two hundred kilometers per hour.

They rode in silence for several minutes until the driver gestured toward the eastern sky. "Antares is coming up, sirs!"

Drake turned to follow the driver's pointing finger. Sixty kilometers to the east was the Colgate mountain range. By day, their snowcapped summits and forested slopes provided a view that was a favorite among the purveyors of scenic holocubes. By night, they were a jagged black wall looming against the horizon. As Drake watched, a single star of eye-searing, blue-white brilliance rose from behind the central peak of the mountain range. In that moment, the scenery around them changed dramatically. The scattered clouds, which had reflected the dull orange glow of the Homeport street lights, suddenly blazed forth with a blue-white fire of their own. The dark forest on both sides of the highway became suffused with an internal silver sheen; long, jet-black shadows leaped westward across the highway.

"Is it always like this?" Drake asked, gesturing to the view beyond the limousine window.

Wilson nodded. "Ever since the nova began rising after dark. Before that it wasn't very impressive at all—just a star bright enough to be visible in daylight."

"It still looks that way from orbit," Drake said. He gazed at the passing scene in silence for several seconds. "Who could have predicted that a disaster of such magnitude would be so beautiful?"

The first person to postulate a rational theory of gravitation was Sir Isaac Newton in 1687. His *Philosophiae Naturalis Principia Mathematica* established the theory that gravity is a force; one by which every atom in the universe attracts every other atom. Newton's views on the subject remained essentially unchallenged for nearly two and a half centuries. The reign of Newtonian physics came to an end in 1916. That was the year Albert Einstein published his general theory of relativity. Einstein suggested that gravity is not a force at all, but rather a curvature in the very fabric of the space–time continuum caused by the presence of mass. No one seriously challenged Einstein's view of the universe until Bashir-ben-Sulieman published his definitive treatise on macrogravitational effects in 2078.

Sulieman was an astronomer working out of Farside Observatory, Luna. He had spent his life measuring the precise positions and proper motions of several thousand of the nearer stars. After two decades of work, he reluctantly concluded that Einstein's simple models of gravitational curvature could not adequately explain the placement of the stars in the firmament. The discrepancies were small and exceedingly difficult to measure; but nonetheless, they were real. Try as he would, Sulieman could not explain them away as data scatter or turbulence, as had earlier astronomers working from deep within the terrestrial atmosphere. The longer Sulieman pondered his data, the more convinced he became that, besides being curved locally in the presence of stellar and planetary masses, space is also folded back upon itself in long lines that stretch across thousands of light-years.

The idea that the space–time continuum is multidimensional is an old one. Classical space–time has four dimensions, three spatial and one temporal: up/down, forward/back, right/left, past/future. However, if four-dimensional space–time is curved (as Einstein postulated), then there has to be at least one additional dimension for it to be curved *into*. For general relativity to be correct, space–time must possess at least *five* dimensions. Bashir-ben-Sulieman's contribution was to add yet another (or *sixth*) dimension. He reasoned that if Einstein's *curved space* was indeed curvature in the fifth dimension, then his own *folded space* must be curvature in the sixth. To keep the two separate, he established the convention of "vertically" polarized curved space—indeed, humanity's very concept of vertical depends on gravity, which is the prime manifestation of curved space—and "horizontally" polarized folded space.

He theorized that the origin of the long, intricately woven *foldlines* was the massive black hole that occupies the center of the galaxy. He went further. Noting that the foldlines stream outward along the spiral arms, he wondered aloud whether the lines of folded space might not be sweeping up interstellar matter as they rotated; in effect, acting as the catalyst for star formation. The problem of the relative overabundance of stellar births in the spiral arms was one that had long plagued astronomers and cosmologists.

Sulieman spent the remainder of his life improving on his theories. At the age of ninety two he proved that the sixth-dimensional foldlines are distorted by the fifth-dimensional curvature that is gravity in much the same way that a lens distorts a ray of light. Sulieman demonstrated mathematically that whenever a foldline encounters a star-size mass, it is "focused" into a restricted volume of space. Usually, the effect is so small as to be indetectable. Sometimes, however, the focus is sufficiently sharp that a weakness appears in the fabric of the space–time continuum, and a *foldpoint* is formed.

Twenty years after Sulieman's death, scientists discovered a practical use for foldpoints. They positioned a spaceship within one of the two foldpoints known to exist within the solar system and released copious quantities of energy in a precisely controlled pattern intended to warp space even further. The energy release caused the ship to drop into foldspace, thereby instantaneously transporting it to the next weak point along the foldline. One moment the research ship was floating high above the sun; the next, it was in orbit about Luyten's Star, some 12.5 light-years distant.

There was no holding the human race back after that. The Great Migration began almost immediately. Over the next several centuries, the leakage of population into space became a flood. The pattern of the migration was determined almost entirely by the shape of foldspace. While some stars were found to possess only a single foldpoint, others possessed two, three, or more. The biggest, most massive stars were discovered to be especially fertile ground for foldpoint production. The red supergiant star Antares was the champion throughout human space. Antares had six foldpoints, which made it the linchpin of a network of star systems on the eastern edge of human expansion.

Since the foldlines were aligned with the spiral arm that contains Sol, humanity found it easiest to expand along the axis of the arm. Distances between colonies were figured not by the spatial distance between their respective stars but by the number of foldpoints between them. In order to reach the star next door, it was sometimes necessary to jump, first, to one five hundred light-years distant, then double back.

Early in the Great Migration, survey ships searching the systems of the Antares Cluster (those stars associated with the foldline hub in the Antares system) found an Earthlike planet circling an unnamed G3 spectral class star 490 light-years from Sol. They named the star Napier, after the ship's captain, and its single habitable planet New Providence. Charter companies were formed and vast quantities of resources were poured into the system. New Providence prospered and attained self-sufficiency in less than a hundred years. As the colony matured, it too began to look for stellar systems in which to invest its excess capital and manpower.

The Napier system was close enough to the stellar giant Antares to be affected by the larger star's warpage of foldspace. As a result of the interaction, New Providence was blessed with more than its fair share of foldpoints. In addition to the foldpoint leading to Antares, there were two additional gateways in the system. Beyond both fold-points were systems containing prime real estate in the form of Earth-class worlds.

With the New Providence colony firmly established, these additional systems became the targets for two competing colonization drives. The better funded of these concentrated on the metal-rich Hellsgate system. The smaller colonization effort was left with the job of establishing a colony in the system of an F8 dwarf identified only by its catalog number. The New Providence colonists in this latter system gave their new home world the name of Alta. They named their star Valeria, and quickly devolved to calling it Val.

The Altan colony grew, although more slowly than Sandarson's World in the Hellsgate system. By Alta's bicentennial year (A.D. 2506), it too was beginning to look toward the surrounding stars. However, the Valeria system possessed only a single foldpoint; Altan starships were thus forced to traverse the Napier system to reach either the Antares hub or its sister colony in the Hellsgate system. In 2510, negotiations were begun with the New Providential government to allow Altan ships unimpeded access to the Napier system. Two years later, with both governments largely in agreement as to terms, the question of access became suddenly moot.

For, at 1732 hours, 3 August 2512 (Universal Calendar), the Altan spaceliner *Vagabond Traveller* reported that its instruments could no longer detect the Val–Napier foldpoint at its charted position. Survey ships were immediately dispatched. In a matter of weeks they had confirmed the extent of the catastrophe. For reasons that no one could explain with certainty, the sole foldpoint in the Valeria system had ceased to exist. Alta was cut off from the rest of human space.

The Admiralty Building was a large, unsightly pile of steel and glass left over from the first years after the founding of the Altan colony. Drake and Wilson exited the limousine in front of the Admiralty's main entrance, acknowledged the salutes of the guards on duty, and stepped briskly through armor-glass doors into the spacious lobby beyond. The building had originally been constructed by the central government of Earth for use as an embassy and ambassador's residence. The familiar continental outlines of the Mother of Men were still visible in the marble tilework of the floor.

The guard at the interior desk was less ceremonial than those at the entrance. He sat within an armor-glass cubicle and required both of them to insert their identity disks into a slot in the cubicle wall. A computer in a subbasement consulted its files, concluded that they were who they said, and flashed a green light on the guard's control panel. The guard saluted them as they retrieved their identification. Wilson led Drake to an old elevator-style lift and ordered the car to the topmost floor. They soon found themselves marching down a quiet hall between portraits of previous first admirals. Wilson stopped in front of a heavy door carved from a single slab of onyx wood, knocked, and was rewarded with a muffled order to enter.

First Admiral Dardan was seated at his oversized desk, his attention focused on a small, white-haired man who stood before a lighted holoscreen. As Commodore Wilson entered, the first admiral rose from his desk and moved to greet the newcomers. His sudden movement caused the white-haired lecturer's voice to trail off into exasperated silence.

"Ah, Richard, good of you to come so quickly. May I present Professor Mikhail Planovich, Chairman of the Astronomy Department at Homeport University." Dardan guided Drake by the arm to where the lecturer stood. "The professor was reviewing what is known of the Antares Supernova."

"Pleased to meet you, Professor Planovich," Drake said, shaking hands.

"Likewise, Captain."

Dardan pulled Drake toward a man who was slouched, drink in hand, on the couch opposite the desk. "I believe you know Stan Barrett, the prime minister's troubleshooter."

"Yes, sir. I met Mr. Barrett when I served as Navy liaison to Parliament two years ago. I'm not sure he remembers me, though."

"Of course I remember you, Drake," Barrett said, shaking hands without rising from the couch. "Your last job, I believe, was the five-year forecast for the cost of fleet operations. We really nailed the lid on old Gentleman Jon's coffin that time, didn't we?"

"We were successful, anyway," Drake replied. The 'Gentleman Jon' Barrett had referred to was the Honorable Jonathon Carstairs, leader of the Conservatives, and no friend of Navy appropriations.

Barrett laughed. "Talented and modest, too! I like that, Captain. I think Luis here has picked the right man for the job."

"Save that for later," First Admiral Luis Dardan said. "Find a seat, Captain Drake, and we'll let Professor Planovich finish his talk."

"Yes, sir."

Planovich turned to the holoscreen and pointed to a bright-red star with a speck of blue-white near it. "As I was saying, Admiral, Antares, otherwise known as Alpha Scorpius, is a supergiant star with a mass twenty times that of Valeria and a diameter four hundred times as great. Antares is..." Planovich looked up from his notes and smiled sheepishly. "Antares *was* an M0 stellar class star that possessed a companion of spectral class A3. You can see both stars on the screen. Stars of the M class range from red to red-orange in color owing to their surface temperatures of 2600 to 3500 degrees Kelvin. The name 'Antares' comes from the Greek, meaning 'Rival of Ares.'"

"What's an Ares?" Barrett asked.

"I believe, sir," Professor Planovich said, "that it is a reference to the reddish color of Sol IV, as viewed from Earth."

"I thought Sol IV was named Mars."

"The Greeks called it Ares, after their God of War. Mars is the Roman name. Now, if I may continue, sir..."

"Sorry," Barrett said without sounding the slightest bit sincere.

"Two months ago, the appearance of Antares changed rather dramatically." The holoscreen view changed. In place of the red speck with the blue-white dot beside it, the screen now showed the retina-searing point of brilliance that Drake and Wilson had watched rise over the Colgate peaks less than ten minutes earlier. "The change, of course, is due to the Antares Supernova of twelve decades ago. Since the distance from Antares to Val is

125 light-years, the wavefront is just reaching us. Our analyses are not yet complete, but it appears as though Antares is the largest supernova on record."

"Larger than the Crab Supernova of 1054?" Wilson asked.

"Actually, the Crab exploded in approximately 4000 B.C., Commodore. It was, however, *observed* on Earth by Chinese astronomers on 4 July 1054. It was visible in sunlight for twenty-three days and for two years thereafter at night. And yes, the Antares Supernova is far larger!"

"I stand corrected," Wilson growled.

"I do not make the distinction to be pedantic, sir," Planovich said stiffly. "The speed-of-light delay between explosion and observation is important. Since we know the distance from Val to Antares, and also the precise moment when we first observed the supernova, it is an easy matter to compute the date on which the star actually exploded. That date, it turns out, was 3 August 2512."

"The same day our foldpoint disappeared," the first admiral mused.

"Yes, sir," Planovich said. "The correlation is as exact as we can make it, considering that we are unable to pin down the exact moment of foldpoint failure closer than a sixteen-hour period on that date. We have long suspected that something catastrophic happened on that day, something large enough to disturb our local foldline sufficiently that the Val–Napier foldpoint lost its focus. Obviously, the Antares Supernova was the culprit."

"Then we weren't the only system affected?" Barrett asked.

Planovich turned to face the advisor. The white glow from the holoscreen illuminated half his face, leaving the other half in darkness. "You may rest assured, sir, that we have not been singled out for Divine Wrath. If anything, we've been luckier than some. I greatly fear for the fate of our parent world."

"Why?" the first admiral asked.

"Surely, sir, you must know that New Providence is but fifteen light-years from the supernova."

"So?"

"Even before the explosion, the New Providential poets spoke of 'the baleful glow of the one-eyed warrior, aglimmer on the snowfields of a crisp winter eve.' They were, of course, referring to the brightness with which Antares shines in New Providence's southern hemisphere before the winter solstice." Planovich strode to the window and pulled back the curtains, allowing the silver glow from outside to flood the room. "Can you imagine what it must be like to have *that* shining sixty-four times as bright in the night sky?"

"Are you suggesting that New Providence could have been placed in danger by the supernova?" the first admiral asked.

"Not 'could have been,' sir. *Was!* A supernova throws out all manner of dangerous particles: everything from gamma and X-rays, to high-speed neutrons, protons, and electrons. There will even be a goodly amount of antimatter in the cosmic wind from such an explosion. In all likelihood, when Antares went supernova, it sterilized New Providence and the entire Napier system!"

"And if their foldpoints were disrupted?"

"Then three billion people died, horribly."

"How the hell could something like this happen without warning?" Barrett demanded.

"It didn't," Planovich replied. "Astronomers have long been aware that Antares is a star well into its dotage. The first explorers of the Antares Hub noted that the red-giant's neutrino production rate was way above normal. That indicated that the star's core was well into its iron-enrichment phase. We knew that it was only a matter of time until it ran low on nuclear fuel, collapsed in upon itself, and exploded. Only, where stars are concerned, 'a matter of time' is usually of the order of a few million years. No one expected it to happen quite so soon."

"What should we expect now?" Barrett asked.

"A good question," Planovich responded. "The radiation from the explosion will be considerably diluted after a century of expansion. Alta's atmosphere should have no problem filtering out the harmful particles. There *will* be a measurable rise in the background radiation in space, however; and it may be necessary to equip all exoatmospheric installations with additional radiation shielding."

"What about foldspace?"

Planovich shrugged. "The effect on foldspace is anyone's guess. There are those who believe that our foldpoint might heal itself once the discontinuity of the nova wavefront passes."

"Really?" Dardan asked as he exchanged looks with Barrett and Wilson.

"That is the theory, Admiral. Personally, I have no strong opinions on the subject one way or the other."

"Perhaps you should."

"I beg your pardon."

Dardan took a deep breath and leaned back in his chair. "It may interest you to know, Professor Planovich, that approximately twenty hours ago, one of our sensor stations picked up an object materializing high in the northern hemisphere of this system. That object is very large. From its radiation signature, we have concluded that it is a starship from outside the Valeria system!"

CHAPTER 2

A starship!

Richard Drake blinked twice, while trying to understand the import of the first admiral's revelation. Strictly speaking, the cruisers that formed the nucleus of the Altan Space Navy were all starships. Twelve decades earlier, *Discovery* and her two sisters had been part of the Grand Fleet of Earth. Except for the bad luck of having been on a tour of the eastern colonies when Val's foldpoint disappeared, *Discovery*, *Dagger*, and *Dreadnought* might still have been in the service of Mother Earth. Nor were the three battle cruisers the only starfarers trapped by the Antares Supernova. Two hundred other interstellar craft— freighters, passenger liners, yachts—had been in the system on that fateful day. But a starship without a foldpoint is a contradiction in terms. With no entry into foldspace, such a vessel is going nowhere.

The appearance of a *starship* in the Valerian system had far-reaching implications. It meant the long isolation was finally over, that interstellar trade would soon be resumed. It meant that Altan society, in near stasis for more than a century, would come alive once again under the stimulus of a hundred years of new ideas and inventions from all over human space. It meant that his own *Discovery* would once again be free to fly between stars— perhaps even to Earth itself.

Drake glanced at Professor Planovich. The academic's

face was frozen in surprise. In stark contrast were the cool, studied looks worn by Dardan, Wilson, and Barrett.

After several seconds of silence, Planovich cleared his throat and asked somewhat unsteadily: "Are you sure, Admiral? No mistake?"

"No mistake. Commodore, please brief our guest."

"Yes, sir," Wilson said. He got to his feet and strode over to take Planovich's place at the holoscreen while the professor sat beside Barrett on the couch. Wilson tapped out a code on the screen keypad and the blue-white nova disappeared. A schematic representation of the Valeria system formed in its place. Deep within the cube, a tiny red arrow floated above the golden point of light representing Val. The orbits of the four innermost of Val's twelve planets showed clearly.

"The ship materialized high in the northern hemisphere, roughly 250 million kilometers from Val. The point is close to the classic position for the Val–Napier foldpoint, but is not coincident with it."

"Are you sure?"

"Quite sure, Professor."

"Then the supernova has disturbed the local shape of foldspace!" Planovich said.

"Yes, sir. That was our conclusion as well. If the disturbance is great enough, then the interconnectivity of the foldlines may no longer be what it was. The Napier system and New Providence may no longer be at the other end of our local gateway."

"Are you saying that our jump charts may no longer be valid?"

"It's a distinct possibility, Captain Drake." Wilson turned his attention back to Planovich. "That is why you are here, sir. It was our thought that you scientists might have the means to remap the foldlines for us."

Planovich stared at the holoscreen for long seconds, his expression pensive, his eyes unfocused. After a moment, he nodded. "It may be possible at that! A series of ultraprecise measurements of the gravitational constant around the foldpoint should do it."

"When can you be ready to leave?" Admiral Dardan asked.

"Leave?"

"Yes, sir. Leave—on an expedition to map the gravitational constant."

"Oh, I can't possibly get away until the end of the current semester. As department chairman, I have administrative duties to perform as well as classes to teach."

"We appreciate your problem, Professor Planovich," Barrett said, "but this is a matter of utmost importance to the government."

The white-haired man glanced at Barrett and then at the first admiral. Having spent the last two months studying the Antares Supernova, he recognized irresistible forces when he saw them. He looked wistful and sighed. "When will this expedition begin?"

"Hopefully, within the next seventy hours. The prime minister has already arranged transportation. We have enlisted a number of other specialists, including some of the top people in multidimensional physics."

"Whom have you got?"

"Dr. Nathaniel Gordon has agreed to go."

"You asked that poor excuse for a lab assistant before you asked me? Why, I've never..."

"Never what, Professor?" Barrett asked.

"Forget it. Just send word where and when you want me and I'll be there."

"Excellent."

"If I'm leaving in three days, I had best begin making arrangements."

"A good point, sir," Barrett said, rising to his feet. "My car and driver will take you wherever you need to go. Of course, you realize that news of our visitor from outside is currently classified as a state secret..." The two civilians left the room, leaving the three Navy men alone.

Dardan smiled from his seat behind the desk. "Barrett

and I have been working the same routine on scientists since noon. That was the fifth recitation of the history of the Antares Supernova I've sat through today."

"Barrett seems very good at getting them to do what he wants," Drake said.

"That he is. Thank God we weren't born to be politicians, eh, Captain?"

"Yes, sir."

"Now, for your assignment. Doug, let's get to the classified data, shall we?"

"Very good, Admiral." Wilson called up another starfield on the holoscreen, this one bright with the false colors of an infrared photograph. The nova was not in evidence. The central star was peculiar, however. It possessed a faint tail like a comet. "This is a telescopic view of our visitor taken just ten seconds after its appearance, Richard. The plume you see is the drive flare from the ship's engines."

"It's maneuvering?" Drake asked.

Wilson nodded. "Doppler analysis gives us an acceleration of one-half of a standard gravity."

"Have we plotted its course?"

"It's shaping an orbit directly away from Val."

"*Away* from Val? Where's it going?"

"We think it might be searching for a second foldpoint."

"A survey ship?"

"Could be."

"But surely they must know we have only the one."

"Haven't you been listening, Captain? That explosion"—he jerked his thumb toward the silver glow that was still flooding in through the open curtains—"has messed up the structure of foldspace. It's possible that there has been considerable reshuffling of the foldlines. That's why we are pushing so hard to get our survey expedition launched. No telling how many foldpoints Val currently possesses until we go look."

"Our visitor from outside may know. Has anyone tried to communicate with him yet?" Drake asked.

"We've been trying to establish contact since this time yesterday," the first admiral replied. "So far our visitor has failed to respond to either radio *or* laser. That is the reason I ordered you down from your ship, Captain.

"Your orders are to plot a maximum-performance intercept and rendezvous with the outsider. You are to make contact and get them talking to us. Use your own judgment as to how you manage that feat, but don't get trigger happy!" Dardan reached into his desk and pulled out a sealed pouch. He tossed it on the desk and gestured for Drake to take it. "Your detailed operational orders are in there, along with some preliminary rendezvous data. Don't remove them from the security pouch until you're back onboard *Discovery*."

"Yes, sir. Why all the security?"

The first admiral looked grim. "Premature release of this information could destroy several major industries, Captain Drake, not to mention the effect on the stock market. The prime minister wants to withhold the news until we can find out more about our visitor."

"I understand, sir. What about support?"

"You won't have any. Neither *Dagger* nor *Dreadnought* can be in position to support earlier than three hundred hours from now."

"Understood, sir. I'm on my own. Thank you for your confidence, Admiral."

"Just don't make me regret my choice. One other thing. Stan Barrett will be going along with you as the prime minister's personal representative. Show him the proper respect, but never forget that you are in command of this expedition. Barrett's advice will be just that—advice. You are not bound to take it."

"Mr. Barrett's going, sir?" Drake asked.

"You sound dubious."

"You *did* say maximum performance, didn't you, Admiral?"

"He did!" a voice called from behind Drake. He turned to see Barrett striding across the office. "Don't worry about me, Captain. I may be developing a paunch, but I'm still basically healthy. Pile on all the acceleration you need to complete your mission."

"I will, Mr. Barrett," Drake said. "I just hope you'll be alive at the other end."

The political assistant laughed. "No more than I, Captain. No more than I."

"Now, then," Commodore Wilson said, "you'll both find a car standing by to take you to the spaceport. Your landing boat is refueled and ready for launch, Richard. It's going to be a long stern chase, and the numbers aren't getting any better while we stand around jawing. Don't let us delay you any longer. Good luck."

"Thank you, sir."

Richard Drake lay strapped into the copilot's seat of the landing boat and watched ANS *Discovery* slowly grow in size through the forward windscreen. When the ship had first come into view, it had been a sparkle of light that hovered above the pale-blue crescent of Alta's horizon. As such, it had been indistinguishable from a star. Over several minutes it had grown, first into a toy spacecraft suitable for a young child to clutch in one pudgy hand, then into a finely detailed scale model. Finally, the battle cruiser had swelled until it filled, and then overflowed, Drake's field of view.

The landing boat overtook *Discovery* from below and behind, giving Drake a good look at his ship. The battle cruiser consisted of a torpedolike central cylinder surrounded by a ring structure. The central cylinder housed the ship's mass converter, photon drive, and jump engines—the latter needing only an up-to-date jump program to once more hurl the ship into the interstellar spacelanes. Also within the cylinder were fuel tanks filled with deuterium- and tritium-enriched cryogen, the heavy antimatter projectors that were *Discovery*'s main armament, and the ancillary equipment that provided power to the ship's outer ring.

The surrounding ring was supported off the cylinder by twelve hollow spokes. It contained crew quarters, communications, sensors, secondary weapons pods, cargo spaces, and the hangar bay in which auxiliary craft were housed.

Drake listened to the communications between the landing boat and the cruiser all through the approach. As they drew close, he noticed the actinic light of the ship's attitude jets firing around the periphery of the habitat ring. When in parking orbit, the cruiser was spun about its axis to provide half a standard gravity on the outermost crew deck. The attitude jets were firing to halt the rotation in preparation for taking aboard the landing boat.

Drake was pleased with what he heard on the intercom during the approach—mostly silence punctuated by terse exchanges of information. The complete absence of chatter was evidence of a taut ship and a good crew. He was suffused with pride as he watched hangar doors open directly in front of the hovering boat just as the cruiser's spin came to a halt.

"Landing Boat *Moliere*. Secure your reaction jets!" came the order from *Discovery* approach control.

"Securing," the pilot said as he reached down to throw a large red switch next to his right knee. The message REAC JET SAFE flashed from the control panel.

"Prepare to be winched aboard."

"Hook extended."

Towing a single cable, a torpedo exited the open hatch and jetted the dozen meters to where the landing boat hovered. The torpedo disappeared from view for several seconds, then the approach controller said, "All right, *Moliere*. Stand by to be reeled in!"

With a barely perceptible jolt as the cable took up slack, the landing boat slid smoothly forward. The curved hull of the cruiser and the open maw of the vehicle hatch swelled to fill the windscreen. The boat passed out of Val's direct rays and into shadow. The dark was short-lived, however. As soon as the bow passed into the hangar bay, the windscreen fluoresced with the blue-white glow of a dozen polyarc floodlamps.

There was a bump as the bow contacted the recoil snubber inside the bay, then the boat was pulled completely inside by giant manipulators and lifted to its docking area while a steady stream of orders issued from the bulkhead speaker.

"Close outer doors. Stand by to repressurize."

Drake unstrapped, complimented the pilot on the smoothness of his approach, thanked the copilot for the use of his couch, then levered himself through the hatchway leading from the cockpit to the main cabin. He collected Barrett and his luggage, then pulled himself hand over hand to where the boat's crew chief was waiting for him at the airlock.

"Any complaints about the docking this time, Chief?"

"Not a one, Cap'n. Couldn't have done better myself. Course, I never worry about *Molly* in the hands of our own winch crew."

A muted rush of air sounded beyond the hull. The crew chief studied his readouts, then opened the airlock. A blast of frigid air entered the lock, bringing with it a swirling mass of condensation fog. Drake shivered involuntarily as he grabbed onto a safety line and pulled himself across the hangar bay to a second airlock leading into the interior of the ship. He helped Barrett into the lock then cycled through just as a voice announced, "Prepare to resume spin!"

Bela Marston met him in the corridor just beyond the airlock. The executive officer's gaze went first to Barrett and then to the security pouch chained to Drake's right wrist. "We didn't expect you back so soon, Captain. Productive trip?"

"You might say that," Drake replied. He gazed at his executive officer with his best "official duty" expression.

"How long will it take you to prepare the ship for space, Mr. Marston?"

"For space, sir?"

"That's the order, Mister."

"Well, Captain," the exec said, rubbing his chin. "The auxiliary engine room computer began reporting a hardware error right after you left for the surface. The chief engineer has its guts spread all over the power pod looking for the problem."

"What kind of error?"

"Improper baud-rate setting to the plasma injectors."

"Fatal or precautionary?"

"The error message was precautionary, sir."

"Then tell the chief engineer to button her up and prepare for space. Now, how long until we can launch?"

"An hour, sir."

"Make it forty-five minutes. I'll be in my cabin with Mr. Barrett. Notify me when you're ready to light her fire."

"Aye aye, Captain."

Richard Drake maneuvered through several long gray corridors, past busy crewmen who moved through the zero-gee ship with the ease of long practice. Stanislaw Barrett followed close behind Drake. The political assistant's movements were noticeably more awkward than those of the spacers, yet he managed to keep up without too much difficulty. By the time they had reached the innermost deck in the habitat ring, sufficient spin had been restored to the ship to provide a spin force equivalent to one-tenth standard gee.

"Just enough to keep our feet on the floor while we prepare for departure," Drake explained as he and his guest walked the last few dozen meters to his cabin.

Drake opened his cabin door, stood back, and gestured for Barrett to precede him. Barrett did so and quickly emitted a low whistle.

"Very nice, Captain! I had no idea the Navy did this well for themselves."

Drake wondered momentarily whether the first admiral hadn't committed a tactical error by allowing this minion of the prime minister aboard. Not wishing to affect the size of next year's appropriation, he was quick to explain: "The decor, Mr. Barrett, is traditional . . . and antique. This cabin is the same as it was when Captain Krueger, the last terrestrial commander, turned the ship over to our colonial forces."

Barrett, who had been staring at an oil painting showing a square-rigged warship of a wet navy of the past, turned and said, "Oh, I'm not criticizing, Captain. Just impressed."

Drake gestured for Barrett to take a seat next to his desk *cum* workstation. "Shall we break open our official orders, sir?"

"By all means."

Drake seated himself behind his desk and unlocked the chain that secured the security pouch to his right wrist. Rubbing his wrist where the handcuff had cut into it, he laid the pouch on the desk and then pressed his thumb against the pale-green surface of the pouch's lockplate. The pouch responded with an audible click and split open lengthwise. Inside a small block of glass like a domino reflected the overhead light in a rainbow of holographically induced color. Drake reached for the block, slipping it from beneath the elastic bands that held it in position within the pouch.

He dropped the record tile into the desk reader and engaged the ship's computer. A momentary whine was followed by a beeping signal. Drake responded by keying in his name, serial number, and authorization code. After a momentary delay, the screen cleared and displayed the message: READY FOR SECURITY ACCESS. Drake typed in a twelve-digit string of alphanumerics known only to himself and the Admiralty master computer. The screen blanked once more. After a second's wait, words of glowing amber began to scroll up the screen:

TO: Captain Lieutenant Richard Drake,
   Commanding Officer,
   ANS *Discovery*

FROM: Admiral Luis Dardan
   Admiralty
   Homeport, Alta

DATE: 14 Hermes 2637

SUBJECT: ORDERS

****MOST SECRET*****MOST SECRET****

1.0 At 2137:42.16 12 Hermes 2637, fleet sensor stations Alpha-7134 and Alpha-9364 detected an artifact at Coordinates 3615/ + 2712/250E6.

2.0 Analysis of sighting records by Admiralty leads to following conclusions:

   1) An operative foldpoint exists once again in the Val system, at the above-noted coordinates.

   2) The artifact is a starship from beyond the Val system.

   3) The vessel's subsequent movements suggest that it may be a survey vessel searching for a second foldpoint.

3.0 The target vessel is under its own power. Current course data follows: 3615/ + 8865 true from previously noted position.

4.0 The target vessel has not responded to Admiralty attempts to communicate with it.

5.0 In light of the above, the commanding officer

of ANS *Discovery* is hereby ordered to take the following actions:

1) You will intercept the target vessel as quickly as is practical without endangering your command.

2) You will identify the origin and nature of the target vessel by any reasonable means at your disposal.

3) You will communicate such information as you may learn to the Admiralty on a priority basis.

4) Insofar as such action does not interfere with your other objectives, you will prevent the subject vessel from leaving the Val system via foldspace transition.

6.0 You will exercise a degree of caution regarding the safety of your command that is consistent with the successful completion of your mission.

7.0 You will seek the advice of the prime minister's personal representative regarding the subject vessel if and when circumstances warrant.

8.0 Good luck, *Discovery*!

[signed]
Luis Emilio Dardan
First Admiral

ATTACHMENTS

****MOST SECRET*****MOST SECRET****

Drake glanced up at Barrett. "Are you aware of the contents of my orders, sir?"

Barret nodded.

"Including paragraph seven?"

This time the political assistant laughed. "Especially paragraph seven, Captain. I wanted a more definite statement regarding my presence aboard your ship, but the admiral refused to give it to me. He even stood up to the prime minister. Still, I hope you will seek my advice 'when circumstances warrant.'"

"So long as it is understood that there can only be one captain onboard ship, Mr. Barrett."

"You'll hear no argument from me."

"Excellent," Drake said. "Shall we get to work?"

Drake called up the attached technical data and began to review it. There were several telescopic views of the intruder similar to the one he had seen in the first admiral's office. He keyed through a series of course projections based on a variety of optimistic/pessimistic assumptions. A few quick calculations by the ship's computer convinced him that rendezvousing with their visitor would be no easy task.

"Why not?" Barrett asked after Drake made the comment to him.

"The starship has been accelerating directly away from Val for the past twenty-two hours, Mr. Barrett. Worse, it has a quarter-billion kilometer head start. At the moment, its velocity has reached 388 kilometers per second, and will be a lot faster when we finally catch it. We're going to have to make up for lost distance and lost time, exceed its maximum velocity by a considerable margin, turn end for end, and then decelerate to match velocities once we've caught the damned thing. Then, assuming it will maintain its acceleration, we'll have to continue boosting to keep from falling behind again. And we'll have to do all this while keeping a large enough fuel reserve to get us home afterwards!

"Now, this particular problem revolves around only two parameters: *Discovery*'s total delta velocity capability and the tolerance of my crew for sustained acceleration.

The two are mutually exclusive, naturally—too little acceleration and we'll run our tanks dry before we catch the starship; too much and we're liable to kill someone."

"And the answer, Captain?" Barrett asked.

"It's going to be close," Drake said, punching additional data into his workstation. "I make it thirty-three hours to turnover; then another twenty-one hours to decelerate for rendezvous. Call it fifty-four hours at three and a half gravities. That will get us to the same point in space as the starship at approximately the same velocity, and leave us with perhaps a dozen hours of stationkeeping reserve before we have to turn for home."

"*Three and a half* gravities for *fifty-four* hours?"

"You said you could take it," Drake reminded him.

"That I did," Barrett agreed, then looked sheepish. "Oh, my aching back!"

CHAPTER 3

There is a common belief among the uninitiated that a spaceship's control room is located somewhere near the ship's bow. In truth, that is almost never the case. *Discovery*, with its cylinder-and-ring design, was particularly unsuited to such an arrangement. Like most warships, the cruiser's control room was located in the safest place the designers could find to put it—at the midpoint of the inside curve of the habitat ring.

Actually, *Discovery* possessed three control rooms, each capable of flying or fighting the ship alone should the need arise. For normal operations, however, there was a traditional division of labor among the three nerve centers. Control Room No. 1 performed the usual functions of a spacecraft's bridge: flight control, communications, and astrogation; No. 2 was devoted to control of weapons and sensors; No. 3 was used by the engineering department to monitor the overall health of the ship and its power-and-drive system.

"Begin your countdown, Mr. Cristobal," Drake ordered as he buckled himself into his command chair in Control Room No. 1. It had been less than an hour since he'd arrived back aboard *Discovery* and five minutes since he'd strapped Stan Barrett into one of the cruiser's acceleration tanks two decks aft. The ship's rotation had been stopped, and the interior of the habitat ring was once again in zero gee.

Drake listened to the quick reports from all over the ship as he waited for the red numerals on the screen in front of him to count down to zero. The voice of Lieutenant Argos Cristobal, *Discovery*'s astrogator, was clear and steady as he called off the seconds remaining: "Ten, nine, eight, seven, six, five, four, three, two, one... Boost!"

An auxiliary screen lit up as a camera mounted on the habitat ring caught the glow that suddenly erupted from the aft end of *Discovery*'s central spire. Theoretically, the cruiser's photon drive should have been invisible in the vacuum of space. However, waste plasma from the ship's mass converters was dumped into the exhaust, causing the drive plume to glow with purple-white brilliance as *Discovery* broke from her parking orbit and headed out into the blackness of deep space.

Drake watched his instruments for several minutes, then, assured that his ship was healthy, keyed for Barrett's cabin. "How are you doing?"

The political assistant lay relaxed in a device that looked like a cross between a waterbed and a bathtub. He grinned up at the camera pickup. "No problem, Captain. This isn't as bad as I thought it would be."

Drake laughed. "That's because we're still at one gravity. We'll maintain this boost until we've cleared the inner traffic zone. You can get up if you like, but don't leave your cabin. Be sure to get back into the tank the moment you hear the first acceleration warning."

"Will do."

An hour later, the ship was accelerating along a normal departure orbit at one standard gravity while crewmen rushed to convert compartments from the "out is down" orientation of parking orbit to the "aft is down" of powered boost. The only compartments that did not need conversion were the control rooms, which were gimbaled to keep the deck horizontal, and the larger compartments like the hangar bay and the engine room, which had been designed to allow access regardless of the direction of "down."

"Traffic Central reports us clear of the inner zone and free to navigate, Captain," Lieutenant Cristobal reported.

"About time! Prepare to turn the ship, Mr. Cristobal."

"Yes, sir. What vector?"

"You'll find the flight plan already in the computer."

Cristobal called up the course setting on his screen and frowned. "I make it due north at three point five gravs, Captain."

"That is correct, Astrogator. Lock it in."

"Aye aye, sir."

Drake had heard the unspoken question in the astrogator's voice at discovering that they were turning ninety degrees to Val's ecliptic. He smiled as he thought of the surprise yet to come. He reached out and keyed for the communicator on duty. "I will be addressing the crew in five minutes, Mr. Slater. Make the announcement."

"Yes, sir." A few seconds later, Communications Lieutenant Karl Slater's voice issued from overhead speakers throughout the ship. "Attention, all hands. The captain will have an announcement in five minutes. Stand by."

The ship began its powered turn, causing Coriolus forces to do strange things to Drake's sense of balance. Two minutes later, Cristobal reported: "Maneuver completed, Captain. Ready for acceleration."

"Very good, Mr. Cristobal. Communications, get me the chief engineer."

"Chief engineer here, sir."

"Heard you had a balky computer, Gavin."

"Nothing we can't handle, Captain."

"Think you can squeeze three and a half gees out of the old girl?"

"No problem."

"Then stand by for sustained acceleration immediately following my general announcement."

"Engineering will be ready, Captain."

Drake quickly ran down the roster of departments,

checking with each department head regarding his status. One worrisome area was manpower. The order to space had come so quickly that there had been no time to recall the personnel on shore leave; *Discovery* was heading out on the most important mission of its long history with 12 percent of its billets empty.

At the end of five minutes, Drake keyed for the communications officer once again. "Put me on the master circuit, Lieutenant."

"Ready, Captain. Press channel six."

Drake gathered his thoughts, wet dry lips, then keyed the circuit.

"Your attention, please! This is the captain speaking. I know that all of you are wondering why we left orbit in such a hurry. We did so because we have been assigned a mission unlike any we have ever had before. Twenty-four hours ago, a starship from outside was detected materializing high in Val's northern hemisphere. We have orders to intercept it!"

Drake paused to let his listeners adjust to the news. After a dozen seconds, he resumed his announcement, reading from the Admiralty's orders regarding their mission, explaining the ramifications of having the foldpoint open again, and concluding with: "We've been training for something like this for a long time. While we are engaged in this mission, I expect each of you to do his job. Now then, prepare for sustained and heavy acceleration. You have two minutes.

"Good luck to you all!"

By any standard, the Valeria system's century and a quarter of isolation had been little more than a giant inconvenience. True suffering—of the kind experienced during a planetwide plague, famine, or nuclear war—had been virtually nonexistent. For Alta, at least, the timing of the Antares Supernova could hardly have been better.

Throughout history, the cost of interstellar shipping had always been a spur to the rapid development of home-grown industry. And so it had been with the Altan colony. By A.D. 2512, Alta had nearly weaned itself from its parent culture on New Providence. The population had grown from a few million hardy pioneers to more than a billion. In many ways, a billion people is the optimum number for a star system—too few mouths to strain the available resources, yet more than enough hands to maintain a modern, technologically advanced society.

With two asteroid belts in the system, raw materials were never a serious problem. Indeed, the only thing that outstripped the production of asteroidal iron was the production of foodstuffs on the plains of Alta's eastern continent. East Continent was blessed with an ideal climate for terrestrial food grains. For fifty years, Alta's breadbasket had produced an unending series of bumper crops.

Even though the loss of the foldpoint had relatively little impact on the colony's physical well-being, the same could not be said for the psychological impact. News of the foldpoint's failure spread like a tidal wave breaking over a low peninsula. Riots broke out within hours. By the end of the third day, the number of suicides had exceeded ten thousand. Over the next fifteen months (the length of time it took Alta to make one circuit around Val) more than a million people were treated for varying degrees of depression.

Not surprisingly, the hardest hit by the news of the failure were those non-Altans trapped in the Valeria system. These included the crews of various out-system starships and Earth's ambassador to Alta. The terrestrial ambassador at the time was a man named Granville Whitlow. Upon his arrival in Homeport in 2510, Whitlow had been the youngest ambassador in human space. His professional plan had called for a two-year stint among the colonists, then home for appointment to more important duties.

Like many of the trapped foreigners (and not a few Altans), Whitlow clung to the hope that the disruption would prove temporary. He passed the time waiting for the foldpoint to heal itself by pretending that nothing had changed. He continued his duties, helping stranded tourists with their passports, giving lavish parties for the small Homeport diplomatic corps, and lobbying the Altan prime minister and Parliament concerning matters of interest to the central government.

One such matter was the supply and maintenance of three units of the Grand Fleet trapped in the Valeria system. For a while Whitlow paid for the maintenance and fueling of the battle cruisers by issuing promissory notes against the central government's credit. This arrangement did not last long. As suppliers began to suspect that the loss of the foldpoint was permanent, they demanded payment in hard currency. Also, about the time his sources of credit began to dry up, Earth's ambassador found himself facing another crisis. As the terms of enlistment of the cruisers' crews began to lapse, individual spacers started to exercise their right to end their military careers on Alta.

When 20 percent of each cruiser's people had chosen life on the planet over perpetual garrison duty in parking orbit, Granville Whitlow approached the Altan Parliament with an offer. He suggested that the power vacuum created by being cut off from the rest of human space (and particularly the services of the Grand Fleet) be filled by the creation of an Altan naval force. As a nucleus for this force, he offered to cede control of the three trapped battle cruisers "for the duration of the current emergency." His reasoning was that once the colonial government controlled the cruisers, they would be obliged to maintain and staff them.

Whitlow had not arrived at his decision to give up the battle cruisers easily. In later life he was fond of saying that it was the hardest thing he'd ever done. For, being a student of history, he realized that the years of separation would inevitably loosen the bonds of kinship between the isolated colony and the central government. Without interstellar trade and mutual interests, the two societies couldn't help but drift apart. He worried that the two might someday find themselves in conflict, even at war!

In the year 2512, the thought of tiny Alta attacking mighty Earth was almost too ludicrous to think about. However, Granville Whitlow was a man trained to take the long view of things, and he took his responsibilities as Earth's representative very seriously. Before offering to cede control of his tiny fleet to the Altan Parliament, he resolved that, should Alta ever decide to fight Earth, they would do so without the assistance of his three battle cruisers.

"Uncle, where are you?"

"Out here, child!"

Bethany Lindquist closed the door behind her and moved through Clarence Whitlow's spacious home toward the sound of his voice. Whitlow was the great-grandson of Granville Whitlow and the older brother of Bethany's mother. When she and Bethany's father were killed in an aircar crash, Clarence Whitlow had taken the ten-year-old girl into his home and raised her as his own. Now, eighteen standard years later, she lived in the city and visited him in his home in the foothills of the Colgate range several times each year.

Bethany found her uncle in the solarium, tending his roses. She threaded her way through fragrant air and spiny stalks to where he carefully pruned red flowers from a plant rising two meters out of the center of a maze of complicated plumbing. She moved to the stoop-shouldered, white-haired man in a dirty gardener's smock and kissed him tenderly on the forehead. "At your plants again, Uncle?"

He nodded. "The Homeport Flower Show is next month and I mean to win a blue ribbon this year."

"You should have won last year!"

He laughed. "I agree, but we're both prejudiced. What brings my favorite niece this far out of town?"

She shrugged. "No reason. I just wanted to visit my family. Is that a crime?"

Whitlow didn't answer immediately. Instead, he made a show of putting his pruning shears aside and pulling off his thick work gloves as he gazed at his niece. What he saw was a young woman of greater than average height, with a well-proportioned figure and an easy, graceful stance. Bethany's face was framed by shoulder-length, auburn hair. Her eyes were green, with a slight slant to them that complemented her high cheekbones. Her mouth was a trifle too large for the rest of her features, but the overall effect was one of quiet beauty. For the hundredth time, he contemplated the transformation that had turned a frightened ten-year-old with skinned knees into the beautiful young woman before him. Where had all the years gone so quickly?

"Your words don't match your manner, child. You're as nervous as I've ever seen you. Now, what's on your mind?"

Her expression became pensive and she took a deep breath before answering. "Carl has asked me to marry him."

"Are you referring to Carlton Aster?"

"Who else?"

Whitlow nodded. Aster was an aide to Jonathon Carstairs, leader of the opposition Conservative Party in Parliament. Whitlow didn't particularly like Aster's politics. However, as hereditary terrestrial ambassador, he had no right to say so out loud. He had met the young man several times on official business and had quickly pegged him as an insincere glad-hander of the type that seemed to gravitate to any legislative body. Gazing at Bethany's face, he quickly decided that he had no right to offer *that* opinion, either. "Do you love him?"

"I think I do."

"You don't sound overly positive."

"I have my doubts sometimes. That's normal, isn't it?"

Whitlow shrugged. "I suppose. Want some advice?"

"From you, Uncle? Of course."

"Take your time giving him an answer. 'Marry in haste, repent at leisure,' as the old saying goes."

"I want you to meet him."

"I have met him."

"I'm not talking about business. I want you two to get to know each other socially. Will you come to Homeport next week and have lunch with us?"

"Too bad I didn't know about this yesterday. We could have had lunch then."

"Oh, were you in town?" Bethany asked.

Whitlow nodded. "I visited the embassy to go over some old files."

Bethany groaned. "Not the Admiralty, Uncle. You didn't!"

Whitlow smiled faintly and spread his hands in a gesture of resignation. His insistence on going about his duties had always been a source of friction between them. Bethany maintained that people were laughing at him behind his back, saying that he was an old man who spent his life dreaming of past glory. He had no doubt that she was right. However, as he had so often insisted to her, the fact that he was an object of his neighbors' ridicule would never stop him from doing his job.

"I'm afraid that I had to, Bethany. Some discrepancies in the old immigration records needed clearing up. If you remember, you yourself obtained copies of a number of files from Alta University last year. I was cross-correlating that data with the records in the old embassy computer. I wasn't able to make much headway, but the trip was far from wasted. There was some sort of crisis going on at the Admiralty yesterday. I spent several enjoyable hours watching the excitement."

"What sort of crisis?"

"I don't know. They wouldn't tell me. But they were running around like a group of *ssatha* in the hot sun. I saw several acquaintences from the Academy of Science taken upstairs to the first admiral's office. That was the most intriguing part of the whole business. They went up with irritated expressions, as though they had been pulled away from something important on short notice. Yet, when they came down, they were changed men."

"Changed how?"

"They seemed . . . preoccupied."

"The Navy's probably asked them to look into the effect of the supernova on fleet communications or something."

"Could be."

"Will you come to lunch next week?"

"Of course, Bethany. I'll even leave my diplomatic sash at home so I won't embarrass you."

"Oh, Uncle!"

"Now that we have that detail out of the way, can you stay for dinner?" he asked.

"I don't know . . ."

"Not even to make an old man happy?"

She smiled. "I suppose I can drive back tonight."

"Excellent," he said, rubbing his hands together enthusiastically. "We'll have a candlelit dinner on the patio around eighteen hundred and watch Antares rise together."

"I'd like that," Bethany said.

"So would I, child. More than you can imagine."

Jonathon Carstairs, champion of the common man, leader of the Democratic Conservative Coalition in Parliament, and—if certain political projects worked as expected—the next prime minister of the Altan Republic, sat in his office and cursed the day he'd ever heard of the Antares Supernova. Not that the damned thing wasn't pretty. Carstairs had been initially enchanted by the nightly phenomenon that the commentators were calling "Antares dawn." Each night at nova-rise, the countryside was flooded with a silver glow that struck a responsive chord in virtually everyone who saw it. By contrast, Alta's four moons were positively drab.

But damn it, pretty or not, the supernova was causing

too great a drain on the treasury! With the blue-white radiance had come a perceptible rise in the background radiation in the Valeria system. It wasn't a problem on Alta itself since the atmosphere shielded the most harmful radiations, but the same couldn't be said for the space habitats. Already demands were being made in Parliament for emergency appropriations to beef up the antirad systems on the space stations.

Then there were the minor irritations. Children refused to go to bed at night with that silver glow beyond their windows. Juveniles had taken to roaming the streets after sunset, with a resulting rise in vandalism. Traffic accidents were up, as were antisocial acts of all sort. Then there was the weather! Farmers in the Brandt Valley were blaming the nova for the lack of rain in the region, while whole villages in the New British Islands were being destroyed in mudslides. Both groups were demanding that the government do something about it. Carstairs had no idea whether or not the nova was affecting the weather, but he knew who would be asked to provide low-interest-rate emergency loans if things didn't change, and quickly! Where the hell was all the extra money going to come from?

Carstairs' somber thoughts were interrupted by the buzzing of the intercom on his desk. He leaned forward. "Yes?"

"Mr. Aster is here, sir."

"Send him in." Carstairs swiveled in his chair to face the door as his assistant entered from the outer office. Carl Aster reminded Jonathon Carstairs of himself, three decades earlier. Carl was good-looking, had an easy speaking style and a way of ingratiating himself to those who could help his career. More important, he seemed to have an instinct for avoiding the missteps that could ruin a budding political career. One such would have been to marry the wrong woman. It was beginning to look as though Aster understood the score on that point. Carstairs heartily approved of his assistant's recent choice of a prospective wife. Bethany Lindquist would be the perfect decoration on the arm of any rising young politician. "Well, what did you find out?" he asked as Aster entered his office.

"The Admiralty isn't talking, sir. They told me the movement of their ships is classified."

"And you let it go at that?"

Aster grinned. "You know me better than that, sir. I called up a friend who owes me a favor. The rumors are correct. *Discovery has* been dispatched to rendezvous with a starship from outside."

Carstairs allowed himself the luxury of a few well-chosen profanities. The news on the parliamental grapevine had been so astounding that he'd felt obligated to confirm it before taking any action. Now it looked as though he'd waited too long.

"What about those other rumors? Is Stan Barrett aboard?"

"My informant wasn't sure, but he thinks so."

"Damn! That means the prime minister has put one over on us, Carl. If we'd caught them before that ship departed orbit, we could have gotten one or two of our own people aboard. Now, as it is, all we can do is pretend we're overjoyed at the prospect of the Social Democrats raking in all the glory."

"I don't follow," Aster replied.

"Don't you? Which party is going to get their leaders' faces before the people most over the next few weeks? Which party will be bragging about how they reestablished contact with the outside universe? And, worst of all, given those two factors, which party is the public most likely to vote for if we go through with our plans to force an early election?"

"What can we do to counter?"

"Hmmm," Carstairs said, "an interesting problem in applied politics, that. There are several ploys we might consider. We could attack their decision to keep this thing secret, basing our case on the public's right to know. Or we might take the opposite tack. We could leak the news ourselves and then attack them for having poor security. Or we might try being really nefarious and cooperate fully with them. That last might get us points for putting the needs of the planet above those of party—as though you could separate the two! As I said, an interesting problem."

The leader of the loyal opposition suddenly sat erect in his chair and slammed his open palm down on the desk with a sound like that of a slab of beef against a butcher's block. "First thing to do is find out how much maneuvering room we have. Carl, get on the screen and set up an appointment with the prime minister for this afternoon."

"And if his secretary asks me for a subject?"

"Tell her that it's a matter of utmost importance to the Republic."

CHAPTER 4

"All hands, prepare for zero gravity! Zero gee in one minute!"

Richard Drake listened to the warning with excitement, and not a little relief. Nor, as evidenced by the sporadic chorus of cheers that erupted over the ship's intercom, was he alone in his reaction. Except for brief ten-minute rest periods each watch, he and the rest of the crew had spent fifty-plus hours strapped into their couches while three and a half gravities of acceleration pressed their bodies into the crash webbing.

"All hands! Zero gravity in thirty seconds. Final warning!"

Drake glanced up at the oversize chronometer on the bulkhead in front of him. Blinking red numerals slowly counted off the remaining seconds of boost. When the numerals reached 00:00:00, the pressure suddenly lifted from his chest. His body was pushed forward into the straps of his harness, then rebounded in a quick series of oscillations. He reached out and began punching keys on his lapboard. Around him, displays on his command console began to change. On the main bridge viewscreen, a hologram that had charted the ship's progress faded into obscurity, to be replaced by a black sky speckled with stars. In the center of the view was the bright, violet-white star that was their target.

Drake switched to a private intercom channel and said,

41

"Battle staff! Link up." Eight faces appeared on screens around him—the members of Drake's staff and Stan Barrett. Each showed the effects of the high-speed run just completed. Eyes had dark circles under them, chins were covered with stubble, faces were drawn. Yet the brightness in their eyes showed their excitement.

"Sensor report, Mr. Marston!" Drake said, glancing at the leftmost screen on his panel.

"We're at a hundred thousand kilometers and closing, Captain," the executive officer said from his post in the combat control center. "The rate of closure is slowing while we maintain zero gravs."

"How long until we match velocity?"

"About three minutes, sir. I recommend that we turn the ship."

"Right! Mr. Cristobal, begin your turn."

"Yes, Captain."

For several hours, *Discovery* had been shedding the excess velocity that had allowed her to catch the starship. To do so, the cruiser had "backed down" on its jets, moving backward through space as it decelerated. Since the starship was still under power, it would be necessary to turn the ship end for end once again and begin boosting forward to maintain station on the constantly accelerating target. As Drake had predicted, *Discovery*'s fuel state was becoming critical. If they couldn't shut off the starship's engines within the next few hours, they would have to abandon the chase and turn for home, or risk running their own tanks dry.

"Are we ready to resume boost, Engineer?"

"Ready, Captain."

"Astrogator?"

"Turn initiated, sir. We'll be ready to resume boost in two minutes. I make it one-half standard gravity to maintain station, and I confirm Mr. Marston's figures regarding time to velocity match."

"Right!" Drake said. "Lock it in. One-half gravity in"—

he glanced at the chronometer—"two minutes, sixteen seconds from now."

"Yes, sir," Lieutenant Cristobal said.

Drake reached out and pressed for the general intercom circuit. "Attention, All Hands! This is the captain speaking. We are going to half a gravity of boost in two minutes. Take all precautions."

Again there was an interminable wait while the chronometer counted down. When the pressure returned, however, it lacked the crushing force they had become accustomed to on the outbound run. After a few moments, Argos Cristobal reported, "Velocities matched, Captain. We are now maintaining station at one hundred thousand kilometers."

"Very good, Astrogator." Drake turned back to the faces of his staff and said, "Now that that's taken care of, gentlemen, your reports!"

As soon as *Discovery* had cleared Alta's inner traffic zone and gone to high boost, Drake had assembled his staff via intercom and briefed them on their mission. The intercom conferences had been reconvened frequently to discuss strategy for making contact with the starship from outside. Tempers had flared as acceleration began to wear them down. Eventually, however, it was agreed that their most pressing duty was to identify their visitor's ship type and system of origin.

From the spectrum of the observed engine flare, it was possible to estimate the power of the outsider's engines. That, coupled with its observed acceleration, made it possible to estimate its mass. The numbers were impressive. After forty hours' observation, *Discovery*'s computer had reported the ship from outside possessed a total mass at just over two hundred thousand tonnes. Only the largest warships of the pre-nova Grand Fleet and the giant colony-transports had been so large.

"Let's have your reports. You first, Engineer."

"Yes, sir," Gavin Arnam replied. At age forty-five, Arnam was the oldest crewman aboard the cruiser. His florid features showed the effects of prolonged acceleration more than anyone except Stan Barrett, who Drake estimated to be closer to fifty. "We've completed the analysis. His photon drive is at least eight percent more efficient than ours. That, coupled with the size of his fuel tanks, explains how he's able to maintain his acceleration."

"How much longer can he keep it up?"

Arnam shrugged. "No way to tell, sir. Longer than we can, no doubt. A ship that size undoubtedly has plenty of legs under it."

"All right. Communicator, any reaction from our visitor yet?"

"None, sir. I've sent messages of friendship in every language in the library. I've tried all channels and our comm laser. Either he's had a communications failure or else he just doesn't want to talk to us."

"Any chance of his not knowing we're here?"

"None, Captain. Besides all the radio noise we've been putting out, we've had our drive flare pointed directly at him for the last twenty hours. To miss us, he'd have to be blind as well as deaf and dumb."

"Combat Control."

"Here, sir."

"Have *you* detected any reaction yet?"

"None, Captain."

Drake continued polling his staff. Everywhere the reports were the same. When he completed the poll, every officer aboard the cruiser had agreed that their original plan for making contact with the visitor was still the best. Finally, Drake addressed the prime minister's representative.

"I am soliciting your opinion, Mr. Barrett."

Barrett grinned. "Pursuant to paragraph seven, Captain?"

"Pursuant to paragraph seven," Drake agreed.

"Then let it be recorded, sir, that I had no opinion to

give. I've studied your plans and can think of no way to improve upon them."

"That settles it," Drake said. "We go as planned." He thanked them, then broke the circuit. Eight screens went dark as one. He stared at the screens for a moment, then keyed for the hangar bay six decks below his feet.

"Lieutenant Hall," a bearded face said from offscreen.

"Launch your ships, Lieutenant. We'll make the approach as planned. Good luck."

"Yes, sir! Launching now."

Lieutenant Phillip Hall, commander of *Discovery*'s small fleet of auxiliary vessels, glanced over the control board of his armed scout one last time. All instrumentation showed green, all fuel tanks indicated full. The only anomaly came from those readouts devoted to weapons inventory. This was one trip where the armed scouts would belie their name. They were about to go unarmed into the unknown.

"Better get pressure tight," Hall ordered his copilot as he reached for his own vacsuit helmet. He lifted it over his head, slipped the helmet into the neck ring of his suit, and deftly rotated it clockwise to lock it into position. Beside him, Weapons Specialist Moss Krueger followed his example. Hall tested the suit by chinning his pressure control. He was rewarded by a satisfying *pop* in his ears. He signaled Krueger with an upraised thumb, then keyed for the scout command circuit.

"This is Hall in *Catherine* calling all boats. Launch status check."

"Swenson in *Gossamer Gnat*, ready for launch, Phil."

"Marman in *Drunkard*, ready for launch, Lieutenant."

"Garth in *Flying Fool*, feeling naked without my pop-guns, but otherwise ready for launch."

"Okay, you all have your flight plans," Hall continued. "The captain just gave us the word to go. Prepare to launch. And for God's sake, don't mess this up!"

"Hangar bay doors coming open, Lieutenant. Beware

the acceleration curve on your way out," the hangar bay controller said into Hall's earphones.

"Will do," Hall responded. "Give us a five-second countdown."

"Stand by. Five, four, three, two, one, launch!"

"In order, follow me!" Hall commanded. He took hold of *Catherine*'s control stick and lifted the scout boat free of its cradle. With *Discovery* under boost, getting clear of the hangar bay would be the most difficult part of the voyage. *Catherine* was a sleek, streamlined arrow designed for high-speed entry into a planetary atmosphere. The armed scout's primary mission was to perform long-range reconnaissance. However, in the event of a fleet action, it could double as a picket ship for the cruiser, a harrier of enemy forces, and a hypersonic bomber.

As *Catherine* cleared the cruiser, Hall shifted from manual control to preprogrammed flight plan. He and his copilot were immediately pressed into their couches by a jolt of nearly five gravities. The cruiser, centered in one of his viewscreens, shrank to invisibility with surprising rapidity. Then came a stomach-wrenching sensation as the scout boat executed a high-speed turn and lined up directly on the drive flare of the outsider.

Richard Drake watched the scouts deploy and wondered if he was doing the right thing. Several members of his staff had advised sending a drone for a close look at the starship before risking any manned vessels. Drake had seriously considered the idea, then vetoed it because a camera drone would look too much like an offensive missile to those aboard the starship. "When in doubt, shoot!" had long been doctrine in both the Grand Fleet and the Altan Navy.

No, he decided, the only sure way to make those aboard the starship understand Alta's peaceful intent was to send men to do the work of machines. He had assigned his staff to plan a scout mission that would provide maximum information at minimum risk. Their recommendation called for the use of all four of the cruiser's scout craft. Three of these were to accelerate away from *Discovery* on divergent courses. Each would fly to widely separated points a thousand kilometers abeam of the starship. Once in position, they would match velocities and begin station-keeping. Their mission was to transmit long-range pictures of the starship back to *Discovery*.

To the fourth scout would fall the job of making a close-in survey of the visitor. When the three camera boats were in position, the fourth would slowly approach the starship, close to within a single kilometer, and match velocities. The contact boat would maintain its position until the starship reacted. Drake hoped that reaction wouldn't involve an attempt to blow the contact boat out of the sky.

"Camera ships are nearly in position, Captain," the communicator reported from his duty station on the opposite side of the control room.

"Let's see what you've got, Mr. Slater."

The main viewscreen split into three sections, each showing a bright plume emanating from a vaguely cylindrical object. Except for variations in the mottling of the barely seen starship's hull, the views might have been taken by a single camera.

"Order all scouts to go to maximum magnification."

"That is max, Captain. That's the best we can do without computer enhancement."

"Get me the view from *Catherine* then."

"Yes, sir."

Like its sister ships, the contact boat had its camera focused on the visitor from the stars. Its stern chase had taken it deep within the expanding cone of hydrogen plasma and high-energy photons that emanated from the starship's drive. The whole viewscreen appeared to be ablaze with violet-white fog. Drake keyed for the ship-to-ship circuit.

"How long before you break out of his drive flare?"

"The flight projection gives us another two minutes

yet, sir," Phillip Hall reported from the cockpit of the contact boat. "I could speed up my approach and get clear in half that time."

"Negative! Let her slide down the groove as planned, Phil."

"Yes, sir."

Drake watched as the fog grew brighter and thicker. Twice the scout pilot had to go to darker filtration to protect his sensors. Then, suddenly, the glowing fog was gone. The screen went black, then lightened perceptibly as the filters readjusted to maximum transparency. The viewscreen showed a rear-quarter view of the starship. The view was accompanied by a chorus of gasps from the control room crew. Before anyone could react, Lieutenant Hall's astonished voice issued from the overhead speakers:

"My God! It's a spacegoing wreck!"

The ship lay centered on the main viewscreen in *Discovery*'s Control Room No. 1. The visitor from outside was basically cylindrical, with a variety of protrusions (too small to have been visible in the telephoto views) jutting outward from the main body. The starship's bulk was oriented such that the axis of the cylinder extended from lower left to upper right on the screen, with the eye-searing brilliance of the drive just out of the field of view at the bottom.

That part of the ship closest to *Catherine* was in shadow with respect to Valeria, but it was brightly enough lit by the ghostly radiance of the nova that Drake had no trouble picking out the weapons blisters that dotted the hull. He noted the business ends of lasers and antimatter projectors, as well as several missile launchers and other things that looked to have a lethal function. There was also an oversize hatch that could well have been a sortie port for armed auxiliary craft. It looked big enough to swallow a full-size destroyer.

But the starship's weapons were not its most striking

feature. Indeed, Drake noticed the extensive armament only in passing. For, as Phillip Hall had already noted, the starship bore the marks of battle on its flanks. The dark mottling that had been apparent in the long-range views was the result of fully one-fifth of the ship's hull plates having been peeled away by a series of internal explosions. Wherever the plates were missing, nova light glinted through layer after layer of exposed beams and decking. In other places, the hull had been smashed inward, as though by a giant fist. In still others, the slashing marks of heavy laser fire had dug impossibly straight furrows along the ship's side.

"Captain, look at the bow!" The speaker was Argos Cristobal. Drake shifted his gaze toward the upper right corner of the viewscreen. The bow of the ship had taken more punishment than the flanks. It had been so badly damaged that it was virtually impossible to discern the original shape of the underlying structure. Indeed, the density of destruction dropped off dramatically toward the ship's stern—which explained why the mass converters, photon drive, and foldspace generators were still operational.

Drake frowned, wondering what it was that he was supposed to be looking for. Then he saw it. Amid the jumbled beams and warped plates, he managed to discern a portion of a single letter. He let his gaze sweep aft until he'd found another, then a third. Obviously the ship's name had once been painted in white block letters on the bow. Much of the name had been obliterated, yet enough remained to make out an underlying pattern:

TS*S C*N*UE**R

SB* 3*1

"I make it TSNS *Conqueror*, Captain."
"You've got good eyes, Mr. Cristobal! Communications!"

"Yes, Captain."

"Pass the word to all hands. Our visitor is a ship from Earth. A Grand Fleet blastship, no less."

"Yes, sir!"

"And get me Lieutenant Hall aboard *Catherine*."

"On the line, Captain."

"Hall!"

"Yes, sir."

"Any sign that someone aboard that bucket of scrap has noticed you yet?"

"None, Captain. We've got our ears turned up to max gain. So far, we haven't even gotten a whisper out of her."

"All right. Set all auxiliary cameras on closeup scan and begin your search spiral when you're ready."

"Will do, sir."

The picture on the viewscreen changed as the starship's hull expanded to fill the screen. New signs of battle became visible with the increased magnification. Here and there on the gray hull, tiny round holes showed where a laser or particle beam had held steady long enough to punch through the thick armor. Small fissures tinged with black identified places where fires had raged until the oxygen that fed them had been vented to space. Electrical cables hung down from the overhead, or spilled out to trail along the hull. In some places, the decking had collapsed under the weight of the ship's acceleration.

Like everyone else in the control room, Drake stared at the screen in astonishment. It was amazing that a ship with such extensive damage could operate at all. The answer, of course, lay in the compartmentalization and maximum redundancy with which warships were designed. The old tales of battle spoke of ships being sliced in two and still fighting on to victory.

Drake was roused from his reverie by the buzzing of the intercom. He turned to find the executive officer staring out at him from one of the screens.

"Take a look at channel three, Captain."

Camera three aboard *Catherine* was slowly panning

across one of the aft sections of the starship's hull. Visible in the view were a series of elliptical indentations spaced regularly around the ship's circumference. At the bottom of each indentation was what appeared to be a man-size airlock.

"Lifeboat berths?" Drake asked.

"Yes, sir. All empty. It appears that the crew abandoned ship."

"Are you suggesting that our visitor is a runaway?"

"It's certainly one possibility, Captain! That would explain why we've had so much trouble communicating with them."

Drake considered the possibility and nodded. "It would explain many things, Mr. Marston. It also leaves us with a problem."

"What problem, sir?"

"We're within eight hours of turning for home if we can't get that drive shut off. If no one is flying that thing, then how are we going to get those engines silenced?"

"We could send a boarding party, Captain. I'd be willing to lead it."

"To do what? Get yourselves trapped in the wreckage while we run out of fuel trying to figure out how to get you out again? You see what it's like over there. The damned thing is *four hundred meters long*! It would take a week just to find the engine room, maybe longer the way things are messed up."

The executive officer looked pensive, then said, "We could exhaust the fuel supply to the mass converters, Captain."

Drake shook his head. "Same objection. You couldn't find the converters in time either."

"We don't need to find them. We'll starve them from the outside. Find the fuel tanks and punch holes in them! Once the cryogen leaks out, everything will shut down due to fuel starvation."

Drake considered, then nodded. "It would work. I hate to damage it further, though."

"What choice have we?" Marston asked.

"None, I suppose. We were sent out here to stop it, and that's just what we'll do. Besides, *Conqueror*'s condition puts an entirely new light on our mission."

"How so, Captain?"

"Obviously, Number One, there's a war going on beyond the foldpoint. Whoever did *that*"—Drake hooked his thumb toward the derelict on the viewscreen—"is no pushover. I think we'd better find out who Earth is fighting, and why. And we'd better do it damned quick!"

CHAPTER 5

By the eighty-second hour after *Conqueror*'s appearance in the newly reconstituted foldpoint, all three major astronomical telescopes in the Valeria system were focused on the drama taking place half a billion kilometers above the ecliptic. The astronomers watched intently as the tiny constellation of violet-white stars continued to recede from the primary at 1500 kilometers per second. As they watched, they wondered when the brightest of the stars would go dark. They were not alone in their concern. Richard Drake wondered the same thing.

For six hours, *Discovery* and its three scouts had matched the derelict starship's movements precisely while they attempted to unlock its secrets. They had photographed the ship in a dozen wavelengths of visible light, scanned its flanks with sidelooking radar and stereoptic lasers, and mapped it with thermographic and ultraviolet scanners. While they studied, they continued their communications attempts, sweeping *Conqueror* with tightly focused beams of electromagnetic radiation composed of every frequency that *Discovery*'s comm system was capable of generating. They even put a vacsuited spacer in one of the scouts' airlocks with a high-powered hunting rifle. He spent a fruitless hour bouncing high-speed projectiles off various parts of the starship in the hope that the resulting clanging noises would be carried by conduction through the ship's structure to any surviving crewmembers.

And while one group tried to rouse the starship's crew, others aboard the cruiser went forward under the assumption that *Conqueror* was, indeed, deserted. Immediately after the thermographic scans were completed, Drake called a meeting in the wardroom to plan strategy. Drake, Bela Marston, Argos Cristobal, and Technician-Second Aliman Grandstaff were already examining the first of the garishly colored thermographs when Stan Barrett arrived.

"Sorry I'm late," the political assistant said. "I've been talking with the powers-that-be back home. Ever try to hold a conversation where there's a one-hour delay between comments?"

"Yes," Drake said. "Doesn't work very well, does it?"

Barrett slid into his seat and sighed. "Doesn't work at all, if you ask me. I was able to learn some things, though. The situation back home is deteriorating fast. News of our visitor is still officially classified, but that isn't going to last long. The Parliament Building has been alive with rumors since shortly after we left. Virtually the whole story has leaked. Several members have threatened to ask questions from the floor. Jonathon Carstairs has even threatened to hold a news conference."

"What about the Admiralty?" Drake asked.

Barrett grinned. "Funny you should ask. Various news organizations have been making inquiries regarding a certain Navy cruiser reputed to have left parking orbit in one hell of a hurry."

"Sounds exciting," Drake replied.

"Bah, you can have it! If I were smart, I'd buy a farm on East Continent and give up politics." Barrett glanced at the screen. "What have we here?"

"We were just about to review the thermographs."

"Looks like modern art. What can these tell you?"

Drake gestured toward the holoscreen where the thermograph was displayed. "*Conqueror* isn't all that different from *Discovery* when it comes to its basic operating principles, Mr. Barrett. It has a lot of evolutionary improvements built in, but no major breakthroughs—at least, none that are obvious at the moment. Both ships utilize photon drives for getting around in normal space; and, presumably, both have similar jump systems for interstellar travel. Now, the heart of any starship is the mass converter. Shut down the mass converter and you shut down the drive. Normally that's done by shutting off the flow of fuel into the converter. Since we have no idea where that particular control is located aboard *Conqueror*, we're going to try something messier.

"Mass converter fuel is deuterium-enriched hydrogen stored at cryogenic temperature. In *Discovery*, we carry our cryogen in tanks in our central cylinder. *Conqueror*'s cylindrical design suggests that we'll find the main tankage complex aft. Once we've located the fuel tanks, we punch a few holes in them with lasers, the cryogen leaks out under the force of the ship's acceleration, the fuel tanks run dry, and the converters should shut down automatically from fuel exhaustion."

"You hope," Barrett said.

"The theory is sound," Drake replied.

"So what are we doing with these thermographs?" Barrett asked.

"Cryogen is stored as close to absolute zero as the engineers can manage. No matter how efficient the insulation on *Conqueror*'s tanks, there will be some cooling of the adjacent structures. Find the cool spots and you find the fuel."

"Got a tank, sir!" Technician Grandstaff said.

"Where?" Drake peered at the picture on the screen. The false colors shaded from scarlet (hot) near the operating drive, to light blue (ambient temperature) over most of the hull, to indigo (cool) in a few spots. The technician had drawn a dashed, glowing line on the screen around one of the indigo sections.

"I make it a cylindrical tank extending approximately to the ship's midpoint, Captain."

Drake nodded. "About thirty percent full, I'd guess."

"Yes, sir."

"How can you tell *that*?" Barrett asked.

"From the temperature profile, sir," Grandstaff said. "Only that part of the tank actually in contact with the liquid fuel shows as indigo on the graph. If thirty percent of the tank length shows cooling, then that's the percent of fuel remaining."

"I see," Barrett said in a tone that made Drake wonder if he really did.

"Have I your permission to check the other views, Captain?" the technician asked.

"Proceed."

There were six fuel tanks in all. Two of them had been sliced open near their forward bulkheads, but *Conqueror*'s acceleration kept the liquid hydrogen away from these potential leak paths. The temperature profiles indicated that the starship still possessed approximately 25 percent of its original fuel supply

"That does it," Drake said when Grandstaff had finished his estimate. "We know we aren't going to outlast it!"

"We'll need to use the ship's secondary battery, Captain," Bela Marston warned from his seat at Drake's right. "The scouts don't carry anything strong enough to carve through that armor in a reasonable time."

"Agreed, Number One. Do you see any problem with using *Discovery* to do the job?"

"I was thinking what I would do if I were aboard that ship and some strange cruiser came up and started carving its initials in my flanks, Captain. I think I'd do my best to carve back! And even if the damned thing's a derelict, there could be any number of automatic defenses still operational."

"I don't see any way around the risk. If we don't get that drive shut down in the next"—Drake's eyes went to the wardroom chronometer—"two hours, we'll be forced to break off the pursuit."

"I haven't any solution to the problem, Captain. Just thought I would mention it."

"Argos, any suggestions?"

"None, Captain."

"In that case, we'll just have to chance it. Thank you, gentlemen. Please return to your duty stations. We go on Red Alert in five minutes."

With all airtight doors closed, and with the crew in vacuum suits and at battle stations, Drake sent *Discovery* hurtling toward *Conqueror*. While the cruiser closed the hundred-thousand-kilometer gap between itself and the starship, the scout boats began to pull back to what Drake hoped was a safe distance.

Once again the control room viewscreen showed a glowing, violet-white fog as *Discovery* encountered the blastship's drive flare. At the same moment, several sensors began behaving erratically, submerged as they were in electrically conductive plasma. He watched the fog grow thicker and brighter, then dissipate as suddenly as before. The filters readjusted to reveal the vast bulk of *Conqueror* less than a dozen kilometers ahead.

"Stand by secondary lasers, Number One."

"Lasers powered up and ready, Captain."

The cruiser surged forward, closing the distance to the blastship until less than a kilometer separated the two spacecraft. Lieutenant Cristobal coaxed the cruiser closer until the mangled hull of *Conqueror* filled the viewscreen.

"In position," Cristobal reported.

"Are you ready, Number One?" Drake asked, trying hard to keep the rising tension from his voice. His mood consisted of equal parts exhilaration and fear.

"Target acquisition complete, Captain," Marston's voice replied in Drake's earphones. The main viewscreen changed to a tactical display showing the aiming point for the number-three laser battery. A close-up of the aft portion of *Conqueror*'s hull filled the screen. A sighting circle was centered on an unbroken section just in front of the photon focusing rings.

Drake gripped the arms of his acceleration couch tightly, licked dry lips, and said, "Fire when ready, Number One."

"Shoot!" Marston ordered.

An intolerably bright spot of light winked into being on the screen. For the space of a long heartbeat, nothing happened. Then, too quickly for human reflexes to react, the pinpoint was gone, replaced by a geyser of liquid hydrogen gushing outward in a curving fountainhead of spray.

"Next firing position, Astrogator," Drake ordered. There followed a series of acceleration surges as Lieutenant Cristobal worked to reposition the cruiser for the next shot.

"In position, Captain."

"Your show, Mr. Marston."

"Shoot!"

Once again the bright point of light sprang forth and was shut off under computer control when the spouting geyser of hydrogen appeared.

"Do you see how long it's taking us to punch through?" Marston asked Drake as the cruiser once again positioned itself for the attack.

"Longer than it should at point-blank range," Drake said.

"About ten times longer, Captain. This baby's tough!"

"Which makes whoever mauled it even tougher," Drake mused.

"Yes, sir. On target, ready to fire."

"Then shoot!"

The secondary battery stabbed out a third time, and once again a geyser appeared. They continued their ponderous dance—move *Discovery* to a new position, aim, shoot, and move on—three more times.

"That's it," Drake said as the last of the *Conqueror's* fuel tanks began leaking its life blood to space. "Pull back, Mr. Astrogator. Let's take a look at our handiwork."

"Yes, sir."

From a distance of five kilometers, it was impossible to see the damage they had inflicted on the giant ship. The only indication was the drive flare, which was now brighter than ever in the thin trailing atmosphere of leaking fuel.

"What now, Captain?" Stan Barrett asked. Without a battle station, the political assistant had watched the operation from the observer's position in the control room.

"We wait, Mr. Barrett. Wait for the tanks to go dry."

They were still waiting an hour later. Thermographs showed the tanks nearly empty, yet the starship's drive showed no sign of faltering. It continued to push the ship along at a constant half gravity, totally oblivious to the presence of the Altan battle cruiser beside it.

"Why hasn't it shut down?" Barrett asked finally.

"There must be an auxiliary fuel tank somewhere inside," Drake growled in frustration. "If that damned *dinophant* doesn't shut down soon, we're going to have a real problem on our hands. We might even have to ... ulp!"

"What the hell?" Barrett exclaimed.

The starship, which only a moment before had been balanced on a violet-white flame, had suddenly gone dark. After the actinic glow of the drive, the white heat of the drive components seemed dim by comparison.

Conqueror had finally run out of fuel!

Somewhere in the blastship's depths, safety systems had sensed the onset of fuel starvation and shut down the drive to prevent its being damaged. *Discovery*'s computer, sensing the change in its quarry, had followed suit, shutting down with equal abruptness. One moment, *Conqueror* and *Discovery* had both been accelerating at five meters-per-second-squared; the next, they were dead in space. Both continued to race away from Val on a fast orbit to eternity; but, at least, they were no longer adding to their velocity.

An impossible situation had suddenly become merely difficult.

A week later, Richard Drake sat in the jumpseat in *Moliere*'s pilot cabin and watched the bulk of *Conqueror* grow in the windscreen before him. The blue-white sparks of arc welders showed aft where spacers were working to seal up the holes that *Discovery* had punched in the blastship's fuel tanks. Centered in front of the landing boat were hatches that glowed with the internal illumination of polyarcs. Vacsuited figures were moving purposefully around inside the starship's hull. The landing boat floated to within a dozen meters of its goal, then fired its attitude control jets to match velocities just beyond one of the lighted hatches.

The landing boat's pilot turned to look at Drake and said, "This is as close as I dare come, Captain. You'll have to go on hand over hand."

"Right," Drake replied. He levered himself out of his seat and floated back into the main cabin where he retrieved his helmet from an overhead rack. The landing boat crew chief helped him on with it. After Drake had tested his suit for pressure integrity, he said: "Lead the way, Chief."

"Yes, sir." CPO Gordon Meyer's voice sounded tinny, coming as it did through the external auditory sensors of Drake's suit. Meyer towed Drake toward the airlock. He helped his captain inside, then waited for the traditional thumbs-up signal before closing the door.

"Ready, sir?" Drake heard over his radio.

"Depressurize, Chief."

"Depressurizing now. Good luck, Captain."

"Thanks."

Drake's suit ballooned around him as the pressure in the airlock dropped to zero. He stood in the crouched stance typical of a man in a pressure suit, listening intently for the sound every spacer dreads most—the ear-popping hiss of an air leak. He heard nothing but his own breathing and the gentle hum of his backpack ventilation unit.

"Door coming open, Captain."

"Understood, Chief." Drake turned to face the outer door of the airlock. The interior lights turned off as a bright crack appeared at the edge of the door. It widened to show a spacer floating just beyond the lock, a gloved hand resting on the safety line attached to a padeye in the landing boat hull. The line extended straight to the blast-ship where it disappeared inside a ten-meter-square opening.

"I'm Spacer Coos, Captain. The exec is waiting for you inside."

Drake moved his hands in the gesture which passed for a nod in a vacsuit. "Just a moment, Coos. I want to see this monster up close."

"Yes, sir," Coos said, the twang of an East Continent accent coloring his words. "That's the first thing most want to do when I greet 'em."

Drake turned to face forward along the blastship. The damage didn't look quite so bad from his vantage point near the stern. By unfocusing his eyes and not looking too closely, it would have been easy to imagine that the behemoth was whole and hale. Just forward of his position, Drake gazed at a weapons blister with the ugly snout of a particle beam projector protruding from it. The blister was silhouetted against the starry blackness and reflected the glow of the polyarcs directly ahead.

"Kind of gets to you, don't it, sir?" Coos asked a few moments later.

"That it does," Drake agreed as a shiver moved unbidden between his shoulder blades. "Take me to Mr. Marston, if you please, Coos."

"Yes, sir."

The compartment beyond the open hatch appeared to be a storage hold—at least, it was filled with a jumble of hexagonal packing containers painted in a variety of colors.

"Welcome aboard *Conqueror*, sir," one of the six vac-suited figures said with Bela Marston's voice. The glare of the spacers' helmet lamps disguised their identities until one figure detached itself from the group and came forward.

"Thank you, Number One. I was getting tired of just listening to your reports. Thought I'd come over and see things for myself."

"Yes, sir. We've arranged a brief tour. Ensign Symes will accompany us."

"Hello, sir," another suited figure said, moving forward.

"Hello, Jonas. Lead on, gentlemen. I want to see the bodies first."

Immediately after *Conqueror*'s drive had been disabled, Drake had nearly stripped *Discovery* of manpower to explore the derelict. The parties had been organized into groups of four, with each assigned a sector to explore. Their orders were to sweep through the ship looking for survivors. They hadn't found any. Most of the hulk was open to vacuum, and those sections that still held atmosphere were heavy with toxic gases and the smell of burned electrical insulation.

Yet, almost immediately, the search parties found traces of the ship's crew. Their personal effects littered the living quarters. From the size of those quarters, Commander Marston estimated that *Conqueror*'s crew had numbered more than a thousand. The scraps of a hastily interrupted meal floated throughout the ship's galley and mess compartment.

By the end of their first twenty hours aboard, *Discovery*'s searchers had accounted for the sixty-three members of the blastship's crew whose remains floated where they had fallen in battle.

Most of the bodies were found in space armor of an unfamiliar design, armor that the Altan engineers quickly reported to be significantly more advanced than their own. In spite of that, the armor had invariably been holed by explosion or laser beam. Those who had not been killed outright had died soon after. Some casualties were found in compartments that still held atmosphere. Many of the latter showed shrapnel wounds. There were also a considerable number of body fragments and large sections of the ship made inaccessible by damage.

Richard Drake had never been in a space battle, but he'd studied the historical records and knew how messy the combination of explosives and vacuum could be. He had also seen the photographs that his people had transmitted from the murdered blastship. Both thoughts crossed his mind as Marston and Symes led him to where the bodies of *Conqueror*'s crew lay. They cycled through into a compartment that the salvage crew had converted into a zero-gee morgue.

As soon as they were inside, Marston began removing his helmet. Drake and the young engineer followed suit. The air in the compartment was a cold shock as Drake lifted his helmet clear. A swirl of exhalation fog surrounded him as he dropped the helmet to float at the end of its tether, and turned to survey the double row of body bags strapped to the deck.

"If you will follow me, Captain," young Symes said.

The assistant engineer led Drake to one of the nearby bags via a safety line that had been strung through the compartment. Drake glanced through the clear plastic to the remains inside.

He blinked, then shifted his gaze to the next bag to the right, and then to the third. "An Earth ship all right!"

"Yes, sir."

On approximately half the worlds colonized by human beings, an overwhelming majority of settlers had consisted of a single racial type. Alta was an example of such a colony. The original inhabitants had been 95 percent Caucasian—a secondary effect of the fact that, two hundred years earlier, New Providence had been colonized almost exclusively by disaffected North Americans and West Europeans. Other planets had been populated by other races. Most of Garden of Harmony's settlers had come from the mountains, steppes, and valleys of Greater China; most of those on N'domo from the jungles and veldt of Central and Southern Africa; most of Noumolea's from the islands and peoples of the Great Pacific Basin.

Anthropologists in search of doctoral theses had found little of interest on these worlds with their homogenous populations. They were far more interested in the other class of worlds—of which Skorzen, Cinco de Mayo, and Roughneck were examples. The original settlers of these planets had been as thoroughly mixed a polyglot as the computers in charge of emigration visas could make them.

Yet throughout history the young of the human species have managed to meet, fall in love, and marry; and to do so without regard to the wishes, customs, traditions, or prejudices of their elders. The result was that the original sharp distinctions between racial types quickly blurred following a colony's founding. By the time of the Antares Supernova, virtually all the planets of human space were inhabited by homogenous populations of a single dominant racial type. The types were different from planet to planet, but the same for any given world.

They were the same, that is, on all planets but Earth. On humanity's home world, the racial genetic pools were deep and their distribution uneven, the result of entire peoples having been isolated from one another for fifty thousand years in widely differing environments. That isolation had ended with the advent of universal air travel in the late twentieth century. The same forces that homogenized colonial populations were at work on Earth, but the sheer magnitude of the task ensured that human diversity would remain a fact for several more millennia.

As Richard Drake pointed the beam of his helmet lamp at the first of *Conqueror*'s dead crewmen, he was greeted by a handsome black face that was deceptively peaceful in repose. The second crewman was white. The open brown eyes of the third were framed in prominent epicanthic folds. Such diversity among a starship's crew could mean only one thing. That ship was manned by people from Mother Earth.

"Have my orders been carried out?" Drake asked, glancing at the bodies.

"Yes, sir," Symes said. "We've disturbed them no more than necessary and the chaplain has given each of them the last rites individually."

"Good, Lieutenant. Make sure that everyone—and I mean *everyone!*—understands that they are to be treated with reverence."

"I'll pass the word again to all working parties."

"I think you'd best look at this, Captain," Marston said, gesturing at a body bag at the far end of the morgue. "Our people found this one about two hours ago. I haven't had time to file my report."

Drake pulled himself hand over hand to the end of the compartment indicated by his executive officer. Once again he positioned himself so that his light played over the transparent plastic bag and its contents. The compartment reverberated with his sharp intake of breath.

"A woman!"

"Yes, sir. We found her in one of the compartments where internal pressure kept us from getting the door open. Indications are that she was killed at the same time as the others. Notice anything strange?"

Drake played his light over the body. The woman had been a pretty blonde. She wore a blue uniform like several of the others. Except for a bruise on her forehead, there was no sign of injury.

Finally, he said, "What am I supposed to be looking for?"

"We found her in a compartment that still held an oxygen atmosphere at approximately thirty degrees C. By this time, there should have been some sign of decay. I don't see any, do you?"

Drake frowned, moved closer, and gave the tanned skin a nearly microscopic examination. Finally, he glanced up at Marston. "You're right. No sign whatever. I wonder what it means?"

"It means that something has killed all the bacteria on

this ship, including the bacteria naturally resident within the human body! Except for the fact that all the lifeboats are missing, I would have said that they took a direct hit from an enhanced radiation weapon. Yet, with a neutron burst that powerful, we should have found everyone dead at their stations and all the lifeboats in their bays."

"I see what you mean, Number One. Record your observation in the log. We'll transmit it back to the Admiralty in the next communication."

"Yes, sir."

Drake straightened up. "Now I want to see the engine room."

"This way, sir," Symes replied.

They were working their way amid massive jumpshift generators, with Lieutenant Symes providing the explanations, when a yeoman from the ship hurried into the stardrive compartment.

"What is it, Murphy?"

"A priority-one message just came in from the Admiralty, Captain!" the spacer said breathlessly.

"Classified?" Drake asked.

"No, sir."

"Then read it."

"Uh, I don't have the flimsy, sir. The second officer just ordered me to get my ass over here, find you, and report in person."

"You've found me. Report."

"Uh, yes, sir. The first admiral has dispatched *Dagger* in company with a cryogen tanker to rendezvous with *Conqueror* and begin the job of slowing her for return to Alta. They'll be here in a month."

"Hardly news, Murphy," Drake mused. "I've been talking to the admiral about the salvage plan for most of this week."

"That wasn't all the message, Captain. Admiral Dardan has also ordered us home."

"Home?"

"Yes, sir. We're to abandon *Conqueror* and begin shaping a maximum-efficiency orbit for Alta within the next twelve hours."

"But, damn it, we just got here! Did the order give a reason?"

"No, sir. Just scoot for home, soonest!"

CHAPTER 6

Outbound, *Discovery* had matched velocities with *Conqueror* a mere fifty-four hours after breaking from parking orbit. Drake wished that the trip home could be made to pass as quickly. Unfortunately, the prodigious expenditure of energy that had allowed *Discovery* to catch the derelict blastship now worked against them. At the moment Admiral Dardan's order to return home reached them, *Discovery* was 1.5 billion kilometers distant from Val and receding from it at a rate of 1500 kilometers per second. In order to return home, the battle cruiser would first have to erase its rather considerable outward-directed velocity. That requirement, along with the ship's fuel state after its earlier herculean effort, ensured that the return home would be a slow one.

Back aboard ship, Drake showed Argos Cristobal the orders and asked, "What deceleration program do you recommend, Lieutenant?"

Cristobal frowned. "We're getting critical on delta V capability, Captain. We'll expend 1500 kilometers per second halting our outbound velocity. That will leave us with only 2200 kps left in the tanks. I recommend a two-gravity deceleration until we've reversed direction and we've built up to a velocity of 1000 kps toward Alta. After that, we shut down the drive and coast until time to decelerate. That will leave us with a total reserve of 200 kps delta V."

"That's only two percent of what we started with, Astrogator."

"Yes, sir. It ought to be enough, though."

"How long to Alta on that program?"

Cristobal busied himself at his console. A few seconds later, he reported, "Four hundred and fifty hours, sir. Shall I lock it in?"

Drake considered the answer. It was worse than he'd hoped, but better than he'd feared. He nodded. "Do so, Mister."

"Yes, sir."

Having finished with the astrogator, Drake turned his attention to wrapping up operations aboard *Conqueror*. Reluctantly, he ordered the work parties to cease their efforts and return to the ship. Drake wished he could give the men a reason for their abandoning the hulk. Unfortunately, the first admiral hadn't offered any.

Grumbling, *Discovery*'s work parties returned to the battle cruiser with their equipment, the records of their explorations, and a variety of small mechanisms that had intrigued the engineers. A crew from the quartermaster's department, under the command of the second officer, waited just inside the hangar bay airlock to take charge of the salvaged equipment. They sealed the samples into packing crates, then directed the work parties to their acceleration stations. When all hands were accounted for, Drake ordered the ship turned to align the photon drive with the direction of flight.

"Ready to go ass-backward into the unknown again, Mr. Cristobal?" Drake asked as he strapped himself into his command chair on the bridge.

"Wish we didn't have to, Captain" came the wistful reply.

"That makes two of us, Lieutenant. Answer the question, please."

"Ready for acceleration, sir."

"Very good. Bring the engines to minimum power. Mind you don't brush *Conqueror* with our flare."

"Aye aye, sir."

A deep thrumming sound emanated from the cruiser's steel bulkheads. Drake sank into his seat with a force one-tenth that which he was used to at home. As he did so, he watched the derelict shrink on the main viewscreen until it was no longer visible.

After several minutes at low power, Drake said, "You may go to your deceleration program when ready, Astrogator."

"Aye aye, Captain."

With the clanging of acceleration alarms, *Discovery*'s photon engines were brought to power and the battle cruiser began putting distance between itself and the starship in earnest. The crew quickly settled down into the routine of powered flight. They stood their watches, did their maintenance, played cards, read books, ate, complained about Navy food, caught up on their sleep, and began the cycle over again. In addition to the usual pursuits, many of the crew were put to work analyzing equipment from *Conqueror*. Drake intended to have a comprehensive report on their findings ready when the ship returned to Alta.

Twenty-one hours after departing the blastship, Drake authorized a brief celebration for the crew to mark the moment when the cruiser finally halted its headlong rush toward infinity. For one brief moment, *Discovery* hung motionless above Val, balanced on its tail of violet fire, before beginning its long plunge back into the inner system.

Eventually, the bright star that had so long been centered on the main viewscreen grew to half-moon shape, then to the familiar blue-white of Alta. Eventually, the cruiser slid into its thousand-kilometer-high parking orbit and the photon engines were silenced.

The ship had barely ceased reverberating when Drake ordered Stan Barrett, Bela Marston, Argos Cristobal, and Jonas Symes to meet him in the hangar bay. Minutes later, they were out in space aboard *Moliere*, poised for a blazing reentry into the atmosphere.

Commodore Wilson met them at the spaceport just as he had done on Drake's previous arrival. Thàt was the only similarity between the two visits, however. This time, Val stood high in the purple Altan sky. In contrast to the deserted terminal building Drake had encountered previously, hundreds of bystanders now crowded the concourse. Most were representatives of Alta's news organizations, all of whom seemed to be jostling for position under the watchful eyes of spaceport police. Outside the terminal building, visible through the concourse's glass walls, several thousand ordinary citizens waited patiently behind police lines or crowded up against the perimeter fence.

Drake had received a dispatch from the first admiral shortly after *Discovery* rendezvoused with *Conqueror*. It had advised him that the government was bowing to legislative pressure and about to release a few, limited details concerning the starship. Drake had been busy with other concerns at the time and hadn't thought much about it. The sight of the crowd made him realize the effect the news had had on the general populace.

"You should have warned us!" Drake shouted at Commodore Wilson as the two men shook hands. The shout was necessary to make himself heard over the background noise.

"Sorry," Wilson shouted back. "Your arrival time leaked somehow. Follow me and we'll get you out of this as quickly as we can." Wilson guided Drake, Barrett, and the three officers briskly past the crowd. As the small group of military men passed, the reporters shouted questions at them:

"Captain Drake, tell us what you found out there... Is it true that the starship is an Earth warcraft?... Why were you along, Mr. Barrett?... Give us your impressions ... Why has the Admiralty thrown a security seal over this? ..."

When they were through the crowd and on their way toward the limousine parked in front of the terminal building, Barrett caught up with Wilson and asked, "Where are we going?"

"Parliament. The prime minister and selected cabinet officials have already been briefed on your findings. We thought we'd leave the Space Committee to you."

Barrett groaned. "Carstairs is on that committee!"

The commodore grinned. "We know. That's one reason we left them for you."

"Thanks."

"Don't mention it."

"How much do they know?"

"Officially? Not much more than the public. We've released a few fuzzy long-range telephotos of the ship and told them that it comes from Earth. As for their unofficial knowledge ... well, there've been a lot of rumors floating around Parliament. Some of them are pretty close to the truth."

The ride into Homeport was made in silence. Marston, Cristobal, and Symes had not been home in almost a year. *Discovery*'s officers sat quietly, letting their eyes drink in the familiar sights, breathing deeply of air that had never seen the inside of a recycling unit. After a fifteen-minute drive, the car pulled into the underground parking garage below the Parliament Building. Once again they were forced to run a gauntlet of holovision cameras and reporters—this time held at bay by men in the uniform of the Government Guard Service. Wilson guided them to a lift that took them to one of the upper floors of the building.

Drake recognized the hearing room immediately. It was the windowless, steel-walled conference room where parliamentary committees held closed hearings. Drake had sat through a couple of classified briefings in the same room during his tour as legislative liaison officer.

It was the one place on Alta guaranteed to be free of electronic listening devices.

The Space Committee was already seated behind the long bench on the raised dais. An audience that included several military men and a number of the prime minister's operatives sat behind a railing. One member of the audience in particular caught Drake's eye. First Admiral Dardan was seated in the middle of the first row behind the railing. He looked at the party from *Discovery* as they entered but otherwise gave no sign of recognition.

Between the dais and the railing were two tables for witnesses. They took their places at the direction of one of the committee's staff members. The Chairman of the Space Committee, who had been leafing through reports bearing the Navy logo, looked up as the witnesses settled into their seats. He leaned forward and locked gazes with the two members seated to his right, then with a like number on his left. After a few seconds, the chairman nodded, straightened, and touched a control on the bench in front of him. Immediately, the amplified sound of a gavel banging wood echoed through the hearing room.

"This hearing will now come to order! Guards, seal the entrance," he growled. The vaultlike doors of the hearing room hissed closed. A *pop* in Drake's ears signaled the switchover to the hearing room's environmental control system. The lights flickered and a quiet *hum* began to emanate from the walls as the antieavesdropping system went into operation. The chairman watched the readouts in front of him for a few seconds, then turned toward the six men seated at the witness tables.

"Welcome, gentlemen. For those of you who do not know me, my name is Olaf Prost, Senior Member from Lower Bero Province. To my immediate right is my colleague, the Honorable Jonathon Carstairs, Member from Sopwell. To his right, the Honorable Alicia Delevan

from the Southridge District of Homeport. To my left
are the Honorable Garcia Porter, Fahrenville Township;
and the Honorable Avram Miller, Rahway, Eastern Continent.

"We of this committee are charged with oversight of
all extraatmospheric activities of interest to this Parliament. You are here because the prime minister has promised to cooperate in this matter of the starship from
outside. Captain Drake, you may now introduce your
little band of adventurers."

Drake got slowly to his feet and cleared his throat.
"I thank the chairman. Now, sir, may I present my
officers: Commander Marston, my exec; Lieutenant
Cristobal, Astrogation; and Ensign Symes, Engineering.
And, of course, you know Stan Barrett of the prime
minister's staff."

"Have you a prepared statement, Captain?"

"Yes, sir," Drake replied. "I didn't know how well
you had been briefed—"

"Not bloody well at all!" Prost answered.

"I have prepared a summary of our mission. I have
a record tile."

"Hand it to the stenographer."

"Yes, sir."

A technician was seated to one side of the hearing
room. At the chairman's order, he rose from behind his
bank of recording instruments and crossed to where
Drake stood. Drake handed him the tile and received a
hand controller in exchange. The technician returned to
his station and slipped the tile into a playback device.

Drake used the hand controller to dim the overhead
lights. As he did so, a holoscreen rose from out of the
floor. Drake began his recitation.

He started with the message he'd received aboard
Discovery ordering him to report to the first admiral's
office, then moved swiftly through the initial briefing,
the rushed departure from orbit, and the long stern chase.
He displayed the closeup views that had convinced him

that the ship was a lifeless derelict. He moved on to a sequence showing the laser surgery that had finally stopped the blastship.

He spoke of the first tentative explorations of the starship's interior and the later effort to survey every compartment and corridor. His audience was unnaturally quiet as the holocam panned across smashed bulkheads and peered into jumbles of twisted I-beams. Drake displayed several views of the casualties that his people had found, and finally ended his talk with a wide-angle hologram of the blastship's gigantic jump engines. When he had finished, he thumbed the control box and brought the overhead lights back to full luminescence.

Prost glanced at the other committee members, then fixed his gaze on the female M.P. next to Jonathon Carstairs. "You may start the questioning, Alicia."

"Thank you, Mr. Chairman. Captain Drake. Was it absolutely necessary for you to attack that ship?"

"We were running low on fuel. If we hadn't stopped it then, we would have been forced to abandon the chase in another few hours."

"What if there had been survivors aboard? You might have killed someone. Indeed, you might have been attacked in reprisal."

"Believe me, ma'am, the thought occurred to me. I won't deny that there was a certain element of risk in our action, but one that I judged to be acceptable at the time. As it was, if we hadn't punctured *Conqueror*'s fuel tanks, we would have lost it forever."

"Surely not, Captain Drake," Garcia Porter said from Prost's left. "We could have sent an expedition with more fuel to make rendezvous if you had been forced to give up the chase."

"No, you couldn't have, sir. With its remaining fuel, and with half a gravity's acceleration, *Conqueror*'s velocity would eventually have gotten so great that none of our ships could have caught it."

"Captain Drake," Avram Miller said.

"Yes, sir."

"If there was no one left alive aboard that ship, how was it able to lead you such a merry chase?"

"It was on autopilot, sir. The last order programmed into the jump computer appears to have been 'Find a foldpoint and jump!' It was stuck in an endless loop and was attempting to carry out its instructions when we caught up with it."

"How? There's only the one foldpoint in this system, and *Conqueror* was headed directly away from it."

"Autopilots are pretty literal minded, sir. Usually they aren't expected to think things through by themselves. The autopilot merely handles the basics of astrogation and engine control, and leaves all the heavy thinking to the main computer. Unfortunately, *Conqueror*'s main computer had its memory obliterated by a strong dose of radiation. The autopilot was trying to accomplish its mission as best it could without help. It was headed for the next nearest foldpoint to make another jump."

"But there isn't any 'next nearest' foldpoint, Captain Drake."

"But there is! It's in the Scirrocco system, some fourteen light-years from here."

"The blastship was trying to get to another star system *through normal space*?"

"Yes, sir."

"The computers were radiation blasted, yet they retained enough data to make an interstellar jump?"

"Not the computers, sir. The autopilot. Starship autopilots are very nearly indestructible. They are constructed using the old crystalline memory techniques. That is why they are relatively stupid, but highly radiation tolerant."

"Did you happen to bring back *Conqueror*'s autopilot?" Porter asked.

"Yes, sir. If we can crack the code, we should be able to retrace its movements."

Olaf Prost leaned forward and glared at Drake. "Captain, what is your assessment of *Conqueror*'s military capability, say as it compares to that of your own ship?"

"It's a *blastship*, Mr. Chairman. There is no comparison. In a fair fight, *Conqueror* would destroy all three battle cruisers in the fleet without ever having to resort to its primary batteries."

"Yet this blastship comes to us damaged and crewless. What is your reaction to that, Captain Drake?"

"My reaction, Mr. Chairman, is that *Conqueror* appears to have been in one hell of a fight. Whoever smashed it is someone to be feared."

Prost glanced at the other committee members as he had done at the beginning of the meeting. Once again, some silent consensus appeared to have been arrived at. He turned back to Drake.

"What would you say if I told you that we are actively considering an expedition to explore beyond the foldpoint, Captain Drake?"

"I would say that you are being very wise, Mr. Chairman."

"Why?"

"Because of *Conqueror*'s condition. We have to find out what is happening out there. Alta may well be in considerable danger now that the foldpoint is open once again."

Chairman Prost looked grim and nodded. "That was our conclusion as well. How quickly can you prepare your ship?"

"My ship, sir?" Drake asked in surprise. Up to that moment, he had been speaking in the abstract, giving theoretical answers to theoretical questions. Suddenly, the reason he'd been called home was obvious. They wanted *Discovery* for the interstellar expedition! "In theory, Mr. Chairman, we could be ready as quickly as we refuel and reprovision—say the day after tomorrow. In practice, of course, we would want to make far more extensive preparations. Check the weapons systems, overhaul the drive, recalibrate the jump engines. If we push hard, we can be ready in a month."

"A month will be entirely adequate, Captain Drake. There are quite a number of scientific studies going on at the moment. They will need the time to bear fruit."

"Uh, I presume, Mr. Chairman, that you have spoken to the terrestrial ambassador about this expedition."

Prost's expression showed his lack of comprehension. "What has he to do with it?"

Drake hesitated, searching for the best way to explain the situation to the legislators. "You need the terrestrial ambassador's permission to use *Discovery* for any out-system expedition, sir. He has the computer codes needed to operate our jump engines. Without them, we are not going anywhere!"

CHAPTER 7

Bethany Lindquist arrived home after a hard day at work to discover Carl Aster sprawled on her living-room couch. He had made himself a drink and was idly thumbing through one of her comparative history journals. Bethany had met Aster at one of the interminable cocktail parties that were a way of life in the capital. She had found him to be a charming man, a good dancer, and a skilled raconteur. They had begun seeing each other. Their relationship had moved from casual, to serious, and finally to a proposal of marriage. It was a proposal that she had not yet answered.

"Hi," he said as he jumped up from the couch, took her in his arms, and kissed her. When the kiss was over, he continued to hold her and asked, "How about marrying me, lady?"

"Ask me next week," she said, sighing. "Right now, I could use a hot bath, a quick meal, and a long night's sleep."

"Didn't I tell you?" he asked. "We're going out tonight!"

"Not tonight, Carl. I had a hard day."

"How could a historian have a hard day?"

She shrugged. "The same as everyone else, I suppose. The damned idiots at the library misplaced my request for a data search on the ancient Mesopotamians. I spent the whole shift doing it manually."

"Why bother?" he asked. "Who cares what happened

a thousand years ago and five hundred light-years from here?"

"It was closer to five thousand years ago, and your question is its own answer," she said. Aster's mocking of her profession had started out as a game between them. It wasn't as funny as it had once been.

"Comparative history is important," she said, "because human beings haven't changed in fifty thousand years. We may have settled other star systems, but deep down, we still react the same as our caveman ancestors. It's the job of people like me to study Earth history looking for parallels to our modern situation. When we find them, we look for how others resolved, or failed to resolve, problems similar to our own.

"For example, Alta is a frontier world that has developed an isolated, posturban society over the last century and a quarter. Every problem your bosses in Parliament face has some analog back in the days before space travel. It's just a matter of finding it."

"Okay, I'm sorry! Your job's important and you've had a rotten day. Let me make it up to you by taking you out tonight."

"Out where?" she asked.

"The prime minister is holding a reception for the Navy."

"What for?"

"Some of the people who chased down *Conqueror* will be there. My boss suspects the whole thing to be a front for some Social Democratic dirty dealing. He wants to make sure that the true faith is adequately represented. Besides, everybody who's anybody in Homeport is going to be there. Which reminds me. Your uncle is coming."

"My uncle? Are you sure?"

"That's what the boss said."

"But why?"

Aster shrugged. "That is one thing he wouldn't tell me. Rumor has it that your uncle refused the first time they asked him and the prime minister had a fit. They had to

send old Rheinhardt out to his place in the country to get
him to change his mind."

"What time is this reception?" Bethany asked.

"Twenty-one-hundred hours."

She sighed. "I'll go."

"Good for you! I'll pick you up no later than twenty
thirty." He reached for the cape that had been draped
over the back of the couch, then kissed her again. "Have
to go now. The boss wants me to see what I can find out
about the guest list. See you tonight."

"I'll be ready."

The men and women who had founded the Altan colony had selected the site for their capital city with the
care of parents choosing the genetic makeup of their first-
born. Experts spent man-years poring over stereographs
of the planet's surface, cataloging the strengths and weak-
nesses of various locations for potential settlements. And
even after the extensive surveys, the first colony ship to
enter the Valeria system was delayed for weeks in orbit
while ground parties examined the half dozen most likely
city-sites firsthand.

Eventually, the expedition managers chose a broad river
valley in the northwest quadrant of the landmass they had
arbitrarily dubbed Main Continent. Literally thousands of
parameters were considered before the choice was made.
Among the most important of these was the fact that the
river—which the original surveyors had named the Tigris
(having already used up the names Amazon, Nile, and
Euphrates)—was navigable from the city-site to the sea,
a distance of more than three hundred kilometers.

To the west of the valley, a range of mountains as tall
as the Sierra Nevadas on Earth broke the force of winter
storms. To the east, a landscape of gently rolling hills
allowed the warm rains of spring to reach the valley unhin-
dered. Beyond the rolling hills lay a vast agricultural plain
destined to be the colony's breadbasket throughout its
first century. Prospector satellites reported a variety of

mineral outcrops within reach of the site, but not so close as to present the future capital of Alta with an air pollution problem. The original village of Homeport had been built on a lightly forested rise above a bend in the Tigris River. The first structures were a dozen log cabins chinked with mud and wild grass, all huddled around a converted space-ship fusion power unit. Three hundred years later, the log cabins were gone. In their place stood the white mansions of their descendents.

Richard Drake gazed out the window of the groundcar as it slowly wound its way up the side of Nob Hill. Down below in the valley, the lights of Homeport seemed wan in comparison to the gleaming metallic sheen of Antares dawn-light reflected off the broad waters of the Tigris River. The nova had dimmed perceptibly in the month since Drake had last been on Alta, but it was still the brightest object by far in the night sky.

"Good to be home, Captain?" Admiral Dardan asked from his place beside Drake in the limousine's backseat.

"Yes, sir!" Drake replied. "Damned good!" It had been forty-six hours (two of Alta's twenty-three-hour days) since Drake had been called to testify before the Space Committee.

"Glad you came?"

"To tell the truth, Admiral, I really should be coming up with those fuel factors for the expedition rather than attending a cocktail party." Drake glanced around at the three other groundcars in convoy behind them. "So should my people."

Dardan shook his head. "This is more important. You and your people are the guests of honor."

"Yes, sir."

"More important, Captain," Dardan said, his voice taking on its official-business tone, "Clarence Whitlow is going to be here. The prime minister invited him personally so that we could talk to him about the problem of the jump codes."

Drake nodded. The revelation that Alta's three cruisers

had long been minus operating jump computers had come as an unwelcome shock to the Space Committee. The Conservatives had accused the Social Democrats of withholding information from them, the SDs had responded by protesting their innocence, and both sides had blamed the Navy. The admiral, obviously unhappy, had answered the chairman's demand for an explanation by saying: "Hell, Olaf, I thought you knew! Old Granville Whitlow wanted to make sure that Alta would never be a threat to Earth; so, before he turned the cruisers over to the Navy, he extracted the jump programs and authorization codes from the computers."

"Where are these codes now?" Prost had asked.

"Filed in the old embassy computer in the Admiralty subbasement. As far as I know, only Clarence Whitlow can gain access to them. If anyone else tries without the proper access codes, it could cause the computer to forget everything it knows."

The hearing had ended shortly afterward amid heated recriminations. After that, everyone acted as though nothing had happened. Drake had been assigned to review the interstellar expedition's preliminary mission plan. When he pointed out that the plan assumed the participation of *Discovery* or one of her sister ships, Commodore Wilson had told him not to worry.

"The problem's being worked on, Captain," he'd said confidently. "You take care of your part and leave the rest to us."

"Yes, sir."

The Admiralty limousine reached the top of Nob Hill and slowed. A large wrought-iron gate came into view on the right, and the driver turned into a long, wooded driveway. One by one, the rest of the cars followed. The woods gave way suddenly to an immaculately manicured lawn bordering a large white mansion. The building was ghost-like by nova-light, with patches of color around its base where colored floodlights were placed in the shrubbery.

The limousine pulled up to a series of broad steps. As

quickly as the car stopped, the door was opened by a liveried flunky. Drake followed the first admiral out. Both stopped to straighten their dress uniform caps, then climbed the steps to the mansion's portico. Waiting under the eaves was a plump, middle-aged woman in an evening gown cut for someone two decades younger.

"Luis! It has been entirely too long since you have accepted an invitation to one of my soirées. I'd almost given you up."

"Good evening, Mrs. Mortridge," Dardan said, bowing to kiss their hostess's proffered hand.

"Mrs. Mortridge, indeed! Call me Evelyn."

"Very well, Evelyn." Dardan turned to Drake. "May I present your guest of honor, Captain Lieutenant Richard Drake of the battle cruiser *Discovery*."

Mrs. Mortridge held out her hand for Drake to kiss. "Thank you so much for coming, Captain. My guests are just dying to hear about your exploits out in the deep black."

"I'm not sure how much I can tell, Mrs. Mortridge—"

"Evelyn, please!"

"Evelyn, then. Parliament has to decide how much of my report to release for public consumption. I understand that they are concerned about how the stock market will react."

"Oh, pooh! If Parliament knows something, everybody knows it. The smart money on the market discounted your findings a week before you got back. Don't pay any attention to those silly security regulations. Nobody else does."

"I'm afraid that I must, Evelyn."

She regarded him with a strange look. Up to that moment, Drake had assumed she was a social butterfly and nothing more. The look the dowager gave him was strangely penetrating, and caused him to reevaluate his first impression. "Have it your own way, my dear."

By the time their exchange ended, the admiral's aides and Drake's subordinates were coming up the steps. Dardan introduced each in turn to Mrs. Mortridge, who immediately slipped back into the role of hostess.

After the introductions, the party went inside. The interior of the mansion was ablaze with color. A string quartet played in the entrance hall as people stood clustered in small groups sipping drinks. The sound of a full orchestra emanated from somewhere deeper within the house. Mrs. Mortridge turned to Bela Marston, Argos Cristobal, and Jonas Symes and said, "I'm going to borrow your captain for a while, gentlemen. You'll find the bar down the hall, second door on the left. There are plenty of unattached women here tonight, so feel free to circulate."

"Thank you, ma'am." Marston bowed.

"Call me Evelyn, Commander."

Drake watched enviously as his officers disappeared toward the bar, then turned to discover that he was alone with his hostess. Dardan and Wilson had somehow managed to slip away in the confusion. He sighed, resigned himself to a difficult evening, and bowed. "I'm at your service, Evelyn."

For the next twenty minutes, Mrs. Mortridge escorted him around the crowd, introducing him to each cluster of guests. Drake lost track after the first fifty platitudes. Just as he was beginning to think that escape was impossible, Mrs. Mortridge was called away to attend to some problem. ". . . Honestly, Richard, you just can't get good servants these days. Will you excuse me?"

Drake muttered that he could manage on his own, then hurriedly backed away. Two minutes later he was ordering a drink at the bar. He took the first appreciative sip, rolled the tart liquid over his tongue, and swallowed. As the pleasant warmth began to spread through him, a well-dressed man moved to stand beside him.

"Captain Drake?"

"Yes."

"My name's Converse. Greg Converse. I'm a manufacturer from Southridge. Mind telling the story of your adventure with this starship one more time?"

"I'm afraid that I can't tell you any more than has been on the news."

"Believe me, Captain, I'm not asking you to give me any classified data. I just want to know what it was like."

Drake picked up his drink and moved to a nearby setee. The manufacturer followed. A small clump of listeners quickly congregated around them. Drake scanned the expectant faces and began to recount his story once more.

"Is it true that you found bodies aboard?" Converse asked after Drake had been speaking for several minutes.

"It's true."

"And that one of them was a woman?"

"Yes."

"What would a woman have been doing aboard a warship?"

"She was wearing the uniform of a weapons tech," Drake replied. "I presume she was a member of the crew."

"Women spacers, imagine that!" someone said.

"It takes no imagination at all!" a contralto voice said from the edge of the crowd. Drake turned to gaze up at the new participant in the discussion. The woman was a reddish brunette, with striking eyes, a heart-shaped face, and an ample figure. She was dressed in a clinging, backless evening gown. She pushed her way into the inner circle and seated herself on the arm of an overstuffed chair that was part of the small conversational grouping around the setee. She turned to face the man who had made the comment about woman spacers.

"The fact is that there have been many women spacers throughout history. The first was a woman named Valentina Tereshkova. By the time Antares exploded, the Grand Fleet of Earth was nearly twenty percent female. Some of the commercial starship crews had an even larger percentage of women. Check your history books if you don't believe me."

"I stand corrected," the man who had made the comment said. He glanced nervously down at the empty glass in his hand, then backed out of the inner ring of listeners.

"It's true, you know," the woman said, continuing in the same lecturing tone. "The Altan ethic restricting women from the so-called risk professions is a result of our ancestors' need to populate this planet. It wasn't unusual for pioneer women to give birth to six, eight, or even ten children each. Raising such a brood leaves very little time for anything else, I assure you."

"We surrender!" Converse said, holding his hands aloft.

The young woman looked sheepish and turned toward Drake. "Forgive me, Captain. I'm a historian by trade and sometimes I get carried away when talking about my specialty."

"Nothing to forgive," he said. "I agree with you. Many's the time on a long patrol that I would have given a year's pay just to hear the sound of a female voice. By the way, my name's Richard Drake."

"I'm Bethany Lindquist," she replied, reaching out to shake his hand. "Please, I didn't mean to interrupt. Continue with your story."

Drake took up where he'd left off, describing his brief visit to *Conqueror*. When he reached the moment when he'd received the recall order, he concluded with "That's about all I'm free to say. Now, I think I'd best circulate before our hostess finds me hiding out in the bar."

His comment was greeted by polite laughter. The crowd broke into small groups. Bethany Lindquist turned to leave. Drake caught up with her as she passed through the portal between the small side room where the bar was located and the main ballroom.

"May I buy you a drink?"

She smiled, showing perfect white teeth. "Why, thank you, Richard. I was on my way to get another when I stopped to listen to your story."

He deposited his own empty glass on the tray of a passing waiter, snagged two full ones, and handed one to Bethany in a single, smooth motion.

"You're a spacer, all right!" she said, laughing.

"What makes you say that?"

"The way you balance those glasses. No one who has stumbled around under Altan gravity all his life could possibly have performed that maneuver without spilling a drop."

"Would you be offended if I asked whether you are here alone?"

"Far from being offended, Richard, I consider it a compliment that you are interested. Sorry, no. I'm here with a friend. He's closeted somewhere with his boss."

"If I were your escort, I wouldn't leave your side."

"You wouldn't?" she asked with a tinge of humor in her voice.

"Never!"

"Glad to hear it because I think Admiral Dardan is looking for you."

Drake turned to follow her gaze. Sure enough, the first admiral was elbowing his way through the crowd in their direction. He sighed, "I suppose one shouldn't be quite so absolute when forecasting the future."

"No, one should not," she agreed.

"Drake!" Dardan said as he reached the couple. "Time to go to work."

Drake turned to Bethany Lindquist and bowed. "Sorry. May I have a dance later?"

"Of course, Richard. Now, go along with the admiral. 'A man's got to do what a man's got to do,' you know."

"Beg pardon?"

"Never mind, just an ancient quotation. Don't worry about me. I'm perfectly capable of fending for myself until my friend finishes his business."

Dardan led Drake to a wing of the mansion that had yet to be invaded by the party. They left the music and dancing behind to trod plush carpeted floors through halls paneled in *zeowood*. The first admiral stopped in front of an intricately carved door, knocked, and was rewarded by a muffled command to enter.

Inside were three men. Drake recognized two of them.

Of these, one was Stan Barrett. The other was the prime minister.

Gareth Reynolds was an old-time politico who had worked his way up through the ranks of the Social Democratic Party. He had begun his career as a poll watcher, then had been promoted to rally organizer and ward captain in quick succession. Having proved himself at the grassroots, he was given the opportunity to run for Parliament. His first election bid had been as a "resigner" from one of the SD safe districts—someone willing to give up his seat for a member of the Cabinet (should one of those worthies fail in his own bid for reelection). Reynolds proved himself an effective MP. By the next general election, he was given a seat of his own, and thus was launched a steady, two-decades-long rise through the legislative ranks. Reynolds had been elected prime minister six years earlier at the last transfer of power between the two major parties.

"Ah, Captain Drake! Welcome," the prime minister said as he stood to greet the two naval officers. "A first-rate job you did on this *Conqueror* thing. First rate!"

"Thank you for the kind words, Prime Minister."

"Not at all. You Navy people get far too little recognition as it is. Now then, I don't believe you know Clarence Whitlow, the terrestrial ambassador."

"Captain," the ambassador said, nodding in Drake's direction from where he sat in a high-back chair.

"I've asked for this meeting," the prime minister said, steering Drake to another chair, "because I wanted Ambassador Whitlow to hear your report firsthand. You'll find your record cube already in the projector." Reynolds indicated a cube reader on the coffee table in front of him. As he did so, Stan Barrett fingered a control, causing a commercial model holocube to drop out of the ceiling.

"Drink, Richard?" Admiral Dardan asked.

"Uh, yes, sir."

When everyone had settled into place, Drake began to recount the history of the mission in greater detail than

he had used for Converse and the crowd of listeners around
the bar. He illustrated his story with the same views of
Conqueror that he'd used before the Space Committee.
He had intended to speak for no more than half an hour,
but found that by the time he'd answered all of the questions put to him, twice that length of time had lapsed.

"Most interesting," Clarence Whitlow said as the holocube went dark at the end of Drake's talk. He turned to
face Gareth Reynolds. "I appreciate your taking the time
to show me this, Prime Minister. However, I must admit
to being somewhat confused."

"How so, Mr. Ambassador?"

"This solicitous attitude by your administration is as
welcome as it is . . . unusual. I have been terrestrial ambassador for quite a number of years now, and this is the first
time the Altan government has consulted me on anything."

"A shortsighted policy on our part," the prime minister
said, "and one I have decided to rectify. Since *Conqueror*
is an Earth ship, we thought it best to bring you up to
date on our investigation."

"Are you saying that you plan to turn control of *Conqueror* over to me as Earth's representative here on Alta?"
Whitlow asked.

There was a low, throat-clearing noise from the first
admiral. "Ah, we intend to salvage the blastship in the
name of the government, Mr. Ambassador. *Dagger* and
a tanker are already en route to begin the long process of
returning it to the inner system."

Whitlow spread his arms in a plaintive gesture. "Then
I fail to understand my presence here."

"Surely," the prime minister said, "you must realize
that the appearance of this blastship is no everyday event."

"Obviously not."

"To state the obvious, Mr. Ambassador, *Conqueror*'s
emergence into this system signals the end of our long
isolation; an event that will not be an unmixed blessing,
I assure you. There are many questions to be answered.

For instance, what will the resumption of interstellar trade do to our economy? Who will benefit and who will suffer? What will happen to the value of the stellar? Will we be able to compete with other systems, or will our technology be so out of date that no one will want to buy our products?"

"All important questions, I'm sure, Mr. Prime Minister. But what have they to do with me?"

"There is a great deal we don't know about this situation, Mr. Ambassador. One thing we do know, however, is that *Conqueror*'s condition strongly suggests that a war is raging somewhere beyond the foldpoint. Furthermore, if one out-system warship can find us, so can others. It seems to me and the leaders of Parliament that it would be better for Alta if we found them first. That being the case, we have arranged to send a scouting expedition beyond the foldpoint, perhaps as far beyond as Earth itself."

"An expedition to Earth?" Whitlow asked. "How wonderful! Will I have time to prepare dispatches to send along?"

"Plenty of time, Mr Ambassador," Admiral Dardan said. "It will take at least a month to ready the ships."

"Excellent. I must begin thinking about my report tonight."

"Ah, there is one other point, Mr. Ambassador," the admiral said.

"Yes?"

"The expedition will include a converted passenger liner and two tankers. The liner will house the scientists and diplomatic personnel, the tankers will carry extra fuel. None of these ships is armed, nor can they be so equipped within a reasonable time. Since they are headed into a probable war zone, we feel it advisable to send a cruiser along for their protection. Therefore, Captain Drake's *Discovery* has been chosen as expedition flagship."

"Obviously," the prime minister said, taking over from

Dardan, "*Discovery*'s jump computer must be restored to operational status before it can go anywhere."

"Obviously," Whitlow agreed.

"I'm glad you see our point, sir. May I assume from your answer that you are willing to provide us with the computer routines and passwords that you hold in escrow in the old embassy data banks?"

Whitlow locked eyes with the prime minister. "I sympathize with your problem, Prime Minister. However, you must recognize that I have sworn an oath to protect Earth's interests, not Alta's."

"I assure you, sir, both coincide in the current situation."

"You can't know that, not until after the expedition returns with their observations. By that time, it would be far too late to rescind my permission, wouldn't it? It is the irreversible nature of returning the jump codes to the cruisers that my predecessors have always feared. To use an ancient allegory of which my niece is fond, 'the genie would be out of the bottle for good.'"

"Are you saying that you *refuse*?"

Whitlow gave forth with a wan smile, set his drink down, and clambered stiffly to his feet. "I am saying that I will have to think about it. Now, gentlemen, if you will excuse me, I have some serious soul searching to do."

Prime Minister Reynolds nodded. "One more thing before you go, Mr. Ambassador."

"Yes?"

"Please think carefully about our request. The fate of this planet may well depend on your decision."

Clarence Whitlow sighed. "That, sir, is what I'm afraid of."

CHAPTER 8

The Antares Supernova was low in the eastern sky when Carl Aster returned Bethany Lindquist to her apartment building in the modern section of Homeport. The building was one of several that had been built in parklike splendor on the western bank of the Tigris. They strolled arm in arm along a winding pathway through a stand of heavily perfumed *cero* trees. The silence of the night was broken only by the gurgling of the nearby river and the occasional flat splashing sound of a pseudofrog leaping after a night-flying insectovoid. Overhead, other small flyers danced around the gauzy globe of a street lamp while silver clouds sailed majestically across the sky.

"Have you forgiven me yet for making you fend for yourself tonight?" Aster asked as they approached the entrance to the building.

"I'm thinking about it," Bethany replied as she stifled a yawn. It was well past midnight and she had been bored for much of the evening. Too bad Admiral Dardan took Captain Drake away, she thought. *There* was an interesting man! "What were you doing all that time, anyway?"

"Making useful contacts," Aster said. "The government has this interstellar expedition coming up, and we're going to make sure that the Alliance is properly represented this time."

"How'd you do?"

"I think I may have swayed a couple of votes."

"That's nice," she said without enthusiasm. Bethany had long ago found that she had a low tolerance for the basic nuts-and-bolts of politics. Her aversion was one reason she'd declined her uncle's request that she succeed him as terrestrial ambassador. Not for the first time, she wondered whether the prospect of being a politician's wife wasn't what had stopped her from immediately accepting Carl's proposal of marriage.

Aster noted her somber mood, slipped a hand around her waist, and drew her close. "What did you do this evening?"

"I met a man."

"Oh?"

"Handsome, too."

"Who was he?"

"The guest of honor."

"You mean Captain Drake?"

Bethany nodded. "He was telling us about *Conqueror*."

"Did he say anything about the upcoming expedition?"

"Not that I can remember."

"How did you like him?"

"He was nice, also considerably younger than I expected."

Aster laughed. "All the active-duty Navy people are young. It has something to do with tolerance to acceleration, I understand."

They reached the lighted entrance of Bethany's apartment building. Aster pulled her close. "Now, about that apology," he said, kissing her.

"Apology accepted," she replied when they were finished.

"Mind if I come up for a nightcap?"

She shook her head. "It's late, I'm tired, and I have to get up in a few hours."

Aster shrugged. "Oh well, can't say I didn't try. I'll call you at work later today."

"I'll be waiting."

She watched him go, then entered the lobby of the

apartment building. Her heels tapped lightly on marble tile floor as she crossed to the lift. Half a minute later and twenty stories higher, she pressed her key against the lockplate of her apartment door. As the door slid into its recess in the wall, she was surprised to discover that the lights were on inside.

Clarence Whitlow sat in her big, overstuffed easy chair with his feet up. A drink sat untouched on the end table beside him and a book lay open in his lap. She noted that the book in his lap was Granville Whitlow's autobiography.

"Uncle, what are you doing here?"

"I hope you don't mind. Some mixup about the hotel reservations."

"Not at all. I'm glad to have you anytime. You didn't have to wait up, you know. You could have taken the bedroom and left a note on the door. Why are you reading a book in my living room at this time of the morning?"

"Speaking of which, isn't it a bit late for you to be getting home?" he asked, arching one eyebrow.

She laughed. "You'd think that I was twelve again, coming home from my first date."

"One of the joys of parenting, Bethany, is never having to admit that the child must eventually grow into adulthood. Did your young man go home?"

"His name is Carl, not 'young man'; and yes, he did." She stared at Whitlow for a moment. "You don't like Carl, do you?"

He started to object, then grinned. "Does it show that clearly?"

"Only to one who knows you as well as I do. What have you got against him?"

"Just call it a difference in style," Whitlow replied. "Nothing for you to concern yourself with. After all, I'm not the one who is thinking of marrying him."

"You're right. I am. Now, you've evaded my question long enough. What are you doing up this late, and why

are you reading great-great-grandfather's autobiography?
I thought you committed it to memory years ago."

"I did. I was hoping to find guidance in here."

"Guidance for what?"

"I had my meeting with the prime minister tonight. I
found out why he wanted to see me."

"Why?"

Whitlow sketched the details of his meeting with Gareth Reynolds and the Navy people.

"Are you going to give them the codes, Uncle?"

"I don't know."

"Surely you don't think the government would use
Discovery against Earth!"

He looked at her. For the first time, Bethany saw how
old her uncle was. It was as though he had aged two
decades in a single night. "In truth, no. To all of us who
have never seen it, Earth is a place of legend and magic.
I can't conceive that any Altan would knowingly harm
the Mother of Men."

"Then where's the problem?"

"There is the small matter of the oath I took. 'Clarence,
son,' my father told me, 'we colonists are interlopers on
this world, rootless aliens living amid strangeness, totally
cut off from the others of our kind. To survive, we need
an ideal, a kind of bedrock into which we can sink the
anchors of our lives. Earth provides us with that ideal. It
is our past. Earth shaped us and made us the way we are.
Even across five hundred light-years of unbridgeable
space, it calls out to us.

"'You are to be the sole representative of Earth on this
planet, my boy. There will come a time, Clarence, when
someone will ask you to compromise your ideals and do
something that may not be in the best interest of that far-
off world that you have never seen. Their reasons will be
good, sound, and logical. You will find yourself sorely
tempted. My advice to you is to ignore all such appeals
to logic. Rely, instead, on what you know is right, and,
above all, be true to your heritage.'" Whitlow glanced up

at his niece. His eyes reflected the light as they filled with wetness. "My father was on his deathbed when he spoke those words. I told him that he could count on me."

"Then you aren't going to give them the codes?" Bethany asked.

"I don't know. Logic tells me to play it safe and refuse. After all, even one of our antiquated cruisers carries enough weaponry to sterilize a planet. What if that planet was Earth? It's not as though I would be keeping Alta from a return to interstellar space. There are dozens of ships in this system with operational jump systems. They could explore space beyond the foldpoint and then report back on conditions there. At least, then I would have some data on which to base my decision."

"You sound dubious, Uncle."

"Do I?" Whitlow asked, with an ironic laugh. "Perhaps that is because I am. The problem is that I am trying to make this decision without any hard facts to back me up. Correction! As the prime minister told me several times tonight, we have one incontrovertible fact—*Conqueror* was virtually destroyed before it entered this system. Apparently, the *Pax Terra* has ceased to exist and Earth is once again at war. What if my refusal means that Earth will be denied our help in her hour of need?"

An unpleasant thought surfaced in Bethany's mind. She considered it for a moment, then decided that it was something that needed to be said. "Maybe Earth has changed, Uncle. More than a century's passed. Maybe it isn't the same place our ancestors swore allegiance to. What if the central government has been taken over by some latter-day Genghis Khan?"

"Do you think I haven't considered that possibility? The thought doesn't seem to have occurred to the government yet. Or, if it has, they are being careful not to say so for political reasons. Which brings me back to my problem. There just isn't enough data on which to make an intelligent decision."

"You could *lend* them the jump codes," Bethany said.

"Once the expedition is over, you could take them back if that seemed the proper thing to do."

"Do you think the first admiral would agree to such an arrangement?"

"He might."

Whitlow's answer was a rude snort. "Once that cruiser's jump engines are operational, the Navy will never let me near them again. I suppose I could go along to insert the passwords manually whenever the ship had to make a transition. That way I could maintain control, yet still allow *Discovery* to lead the expedition."

"You can't!" Bethany said, horrified at the thought.

"Why not?"

"Your heart would never stand up to high boost."

"Have you a better idea?"

"Send someone else."

Whitlow screwed up his face as though he'd bitten into a sour *gravafruit*. "That's a problem. There is only one person who I would trust with such a responsibility."

"Send him . . ." Bethany's voice trailed off to a whisper as she noted the look on her uncle's face. The kindly old man who had raised her was gone. In his place was a mover of worlds. Intent brown eyes peered up at her from the depths of a granite visage.

"Captain Drake. There's a gentleman and lady here to see you," the yeoman on the Admiralty desk said from out of Drake's workscreen.

"Who is it, Kraeler?"

The yeoman glanced over his shoulder as though to make sure that he would not be overheard, then leaned close to the phone pickup and said, "You know that crazy old man who spends all his time down in the subbasement?"

"Are you referring to His Excellency, the terrestrial ambassador, Yeoman?" Drake asked gruffly.

"Uh, yes, sir. Ambassador Whitlow and his niece, sir."

"Kraeler, it may interest you to know that the ambassador holds the key to the upcoming expedition into fold-space. If you have offended him in any way by your display of disrespect, the first admiral will see that you are assigned to the liquid helium inventory on Frostbite, which is nothing compared to what I will do to you first."

Kraeler blushed visibly. "Uh, sorry, Captain. I didn't think—"

"Damned right you didn't! I'll be down in a minute. In the interim, try to be civil to our guests." Drake didn't wait for an answer before cutting the phone circuit. He immediately keyed for the first admiral.

"What is it, Drake?"

"Ambassador Whitlow is here, sir."

Dardan's eyebrows lifted in surprise. "Is he alone?"

"No, sir. The yeoman on duty says that he has his niece with him."

"Well, have them sent up— No, better yet, you go down and get them."

"I was about to, sir."

"Bring them to my office."

"Shall I have someone notify the prime minister's office, sir?"

"Not yet, Captain. Let's see what they want first."

"Yes, sir."

Drake informed the duty officer where he would be, then hurried down to greet Clarence Whitlow. He found the ambassador in the lobby. With him was a woman. Even though she had her back to Drake as he stepped from the lift, there was something familiar about her.

"Welcome, Mr. Ambassador. Glad you could come... Why hello!"

The woman had turned around at the sound of his voice, revealing the enchanting face that he had admired the previous evening at Mrs. Mortridge's party.

"Hello, Captain Drake," Bethany Lindquist said.

"Do you two know each other?" Whitlow asked.

"We met last night, sir," Drake said. "However, I didn't know that Bethany was your niece."

"You didn't ask," Bethany said, smiling.

"I guess I didn't." Drake turned back to Whitlow. "The admiral has asked that I accompany you to his office, Mr. Ambassador."

"That is the reason we are here."

"Yes, sir. Please follow me."

Drake led them to the lift. Once the three of them were inside, he punched for the first admiral's office. He spent the next few seconds admiring Bethany Lindquist's reflection in the polished stainless steel of the closed lift door.

The first admiral shook Whitlow's hand and kissed that of his niece before ushering them to the area of his office where several high-back chairs covered in *zzoro* leather faced each other.

"Coffee, Mr. Ambassador?"

"Please, Admiral. I take mine straight."

"How about you, Miss Lindquist?"

"Cream only," Bethany said.

The admiral spoke a few quick orders into the air. A minute later, a steward in a white coat entered with a tray bearing four cups of coffee—actually an Altan substitute, which many of the Founders had found unpalatable. When everyone had been served, the admiral took a sip from his cup, then set it down on the table in front of him.

"How may I help you this morning, Ambassador Whitlow?" Dardan asked.

"I spent most of last evening thinking about the prime minister's request that I relinquish *Discovery*'s jump codes, Admiral. Frankly, I am inclined to do so, but only on my own terms."

"Which are?"

"I propose to provide *Discovery*'s basic jump routines to your people, but to keep control of the security passwords that are required to validate orders sent to the jump system computer."

"I fail to see the point, Mr. Ambassador. What good

are jump codes if the computer refuses to acknowledge orders?"

"The passwords will remain in the possession of my personal representative, who will manually input them into the computer just before each foldspace transition. After transition the passwords will be removed until the next time they are needed."

"Giving your representative an absolute veto as to where this expedition goes and what it does," Dardan mused.

"Precisely!" Whitlow agreed. "When I assumed my position as terrestrial ambassador, I took an oath to protect Earth's interests. This arrangement is the only way I can think of to discharge my obligations honorably."

"Are we to be informed of the identity of this paragon of integrity on whose shoulders will rest the fate of this planet?" Dardan asked.

"Hardly a paragon, Admiral," Bethany Lindquist blurted out.

Dardan turned toward Bethany, a questioning look on his face.

Embarrassed, Bethany cleared her throat and cast her eyes downward to where her hands fidgeted in her lap. "Excuse the interruption," she muttered.

"I take it, Miss Lindquist, that you know this person."

"You might say that, Admiral," she said with a note of defiance in her voice. "My uncle has asked me to represent him on this expedition. I have agreed to do so."

"Impossible!" Drake growled.

"Why, Captain?" Clarence Whitlow asked.

"Because your niece's presence aboard would be disruptive, sir. Be sensible! Most of my crew has been in space for more than a year! Besides, we have no facilities for women aboard, and if we have to fight, it may not be healthy aboard *Discovery*. Believe me, this expedition is no place for a woman."

"Captain Drake. Unless my niece accompanies you, there will *be* no expedition."

Bethany said, "You expressed a different opinion last evening, Captain Drake."

"Making coversation with a pretty girl at a party is one thing, Miss Lindquist. Riding herd on two hundred crewmen with overactive libidos is quite another." He turned to Admiral Dardan. "Sir, we can't let them do this to us!"

Dardan scratched his chin and sighed. "I fail to see how we can stop them, Richard. We need those codes and this appears to be the only way to get them."

"But . . ."

Dardan stared at his subordinate, then growled, "That's an order, Captain!"

"Yes, sir. I suppose we can put her up in Mr. Marston's cabin."

"Am I to take it, Admiral, that you are agreeing to my proposal?" Clarence Whitlow asked.

"Do I have any choice?"

"No, sir."

"Then I'm agreeing. Naturally, I will have to check with the prime minister."

"Naturally."

"Once that's done, we can formalize things."

First Admiral Dardan reported in person to the prime minister regarding his meeting with Clarence Whitlow. The PM listened in silence as Dardan explained the terrestrial ambassador's request, and his (Dardan's) tentative acquiescence. When the admiral had finished his report, the prime minister leaned back in his chair and regarded him with a weary gaze.

"Was it wise to agree so quickly to such an arrangement, Luis?"

"I thought it best, Prime Minister. If a war is raging beyond the foldpoint, we're going to need all of our cruisers' jump engines reactivated. This seemed a good first step toward that goal."

"I fail to see how," Reynolds replied.

"Clarence Whitlow is suffering from the same malady

we are, Prime Minister. He lacks information with which to make intelligent decisions. By agreeing to his terms, we provide him with a source of information in the person of his niece. Hopefully, once he—and we—are better informed, we'll all come to the conclusion that our interests are compatible. If so, it is likely that he will release the remaining cruisers' jump codes and passwords of his own volition."

"What if he decides that our interests are diametrically opposed?"

"Then we will have Bethany Lindquist on our side to help convince him."

"What makes you think that?"

"I had a talk with Captain Drake after Whitlow and his niece left my office. He has orders to give the woman full access to all data obtained during the expedition."

"*All* data, Admiral? Is that wise?"

"Yes, sir. We can't afford having her think that we are hiding anything from her. If we treat her properly, she can't help but view our efforts sympathetically."

"What do we know about this Bethany Lindquist?" Reynolds asked.

Dardan pulled several printouts from his briefcase. "She's a comparative historian at Alta University. Her fitness reports are all superior. I've talked to her supervisor and he seems to be very impressed with her competence."

"What about her politics?"

"She doesn't seem to have strong opinions one way or the other. We know that she has resisted her uncle's desire that she succeed him as terrestrial ambassador. Poll records indicate that she votes regularly, but that's about all . . . at least, until quite recently."

"What happened recently?"

"She became involved with Carl Aster."

The prime minister sat suddenly erect in his chair. "Aster? Jonathon Carstairs' aide?"

"Yes, sir."

"Most curious. Just this morning, Carstairs submitted his list of personnel for the expedition. The scientists are all strong supporters of the Conservative Alliance, of course—I would have been surprised if they were otherwise. Of the nonscientists, two were of particular interest. Carstairs is nominating Alicia Delevan as coambassador and Carl Aster as her aide. Furthermore, Gentleman Jonathon hinted that there will be trouble if Delevan and Aster aren't picked to go along. Now, Admiral, you tell me that Clarence Whitlow's representative is Aster's girlfriend? If I were a suspicious person, I would think that the Alliance is trying to take control of this expedition."

"As a military man, Prime Minister, I am not allowed to take sides in politics. However, if you are asking for my professional opinion regarding the expedition—"

"I am, Luis."

"Then, sir, my recommendation remains the same. Whatever the political liabilities of Bethany Lindquist's relationship with Aster, it doesn't change our situation regarding her uncle. We should accept his offer before he raises the ante."

The prime minister thought about it for a moment, then nodded. "Agreed. It may surprise you, Admiral, but there are still some of us vote scratchers around who place the interests of the planet above those of party. I have already decided to accept a number of Carstairs' kept scientists on this expedition. To do otherwise would spark a needless battle in Parliament, one that we might well lose.

"Begin your preparations. I'll order a formal treaty drawn up outlining the terms of our agreement with the Earth ambassador. Tell Clarence Whitlow that it will be ready for signatures within the week."

"Yes, sir."

Alicia Delevan was a small woman with coal-black hair and a face that looked pinched if she wasn't careful about the expressions she used. She was a sociologist by training and a socioeconomist by profession. It had long been her

opinion that the Industrial Guild was purposely manipu-
lating public policy to drive smaller businesses into tax
bankruptcy. Unable to get her Social Democratic member
of Parliament to listen to her complaint, she had begun
working for the Conservative Alliance to pass a bill that
would have lowered the tax rate on single-proprietor business. Eventually, she had run for Parliament herself.

That had been six Altan years ago. She had been
appointed to the prestigious Space Committee the previous year as a reward for orchestrating the successful
overthrow of a Social Democrat public works project. The
appointment had been a sign that the party was grooming
her for higher office. She'd found the work interesting
and had impressed Jonathon Carstairs with her political
savvy. She was, therefore, flattered when he recommended her to represent the Alliance on the interstellar
expedition.

She was flattered, but far from happy.

Alicia Delevan had never had any desire to go to space.
In her opinion, there was more than enough to worry
about on Alta to be concerned with the heavens. Like
Carstairs, she considered the Antares Supernova to be a
nuisance, and had greeted the news that the foldpoint was
once again open with something less than enthusiasm. In
fact, Alicia considered an expedition to the Napier system
to be little more than an attempt to relive past glory.

"Why me?" she had asked Carstairs when he suggested
that she represent the Conservative Alliance on the interstellar expedition.

"Because you are smart, because you are intelligent
enough to know when to cooperate with the opposition
and when to fight, and because I trust you."

"But I've got work to do here. We're trying to force a
general election, remember?"

"This *Conqueror* business is going to delay our plans,
Alicia. The electorate is too damned excited by the prospect of a return to interstellar travel. If we ask for an
election today, the general air of good feeling will sweep

Reynolds and his cronies back into office for another five years. We can hardly risk that, now can we?

"And that's the reason we need you on this expedition. The Social Democrats are going to milk this thing for everything it's worth. We need you out there to remind the people that the SDs aren't alone in ending our isolation."

"But what am I supposed to *do*?"

"You're to be my eyes and ears. Keep alert for opportunities. Cooperate with the SDs if that makes sense, oppose them otherwise. But primarily, bring me back an accurate report of the situation out there."

Alicia sighed. "I suppose there's no arguing the point with you."

Carstairs smiled humorlessly. "None at all. I need someone I can trust out there, and you're elected."

CHAPTER 9

There is an old saying among those who fly the ships of space: "No vessel ever leaves port until the mass of the authorizing paperwork exceeds the body weight of the largest man aboard." In the month that followed *Discovery*'s return to Alta, Richard Drake found himself contemplating that piece of folk wisdom more and more often. If anything, he was beginning to wonder if it didn't seriously understate reality.

The signing of the protocol between the Altan planetary government and Clarence Whitlow took place in the Great Hall of Parliament six days after the meeting in the first admiral's office. Prime Minister Reynolds, Jonathon Carstairs, and First Admiral Dardan represented the government in the televised ceremony. Clarence Whitlow, resplendent in the uniform of a commander in the Grand Fleet of Earth (Granville Whitlow's reserve rank at the time of the supernova), represented Earth. Both sides signed with proper solemnity. When the protocol was safely sealed into the old embassy computers in the Admiralty subbasement, Whitlow reached into his pocket, extracted a record crystal, and handed it to the prime minister as the two hundred invited guests broke into applause.

The successful turnover had been the excuse for a day-long celebration and formal ball. Richard Drake attended reluctantly and, to his own surprise, enjoyed himself thoroughly. Much of his enjoyment came from the several opportunities he took to dance with Bethany Lindquist. Both avoided mentioning their disagreement over her presence aboard *Discovery*; and in the course of the evening they found that they had a number of interests in common. Drake would have gladly monopolized her company into the early-morning hours, but found himself the recipient of progressively less friendly looks from Carl Aster. Around midnight, Drake excused himself and left the party. Early the next morning he boarded *Moliere*. Two hours later, he delivered a record tile containing the jump codes to the engineers aboard *Discovery*.

Bringing the jump computer online was more difficult than originally expected. For 125 years, cosmic rays had rained down on the cruiser. Occasionally, one of these microscopic bullets would impact something important in the jump engine control circuitry. Sometimes the change was sufficiently gross to show up in the periodic, but relatively crude, maintenance checks (the only checks possible in the absence of the computer's operational codes). Other times, however, the damage was too subtle to be easily detected. The result was a slow accumulation of incipient failures in the computer and its peripheral equipment. Fully 10 percent of the jump computer's circuits failed the self-test checks on initial power-up, with a like percentage downchecked during the continuous maintenance evaluations run over the next two weeks.

Drake found that he was forced to assign more skilled technicians to the computer effort than he'd originally anticipated. This resulted in a shortage of people to check out the rest of the ship's systems. Therefore, he improvised. Communicators were assigned to check life-support equipment. Weapons techs found themselves tearing into radars and infrared scanners. Photon drive specialists helped balance mass converter containment fields. In spite of the manpower shortage, Drake insisted that every part of the ship be gone over with painstaking thoroughness. Any part that was even slightly suspect was replaced, right down to the urn in the enlisted men's mess.

Nor was *Discovery* Drake's only worry. As expedition commander, it was his responsibility to oversee the preparations of the scientific and commercial contingent aboard the passenger ship that would accompany the cruiser.

In 2512, *City of Alexandria* had been an overage passenger liner plying the Antares Cluster. It had been on one of its twice-yearly visits to the Valeria system when the foldpoint disappeared. Unlike the cruisers, the newly cut-off colony had found no compelling reason to keep *Alexandria* operating. The liner had gone immediately into orbital storage to await the day when it would be needed for interplanetary transport within the Val system. After a hundred years, a syndicate of investors had purchased the ship. They had planned to convert it to a spacegoing pleasure palace and take it out to the asteroid belts, but had run out of money before the refit was completed. For the next two decades, the old liner had been something of a white elephant, passing from one owner to the next. By the time *Conqueror* appeared in the Altan sky, the ship had been on the resale market for more than a year.

Richard Drake and Bela Marston, encased in vacsuits, sat side by side, strapped to the bench seat of an orbit-to-orbit bug. The bug, a small egg-shaped craft used for short jaunts between ships and stations in orbit, was little more than a cabin surrounded by fuel tanks and thruster-clusters. However, what the craft lacked in comfort was more than offset by the spectacular view through the transparent plastic of its hull.

The bug was oriented with its landing skids toward the sky and its bubble-cabin toward the planet. As a result, Alta hung overhead, a jewellike orb on a cloth of black velvet. Directly ahead lay a paintpot swirl of white clouds and blue seas that extended unbroken to the planetary limb. Above and to the left was the gleam of the southern polar ice cap. To the right, Main Continent seemed a giant ship making stubborn progress across the Voss Sea, trailing the Islands of Paradise in its wake.

"*City of Alexandria* reports the docking portal is now clear, Captain," Marston said from beside Drake. "We've been authorized to begin our final approach."

"Take us in, Number One."

"Yes, sir."

Drake gazed directly ahead, looking over the jutting nozzles of the bow thruster-cluster. He scanned space just beyond the planetary limb, searching for a tiny, geometric shape. After a few moments of searching, he was rewarded by the sight of a tiny cylinder hanging in space. Over the next several minutes, the cylinder grew slowly larger. As it did so, smaller shapes began to appear around it. As they closed still farther, it became obvious that the cylinder was rotating about its central axis several times each minute.

City of Alexandria was approximately the size of *Discovery*. Unlike the battle cruiser, however, the liner had been built on the cylindrical plan. Living quarters were located in the high-gravity section around the periphery; cargo holds were inboard, near the axis of the ship; engines and tankage were aft. Around *Alexandria*'s waist, several large hatchways opened onto deep wells into the ship's cargo holds. Another hatch, located at the axis of rotation at the ship's bow, was used as a docking portal while the ship was rotating.

The liner grew massive as the orbital bug made its final approach. Shuttles were clustered around *Alexandria*'s prow, each waiting its turn at the docking portal. Marston edged the bug through the gathering of winged shuttles and lined up on the closed docking portal doors. As they approached, the doors swung wide to reveal the portal interior. Marston watched the rotating portal for a few seconds, then gave his control stick a deft twist. With a sudden burst of subdued sound, the attitude jets fired. Over a span of several seconds, the liner's rate of rotation seemed to slow, then stop completely. Marston confirmed by both eye and instrument that the bug's rotation was synchronized with that of the liner, then nudged his control stick forward. There was another faint muttering of control jets as the bug slowly slid into the liner's maw.

Once inside, they were directed to a tiedown point well back from the main hatchway. When their steed had been secured, Drake and Marston checked their suits for pressure integrity, then spilled the bug's air to vacuum. Drake unsnapped his harness, levered himself up out of the close confines of the bug's cabin, then slowly pulled himself hand over hand along a safety line in the nearly weightless compartment. Glancing to make sure that his executive officer was following, he made his way to an airlock. Kenil Fallan, *Alexandria*'s commanding officer, was waiting for them on the other side.

"Permission to come aboard, sir?" Drake asked.

"Permission granted, and welcome, Captain," Fallan replied.

Marston repeated the ancient formality and received the same response. The needs of custom satisfied, Drake and Fallan grinned and shook hands.

"Those new bars look mighty impressive, Kenil."

"I hear you recommended me for them, Richard."

Drake shrugged. "The admiral made the final decision."

"Anyway, thanks."

"You're welcome. Now, how is your new command shaping up?"

"Not exactly like our spit-and-polish midshipman days aboard *Dagger*, I can tell you that. The crew is first-rate. They've torn down everything that can be taken apart, run maintenance checks until they're blue in the face, and generally done a fine job. The civilians are another story. They don't seem to realize that they can't go anywhere and do anything they want, anytime they want. I have to referee some silly-ass dispute between the scientists about two or three times each watch."

Drake nodded. "That's the reason we're here. Is everyone assembled?"

"Yes, sir."

"Then give us a few minutes to get out of these suits and we'll proceed with the object lesson."

"Very good, sir. This way to the suit lockers."

TO: Fleet Captain Richard Drake
    Commanding Officer
    Interstellar Expedition One

SUBJECT: Operational Orders
              Interstellar Expedition One

1. You are hereby directed to join Altan Navy vessels *Discovery* and *City of Alexandria* with Commercial Cryogen Tankers *Sultana* and *Haridan* to form Task Force 001, Interstellar Expedition One.

2. You will take command of Task Force 001 and prepare it for space.

3. When ready, you will direct your command to the Val—Napier foldpoint, where you will proceed to the Napier system via foldspace transition.

4. You will fulfill the following mission objectives:

    4.1 *Primary Objective* : You will evaluate the current sociopolitical situation in human space. Specifically, you will determine whether interstellar warfare is now taking place beyond the Valeria system. You will determine, insofar as you are able, the identity of belligerents, their relative strengths, and the cause (or causes) for such warfare.

    4.2 *Secondary Objective* : You will determine the effect of the Antares Supernova on the structure of foldspace.

    4.3 *Tertiary Objective* : You will determine

the effect on the Napier system of the Antares Supernova.

4.4 *Quaternary Objective* : You will render all reasonable assistance to those persons assigned to your command holding parliamentary charters.

5. Task Force 001 may undergo additional fold-space transitions if, in the opinion of the expedition commander, such are required to fulfill the primary mission objective. Additional transitions shall not be undertaken solely for the fulfillment of secondary, tertiary, or quaternary objectives.

6. Task Force 001 is authorized to use the minimum force necessary to fulfill the primary mission objective, or to act in self-defense should belligerent military forces be encountered.

7. All data concerning the Earth Fleet Blastship *Conqueror* shall be considered an Altan state secret, and shall not be revealed to non-Altan personnel.

8. Task Force 001 shall return to the Valeria system upon completion of the primary objective, or by standard day 181 after the initial foldspace transition, whichever shall occur first.

(Signed)   (Signed)
Gareth Reynolds   Luis Emilio Dardan
Prime Minister   First Admiral
Altan Republic   Altan Space Navy

As originally planned, the expedition beyond the fold-point was to be a military and scientific reconnaissance-in-force. Since it would be penetrating potentially hostile space, the Navy had been given overall command responsibility.

The expedition's major objectives were fairly straightforward: Find out what happened to *Conqueror*, map the changes in the structure of foldspace, and determine the fate of New Providence after the supernova. If those had been the only objectives, Task Force 001 could have been pared to *Discovery* and a single tanker for refueling. The Admiralty worked with Alta University to put together two small scientific working groups. The first included experts in the fields of anthropology, archeology, history, political science, psychology, and sociology. Their job was to assess the human impact of the supernova on the other systems of the Antares Cluster. The second working group included the astronomers and physicists originally recruited by Admiral Dardan and Stan Barrett to map the structure of foldspace within the Val system. They would perform the same task in each system encountered, and thereby build up a picture of the large-scale effect of the supernova on the structure of foldspace.

Unfortunately, the Navy's idea of a lean expedition hadn't sat well with a number of influential people. The announcement that the foldpoint was once again open had sent a shockwave of excitement through Altan society. It hadn't taken long before the requests to join the expedition began pouring in.

The first request for space aboard *City of Alexandria* came from the Holy Ecumenical Church of Alta. His Eminence, the Bishop of Homeport, personally put in an appearance at the Admiralty to plead his case.

"I am sure you realize the importance of reestablishing contact with Mother Church on Earth," the bishop had told Admiral Dardan.

"I'm not sure I do, Your Eminence," Dardan had replied.

"There is the matter of modernizing our canon law, not to mention the need for Mother Church to reaffirm the right of our priests to say Mass and perform baptisms. Why, we've a century of religious doctrine to catch up on. No telling what sins we are committing through ignorance."

"But surely this can all wait for a future expedition, Your Eminence."

"I think not, Admiral. At the very least, the whole of the priesthood should be examined by a cardinal of the Church to determine our fitness to serve. Then there is the matter of petitioning the Holy Father for a cardinal of our own."

Dardan had sighed. "How many emissaries do you propose sending?"

"Not many, my son." The bishop had placed his fingers together in a steeple gesture. "No more than thirty."

Dardan had exploded. "You'll see me in hell before you pack my ships with thirty churchmen, Your Eminence!"

"That may well be, my son," the bishop had replied blandly.

The next demand for representation had come from the Industrial Guild. The guild represented the fifty largest manufacturers on Alta. Having heard of the reception provided the bishop, they bypassed the Admiralty and went instead to Parliament, where they requested a delegation of twenty-two guild representatives be sent along "on this first interstellar trade mission in more than a century."

By the end of the first week after the signing of the Whitlow/Alta agreement, no fewer than sixty-three similar requests had been introduced onto the floor of Parliament.

The Navy countered the industrialists and the other petitioners by pointing out that an expedition into a war zone was no place for supernumeraries. Parliament took the matter under advisement, setting up a committee to study it. The committee, noting the considerable political clout of some of the petitioners, decided to grant a limited

number of parliamentary charters—in effect, directing
the Navy to find room aboard *City of Alexandria* for those
so favored.

So it was that Richard Drake found himself saddled
with fifty "chartered representatives" and orders to "render all assistance." In addition to two each from the two
major political parties and a delegation of four churchmen,
there were two chartered representatives each from the
Industrial Guild, the Labor Council, the Educator's Union,
the Independent Traders, and the Physicians Association.
Smaller groups were allowed only a single representative.
Each charter holder was given a berth assignment and a
shipboard job. Some of the jobs were even useful. The
physicians, for example, were assigned as ship's doctors
aboard *Alexandria*, allowing the Navy doctors they'd displaced to be transferred to the two commercial cryogen
tankers.

The four politicians aboard the liner were to act as
diplomatic staff, if and when the expedition entered an
inhabited system. It had been agreed that the two parties
would share in the expedition's diplomatic efforts. Stan
Barrett and Alicia Delevan, the female member of the
Space Committee, were to be coambassadors. Drake had
frowned at the thought of diplomatic authority being split,
but kept his opinion of the arrangement to himself.

Several days earlier, Drake had received a visit aboard
Discovery from one member of the diplomatic staff. He'd
been engrossed in catching up on his official reports when
someone had knocked on his cabin door. He'd looked up
to find Carl Aster standing in the doorway.

"What may I do for you, Mr. Aster?"

"I want to be reassigned to this ship, Captain," Aster
had said, stepping into Drake's cabin.

"Sorry, I've no place to put you. With all the spare
parts and supplies we're taking aboard, we're about to
burst at the seams as it is. Even the showers are filled
with foodstuffs. It'll be a month before we'll be able to
eat our way into them enough to resume washing."

"Damn it, man! My fiancée is aboard this ship."

"Are you and Bethany to be married?" Drake asked. "Congratulations, I hadn't heard."

"It isn't official, yet. However, we have a clear understanding. Surely you can understand my wanting to be with her."

"I understand perfectly, Mr. Aster. However, that doesn't change anything. Personally, I'd just as soon see Miss Lindquist transfer to *Alexandria*. At least, she would be with other women there."

Aster had chewed his lower lip and said, "I was hoping we could keep this between us, Captain. However, if I have to go over your head, I will."

"The answer will still be no. Now, if you will excuse me, I have work to do."

Aster had stomped off. Drake had half expected to receive orders ordering the politician's transfer to the expedition flagship. When they didn't come, he found that the thought of Bethany Lindquist and Carl Aster on different ships cheered him considerably.

CHAPTER 10

As Fallan led Richard Drake and Bela Marston down a series of stairwells into ever-increasing gravity, Drake noticed that *City of Alexandria* had a shabby look to it. Where *Discovery* was all shiny metal and brightwork inside, *Alexandria* reflected twenty years of neglect. The corridor walls had once been lined with expensive hardwoods and solid brass lighting fixtures. The wood was gone, stripped by a previous owner for resale to a rich apartment dweller in a wood-starved space habitat. The occasional brass fixture that remained in place was barely recognizable under a thick layer of black tarnish. The corridor walls had been painted a uniform gray after the wood was removed, but whoever had done the job hadn't taken the time to properly prepare the surface. Large feathery flakes of paint now hung loose everywhere Drake looked. Beneath the peeling paint were dingy cream-color splotches of dried paneling adhesive.

"Sorry about the condition of my ship, sir," Fallan said as they skated down a low-gravity corridor between stairwells. "We've been too busy getting her spaceworthy to take care of the esthetics."

"It's going to be a long mission, Mr. Fallan. There will be time for that after we get underway."

"Yes, sir. I've told my section chiefs to get the men busy chipping and scraping as soon as we clear orbit."

Their destination was *Alexandria*'s main ballroom. Situated on the outermost level (where gravity was highest), the ballroom was large enough for the deck underfoot to show a perceptible curve. In order to use the large compartment, however, it was necessary that ship's spin provide the pseudogravity. During powered flight, when gravity was "aft" rather than "out," the compartment was a deep arc-shaped well of limited utility. Since no spaceship can afford to waste that much space, the architects who designed the liner had installed four levels of retractable decks. Once extended from their recesses in the walls, they turned the oversize compartment into a series of smaller spaces.

In the two weeks since the scientists and other civilians boarded *Alexandria*, Captain Fallan had reported receiving a steady stream of complaints concerning cabin assignments, work-space allocations, and living conditions in general. To his surprise, Drake responded to his report by asking for a complete list of complaints.

"You shouldn't trouble yourself with such trivia, sir," Fallan had said. "Most of the time, the complainer is just trying to establish his status in the pecking order. We listen, utter soothing noises, then forget about it."

"They aren't trivial, Captain Fallan, nor should you treat them as such. They're symptomatic of a problem we must resolve before it gets out of hand. I want you to call an assembly of all your officers and civilian personnel at oh eight hundred tomorrow. I'll see to it that the tanker captains are notified."

"Yes, sir."

Two Marines from *Alexandria*'s fifty-man contingent flanked the main entrance hatch into the ballroom when the three officers arrived. The Marines snapped to attention and saluted. Drake returned their salutes, then stepped over the raised coaming into the ballroom.

The large compartment had been configured as an auditorium, with rows of seats arrayed in front of a raised dais and podium. As Drake stepped over the threshold, there was a cry of *"Ten-hut!"* from one of the Marines. Scattered figures, all in uniform, jumped to their feet, ramrod straight and eyes facing front. An occasional civilian figure also stood, although in a much more relaxed manner. Most of the hundred-plus occupants of the compartment merely glanced up, then went back to their individual discussions.

Drake strode down the aisle at the side of the compartment, mounted the dais, and moved to the podium. While waiting for the noise to subside, he let his gaze sweep across the compartment. He noticed Bethany Lindquist and Carl Aster holding hands in the second row and felt a momentary pang of jealousy at the sight. Professor Planovich was also seated in the second row, three seats to Aster's right. Drake recognized a dozen other members of the scientific staff, including several women. Standing toward the back of the crowd were the captains and executive officers of the cryogen tankers, as well as several scout and landing boat pilots from *Discovery* and *City of Alexandria*.

Drake ordered those standing to be seated. The military personnel sat down, and the buzz of conversation slowly began to subside. Drake waited until the crowd had grown silent before beginning to speak.

"Thank you for coming, ladies and gentlemen. I asked Captain Fallan to call this meeting in order to get a few things straight before we leave orbit for the deep black. First of all, I would like all those who did not stand when I entered the compartment to please do so now."

There was a renewal of the crowd noises and no one moved for a second. Then, slowly, hesitantly, the powerful of Alta began to climb to their feet. First one, then two, then small groups, until finally, the scene was exactly reversed from that of a minute earlier.

"For the next several months, you will all be living and working aboard this ship. As I am sure you have noticed already, we are too many people crammed into too little space, and there is little opportunity for incompatible personalities to get away from each other. This is quite normal, and we spacers long ago developed a code of conduct to minimize the stresses of shipboard life. The code is based on three principles: respect for one's fellows, common courtesy, and the fact that a ship in space is no democracy.

"One of the most basic principles of this code involves the respect given a commanding officer aboard ship. For many of the same reasons that one stands when a judge enters a courtroom, so too should you stand when a captain enters a compartment. The act is intended to show your respect for the position rather than for the man who fills it. Since each of you now standing has chosen to ignore this simple courtesy, you will pay for the oversight by reporting to Captain Fallan immediately after we leave orbit. He will assign you to forty hours of ship's maintenance as a penalty."

There were several seconds of shocked silence, followed by an explosion of protests. Drake let the noise wash over him, making no move to stop it. Eventually, all was quiet once again.

"I take it from your reaction that you think I'm being overly harsh," he said.

"Damned right!" someone yelled from the back row.

"You should be thankful to get off so easily. True, I could have ignored the unintentional insult you gave me. I could have explained why we have these quaint customs aboard ship and asked you to humor us by complying with them. I could have, but I didn't. In an emergency, your lives may well depend on your immediate, unquestioning obedience to my orders or those of Captain Fallan. Since such obedience does not come naturally to anyone, I have chosen to educate you in a way that you will remember."

"What if we refuse to knuckle under?" one white-haired man in the fifth row asked.

"Your name, sir?"

"Greg. Tobias Greg, Labor Council Chartered Representative."

"Well, Mr. Greg. My response to willful disobedience of orders depends on the stage of the mission we are in at the time. For instance, if you are refusing my order at this moment, I will have the Marines put you bodily onto one of the supply shuttles and have you returned to Alta. Should your refusal come after we've left orbit, however, I just may have you shot as an example to others."

Several Adam's apples bobbed up and down as their owners swallowed hard, but no one spoke up. Drake continued: "Now, then, enough of this. Shall we get on with the real reason for this assembly? Commander Marston will read you the expedition orders."

Marston exchanged places with Drake and began to read in slow, measured syllables. While his executive officer read, Drake surveyed the crowd. Compared to a few minutes earlier, they were much subdued. When Marston had finished, Drake returned to the podium.

"Are there any questions concerning these orders?" When no one answered, he stated, "Let the record show that there were no objections. Captain Fallan!"

"Yes, sir!" Fallan replied.

"Will your ship be ready for space three days hence?"

"It will, Captain Drake."

"Captain Trousma."

"Yes, sir," the commander of cryogen tanker *Haridan* said, rising to his feet.

"Will your vessel be ready at that time?"

"Yes, sir."

Drake went down the roster of ship's officers, asking each the same question in turn. Every answer came back affirmative. He then started on the scientists.

"Professor Planovich."

"Yes, Captain Drake."

"Is all your equipment aboard and stowed?"

"It is."

"I understand you've a complaint about your cabin."

Planovich looked hesitant, then said, "Well, yes, I do. It stinks! The smell is so bad that I can't sleep nights. I've requested that Captain Fallan find me another one."

"Captain Fallan!"

"Yes, sir."

"Do you have a spare cabin for Professor Planovich?"

"No, sir. Not unless he wants to move into one of the bunkrooms."

"Care to sleep with the Marines, Professor?"

"I think my rank entitles me to a private cabin." Planovich sniffed.

"Of course it does. But you have a private cabin, sir."

"But it stinks!"

"Request denied. If you can't stand the smell, pack your bags and report to the quartermaster's office. He'll get you on one of the returning shuttles." Drake looked away from the wizened astronomy professor, pretending not to see the sudden reddening of his face.

"I'm sorry if any of you are experiencing similar discomforts. But this is an old ship with a checkered past, and it is full of unpleasant odors. The sooner we get it cleaned up, the sooner the problem will be alleviated.

"Now, then, Mr. Hamadi, I believe you had a complaint . . ."

After the going over he'd given Planovich, Drake discovered that no one else seemed to be disturbed by anything. He continued his roll call, asking each person in turn whether they were ready for space. All professed to be ready. He ended with Bethany Lindquist.

"Miss Lindquist, is the terrestrial representative ready for space?"

"I am, Captain Drake," she said in a clear, steady voice.

"In that case, ladies and gentlemen, I hereby issue the following order for all vessels: Task Force 001, Interstellar Expedition One, will leave Altan orbit at twelve hundred hours on fifteen Apollo 2637, three days from now. I urge each of you to study your needs. If it isn't aboard by the time we launch, you'll have to do without for half a standard year. If there are no further questions, I order this assembly adjourned. Please rise and wait for my departure."

This time there was no shortage of people on their feet. Drake strode out into the corridor. He was followed close behind by Captain Fallan and Commander Marston. When they had rounded a turn in the corridor, Drake turned to Fallan.

"Well, Captain, what did you think of my performance?"

Fallan grinned. "I thought several people would drop their teeth when you ordered them to report for maintenance duty, sir."

"What about you, Bela? Do you think I was too hard on Planovich?"

"You had to do it to someone, Captain. It was his bad luck to be first on your list."

Fallan nodded. "I agree, sir. An object lesson was needed."

"Perhaps, Captain Fallan. However, in so doing, I've left you with a problem. You have at least one very angry scientist on your hands, and probably a lot more. I think we'd better plan how you are going to return your passengers to a cooperative mood."

"Yes, sir. My office is this way."

"Lead on."

Two days later, Carl Aster found himself in front of Mikhail Planovich in *City of Alexandria*'s mess. Both men were awaiting their turn at the coffee urn. Their relative positions were no accident. Aster had known where Planovich was headed and had hurried to beat him there.

"Hello," Aster said, handing Planovich an empty cup and saucer before taking one himself.

"Hello, yourself," Planovich replied.

"I've been meaning to tell you that I thought you got a raw deal about your cabin. How's the smell?"

Planovich shrugged. "I've been working on it. It's bearable."

"Drake shouldn't have treated you like that. He shouldn't have treated any of us like that! We've got better things to do than chip paint for the military!"

"Oh, I don't know," Planovich replied. "I enjoy working with my hands. I find it gives me time to think."

"I can tell you that I won't enjoy it! Not one bit," Aster said as he filled the cup that Planovich held under the urn's spigot. When both cups were filled, Aster directed Planovich to a table.

"Is there something I can do for you, Carl?" the astronomer asked.

Aster leaned forward and let his voice drop to a conspiratorial whisper. "As a matter of fact, there is. I'd like you to meet someone."

The astronomer glanced around the mess compartment. "Where are they?"

"Not here. Let's go somewhere we can talk in private."

Planovich shrugged. "Why not? I'm at loose ends for an hour or so."

Aster led the astronomer halfway around one of *Alexandria*'s circumferential decks and down a ladder to that part of the ship where the private cabins were. As they walked, Planovich commented that low gravity made him feel ten years younger.

Aster stopped at a cabin door and knocked. A muffled female voice commanded him to enter. He opened the door and ushered Planovich through. Inside, seated at a tiny desk, was Alicia Delevan.

"Welcome, Professor Planovich. Please, have a seat," she said, gesturing to an easy chair that nearly filled the cabin. Planovich sat, while Aster plopped down on the bunk. "I asked Carl to arrange this meeting because I didn't want certain people to see you talking to me."

"What people?"

"Why, Stanislaw Barrett, for one. Captain Fallan for another. I believe we both find ourselves in a situation where we have a mutuality of interest. Perhaps we can help each other."

"What interest?"

"You do not seem too happy with your lot aboard this ship as Dr. Gordon's subordinate."

"If I'm not, that's my business."

"So it is," Alicia Delevan continued smoothly. "In my case, I am unhappy because this expedition was organized by the Social Democrats and stands to benefit them at my own party's expense."

"I thought this was a Navy operation."

"It is. But the Navy takes orders from the prime minister, who is an SD. And it is the prime minister who is attempting to turn this bipartisan expedition into a propaganda bonanza for himself and his party."

"How could he do that?"

"By making his people look good and my people look bad. Believe me, Professor, the techniques are ancient and they work fine—that is, so long as one side has complete control over the release of information. However, if both parties have access to the same information, the fight tends to be more equal.

"That is where you come in. I need some honest brokers in the scientific community aboard this ship who will provide me with the same information that Stan Barrett is getting via Captain Drake. I ask nothing dishonest, only that you help me keep the competition fair."

"What do I get out of it?"

"The satisfaction of knowing that you've kept the prime minister's representatives honest and that you will have an influential friend in government should you ever need one. After all, this won't be the last expedition we send out to map the structure of foldspace. I would think the top science job on some future trip would be within the reach of a man of your accomplishments."

Planovich frowned. "I'll have to think about it."

"Of course," Alicia Delevan said. "You can give me your answer tomorrow, if you like."

To save fuel, the journey to the Val-Napier foldpoint was made at a relatively conservative half a standard gravity. The journey took 125 hours.

"What's *Alexandria*'s status, Mr. Slater?" Drake asked the chief communicator from his command chair on *Discovery*'s bridge.

"*Sultana* is just about through replenishing her tanks, sir. *Haridan* is standing by to do the same for us."

Drake nodded. "Tell Captain Trousma that we will be cutting power in two minutes. He can begin his approach as soon as he sees our drive flare go dark. Make the announcement."

Karl Slater's voice echoed through the ship a moment later. "All hands. Zero gravity in two minutes. I repeat, zero gravity for refueling. Two minutes."

Drake turned back to the main viewscreen on the far bulkhead of the control room. The screen showed a three-dimensional schematic diagram. The foldpoint was represented by a sweeping family of contour lines. The lines, which mapped minute variations in the local gravitational constant, converged to a single point and then separated once more. Drake ordered the schematic centered at the point of convergence and magnified. An instant later, the diagram changed. The convergence point nearly filled the screen. Centered around it was a fuzzy red ellipsoid. The ellipsoid showed where the local curvature of foldspace exceeded the critical value. It was, in effect, an outline of the foldpoint itself.

On the screen, two pairs of small golden sparks could be seen slowly moving toward the red ellipse. These were the ships of Task Force 001. They were following a 0.5 standard gravity deceleration curve, one that would, in another few minutes, bring them to a halt in space relative to the foldpoint. By that time, however, they would be within the body of the foldpoint itself and, if all went well, would depart the Valeria system for Napier more than a hundred light-years distant. The lead pair of golden sparks were *Discovery* and *Haridan*. The pair farthest from the foldpoint were *City of Alexandria* and *Sultana*.

"Ready for zero gravity, Captain," Lieutenant Cristobal said from the astrogator's station.

"Cut your power when ready, Astrogator."

"Cutting power now, Captain."

A series of alarms sounded and then the familiar, momentary sensation of falling as Drake surged against his acceleration harness. The view on the screen switched to a camera on the hull. A small silver globe lay centered in the picture. Tiny sparks of attitude control jets flashed on the globe, and it began to grow. *Haridan* was a ship fully four times as large as *Discovery*. In spite of its bulk, however, the tanker required only a dozen crewmen to run it. Most of its volume consisted of insulated tankage filled to capacity with cryogenic hydrogen.

The tanker moved smoothly up to match velocities. As it did so, a teleoperated, insulated line snaked across the two hundred meters of space that separated the two ships, seeking the battle cruiser's fueling connection. It found it with the unerring accuracy of computer control and plugged in. For the next ten minutes, hydrogen maintained within two degrees of absolute zero flowed through the line to top off *Discovery*'s tanks. Then the tanker uncoupled and slowly drifted to a safe distance.

"Captain Trousma reports refueling completed," Slater said over the intercom.

"Very good. Set up a captain's conference."

"Aye aye, sir."

In less than a minute, Drake found himself staring at the faces of Captains Fallan, Trousma, and Lee—the last being *Sultana*'s commanding officer. "Well, gentlemen, it looks as though we've arrived. Status report, please."

"*Alexandria*, ready to jump."

"*Haridan*, ready to jump."

"*Sultana*, ready to jump."

"And *Discovery*'s ready to jump, gentlemen," Drake finished up. "All right, you know your orders. We go first.

City of Alexandria follows us one minute later. Then *Haridan* and *Sultana* at the same interval. Slave your computers to me and we'll begin our final approach."

There were three acknowledgments before the screens went blank. Drake punched for his chief engineer. "Are you ready, Mr. Arnam?"

"Ready, Captain. Mass converters are holding steady. Radiation shielding has an attenuation factor of ten to the sixth."

"Ready, Mr. Marston?"

"Battle stations are manned and ready. Foldspace generators are energized. Jump computer is awaiting the introduction of authorization codes to become operational."

"Stand by. Mr. Cristobal."

"Yes, Captain?"

"Bring the ship to half a grav."

"Aye aye, sir."

There was a further clanging of alarms, and weight returned. The view on the main workscreen changed again. The closeup schematic of the foldpoint reclaimed the screen. This time, the golden sparks were considerably closer to the red ellipsoid. Drake keyed his intercom.

"We're ready for you, Miss Lindquist."

Bethany, who occupied the duty station next to the astrogator, glanced over her shoulder at Drake.

"I'm ready also, Captain Drake."

"Two minutes to transition. Please authorize our use of the jump computer."

"Authorizing now," Bethany said. She turned back to her workstation. The station was a standard design, with one exception. Bethany's keyboard had an opaque plastic shield over it that prevented anyone from seeing what keys she pressed. In Drake's opinion, the precaution was unnecessary. Each successive foldspace transition would require a different fifteen-digit alphanumeric authorization code known only to Bethany Lindquist and Clarence Whitlow. Knowing the last legal code would not help the next transition at all. However, Clarence Whitlow had insisted on the extra security of a visual shield, so Drake had ordered one installed.

Drake's command chair was positioned to give him a view of all the workstations in the control room. He watched Bethany's wrist flex as her fingers moved beneath the shield. A moment later, a message flashed on the large workscreen:

FOLDPOINT TRANSITION AUTHORIZED!

"Thank you, Miss Lindquist. As soon as we pop out on the other end, please authorize our immediate return in case we have to beat a hasty retreat."

"No problem, Captain," she replied. "The return authorization is always active."

On the screen, the first tiny golden spark crossed over into the red ellipsoid. The marker began to blink rapidly.

Drake keyed for the astrogator. "All right, Mr. Cristobal. It's all yours. Jump when ready."

"Yes, sir. Fifteen seconds to transition . . . Generators to power. The jumpfield is building nicely. Ten seconds . . . Five, four, three, two, one . . . Jump!"

CHAPTER 11

Records from the days of interstellar travel made no mention of any physical sensation accompanying fold-space transition. Richard Drake was therefore surprised when the hair on his arms began to tingle and his ears started to ring. Then after a momentary sensation akin to the surge that accompanies the onset of zero gravity, everything returned to normal. He reached out to punch up the general intercom circuit, opened his mouth to speak, and realized that he had been holding his breath. After two deep breaths, he said, "All departments, report status!"

The roll call went with gratifying smoothness. Drake could hear the relief in the voices of his department heads as each reported no damage or casualties. Left unsaid, but never far from anyone's mind, was the fact that *Discovery*'s jump engines had had no proper test in 125 years. The chief engineer seemed to Drake to be especially relieved.

"Did you feel a sort of *bump* when we jumped, Gavin?" Drake asked Arnam after the roll call had been completed.

"I would say that our jump engine is a bit out of tune, Captain. I wouldn't advise trying to fix it unless it gets worse. If one of my people made a mistake, we might find ourselves stranded."

"Recommendation accepted." Drake punched for

Lieutenant Cristobal's station. "Where are we, Astrogator?"

"Checking now, sir. I have a telescope focused on this system's primary. I'll have its spectrum in a moment."

"We're not still in our own system, are we?"

"Not a chance, Captain. This star's the wrong color for Val."

"Put it on the screen."

"Aye aye, sir."

The main screen cleared to the mottled disk of a star. Valeria was an F8 spectral class star, fairly close to Sol in size but somewhat hotter than humanity's home star. Napier, on the other hand, was spectral class G8 and significantly larger than either Sol or Valeria.

"It's Napier, all right, Captain," Cristobal said a moment later. "No doubt. The spectrum has all of the right lines and none of the wrong ones. However, the background stars are wrong."

"How wrong?"

"They aren't the right stars if this is the Napier–Val foldpoint. Unless the records are wrong, we should have emerged a full ninety degrees to the celestial east of our current position."

"Obviously, foldspace has been altered significantly this close to the nova," Drake said, nodding. "See if you can find Antares for me, Lieutenant."

"Antares coming up, sir."

Napier drifted out of the field of view as Cristobal reprogrammed the hull telescope to seek the nova. Stars crossed the viewscreen with dizzying speed. Then the movement stopped and the Antares Supernova lay centered in the screen.

The supernova had been triggered by the exhaustion of the hydrogen fuel deep within the red-orange supergiant's core. Without fuel to feed it, the fusion reaction that had powered the star for tens of millions of years had suddenly gone out. With its internal source of energy gone, Antares could no longer fight off gravity. It had collapsed in upon itself. But a star is more than a ball of fusing hydrogen. It possesses vast quantities of potential energy locked up in its gravitational field. As soon as the collapse began, the energy of collapse reappeared as pure heat. The core, which moments earlier had been energy starved, suddenly found itself with more energy than it could use in a million years under normal conditions. But conditions within Antares were no longer normal. The star's internal temperature had risen to a level where neutrino production became the dominant atomic reaction.

Normally it takes thousands of years for the energy produced in a star's core to reach the surface and be radiated away as light and heat. But the neutrinos were able to penetrate the superdense plasma in seconds. Antares' rate of energy leakage to the surrounding cosmos skyrocketed, and its rate of collapse accelerated. The core temperature increased even further, causing ever larger quantities of neutrinos to be produced. It was a regenerative cycle that could not endure forever.

As the core temperature rose toward infinity, it heated the middle layers of the star's atmosphere above the light-off point for the hydrogen fusion reaction. Unlike the core, Antares' atmosphere still contained enormous quantities of hydrogen fuel. A furious fusion reaction suddenly broke out, generating in a single second more energy than Antares had previously generated in all of its history. Unable to dissipate this new energy to surrounding space, the star had taken the only course open to it.

Antares had exploded!

The explosion had had two fundamental effects: The core, which was already in a superdense state, had collapsed entirely under the pressure. The star's core, which an instant before had measured more than half a million kilometers in diameter, was now a rapidly rotating ball of neutrons with a diameter of less than fifty kilometers.

The second effect was even more spectacular. Antares' outer layers, which had been relatively unaffected by the cataclysm deep within the star, were suddenly blasted into surrounding space. A shockwave consisting of visible light, heat, X-rays, gamma rays, and neutrinos had raced outward at the speed of light. Not far behind had come a second shock wave, this one composed of individual protons, neutrons, and electrons. And finally, 30 percent of the star's original mass had been thrown outward at speeds in excess of seven-thousand kilometers per second.

Since Antares had lit up the sky in the largest blast ever observed by human beings, 125 years had passed. For all that time, the globe of cooling plasma had expanded away from the ball of neutrons that Antares had become. By 2637, the glowing globe—its periphery moving at better than 2 percent of the speed of light—had expanded to cover a volume of space six light-years in diameter.

The Napier system was only fifteen light-years from Antares. Thus, on *Discovery*'s main viewscreen, the supernova's gas cloud covered a full 23 degrees of arc. It took Drake a few seconds to comprehend the scale of the object. He gasped in astonishment when he realized the full enormity of the thing. His gasp was followed by several others around the control room.

Antares had been transformed from a point of light into a perfectly round sphere that seemed to cover half the sky. The gas was thickest around the circumference, where it glowed blue-white. The seemingly solid periphery faded gradually as one looked radially inward toward the center. The color changed as well. Nearest the blue-white ring, the gas shaded down from blue, to green, to orange, and finally to a very dim red. In the center of this multicolor globe, a starlike object radiated furiously. The filter circuits on *Discovery*'s cameras made it impossible to tell the intrinsic brightness, but Drake suspected that the central patch of radiance was bright enough to damage an unprotected eye. He made a mental note to work out safety precautions for exploration parties before allowing anyone to leave the ships.

It was more than a minute before anyone spoke. Bethany Lindquist finally broke the spell of silence by whispering, "My God, it's the most beautiful thing I've ever seen!"

Drake cleared his throat, angry at himself for allowing his attention to be stolen by the supernova remnant when he had more important things to do.

"Mr. Marston," he growled.

"Uh, yes, sir!" came his exec's voice.

"*City of Alexandria* should be coming through any second. I want a report on her position as soon as she materializes."

"Will do, Captain."

There was a long, stomach-churning wait. Even though the entire Task Force would jump from essentially the same position within the foldpoint in the Val system, that was no assurance that they would arrive in the Napier system in the same good order. The point of emergence within a foldpoint was controlled only by the laws of probability. More than a dozen seconds after the moment when the liner should have appeared on the battle cruiser's screens, Bela Marston reported:

"We have a contact, Captain. Bearing 189/22. Range 600,000 kilometers." Then, over the next two minutes, Marston reported two additional contacts. All were spread over a similar volume of space.

Drake ordered Slater to establish contact with the other ships. When he had done so, Drake keyed for the ship-to-ship circuit and said, "All captains! Close on *Discovery*. Captain Fallan, start your scientific surveys. I want a teleconference to review preliminary findings in four hours. Drake out!"

Richard Drake, Bela Marston, Karl Slater, Gavin Arnam, and Bethany Lindquist gathered in the officers' mess on Beta Deck five minutes before the appointed hour. When not used for serving meals, the mess compartment doubled as a wardroom and conference room. *Discovery*'s representatives to the teleconference sat on both sides of the long steel mess table, drinking coffee from porcelain cups. At the far end of the compartment was a viewscreen only slightly smaller than those in the control rooms.

"Thank you for inviting me," Bethany said to Drake from her position across the table from him. "I was wondering if you would. After all, I *am* the representative of a foreign government."

"Hopefully, a friendly foreign government, Miss Lindquist."

Bethany responded with a wan smile. "It was friendly the last time we looked, Captain."

"They're ready aboard *Alexandria*, sir."

"Fine, Mr. Slater. Put them on the screen."

The viewscreen at the end of the mess compartment came to life. In its depths was one of the conference rooms aboard *City of Alexandria*. Captain Fallan, several members from both natural and social science teams, and the entire political staff were crowded around a mess table very similar to the one in front of Drake.

"Captains Lee and Trousma?" Drake asked.

"Tied into the circuit from their ships, sir," Slater responded. "Do you want me to put them on the screen?"

"Not necessary." Drake turned toward the screen. He looked directly into the camera pickup and said, "Ladies and gentlemen, this conference is being recorded for the expedition log. Please state your name and title clearly when it comes your turn. Please start us off, Captain Fallan."

"Yes, sir. Captain Lieutenant Kenil Fallan, Commanding Officer, ANS *City of Alexandria* ..." The roll call proceeded around the table. When everyone aboard the liner had spoken up, Drake asked the two tanker captains to identify themselves, then signaled for Bela Marston to begin the roll aboard *Discovery*. The roll call quickly rounded the table, and Drake found himself saying "... Fleet Captain Richard Drake, Expedition Commander, Commanding Officer ANS *Discovery*." He man-

aged to give his new rank, which he had recei~~ve~~
with command of the expedition, without stumbli~~ng~~

"Are your people ready to report their findings, C~~ap~~
tain Fallan?" he asked.

"They are, sir."

"Then please begin."

Fallan turned to a middle-aged man with dark hair and
a full beard. Drake recognized him as Dr. Nathaniel Gordon, the astrophysicist who had commanded the original
survey mission to chart Val's foldpoint. "Dr. Gordon, will
you review our preliminary findings?"

"Why, yes," Gordon said. He retrieved a pocket computer and used a stylus to scroll through his notes. Then
he looked up and said, "Four hours isn't much time to
do anything but a quick survey. However, we have managed to collect quite a lot of raw data.

"First of all, we have detected the presence of the
neutron star that is at the heart of yonder nebula. No
surprise there. Our orbital observatories at home have
been watching the newborn Antares pulsar for the past
three months. The only discrepancy between those read-
ings and our own is in the rotation speed of the neutron
star. At home, it was pulsing 620 times each second. Here
in the Napier system, the rate is down to just under 600
pulses per second—598, to be exact. The difference is
due to the fact that we are now seeing a star that is 110
years older than the one we have been viewing back home.

"Our second observation concerns the local level of
background radiation. As you no doubt have already noted
aboard *Discovery*, it's damned high! I've calculated the
lethal dose for an unprotected man to be approximately
twelve hours. We are safe behind our shields, but I wouldn't
venture out without my lead underwear."

"What does that level of radiation say about the fate
of this system's inhabitants?" Dr. Warton, leader of the
social science team asked from *Alexandria*'s conference
room.

"It doesn't bode well for them, sir," Gordon replied.

"Not well at all when one extrapolates backward to the first years after the supernova. The radiation level was much higher then—high enough to kill in a matter of minutes. No, if anyone has survived in this system, they've either relied on some very efficient radiation screens or else they've burrowed underground. As for the New Providential animal and plant life, the whole planet has undoubtedly been sterilized by radiation."

Gordon turned his attention back to the people aboard *Discovery*. "The last observation my working group has to report involves the nebula itself. An absolutely fascinating sight that! When viewed at certain wavelengths, there is a very definite structure to the cloud. Much of that structure is due to the influence of Antares' A3 companion, which was very nearly destroyed by the supernova. By studying the interactions between the gas cloud and the remains of the two stars, we may be able to learn quite a lot about the dynamics of the supernova."

"Professor Planovich, I believe you were in charge of observations concerning the local structure of foldspace," Drake said into the screen.

The older astronomer got stiffly to his feet. It was obvious from his manner that he still nursed a grudge over the treatment he'd received at Drake's hands during the last prelaunch assembly aboard *Alexandria*. Even so, his professional pride had kept him working, and his native caution muted his defiance to a single surly glance.

Like Gordon, he consulted his notes before beginning his report. "The fact that we came out where we did is an important clue, Captain. Obviously, the local structure of foldspace has undergone considerable distortion compared to that in our own system. That is hardly surprising, of course, when one considers the proximity of Napier to Antares.

"Prior to the supernova, Napier possessed three fold-points—one direct to Antares, one to our own Alta, and a third to our sister colony on Sandarson's World. That number may have grown or diminished as a result of the explosion. We will have to do considerable mapping of the gravitational constant before we can say for sure. That concludes my report."

Drake turned his attention to his executive officer. "Commander Marston, your report, please."

"Yes, sir. For the record, I was in charge of surveying the system for signs of life. I'm afraid the news is bad. In more than two hours of scanning the electromagnetic spectrum, we were unable to detect artificial energy release of any kind. We surveyed New Providence itself and three of the other planets known to be inhabited before the supernova. The airwaves are dead everywhere. No broadcast signals, no electric power generation noise, no groundcar static discharges. Nothing!"

"Would we be able to hear such things if they've gone underground to get away from the radiation of the nebula?" Alicia Delevan asked.

"I would think there would have been *some* indication," Marston replied.

When no one else spoke up, Drake asked, "Is that the last of the preliminary reports?" The question evoked a general chorus of nods. "In that case, I want your opinions as to whether the fleet should risk traveling to New Providence."

There followed a long discussion of the pros and cons of making closeup observations of New Providence. It quickly became obvious that no one had any substantive objection, and, in fact, most were eager to see the home of their ancestors.

"Then you are all agreed?" Drake asked, cutting off the one-sided debate after twenty minutes. "So am I. Ladies and gentlemen, we are going in!"

CHAPTER 12

NAPIER :

BASIC DATA: G8 spectral class star in the
Antares Cluster, Type III Giant
(Capella Class). Position (Sol
Rel.):1632RA,-2626DEC,335L-
Y.

Number of Foldpoints: 3.
Foldspace Transition Sequences:
  Primary: Sol, Goddard, Antares, Napier.
  Secondary: Vega, Carswell, Sacata,
Hermes, Aezer, Hellsgate,
Napier.
  Tertiary: Valeria, Napier.

The system contains thirteen planets, 120 moons,
and 1 asteroid belt. Planet VII, New Providence,
is an Earth-type world with indigenous lifeforms.
The planets, in order of their distance from the
system primary, include...

HISTORY: First explored in 2216 by C. Napier
and L. Gruen. The seventh planet was
found to possess nearly optimum
Earthlike conditions. (See entry for
NEW PROVIDENCE.) Settlement
rights for the Napier system were
obtained by the New Revivalist Church
of North America in 2256, with initial

immigration restricted to church members. The system was opened to premium immigration by the Boston-Toronto Trading Corporation, Ltd. in 2275. Immigration was curtailed in 2315, and the colony declared self-sufficient in 2385.

THE PEOPLE: The population of the Napier system is 3,287,654,000 (2500 census). The population is predominantly of North American and European ancestry.

— Excerpted from *A Spacer's Guide to Human Space, Ninety-seventh Edition*, Copyright 2510 by Hallan Publications, Ltd., Greater New York, Earth.

Napier was a much larger star than Valeria. One of the consequences of its greater mass was a larger gravitational lens effect. This, in turn, placed the Napier–Val foldpoint considerably farther from the primary than was the foldpoint in the Valerian system. Also, Napier VII was on the opposite side of the star from where the fleet had emerged, further aggravating the unfavorable celestial mechanics. At one-half gravity of acceleration, it would take the fleet twenty-one days to cover the distance between the foldpoint and New Providence.

By the sixth hour after breakout, the ships of Task Force 001 were arrayed in line-astern order, accelerating toward the system primary. The flight plan called for a fast cometary orbit with a relatively close approach to Napier, a change-of-plane maneuver, then deceleration to intrasystem velocity. The fleet would arrive at its destination with just enough velocity to enter a planetary parking orbit.

Drake put every long-range instrument aboard *Discovery* and *Alexandria* at the scientists' disposal while the fleet was in transit. Their orbit took them close to two of the system's outer worlds—gas giants midway between Sol's Jupiter and Val's Barbacane in size. The old records spoke of bases for "Jupiter-diver" mining operations on the satellites of both worlds. Gas giant atmosphere mining was a primary industry in virtually every inhabited system. If there were still a technologically advanced society anywhere in the Napier system, they would likely be exploiting the outer worlds as a source of raw materials.

The surveys of the two worlds' moons proved fruitless. In spite of the questing telescopes, infrared sensors, and high-gain radio antennas, no evidence of human activity was detected. The moons, which the charts labeled "Snowball" and "LaGrange," were empty of life.

The next target of opportunity for scientific observation was the system primary itself. At midvoyage the fleet's orbit took it within 60 million kilometers of the star's surface—close enough for the engineers aboard *Haridan* and *Sultana* to be concerned about keeping their cargoes at cryogenic temperature. Because the Napier–Val fold-point was high in the southern hemisphere of the system, it was also necessary to change the plane of the fleet's orbit as it closed to perihelion. For nearly a day, the four ships' photon drives thrust at right angles to their line of flight, twisting their orbit into plane with Napier's ecliptic. Then it was time to turn end for end and begin decelerating for rendezvous with the still-distant seventh planet.

Immediately following the fleet's rounding of the system primary, the scientists turned their instruments outward toward New Providence. They worked ceaselessly in an attempt to peer ever more closely into the mysterious silence that shrouded their destination. As in their previous attempts to find signs of artificial energy sources, they were unsuccessful. All that their questing instruments returned to them was the quiet hiss of their own ships' drive flares.

Drake ordered *Discovery* to full alert twenty days and sixteen hours after leaving the foldpoint. As the General

Quarters alarms wailed through the ship, New Providence was a blue-white marble on the main control room viewscreen. Off to one side was Laertes, New Providence's rather sizable moon, a gray-white sphere that early New Providential poets had compared to Earth's Luna.

Shortly after the fleet had rounded Napier, Drake had met with *Discovery*'s scout pilots. "Before I commit the fleet to a close orbit of New Providence, gentlemen, I want to make damned sure that it's safe to do so. Therefore, we will launch all four armed scouts while the fleet is still two million kilometers from the planet. *Catherine* and *Drunkard* will make a quick pass just outside the atmosphere to obtain reconnaissance views of two major urban areas on opposite sides of the globe. You can use the old maps to pick your targets. *Flying Fool* and *Gossamer Gnat* will follow close behind, but will decelerate sufficiently to enter opposing north-south polar orbits. I want at least two complete circuits of the planet before the fleet arrives.

"Unless one of you waves us off, *Discovery* will take up a high-guard, north-south parking orbit while *City of Alexandria* does the same close in. The two tankers will take up positions at the New Providence–Laertes L4 and L5 points, where they will act as ground-to-orbit communications relays, if and when such are required."

The scouts had spent the rest of the voyage refining the basic plan. By the time *Discovery* reached the specified distance from New Providence, they were eager to be on their way.

"Are you ready, Lieutenant Hall?" Drake asked.

"Ready, sir," the commander of *Discovery*'s scout force said from out of the screen at Drake's console. As in the approach to *Conqueror*, Drake planned to send his scouts in before risking any of the fleet's ships. He wondered if he was once again sending them to rendezvous with a derelict.

"You may launch when ready," Drake said to Hall.

"Understood, Captain. We are launching now. Open hangar bay doors!"

The first pictures from *Catherine* and *Drunkard* began coming in some four hours later. *Discovery*'s crew had been on full alert for all that time, scanning their instruments and checking their weapons. And, for all that time, the tension had been building aboard the battle cruiser. Every second that passed without someone detecting the presence of man on the ancestral home of all Altans brought with it a firmer realization that their worst fears might well be confirmed. New Providence had been a world of three billion souls; and now it was as silent as a tomb.

The first long-range televiews came from Scout Boat *Drunkard*. It showed a planetary limb, a blue ocean, and the unfamiliar shoreline of a continent. As they watched, the continent grew with surprising rapidity, an indication of the speed with which the scout was closing on the planet.

"What is *Drunkard*'s target?" Drake asked.

"Regensburg," Lieutenant Cristobal answered. "The records indicate that it is the major metropolis in the northern hemisphere. *Catherine* will arrive five minutes later and will overfly a city named Terra Nova."

"One of my great-great-great-grandfathers came from Terra Nova, I think," Bethany Lindquist said from her position beside Cristobal.

"I thought your family was from Earth, Miss Lindquist," Argos Cristobal said.

She swiveled to face the astrogator. "Only *some* of my ancestors, Mr. Cristobal. You'll find that I have quite a lot of Altan in me."

The view jumped once as Scout Pilot Marman ordered a switch to a higher magnification. The scene was suddenly frozen on the screen as the computer chose a single frame from *Drunkard*'s orbital mapping camera. The view was of the outskirts of the city of Regensburg taken at a slant angle of 45 degrees.

Regensburg had been built on a series of rolling, forested hills. The screen showed equal parts of city and forest. The forest was dead. Bare trunks jutted skyward, sprouting sticklike branches in geometric symmetry. Many trees had been uprooted by windstorms. Their corpses lay scattered randomly among the upright bodies of their brethren. In some areas, the tangle of deadwood approached jungle proportions, as if the natural process of decay had been halted.

"No microorganisms," Drake muttered to no one in particular. "The planet must be sterile."

He switched his gaze to the city. It, too, was the color of dead plants and, like the forest, showed signs of weather damage, yet with a degree of preservation unexpected in a hundred-year-old ruin.

"Scout Marman reports his flyby complete. He is headed out into space," Slater reported from the communicator's station.

"How many frames did he get?"

"Fifty thousand, Captain, all received and ready for processing. *Catherine* reports coming up on Terra Nova."

Drake turned his attention back to the main viewscreen. Once again there was a view of the planet's limb. Once again, the camera was switched over to high magnification, and a single frame was frozen on the control room viewscreen. This time the view was centered on a large city. But where Regensburg had looked as though its inhabitants had stepped away for a moment, Terra Nova was a shambles. Everywhere, blackened steel frameworks jutted skyward from piles of masonry, toppled towers lay where they had smashed across parked groundcars, and hollow shells stood guard over collapsed interiors. The sight of the destruction sent a shiver through Drake's soul.

"Some kind of out-of-control fire?" Argos Cristobal asked.

"It was an out-of-control fire, all right," Bethany Lindquist responded, her voice filled with horror. "Look at the way the outlying buildings all seem to have toppled away from the central point. I've seen that pattern before in history tapes. That city didn't burn of its own accord. Someone exploded a nuclear weapon on it!"

It had taken the fleet four hours after the initial flybys to reach New Providence. For half that time, the expedition's scientists had pored over the panoramic views transmitted by *Drunkard* and *Catherine*, or had watched the unfolding of still greater panoramas as the other two armed scouts took up their stations just outside the atmosphere. The additional observations confirmed what they had already surmised. New Providence was indeed a dead world.

Everywhere they looked they found desolation and the remains of once-living things. So far as could be seen from orbit, nothing lived on the planet's surface. Nor had the world died peacefully. Terra Nova was not the only city that had died by the sword. The orbital survey crews counted more than five hundred blast-damaged areas on the planet, including many that had been the victims of more than one strike. When he had seen enough, Drake ordered another ship-to-ship teleconference.

"What do your people make of it, Dr. Wharton?" he asked the head of the social sciences team as soon as the link between ships was established.

"Other than the obvious fact that there was unrestricted warfare in this system sometime after the Antares Supernova and that the conflict went on for quite some time, we have no conclusions, sir."

"How do you know how long it lasted?" Stan Barrett asked from *Alexandria*'s conference room.

Wharton turned to face the politician. "A close examination of Terra Nova reveals secondary plant growth and attempts to repair the damage, Mr. Barrett. It was probably destroyed early in the conflict. In the city of Durbanville, on the other hand, there are human remains visible and the vegetation apparently had no time to grow back after the blast. The logical conclusion is that Durbanville was destroyed shortly before the wavefront from the supernova arrived."

"What do you suppose started the war?" Alicia Delevan asked from her seat opposite Wharton.

Wharton shrugged. "I have no idea, dear lady. I'm afraid we'll have to go down and dig through the ruins to find the answer to that question."

Drake, who had been listening to the discussion in silence, interrupted from *Discovery*'s conference room. "I have a more immediate problem, ladies and gentlemen. We are within an hour of orbiting New Providence. I must have your opinions as to whether it is safe to do so."

"We'll learn nothing out here in deep space, Captain Drake," Wharton said. "We *have* to orbit."

"What if there are computer-controlled defenses?"

"They probably corroded into uselessness long ago. Besides, the radiation from the Antares Nebula will have turned any defense system computer into so much inert mass by now."

"Other opinions?" Drake asked.

"Orbit," Stan Barrett said. "We must find out what happened down there."

There was a general murmur of assent from the scientists aboard *Alexandria*.

Drake nodded. "Very well, then. We orbit as planned!"

The first Marine ground party landed on New Providence three days later, much to the chagrin of the scientists. Richard Drake had decreed that none of the scientists would be allowed on the surface until the Marines completed a radiation-shielded base camp large enough to house a hundred occupants. Construction of the shelters, their support equipment, and a perimeter fence—in case the planet wasn't as dead as it looked—took five days. Not until the camp was declared ready for occupancy did Drake finally relent and give his permission for the first scientist to join the Marines on the surface.

Ground operations quickly settled into a fixed routine

pegged to the thirty-eight-hour New Providence day. For nineteen of those hours, the Antares Nebula was below the horizon and the background radiation dropped to a safe level. While the nebula was absent from the sky, small working parties scoured the deserted city in the hope of finding some clue as to the course of events on New Providence after Antares exploded.

The searchers were lucky in one respect. The periods of low radiation were roughly synchronized with the rising and setting of Napier, allowing the search to take place in daylight. Drake issued orders that everyone was to return to the shelter at least one hour before the first glimmer of the nebula's outer ring rose above the horizon. The "nebula-up" periods were spent poring over the day's findings, eating, and sleeping off the exhaustion brought on by the eighteen-hour-long workdays.

The expedition's archeologists quickly discovered that finding out what had happened to New Providence wouldn't be an easy task. Like most modern societies, the New Providentials had stored their records as electronic impulses. A century of daily radiation storms had wiped the planet's computer banks clean. Even the normally radiation-resistant crystal memories had long since surrendered their precious cargo of information to the rain of cosmic bullets.

With the primary information sources rendered useless by radiation, Dr. Wharton set his work parties to collecting the vestigial remains of precomputer technologies. They combed the ruins for anything that had survived the dual catastrophes of war and nature. What the search teams found mostly was paper: newsfax printouts, personal mail, and books of the printed-and-bound variety.

To facilitate the search, the base camp had been constructed in a park in the center of a medium-size city in New Providence's northern hemisphere. Hecate had been a regional transportation hub since the founding of the colony. It had escaped the large-scale bombardment that had destroyed so many other New Providential cities.

On the third day of searching the deserted city, one of the work teams uncovered a cache of newsfax printouts. The first, dated 5 August 2512, carried a report that several scheduled starships were overdue. Two days later, another printout confirmed rumors that the Napier–Val foldpoint had failed. The stories quoted several leading scientists, none of whom had any explanation for how such a thing could happen.

The same accounts that told of Alta's being cut off confirmed that the foldpoint to Sandarson's World was still open. An even later newsfax printout editorialized that the government should mount an expedition to investigate why ships were able to leave the system via the Antares foldpoint but no traffic seemed to be coming the other direction.

"Small wonder," Wharton said, showing the article to one of his assistants. "They must have been vaporized the moment they jumped!"

As the days went on, Gregory Wharton became more frustrated over the pace of the search. It wasn't that they weren't finding records. They were. And, in fact, there seemed to be no shortage of information from the prenova and immediate postnova periods. But of the war, they could find no mention.

Drake was working on his log a week after the first scientists had gone down to New Providence when he was interrupted by a knock on his cabin door.

"It's open!" he yelled.

The door slid into its recess to reveal Bethany Lindquist standing in the corridor beyond. "I'm not bothering you, am I, Captain?"

"Heavens, no! Glad for the interruption. Come in and have a seat. What can I do for you?"

Bethany took the proffered chair next to his workstation, hesitated, then said, "I'd like to go down to the surface."

Drake blinked in surprise. "What?"

"I want to join the ground party."

"Out of the question!"

"But why?"

"I'll turn the question around for you. Why do you want to go?"

"I'm a historian by trade. I could be useful. There will be bookfilms to work through, newsfax printouts to salvage, even computer banks to tap into, if any survive. That's what I do for a living."

"The ground party already has two historians with it."

"One more set of hands is always useful, Captain."

"Thanks to your uncle, Miss Lindquist, you are considerably more than 'a set of hands' to me. In fact, you are the one irreplaceable person aboard this ship. If something were to happen to you, this expedition would be over."

"No more so, Captain Drake, than if I should decide not to authorize the next foldspace transition." She regretted her words immediately when she saw his scowl. "I'm sorry. I didn't mean it. It's just that I'm tired of sitting in my cabin while others work. Besides, I don't want to come all this way and then never leave the ship."

Drake sat back, chewed his lower lip, and thought about his orders from the first admiral that he was to win Bethany Lindquist over to the Altan viewpoint regarding *Discovery*'s jump codes. It certainly wouldn't hurt the cause to grant her wish. Also, he knew just how she felt. It was frustrating to have to sit in orbit while others uncovered New Providence's secrets. On the other hand, there were definite dangers down below and without her there would be no expedition.

Drake considered his competing imperatives for half a dozen seconds before speaking. "If I allow it, I'll demand certain concessions."

"Such as?"

"I want you to record the jump code for the next transition in the computer before you go. You can put any security classification you want on it. Only, if you haven't countermanded the code within a reasonable time—say, thirty days—I want the computer to release it to me."

Bethany hesitated for a moment, then nodded. "Agreed, Captain."

"I also insist that you have an escort the whole time you are down there. And, if we discover conditions on the surface to be even slightly dangerous, I'll order you back up here instantly."

"I agree to that also."

He leaned back in his chair and said, "In that case, have an enjoyable trip. I only wish I could go with you."

CHAPTER 13

"We really ought to be getting back, Miss Lindquist."

Bethany Lindquist looked up from where she knelt in a deserted hallway in front of a locked door. Standing over her, holding a large hammerlike implement, was a hulking figure in the mottled-green of the Altan Space Navy Marines. Bethany got to her feet and brushed light-color dust from her knees. "All right, Corporal Vargas. Let's pop this one last door and then head for the barn."

"Right, ma'am. Stand clear."

Bethany retreated to the opposite side of the hall and watched while Vargas raised the sledgehammer. He smashed the heavy head into the door just above the lock box with a practiced swing. The sound of rending metal and a cloud of century-old dust accompanied the opening of a three-centimeter-wide gap between door and frame. Vargas spat to clear the taste of musty disuse from his mouth, eased his hand into the gap, braced himself as best he could, and shoved. The recalcitrant door slid slowly into its recess amid more sounds of tortured metal.

"Well done, Corporal," Bethany said. "This breaking-and-entering isn't as hard as it looks."

"If only old Judge Waring could see us now, miss."

"Who?"

"The city magistrate back where I come from. It was him who sort of talked me into joining the Marines. Gave me a choice between that and a stretch in juvenile hall, he did!"

Bethany laughed. "I won't tell him about your recent life of crime if you won't." She gestured toward the now open door. "Shall we get on with it?"

"Just a second, ma'am, while I collect the rest of my gear."

She watched the giant Marine sling the strap of his wrecking tool over his shoulder. As he reached for his backpack, she couldn't help thinking that a more unlikely nursemaid would have been difficult to find.

As Richard Drake promised, she had found a Marine escort waiting for her as she stepped off the landing shuttle at base camp some five New Providential days earlier. That escort had been Corporal Garrold Vargas. From that moment on, he had been her constant companion each time she ventured outside the protection of the radiation-shielded Hecate Base. Like the rest of the ground party, the two of them had quickly fallen into a routine governed by the rising and setting of the Antares Nebula. Each morning they piled food, water, and two backpacks full of burglar tools into a small rover vehicle and set out for their assigned search area. Once in the area, Bethany would choose the buildings and rooms to be searched, and Vargas would make sure that no locked doors impeded their progress. It was a perfect division of labor, and, to their mutual surprise, they found that they worked well together.

Their assigned area for the day was identified on 150-year-old Altan maps as Hecate University. Bethany had hoped that their luck would change in an institution of higher learning. However, so far the campus had proved more devoid of paper scraps than had the residential areas near the base. It was frustrating to walk among the thousands of information terminals scattered about the campus and know that a century of radiation had turned them all into useless lumps of silicon and glass.

They stepped through the doorway that they had just

opened. As expected, they found themselves in a class-room. The room was identical to a hundred others they'd seen during the day. Fifty computer stations were arrayed in parallel rows, each facing a much larger and more complicated station on a raised dais. They quickly fell into their standard routine. Bethany began searching the work-station closest to the door while Vargas took the one situated in the farthest corner of the room. They worked quickly down the rows, searching desk drawers and knee-holes for any scrap of written or printed material. As usual, there were numerous crystalline record tiles—all turned a smoky gray by the radiation—but no paper of any sort.

When they had finished the students' stations, Bethany moved to the instructor position. Vargas glanced around the room, saw nothing left to search, and moved to stare out the window. They were on the tenth floor and the window gave them a good view of the sprawling campus and of Napier, which was low in the sky. Bethany concluded her search of the instructor station, found nothing, and moved to join the Marine.

"Kinds of reminds you of home, don't it, Miss Lind-quist?"

"That is because most Altan architectural styles are copies of New Providential originals," Bethany said. She glanced out at the rest of Hecate University. The school had been built on four sides of a large quadrangle—a place where trees and flowers had once been interspersed with fountains and benches amid pedestrian paths. Surrounding the quadrangle were buildings similar to the one they were in. "God, look at this place! It'll take a year to search it properly."

"Are Earth universities like this one?" Vargas asked.

"I've only seen pictures, of course," Bethany replied. "However, on Earth they tend to build tall, with less open space. Land is a lot more valuable there because of their population. *That*"—Bethany gestured toward the quadrangle below—" would be a wasteful extravagance on the Mother of Men."

"Look at those statues," Vargas said, gesturing toward two stone-color shapes in the center of the quadrangle. "What kind of animals do you suppose those are?"

Bethany's gaze followed the Corporal's pointing finger. The reclining shapes flanked a small, kiosklike structure that looked something like a subway entry portal back home.

"Hard to tell at this range. Give me your binoculars, Corporal."

Vargas handed her his electronic glasses. Bethany used them to zoom in on the figures. After a long pause, she said: "Why, they're lions!"

"What's that, a New Providence beast of some sort?"

Bethany lowered the glasses to reveal a deeply furrowed brow. "Surely your mother told you about Earth lions, Corporal. You know, big versions of house cats."

Vargas scratched his chin. "Oh, yeah. Lions."

"I wonder what a statue of a lion is doing here on New Providence," Bethany mused, as much to herself as to Vargas. "It couldn't have meant anything to the locals unless they had a particularly well stocked zoo." She handed the binoculars back to the Marine and said, "I think we'd better check this out."

"Can't do it, Miss Lindquist," Vargas replied. "Sun's going down. That means nebula-rise is less than ninety minutes off."

"It won't take long, Corporal. Relax, we'll make curfew with plenty of time to spare."

While the social scientists sifted through the detritus of the dead planet, the astronomers in orbit worked to map the local structure of foldspace. For centuries teachers of multidimensional physics had searched for an apt analogy with which to describe foldspace to their students. The most common involved comparing it to a piece of paper that has been crumpled into a tight ball and then straightened flat again. In the process of transformation from two-dimensional sheet to three-dimensional sphere, the paper picks up a complex pattern of folds and creases. By studying the pattern, it is possible to fully describe the crumpling process. In effect, foldlines are the "creases and folds" left over after the space–time continuum has been "crumpled up" by a supermassive black hole.

The expedition's scientists had two clues to help them understand the postnova structure of foldspace. The first involved the detailed maps of foldspace structure prior to the nova. The second was the knowledge of how far the Napier–Val foldpoint had moved from its prenova position. By starting with the old maps and skewing them to account for the observed shift in the foldpoint's position, the scientists were able to construct a computer model that accounted for the shift. The computer model, once completed, then allowed them to predict the position of the other surviving foldpoints.

In science, however, a prediction is no good unless confirmed by experiment. Confirming the position of a foldpoint is a difficult business at best, one requiring many thousands of delicate measurements of the local gravitational constant. *Alexandria* carried several hundred free-flying gravitational detectors for just that purpose. The detectors were to be launched on precise trajectories that would take them near each of the theoretical positions of the system foldpoints. While in flight, they would measure the gravitational constant in the region and transmit the data back to *Alexandria* for analysis.

The continuous whine of the telemetry streams filled the plot room aboard the liner for a hundred hours or more. When the principal investigators had developed a preliminary map confirming the position of foldpoints leading to the heart of the Antares Nebula and to Alta's sister colony of Sandarson's World, Nathaniel Gordon and Mikhail Planovich requested an audience with Richard Drake in his cabin aboard *Discovery*.

"I believe we have located all the foldpoints in this

system, Captain." Gordon pointed to three widely separated locations—including the one marking the Napier–Val foldpoint—in a three-dimensional globe. In addition to the star, planets, and foldpoints, the globe showed a series of isogravity lines.

"Are you sure of that number?" Drake asked.

Professor Planovich nodded. "Quite sure, Captain. We now have a much better understanding of what the nova did to foldspace. In fact—"

Planovich was interrupted by the buzzing of the intercom on Drake's desk. He reached out and accepted the call.

"Yes, Mr. Slater?"

"Call from Dr. Wharton on the surface, Captain. I wouldn't have bothered you except that he says it's urgent."

"Put him on."

The screen cleared to show the pudgy, reddish features of Gregory Wharton. The man was obviously disturbed about something.

"What can I do for you, Dr. Wharton?" Drake asked.

"Ah, night has fallen here, Captain Drake, and the nebula has just risen."

Drake glanced at the chronometer on the wall. In addition to ship's time, it displayed the status of both the day/night and high/low radiation cycles at Hecate's longitude. "We're aware of the time up here, Doctor. What's your problem?"

"Bethany Lindquist and that corporal you have guarding her went out as usual this morning. They haven't returned."

Drake felt a knot begin to form in his stomach. "Are you sure? Have you checked all the shelters?"

"We have, sir. I've called the complete roster. No one has seen them and their vehicle is not in the motor pool."

"What about communications?"

"They checked in by comm laser via *Sultana* relay

when they arrived at their search area this morning. We've heard nothing since. What shall I do?"

Drake thought about it for a moment, acutely conscious of the sick feeling in the pit of his stomach. A city is a dangerous place anywhere, anytime. A dead city on a dead planet is more so by several orders of magnitude. He could imagine Bethany lying injured somewhere, watching the deadly glow of the Antares Nebula rise slowly over the horizon.

Drake stared at the panicky face in the viewscreen, mulled over his options, then said:

"I'm coming down! Don't do anything until I get there."

Bethany and Vargas drove their rover to the center of the quadrangle where the statues flanked the kiosk. As they approached, any doubts Bethany had concerning their nature were dispelled. They were lions, all right, and not just any lions. The animals lay in a reclining position, their paws stretched out before them and their tails wrapped close in at their sides. Their manes were full and bushy, and four stone eyes seemed to be staring intently into the distance. Between the two animals, a concrete ramp slanted downward, disappearing behind a large steel door that sealed the kiosk's entrance.

"Smash it down, Corporal!" Bethany ordered, pointing to the door.

Vargas frowned, opened his mouth to speak, then thought better of it. He unlimbered his sledgehammer and went to work. Two minutes later, the quadrangle still rang with the resonant clanging of his hammer.

"Wait a minute," Bethany called out as Vargas prepared to swing for the twentieth time. "Let me in for a look."

Vargas ceased his attack on the door and wiped sweat from his brow. "I don't think we've got the proper equipment here, miss."

"Try a couple of more," Bethany replied, stepping back

from her inspection of the lock. "It looks like it's beginning to give."

Vargas lifted his wrecking tool once more and slammed it into the door with all the force he could muster. The door emitted a metallic shriek. He hit it twice more. On the final blow the hinges gave way and the steel barrier crashed inward. Inside the kiosk was a ramp leading underground. Beyond the heavy steel rectangle, an escalator led downward, disappearing into blackness some thirty meters below ground.

"Give me your light."

Vargas did as he was told with a nervous glance at Napier's position low on the horizon. "We're almost out of time, Miss Lindquist."

"Trust me, Garry. This could be important. We'll check it out, then run for home. I promise!"

The two of them slowly descended the motionless steps of the escalator. At thirty meters of depth, they came to a landing where the escalator ended. Another escalator continued down a few meters away. Bethany led Vargas to it and started down before he could protest. In seconds they found themselves in a complete blackness relieved only by the beams from their handlamps. They continued downward to a second landing, and then to a third escalator, before eventually coming to an underground hallway. The hall was too long for their lights to reach either end.

"It must run under the entire quadrangle," Bethany said, her voice echoing hollowly from the surrounding walls.

"What do you suppose it is?"

"An underground passageway across campus, among other things," she replied.

"Which way?" he asked.

She let her light play first along one wall, then another. "Let's try to the right."

They moved gingerly along the underground corridor

until they came to a door with the silhouette of a reclining lion on it.

"This is what I'm looking for," Bethany said. "Let's crash it!"

"Not necessary," Vargas replied as he slowly pushed the inert door into its recess. "It's open."

Inside they found a spacious underground room with the ubiquitous information terminals scattered around on various tables. Bethany ignored the room and moved to a far doorway. This door too opened easily and she moved through. In spite of five long days of exploring deserted ruins, she couldn't help feeling the solitude of the place.

The second room contained a desk-size machine. Bethany held her breath as she searched the unobstructed front panel of the device with the beam of her handlamp.

"What is it?" Vargas asked, adding his own illumination to the object.

"I'm not sure," Bethany replied, "but I think it's a computer."

"Could be. It looks like other computers we've found. Come on, let's go."

"Go?" Bethany asked in surprise.

"Sure. The sun's going down, remember? We've found lots of computers during our explorations."

"Have you found any that happen to be a hundred meters underground?" Bethany asked.

Vargas shook his head. "No, most of 'em have been on the upper floors of buildings. Why?"

"Because a hundred meters of soil is more than enough to shield against the radiation from the nebula."

Vargas stared at her. The light from the lamps gave his face a craggy look. His eyes were white circles staring out of two pools of shadow black. "Are you saying that this machine may be in working condition?"

"Could be. I think we've found the university's library computer."

"You knew this was down here, didn't you?" Vargas asked, a hint of awe in his voice.

Bethany nodded. "I had my suspicions when I saw those lions upstairs. For some reason, lions have always been associated with libraries. Those statues are copies of two very famous lion sculptures that once adorned the steps of the New York Public Library on Earth. If Hecate University had copies, I figured they were using them to mark the entrance to the library. Besides, it didn't make sense that they'd build that big quadrangle up above and not put anything under it."

"We've got to report back," Vargas said urgently. "The sarge told us that if we could find a working computer, we could forget all that scrap paper we've been collecting."

"We will, but not until I check one more thing." Bethany moved to a door at the back of the computer room. This time it refused to open. She turned to Vargas. "Unlimber your hammer and go to it, Corporal."

The door yielded after a single blow. Bethany pushed her way inside the room beyond. She flashed her lamp beam over a series of file cabinets. Inside were dozens of small record tiles.

"What is this?" Vargas asked.

"Backup records," Bethany replied. "This is where they filed everything they didn't want cluttering up their working memory. All right, Corporal, I've seen all I need to see. Let's get back to camp and report."

"Yes, ma'am!"

The western horizon was aglow with color when they finally emerged from the underground tunnel. Fingers of red and orange climbed the sky, fading to blue and then to blue-black directly overhead. A few stars had begun to appear in the vault of the heavens, while to the east, a milk-white glow was brightening in a gap between two buildings. The sight of that glow sent a shiver of fear down Bethany's spine. It signified that the Antares Nebula would soon bathe the city of Hecate once more in its deadly light.

The two of them moved to their vehicle and shrugged off their packs and other equipment. Bethany climbed into the passenger side of the rover while Vargas stowed the equipment in the back. She slouched in her seat and concentrated on regaining her breath after the long climb up the stalled escalator. It was several seconds before she noticed that Vargas had made no move to take his seat behind the rover's controls. Instead, he had moved to the front of the vehicle and was staring toward the burgeoning glow in the east.

Bethany slid across the bench seat to the driver's side and palmed the control that retracted the window. "Get in, Corporal! We've just time enough to make it back."

Vargas turned to look at her. There was a frown on his face. "I'm afraid it's already too late, Miss Lindquist."

"What are you talking about? The radiation won't get bad for another twenty minutes. It only took us fifteen minutes to get here from camp this morning."

"That was this morning, in daylight. It'll be full dark in another ten minutes." He shook his head. "Too much chance that we'll make a wrong turn, or run over a piece of debris, or fall into a hole in the dark. We'd be cutting it too close to recover before nebula-rise. Even if nothing happens and we make it, Sergeant Crocker will have me shot for taking such a damnfool chance with you along."

Bethany opened her mouth to retort, saw the look in Vargas' eye, and nodded instead. He was right, of course. Exploring the library had taken more time than she'd planned. And even though their packs were jammed with record tiles, it wouldn't do anyone any good if they were caught in the open by nebula-rise. Bethany resigned herself to spending the night in the tunnels they had just vacated.

"If we're going to hole up, we'd better report in."

"Can't," Vargas replied, gesturing toward a row of glowing numbers on a screen in the rover's instrument panel. "Both relay ships are below the horizon just now."

"Damn!"

One of the first discoveries of the original ground party had been the fact that radios didn't work well on present-day New Providence. As in most of the planet's problems, the nebula was to blame. The constant rain of charged particles against the ionosphere resulted in a continuous howl of static across the communications bands. To keep in contact, the ground parties relied on comm-laser links to the two orbiting cryogen tankers. With the tankers somewhere over the horizon, Bethany and Vargas were effectively isolated.

Bethany gazed up at the surrounding buildings. "Think we have time to go up on the roof and beam the camp directly?"

"No!" Vargas growled. "The only thing we've time for is to get under cover."

"All right. We forget reporting in, then. How long to dismount the rover's energy pack?"

"What for?"

"It might prove useful down below. Besides, the radiation will ruin it if we don't get it into the tunnels. The same goes for the laser and the other solid-state controls on the rover."

He nodded. "I'll dismount the fixed equipment. You start moving the supplies. And, Miss Lindquist..."

"Yes, Corporal?"

"No matter how much we have to do, we knock off five minutes before nebula-rise and get our butts underground. Agreed?"

"Agreed."

They beat their self-imposed deadline by two minutes. Bethany made one last trip to the surface to help Vargas gather the tools he'd used to dismount the rover's navigation package. As she did so, she glanced at the eastern horizon.

The glow had brightened considerably, and the edge of the nebula was now visible as a misshapen white arch silhouetted against the black sky. Atmospheric distortion made it look as though the arch were hanging a few degrees above the dark line of the horizon. Below the arch, a starlike image burned with the light of a fluorescent lamp. The image was that of the Antares pulsar refracted over the horizon by the atmospheric lens effect. Bethany knew from watching the phenomenon on previous nights that the real star was never far behind its phantom image.

"Time to go." Vargas grunted as he picked up the instrument cluster and slung it over one shoulder. "Grab my pack and follow me."

She followed him at a run. They hurried through the kiosk, over the fallen portal gate, and down the sloping tunnel to the first escalator landing. Vargas carefully lowered his burden and then sat down next to the stack of equipment that Bethany had moved into the tunnel. Overhead, at the entrance to the subterranean passageway, a radiation detector began to chatter furiously.

CHAPTER 14

It took another hour, with frequent stops for rest, to move their supplies down to the library level. Because of its weight, the rover power pack was the last to go.

"What do you want with this thing?" Vargas asked, nudging the heavy case with his toe.

"I thought we might be able to power up the library computer and read some of the old records," Bethany said. "So long as we're marooned down here until morning, we might as well get some work done, right?"

Vargas grunted his assent, then stoically carried the pack down to the computer room. He propped it up to allow Bethany access to the output controls, made sure the pack was switched off, then turned to heating up two ration packets over a small camp stove. While tantalizing odors filled the old library, Bethany removed the computer's access panels and began tracing circuits. She had just managed to locate the computer's main power supply cable when Vargas announced dinner. Bethany ate hurriedly, then returned to work. Two hours later, she had the power pack's output hooked up to the computer via two leads salvaged from one of the library information terminals.

"Let's try it!"

"What voltage?" Vargas asked.

Bethany read the computer's electrical requirements off a maintenance plate at the back of the machine. The

Marine manipulated the manual control set in the face of the powerpack, then looked up.

"Ready?"

"Go ahead."

Vargas energized the pack. Instead of a spark or the smell of burning insulation, they were rewarded with the sudden illumination of the computer's terminal screen.

"I'll be damned, it works!" she said. The sound of her voice made it obvious that she had been holding her breath. She reached for one of the computer tiles they'd liberated from the file cabinet and inserted it into a domino-shaped slot in the computer's face.

Vargas looked at her haggard features made more so by the harsh camp light they were using to illuminate the chamber. "You must be about ready to drop. Why don't you knock off for a few hours? You'll be more efficient if you get some sleep before trying to read this stuff."

"I'm too excited to sleep," Bethany replied without looking up from her work. "You go ahead and stretch out in the next room if you like. I'll be all right in here."

"Are you sure?"

"Of course. Go ahead."

Vargas left to arrange his sleeping bag while Bethany began experimenting with the information terminal. The Marine wrapped himself in the light fabric, sealed the electrostatic closure on the side of the sleeping bag, rolled over to face the wall, and was asleep within a dozen seconds.

He awoke four hours later to find the main library room dark except for the ghostly flicker of the terminal screen in the adjoining computer room. He opened the sleeping bag, got to his feet, and padded quietly to the open doorway. Bethany sat crosslegged in front of the terminal. Her back was braced against the wall while her eyes scanned the quickly scrolling text that rolled up the screen.

"Are you all right, Miss Lindquist?" he asked.

Bethany turned to look at him. She stretched, then rubbed her eyes. "Nothing wrong with me that a year's sleep won't cure, Corporal."

"Then why don't you quit and take a nap?"

"I'm almost done." She pointed to three clusters of record tiles. "I've been separating our treasure trove into categories. The largest stack contains prenova records; the medium-size, general information from the postnova period; the smallest, news reports and commentaries, most of which mention the nebula."

"Find anything interesting?"

"You might say that." She looked up at him with an expression that seemed equal parts fatigue, excitement, and awe. "I know where and how the war started!"

Richard Drake sat in the right-hand pilot's seat of one of *City of Alexandria*'s landing boats and gazed at the night face of New Providence some thirty thousand meters below. The planet had taken on a fairyland look under the nebula's baleful glow—a light much softer and more diffuse then the incandescence of Antares dawn at home. Nor was the nebula the only source of illumination. The constant rain of charged particles against the planet's magnetic field triggered massive, night-long auroral displays. Sheets of softly glowing celestial fire swept across the sky as streamers of red, green, and blue chased each other from horizon to horizon. Except for the continuous growl of the radiation detector, it would have been easy to forget that the scene was deadly.

"We're coming up on Hecate, Captain," the landing boat pilot said, pointing to a bright red beacon that had just appeared on the horizon.

The boat swept over the city and banked steeply. Below, a dozen temporary buildings stood in a pool of polyarc illumination amid the dead shrubbery of a park. The landing boat completed a sweeping turn, slowed to a hover over the camp, then slowly settled to the ground in a billowing cloud of dust.

"We're down, sir," the pilot said after a few seconds. "We'll have to wait until they get the portable rad-shield erected before we can disembark."

Drake nodded. It took ten minutes for a remotely operated meshwork shield to be maneuvered into position between the landing boat and the nebula. As soon as it was in place, Drake hurried to the nearest shelter at a quick trot. Gregory Wharton and Fleet Sergeant Vin Crocker were waiting for him just inside the shelter's radiation lock. Crocker was the commander of *Alexandria*'s Marine contingent.

"Any news?"

"Nothing since I called you four hours ago, Captain," Dr. Wharton replied.

Drake turned to face Crocker. "All right, Sergeant. How did it happen?"

"We don't know, sir. Everything was fine when they left camp this morning. Miss Lindquist was even joking while they loaded their gear aboard their scout vehicle. They checked in when they reached their search area. All we know is that they didn't show up for evening muster."

"Is this Vargas competent?" Drake asked.

"He's one of my best, sir. That's why I made him Miss Lindquist's escort."

"Where was their assigned search area?"

"I can show you on the map in my office, Captain," Wharton replied.

Drake and Crocker followed the sociologist into an adjoining shelter and a small cramped office. A map of the city covered one wall. It had been marked with strips of colored tape to chart the progress of the operation.

"They were scouting Hecate University," Wharton said, pointing to an area bordered by red tape on the map. "I was going to assign one of our larger teams there in a few days, but Miss Lindquist insisted on getting an early start."

"And you let her?"

"If you remember, Captain, your orders were to extend her every courtesy so long as she was in the company of an escort."

Drake took a deep breath, then slowly settled into the chair behind Wharton's desk. "All right, gentlemen, enough looking backward. What are we going to do now?"

"I recommend we search for them, sir," Crocker said. "We've been installing shield generators in two ground vehicles. They won't be anywhere near as efficient as a fixed installation, but they'll be better than nothing."

"What attenuation factor do you expect, Sergeant?"

"At least a thousand."

"That means the vehicle occupants will reach the safe limit for radiation exposure in approximately four hours."

"The exposure limit is conservative, sir. I think a man would be safe for at least twice that long, maybe longer. Anyway, I've got four volunteers willing to try it."

"Yourself included, Sergeant?"

"Yes, sir."

"Well, forget it. Assuming they aren't dead or too injured to move, they should have found themselves a hole to hide in as soon as they realized that they were going to be caught by the nebula. If they made it underground, then they're safe until morning. I don't want anyone running up his cumulative rad-dose for no good reason in the meantime."

"And if they aren't under cover, Captain?" Wharton asked.

"Then they will be dead in another eight hours. Either way, the chance of finding them in the dark is nil. We'll just have to wait until the radiation subsides in the morning."

When Napier rose the next morning, it shed its rays on a haggard rescue expedition. Minutes later, the Antares Nebula's ghostly form finally slipped below the opposite horizon. The disappearance of the nebula was the signal for furious activity in the camp. The doors on the big

motorpool shelter swung back and a line of vehicles pulled
forward into the light. Moments later, a dozen men left
the shelters and began to load equipment. Richard Drake
was just climbing into the passenger seat of the lead vehicle when the base communicator yelled, "I've got them,
sir! They're calling via *Haridan* relay. Miss Lindquist is
on the line."

Drake muttered an oath under his breath and ran for
the base communications center.

"It was all my fault, Captain," Bethany's voice said
as soon as Drake identified himself. "Corporal Vargas
wanted to start back, but I just had to look down one
more hole. By the time we got back to the surface, it
was too late."

"Slow down," Drake said, momentarily diverted from
the tongue-lashing he'd been planning for the past fifteen
hours. "Start at the beginning."

Bethany hurriedly told him about the library computer
and the record tiles they had found, and concluded with
"I've spent most of the night skimming the records. Several of them discuss the postnova war in detail. By the
way, we were wrong."

"About what?"

"We thought the New Providentials fell to fighting
among themselves. Nothing could have been farther from
the truth. They were attacked."

"Attacked by whom?"

"Aliens."

"I beg your pardon?"

She grinned out of the screen at him. "You heard me.
The New Providentials called their attackers the Ryall.
They entered the system through a temporary foldpoint
opened up by the supernova. The records say they attacked
without provocation."

"Wait a minute!" Drake growled into the screen. "Are
you seriously saying that *New Providence was attacked
by intelligent, starfaring aliens*?"

"I just said so, didn't I?"

"Where are you?"

"We're in the big quadrangle in the center of Hecate University. Corporal Vargas is putting our car back together."

"Don't move. We'll be there in twenty minutes. I want to see these records for myself!"

It hadn't taken the New Providential astronomers long to decide that the events of 3 August 2512 could best be explained by a supernova explosion somewhere in the Antares Cluster. To their horror, they quickly concluded that the only star which fit all of the observed phenomena was Antares itself. New Providence, they realized, was under a sentence of death.

The first reaction of the general public was to deny that the supernova had occurred at all. The astronomers' work was denounced as baseless speculation by some and as intentional scaremongering by others. Learned scientists in dozens of fields unrelated to astronomy went on the mass media to explain with great certitude why the doomsayers were mistaken. Other experts, no less certain, concluded that: "Yes, Antares has exploded, but we have nothing whatsoever to fear from that far-off event. There are fifteen light-years of vacuum between us and the nova. No explosion, no matter how large, could possibly bridge such a gulf."

The denial phase lasted for three of New Providence's long days. Slowly, however, the protests turned to thoughtful analysis as commentators noted that the astronomers were holding firm to their prediction of disaster. The molders of public opinion began to ask "What if?" then "What will?" and finally, "When?" An eerie calm settled over the planet, a calm that lasted for two more days.

On the fifth day, public anger began to surface—anger not against the nova but rather against those who brought the bad tidings. Mobs formed around major universities to demand that the astronomers be forced to recant their predictions. The demands turned violent. Buildings were set ablaze and several academics killed.

After a long week of rioting, cooler heads began to assert themselves. The catharsis was over and the facts remained unchanged. Nature had taken no notice of the tantrum. The shockwave from the exploding star still raced toward Napier at the speed of light. So, reluctantly, and with considerable wistfulness for what might have been, the people of New Providence turned their full attention to preparations to evacuate their planet.

By the end of the first standard year, the system's entire industrial base had been turned to building an evacuation fleet. The basic ship design was a globe nearly a thousand meters in diameter. Each ship was to carry a million people and their belongings. The master plan called for a hundred such vessels to be built, and for each to make at least thirty trips to the colony on Sandarson's World.

While the engineers raced to build the evacuation fleet, New Providence's scientists studied the changes that the supernova had wrought in the local structure of foldspace. Prior to the star's eruption, the Napier system had possessed three interstellar portals, one each leading to Antares, Valeria, and Hellsgate—the star of Sandarson's World. The nova had dramatically revised the foldspace map of the Napier system by collapsing the foldpoint to Valeria and rendering the Antares foldpoint unnavigable.

New Providence's astonomers were therefore surprised when they detected the characteristic clumping of isogravity lines that normally mark a foldpoint in a part of the system where none had previously existed. The new foldpoint was situated nearly three times as far from Napier as the system's prenova foldpoints. Analyses of the newly formed foldpoint showed it to be a temporary phenomenon, the result of a long-range focusing of the foldlines by the expanding nova shockwave. Once the shockwave passed the Napier system, its focusing effect would be lost and the new foldpoint would disappear.

In the meantime, however, the scientists who had discovered the new foldpoint recommended an expedition to explore it. The government, decreeing that nothing would impede evacuation fleet construction, took the matter under advisement. It wasn't until the second year after the supernova that they were able to free up the necessary ships and men for the expedition.

Three ships were launched amid considerable fanfare on the second anniversary of the nova. They reached their goal a month later. After a series of preliminary measurements, two of them jumped to the system beyond the foldpoint. The third vessel, a chartered freighter named *Aldo Quest*, stayed behind to make precise isogravity measurements of the foldpoint.

Twelve days later, a panicky voice broke into a routine status report to scream that *Aldo Quest* was under attack by a dozen spacecraft of unknown type. There was no chance to say more. A few moments later, the comm link went dead in midsentence.

With *Aldo Quest*'s cry for help as a spur, the New Providential Council of Elders met in emergency session to decide their course of action. They were fortunate in that an entire flotilla of the Grand Fleet of Earth had arrived just a week earlier to aid in the evacuation effort. The flotilla had been dispatched direct from Earth and had reached the Napier system through the system's secondary sequence of foldspace transitions. Flotilla XVII of the Grand Fleet consisted of nine ships ranging in size from small destroyer-escorts to the flagship, the Heavy Battle Cruiser *Dartmouth*. Upon hearing *Aldo Quest*'s fragmentary report, the flotilla commander ordered his ships to space immediately to intercept the unknown invaders.

It took ten standard days of high acceleration for the two fleets to close the distance between them. As they flew, instruments onboard the ships of Flotilla XVII studied their potential adversaries at long range. As a result of these observations, the flotilla commander quickly became convinced that he faced alien invaders. The invading ships were disk-shaped and driven by drive flares that emitted much too great a portion of their power in the ultraviolet portion of the spectrum.

The two fleets encountered each other more than three billion kilometers from New Providence. In spite of the loss of the *Aldo Quest*, Flotilla XVII had broadcast messages of friendship throughout its approach. They continued to do so even as the alien disks opened fire with lasers and antimatter projectors. The flotilla returned the aliens' fire with long-range missiles, lasers, and neutron beam projectors. By the time the two fleets had interpenetrated, each had lost half of its initial strength.

The surviving alien warships slipped through the gaps they had torn in the ranks of the human defenders and continued on toward New Providence. The vice admiral in command of the interception fleet ordered his forces to begin savage braking maneuvers. They halted their outbound flight and gave chase to the aliens.

A long, brutal fight ensued all the way to the planet. There were only seven operational warcraft—three alien and four human—when the disks came in range of New Providence's planetary defense system. Century-old defense satellites added their fire to that of the surviving human ships. The three aliens were quickly destroyed in the crossfire; but not before one of them was able to launch half a dozen missiles against New Providence itself.

A single disk-shaped ship spat forth six missiles and six New Providential cities died violent deaths.

"That was the first raid," Bethany Lindquist said to Richard Drake. Both were in the library computer room staring at the terminal screen that Bethany had jury-rigged the night before. "There was another raid approximately three years later. By that time, the New Providentials had turned some of their shipbuilding capacity from evacuation craft to warships. Also, Earth sent in reinforcements. They caught the second Ryall fleet and destroyed it before it got much beyond the foldpoint."

Drake frowned. "If the first raid cost New Providence half a dozen cities destroyed, and the second raid was stopped so quickly, why have our surveyors counted more than five hundred major nuclear strike points on the surface of this planet?"

Bethany shrugged. "There must have been another attack after these records were made, one that was more successful than the first two."

"To judge by the evidence, it must have been a major breakthrough just before the nova wavefront swept through this system."

Bethany nodded. "That is the way I read it, Richard."

"How much did the New Providentials know about these Ryall?" Drake asked.

Bethany didn't answer. Instead, she manipulated the controls of her viewer. The screen cleared and an image formed in its depths.

The scene showed an alien being lying on an autopsy table. Drake fought down a feeling of unreality at the sight of the creature, and studied its form with all the detachment he could muster. He couldn't say that it was a pretty sight, but then, a man in a similar situation would hardly have been displayed to his best advantage either.

The being was a six-legged, two-armed centauroid whose appearance suggested a reptilian ancestry. It lay sprawled awkwardly across the autopsy table on its right side, with its head at the top of the screen and a meter-long tail dangling over the end of the table at screen-bottom. The hide was gray-green and lightly scaled.

As Drake watched, a set of disembodied human arms reached into the scene and lifted the creature's head up from the table, twisting it nearly 180 degrees to face the camera. Either the creature's long neck had been broken or it had considerable flexibility.

The head displayed a bulging cranium atop a toothy snout. The eyes were set on opposite sides of the skull and set under a heavy ridge of bone. Drake noted that the being would have found it difficult to look straight ahead. The ears were holes in the top of the skull around which mobile-looking flaps of skin lay stretched on a framework of small spikes.

The camera zoomed in to show a close-up of one of the creature's eyes as the unseen human biologist turned its head to give a better view. At first, it seemed as though the Ryall's eyes were two obsidian spheres sunk deep within its skull. However, a new set of hands moved into the picture and shined a flashlamp into the eye. There was a flash of reflection from a black pupil within a jet-black eyeball. There was no evidence of either an eyelid or a nictating membrane to cover the eye.

The camera pulled back and refocused on the creature's mouth. A tri-forked tongue hung limply between double rows of sharp, conical teeth. The camera then slowly panned across the creature's flank, revealing a six-fingered hand with vestigial webbing between the grasping digits, then six legs that culminated in slightly webbed feet.

"Not very pretty" was Drake's only comment after the display had been going on for several minutes.

"I don't know," Bethany replied. "It has a certain intrinsic beauty of its own, I think. Do you want to see any more? They'll be starting the autopsy in another minute or so. I can fast-forward to the results, if you like."

"Don't bother," Drake said. "It would be wasted on me. We need to get it onboard *City of Alexandria* so the real experts can take a look at it."

Bethany nodded and reached for the hand communicator that she'd left on the top of the computer housing.

"Shall I have the salvage crew start dismantling the library?"

"Not just yet," Drake said. "I have something to say that I don't want anyone else to hear."

Bethany sensed his sudden change in mood and frowned. "If it's about my getting caught by the nebula last night, I'm sorry."

"You should be," he said, his tone suddenly icelike. "It was a damned stupid thing to do..."

CHAPTER 15

Two standard days after the discovery of the Hecate University library, Richard Drake ordered ground operations on New Providence brought to an end. It took several more days to repack the ground party's gear and transport its personnel back to orbit. Bethany Lindquist delayed her departure as long as she could by the simple expedient of making herself as useful as possible. She packed records, disassembled equipment, and sorted through the mountain of specimens that the search parties had collected. Eventually, the repacking was completed and all that remained was for the Marines to dismantle the shelters. Bethany climbed into a landing boat with the last of the scientific personnel and watched as men in mottled green began to take apart the buildings of Hecate Base.

The landing boat climbed to orbit and docked with *City of Alexandria* without incident. The passengers waited patiently for docking tubes to be attached, then disembarked single file through the forward airlock. Bethany was the next-to-last passenger to leave the boat. She floated into the docking tube headfirst, then pulled herself along using handholds affixed to the tube walls until she reached its mouth. She halted a moment and surveyed the organized chaos in the axis passageway beyond.

A line of spacers, their boots anchored to meshwork, passed large, weightless, hexagonal shipping crates from the landing boat's aft airlock toward an open hatchway leading to one of the liner's cavernous cargo holds. Interspersed with the moving cargo were Bethany's fellow passengers. They nimbly dodged crates while working their way aft toward the three outward radiating stairwells that led to the lower decks. Adding to the confusion were a number of people who were trying to keep out of everyone else's way by clinging to the walls of the passageway. Carl Aster was a member of this latter group.

"Bethany!"

Bethany waved with one hand while keeping a careful grip with the other. Aster pushed off from his perch, floated across the line of cargo handlers (triggering several oaths in the process), and grounded next to Bethany. He encircled her waist with his arms and kissed her lightly on the lips. The kiss was accompanied by a rough chorus of appreciative cheers from onlookers.

Bethany let the kiss go on for a few seconds, then struggled to break free. "Stop it," she said in an embarrassed whisper. "Everyone's watching!"

"So what?" Aster asked in a normal conversational tone. "I'm sure they've all seen a man kissing his girl before."

"Please, you're embarrassing me."

Aster grinned at her. "All right, but I think you are being terribly parochial about this." He turned to face the cargo handlers. "The show's over, people. Back to work."

The compartment suddenly echoed with laughter as the crates began to move once more. Bethany felt a tap on her shoulder and heard a throat-clearing noise. She turned to see Dr. Wharton hanging patiently inside the docking tube behind her. "I don't want to seem unfeeling, Bethany, but would you mind if I squeeze past you and your young man?"

"Sorry, Dr. Wharton."

"Come on, let's get out of this crowd. I've reserved a table in the scientists' lounge."

"I wish I could, Carl, but I'm just passing through. I have to report aboard the shuttle boat for *Discovery*."

"No problem. I've got orders for the same shuttle. It won't be docking for another hour yet."

"Why are you going to the cruiser?" Bethany asked.

"Our esteemed expedition commander has called a full conference of the scientific staff. They're going to tell him what they've learned from those records of yours before we head out again."

"Then the decision to break orbit has been made?"

"That's the rumor on the grapevine."

"When and where to?"

"Almost immediately, if you believe the second assistant cook's version. As for the destination, opinions vary. Some are sure that Drake will order us home to warn Parliament about the Ryall threat. Others are equally positive that he'll choose to make the foldspace transition to Sandarson's World. On the other hand, some of the scientists are hoping we don't go anywhere. They're too absorbed in studying the nebula at close range. But enough of this gossip. How about that drink?"

"Drink? As in alcohol?"

Aster laughed. "You've been living aboard that damned warship too long!"

He escorted her down to Alpha Deck and to the compartment which the scientists had turned into a place to relax and exchange gossip and data. Bethany was surprised to find Alicia Delevan waiting for them as Aster guided her to a booth in a secluded corner of the lounge.

"I believe you know my boss, Special Ambassador Delevan," Aster said formally.

"I'm honored, Mrs. Delevan," Bethany said, extending her hand.

"Call me Alicia, Bethany. All of my friends do."

"All right, Alicia."

"What will you be drinking, my dear?"

"Martini, please."

"I'll have the same. Will you do the honors, Carl?"

"Sure thing, Boss." Aster wandered off to get the drinks while Bethany slid into the booth opposite the ambassador from the Conservative Alliance.

"I've been looking forward to meeting you, Bethany," Alicia said. "Carl talks about you all the time. I hope I'm not intruding on your homecoming celebration."

Bethany smiled slightly. "With less than an hour until shuttle departure, it wouldn't have been much of a celebration anyway."

"Still, it's inconsiderate of me. I wouldn't have done it if it wasn't my job."

"Your job? I don't understand."

"You are an important person, Bethany. It's the job of politicians like myself to get to know important people. And, since I couldn't be sure that I'd have a chance to talk to you later, I asked Carl to arrange this meeting."

"I think you overrate me, Alicia."

"Do I? Who else on this expedition holds an absolute veto over Richard Drake's decisions? Believe me, young lady, that security code which you have in your head gives you power. All you need do is decide to use it."

"Really, it isn't like that at all."

Alicia smiled. "And you're modest, too. No wonder Carl loves you so much. I understand now why he was so angry when Captain Drake refused him a berth aboard *Discovery*."

"Carl asked for a berth on the cruiser?"

"Didn't you know? I gave him my permission to transfer before we left parking orbit. He wanted to be near you, and I wanted someone aboard the flagship to keep me apprised of developments. As it is, I have to stoop to plying the shuttle pilots with drinks to find out what's happening over there. Carl went to Richard Drake and asked for a transfer. Drake refused. He claimed overcrowding. Carl thinks he had another reason for not wanting Carl onboard *Discovery*. Now that I've met you, I tend to agree."

"Are you saying that *I* was the reason?"

"You *are* the best-looking woman within several light-years. And our esteemed commander is in a position to . . . shall we say, limit the competition?"

Bethany sighed and shook her head. "You couldn't be more wrong. The last time I saw Richard Drake, he was telling me how stupid I was to allow myself to be caught by nebula-rise the night we found the library."

"Sounds like true love to me."

"What does?" Carl Aster asked as he returned with the drinks.

"The way you and Bethany talk about each other," Alicia replied smoothly.

"Sorry I missed it. The damned dispenser is out of order and I had to make the drinks by hand. Hope you like them."

Bethany took the deep, low-gravity glass and sipped at the clear liquid. "Perfect."

"Not bad, Carl," Alicia agreed, placing her glass on the table. "Now then, enough girlish chitchat. Some of us weren't lucky enough to get shore leave, Bethany. Tell us what it was like down on the surface. Did you see any of the cities the Ryall destroyed?"

Bethany shook her head. "Some of the Marines mounted a quick expedition to the ruin closest to Hecate. I wanted to go along, but Dr. Wharton wouldn't let me. I saw the pictures though. The city was a sea of rubble from horizon to horizon. It reminded me a bit of the pictures of Hiroshima."

"Beg your pardon?" Alicia said.

"City on Earth," Carl Aster replied. "Japanese islands. Has the distinction of being the first place nuclear weapons were ever used. First World War, I believe."

"Second," Bethany corrected.

Aster put his arm around her shoulder and hugged her one-handed. He turned to Alicia Delevan and said: "You'll get used to it. She's a cornucopia of interesting historical trivia."

"That's right. You are a historian by profession, aren't you?"

Bethany nodded. "Comparative historian."

"Have you a professional opinion as to what we should recommend to Parliament concerning this alien threat you discovered?"

"We don't know that the Ryall are a threat to us," Bethany replied. "Those ruins are a hundred years old, and the foldpoint the Ryall used to enter the Napier system is long gone. Besides, if their home system is close by, the problem may have resolved itself."

"How so?" Alicia Delevan asked.

"Isn't it obvious? If their star system is anywhere nearby, then their planet has been sterilized by the nova just as thoroughly as New Providence was."

"Hmmm, an interesting hypothesis that hadn't occurred to me. Still, I think you will agree that it would be better if we took no chances regarding these aliens. That we should protect ourselves until we know that there is no need to do so."

"I agree."

Alicia took a sip of her drink and regarded Bethany. "So, now that we have learned of their existence, what is our next step?"

"I suppose we'd better find someone who can tell us what is going on."

"That was my own first reaction," Alicia said, smiling her most disarming smile. "However, after having given it more thought, I've concluded that would be the worst thing we could do at the moment."

"Why?"

"Because I don't think we realize how lucky we've been. For more than a century we've looked upon our enforced isolation as a curse. We've moaned and groaned for so long that we've come to believe that. Yet, having discovered what happened to New Providence after the Antares Supernova, I'm beginning to think that our long isolation was a blessing. If our foldpoint had been open a hundred years ago, our world might lie in ruins today."

"I hadn't looked at it that way."

"No one appears to have done so," Alicia replied. "Let's take that thought one step further. So far as the outside universe is concerned, our foldpoint is *still* closed and will remain so until there is evidence to believe otherwise."

"Do you see what Alicia is driving at?" Aster asked Bethany. "So long as we don't reveal our presence, no one—not Ryall or human—will have any reason to come looking for us. We'll be as safe as we always were."

"Are you suggesting that we hide?" Bethany asked.

"Not necessarily," Alicia replied. "What I'm suggesting is that the decision to reveal ourselves to the outside universe is not one that we on this expedition can make. It rightfully belongs to Parliament. I bring this up because rumor has it that Captain Drake is planning to push on to Sandarson's World. I want to stop him. If Parliament wishes to authorize a second expedition to Sandarson's World—or anywhere else, for that matter—so be it. But we should not arrogate that responsibility to ourselves."

"If the expedition commander wants to push on, how can anyone stop him?"

"As I said earlier, Bethany, you are the one person who can veto Richard Drake's decisions. You hold *Discovery*'s jump codes. Without them, he isn't going anywhere."

"Are you asking me to force a return to Alta against Captain Drake's wishes?"

"Nothing so drastic," Alicia assured her. "We merely ask that you consider carefully what I have said and, when the time comes, help us talk sense to him."

Bethany chewed her lower lip. "I'll have to think about it."

"Of course. That's all we ask."

An overhead speaker announced the arrival of the shuttle from *Discovery*. The three of them finished their drinks, slid out of the booth, and headed back up toward the axis passageway.

The shuttle was crowded as it approached *Discovery*. Bethany found herself seated next to a window with Carl and Alicia Delevan beside her. The two of them talked about the upcoming conference and the strategy they would use to argue for an immediate return home. Bethany half listened to their conversation while she gazed out the window at the tiny scintillations that charged particles from the nebula sparked in the shuttle's antiradiation field. Mostly, however, she thought about Alicia's suggestion that they return to their pre-*Conqueror* isolation.

After the orbital boat had docked with the cruiser, they waited their turn while two dozen other passengers floated out through the forward docking tube. Not all of the passengers were bound for the scientific conference. Some were military spacers whose duties had taken them to the liner and who were now returning to their ship. Among the obvious conference attendees, however, were Dr. Wharton, Professor Planovich, and three others from *Alexandria*'s scientific community.

Beyond the tube mouth, there was none of the disorganization that had been apparent earlier in the day aboard the liner. Spacers were on hand to help arriving scientists, politicians, and the few chartered representatives who had been invited to attend the conference. Bethany watched the purposeful activity around her and was surprised to realize that she was glad to be back aboard the battle cruiser. It had the feeling of home about it.

"I count only eight people headed for the conference, including us," Bethany said. "Where are the others?"

"Most came over on an earlier flight," Carl replied.

"Where are we going?"

"Gamma Deck mess hall," Alicia answered. "Know where that is?"

"Sure. They hold Sunday services there. Follow me."
Bethany led them to the nearest spoke lift, down to

Gamma Deck, then a quarter turn around *Discovery*'s habitat ring to reach the large compartment where the conference was to be held.

The mess hall furnishings had been rearranged since the last time Bethany had attended one of *Discovery*'s weekly devotional services. Instead of the parallel rows of seats bolted to the deck, there was now a long table with a row of chairs on each side. Other chairs were arrayed around the periphery of the compartment.

A Marine sergeant in gaudy dress reds consulted a seating chart, then directed Bethany and Alicia to sit at the table. He pointed Carl Aster to a chair along the far wall, then turned to greet the next group of attendees. Ten minutes later, the compartment was nearly full of people. Precisely at 1400 hours, the sergeant snapped to attention and ordered the crowd to do likewise.

There was a hurried scraping of chairs against metal as people climbed to their feet. Richard Drake strode into the compartment, followed closely by Bela Marston. Both men wore the blue-and-gold full dress uniform of the Altan Space Navy. Drake moved quickly to the head of the table while his executive officer took the seat at the opposite end.

Drake waited for everyone to be reseated and for a dozen conversations to slowly drift to a halt. He then let his gaze drift down the rows of expectant faces and said:

"Good afternoon, ladies and gentlemen. Thank you for coming. I have called this conference to review the findings of the scientific staff regarding what we have learned during our six weeks in the Napier system. Please confine any remarks that you wish to make to that subject. Dr. Wharton, I believe you are first up today."

"Yes, sir," the sociologist said. He stood at his place and leaned both clenched fists on the table. "We came to this system expecting to find a dead world. What we *didn't* expect, however, was the sight of most of its cities blasted by weapons of mass destruction." Wharton quickly sketched the details of the Ryall raids for those who had not yet had a chance to hear the entire story. His report included more detail than had Bethany Lindquist's, but was otherwise similar. He concluded by saying "As many of you have already pointed out, the majority of the cities on this world died in some later battle of which we have found no record. However, with these records from Hecate University, I think we can be confident that we know what happened to this world."

"Professor Planovich," Drake said when Wharton had finished. "Your report, please."

"My team was assigned to evaluate the New Providential analysis concerning the foldpoint through which the Ryall attacked this system. We can find no error in their methodology. Therefore, we must assume that such a foldpoint existed for the fifteen years between the moment of Antares' explosion and the time when the expanding shockwave swept through this system."

"But it doesn't exist now," Drake said.

"Oh, no!" Planovich exclaimed. "We have been quite thorough in mapping this system. The modern foldpoint count is three—the same as before the nova. If you want to leave, you have your choice of Alta, Sandarson's World, and the heart of yonder nebula. I do not recommend the latter destination, however. Conditions on the other end are decidedly unhealthy.

"As for the fourth foldpoint through which the Ryall attacked, the special conditions that caused the Napier system to be temporarily connected to some unknown, Ryall-inhabited star system have long since changed."

"Then we don't have to worry about the Ryall returning to this system?" Drake asked.

"We do not, Captain Drake."

"But how can a foldpoint just disappear?" one of the anthropologists who had been with the ground party asked.

"Precisely the way our own foldpoint did," Planovich replied. "Antares' blow-up disrupted foldspace all over this region of the galaxy. It may well have changed half the prenova interconnections. This particular connection

was special. It required the foldlines to be refracted by
the nova shockwave. Once the wave swept past this system, the focus was gone and the foldpoint disappeared.
A similar phenomenon caused our own foldpoint to heal
itself."

"Do you have any idea as to the location of the Ryall
system, Professor Planovich?" Stan Barrett asked.

"Not really," the astronomer replied. "We need to know
much more before we can answer that question. We may
be able to divine some of the data we need from further
study of the nebula, however. That is, if we are able to
delay our departure from this system."

Several pairs of questioning eyes turned to Richard
Drake. He scanned the anxious faces before saying "I'm
sorry, Professor, but we will be leaving this system immediately."

"Do you mind if we ask where to?" Alicia Delevan
asked.

"Not at all," Drake replied. "I have consulted my orders,
which charge me with the responsibility to determine
whether or not warfare currently exists in human space.
Our studies of New Providence have been quite useful
but, unfortunately, are not sufficient to answer the question. Therefore, I have decided to press on to Sandarson's
World."

"I object!" Alicia Delevan said.

"State your objection, Madame Ambassador."

Alicia quickly recounted the recommendation she'd
made to Bethany onboard *Alexandria*. She emphasized
the fact that Parliament had no way of knowing about the
Ryall when they approved the expedition orders, and that
it was the expedition's duty to report home for new orders.
After nearly fifteen minutes of impassioned pleading, she
concluded by saying "You have no right to take this decision into your own hands, Captain Drake."

Drake regarded Alicia Delevan for long seconds, then
said, "I have every right, Madame Ambassador. I took
an oath that, among other things, requires me to carry

out my orders. I can best do that at Sandarson's World, and that is where we are headed."

Alicia Delevan turned to Bethany. "You've got to stop him!"

Bethany glanced from Alicia's angry expression to Drake's stern visage and felt the weight of responsibility descend upon her. She thought about her quandary for a long minute, then turned back to Alicia.

"I'm sorry, Madame Ambassador," she said formally. "I took an oath as well. I promised my uncle that I would deliver his dispatches to a diplomatic representative of Earth. I agree with Captain Drake that my best chance for doing that is Sandarson's World."

CHAPTER 16

Richard Drake sat in his command chair on *Discovery*'s bridge and watched as Cryogen Tanker *Sultana* uncoupled its refueling line from the battle cruiser. There were sudden bright sparks of attitude control jets at several places on the tanker's hull and the giant globe began to recede on the viewscreen.

"Captain Lee reports refueling complete, Captain," Communicator Slater's voice said in Drake's ear. "He is returning to station. Also, we have just received a message from Captain Trousma. He reports *Haridan* ready to jump. He wishes us luck."

"Is there time for a reply?"

"Negative, sir. The communications delay at this range is ninety-seven minutes. By the time our message arrives, *Haridan* will be long gone."

"Thank you, Slater. Carry on. You may return to powered flight at your leisure, Mr. Cristobal."

"Aye aye, sir. Engines to power in thirty seconds."

Drake punched up a schematic display of the Napier system on one of his private screens. In addition to the primary and its wide-ranging family of planets, the screen showed the locations of the three currently active foldpoints. The foldpoints for Alta and Sandarson's World were in the same celestial hemisphere, but were otherwise separated by more than 80 degrees of arc. His gaze was drawn to the Napier–Val foldpoint and the tiny symbol beside it that marked the current position of Cryogen Tanker *Haridan*.

Even though Drake had turned down Alicia Delevan's plea that Task Force 001 return to Alta, he agreed with her that Parliament should be warned about the Ryall as quickly as possible. After consulting with his operations staff, he selected *Haridan* to carry the news. The cryogen tanker had departed New Providence orbit three weeks earlier after having offloaded the remainder of its cargo to *Sultana*. In addition to official reports, it carried a dozen chartered representatives who had requested passage home. Drake suspected that most of them were going home to take advantage of the controversy that news of the Ryall would undoubtedly provoke. Whatever the reason, he was glad to be rid of them.

There was a sudden clamor of acceleration warnings aboard *Discovery*. Seconds later, gravity returned to the ship.

"Put the foldpoint display up," Drake ordered his astrogator.

"Aye aye, sir."

The main viewscreen changed to show the isogravity contour lines that converged to mark the position of the Napier–Hellsgate foldpoint. The display changed once more and a fuzzy red ellipsoid appeared in the center of the screen. Three small golden sparks were nearly at the edge of the ellipsoid. The sparks moved slowly inward as he watched.

"Set up a captain's conference, Communicator."

"Yes, sir."

When Captains Fallan and Lee had been connected to Drake's console, he ordered: "Status report, gentlemen!"

"*Alexandria*, ready to jump, Captain."

"*Sultana*, ready to jump, sir."

"Slave your computers to the flagship. The order of transition will be the same as last time. Good luck!"

The screens went blank. Drake signaled for Bela Marston in Combat Control. "Ready, Commander?"

"Ready, Captain. All battle stations are manned. Mass converter output is steady. Foldspace generators are ready for authorization codes."

"Miss Lindquist!"

"Here, Captain," Bethany reported from her duty station next to the astrogator.

"Two minutes to transition. Enter your authorization codes now."

"Yes, sir." Bethany's fingers touched hidden keys in quick succession. The main viewscreen flashed its message that the foldspace generators had been unlocked and were ready for use. Above the glowing letters, the golden spark representing *Discovery* crossed the boundary of the foldpoint and began to blink rapidly.

"All right, Mr. Cristobal. She's all yours. Jump when ready."

"Yes, sir. Thirty seconds to transition... Generators to power. The jumpfield is building nicely. Twenty seconds... Ten seconds... Five, four, three, two, one... Jump!"

HELLSGATE:

BASIC DATA: FO spectral class dwarf star in the
              Antares Cluster. Position (Sol
              Rel.): 1712RA,-2513DEC,560L-
              Y.

Number of Foldpoints: 2.

Foldspace Transition Sequences:
  Primary: Sol, Goddard, Antares, Napier,
            Hellsgate.
  Secondary: Vega, Carswell, Sacata,
             Hermes, Aezer, Hellsgate.

The system contains eight planets, 56 moons, and 1 small asteroid belt. Planet IV, Sandarson's World, is an Earth-type world with indigenous life-

forms. The planets, in order of their distance from
the system primary, include...

HISTORY: First explored in 2315 by Carl Sandarson. Colonization was delayed until
2365 due to the marginal economics
associated with the system's complex foldspace transition sequences.
The fourth planet is habitable in its
temperate regions (see separate
entry for SANDARSON'S WORLD)
but is considered too cold to be
classed as prime real estate. The colony was established by New Providential mining interests for the
purpose of exploiting the abundant
mineral resources of Hellsgate IV.

THE PEOPLE: The population of the Hellsgate
system was estimated to be
1,480,000 during the 2500 census, and is predominantly of
North American and European
ancestry.

— Excerpted from *A Spacer's Guide to Human
Space, Ninety-seventh Edition*, Copyright
2510 by Hallan Publications, Ltd., Greater
New York, Earth.

The expected sensation of foldspace transition washed
over Richard Drake. When it had subsided, he keyed for
the general intercom circuit. "All departments, report status!"

As the reports came flooding in, he was struck by the
difference in tone from the ship's previous foldspace transition. Then the department heads' voices had been terse,
with an obvious undercurrent of tension. Now, however,
the reports were calm and businesslike, as though each

officer were announcing the imminent arrival of the daily mail barge. Drake wondered whether they had grown bored with interstellar flight, or were merely better at hiding their anxiety. Judging from his own mood, he suspected the latter.

"Where are we, Astrogator?"

"Hellsgate, sir. The spectrum matches to six significant figures."

"Put Antares up on the screen, Lieutenant."

"Yes, sir."

There was a moment's delay before the main viewscreen flashed to show a black background with dozens of points of light sprinkled across it. In the center of the screen was a star the color of dying embers. It was a sight that Richard Drake had never expected to see again.

Since Hellsgate was twice as far from Antares as Valeria, the expanding wavefront of nova light had yet to reach Alta's sister colony. In this system, at least, Antares was still the blood-red star of old, the ruddy spark that had lit the night during many a winter camping trip when Drake was a boy. Antares dawn would not come to Sandarson's World for more than a century.

"Mr. Marston."

"Yes, sir!"

"Keep an eye out for *City of Alexandria*. Report the moment she materializes."

"Aye aye, sir."

The seconds ticked away before the executive officer reported: "We have a contact, Captain. Bearing 17/93 true. Range 280,000 kilometers." Another wait ensued, and then: "Contact. Bearing 165/12 true. Range 820,000 kilometers."

"Mr. Slater. Order Captains Fallan and Lee to home on us. And put me on 'All Hands' circuit."

"You're on, Captain."

"Attention, all hands! This is the captain speaking. We have arrived in the Hellsgate system in good order. Keep alert. Departments assigned to survey duty are to commence their activities immediately. Report findings as you get them. Captain, out."

If Drake had had any concern that they would find Sandarson's World as dead as New Providence, that fear was quickly dispelled. Even without the aid of astrogation tables more than a century and a quarter out of date, it would have been difficult to overlook the planet. Sandarson's World was a radio star of the first magnitude and the source of unusually high neutrino emissions. Similar emissions from a number of other planetary bodies within the system betrayed the presence of several thriving subsidiary colonies.

"We're intercepting strong broadcast signals, Captain," Slater reported shortly after the planet was pinpointed by questing radio telescopes.

"Human or Ryall?"

"Definitely human, sir. They are speaking Standard. The accent is a bit thick, but I have no trouble understanding them."

"What are they saying?"

"It's all commercial broadcasting so far, sir. Entertainment programs mostly."

"Let me know if you intercept anything that sounds like military traffic."

"Yes, sir."

Other observers reported detecting the drive flares of spacecraft in transit between several of the system's inner planets. So far as could be told from long-range spectroscopic analysis, the ships' flares were virtually identical to those of the Altan fleet—indicating a roughly comparable technology base. In Richard Drake's mind, that one fact alone justified the decision to push on to Hellsgate. It proved that Alta had not fallen hopelessly behind the rest of human space during its long isolation.

Four hours after breakout, *Alexandria*'s astronomers noticed a cluster of some sixty separate space installations high above the ecliptic on the opposite side of the system primary. The location was so far removed from Hellsgate's planets, and the cluster so large, that they began immediately to investigate with long-range instruments.

"That's approximately where the foldpoint from the Aezer system was prior to the nova," Nathaniel Gordon told Drake when he reported the discovery.

"Space stations around a foldpoint?" Drake asked. "Why? I would think it more economical to offload cargo at Sandarson's World."

"Perhaps the economics of cargo handling aren't quite the same here as they are at home," Gordon theorized.

Bethany Lindquist, who had been listening to Drake's conversation, strode across the bridge to his command chair. "Cargo facilities, my eye! I'll bet you anything that those are military."

"What sort of military?"

"I would imagine they're orbital fortresses designed to discourage intruders from using the foldpoint."

"How do you come to that conclusion, Miss Lindquist?"

"You've studied military history, Captain. Where do you build fortifications? At navigation chokepoints, of course, which is precisely what any foldpoint is. Circle a foldpoint with enough firepower and you can keep anyone you choose out of your system."

"If that's the case, we should see similar installations quite close by, Bethany," Dr. Gordon said from *Alexandria*. "Where are they?"

"They aren't there, Nathaniel. Why should they be? So far as the inhabitants of Sandarson's World know, the only place *this* foldpoint leads is to the dead world of their ancestors. Why guard a cul-de-sac?"

"Who do you think they're defending against?" Drake asked. "The Ryall?"

"Could be."

"Whoever it is," Dr. Gordon said, "we can assume that this system's inhabitants may not be overjoyed to see us. I recommend that we exercise extreme caution until we know more about the situation here, Captain."

Drake nodded. "I'll keep it in mind, Doctor."

The first indication that their presence had been noticed came two hours later. Drake was reading and initialing communications intercept reports when Karl Slater buzzed for attention.

"What is it, Communicator?"

"We are being scanned, sir! Sensors just picked up a surprisingly powerful electromagnetic pulse from the inner system."

"Radar?"

"That's the way I read the waveform, Captain. Probably a sophisticated search radar."

"Do you suppose they can get an intelligible return at this distance?"

"They can get range data. Whether they'll be able to decipher much more depends on their signal-processing capabilities."

"Could it be some sort of traffic control radar?"

"Civilian traffic control usually relies on ships' announcing themselves as they enter a system, sir. Long-range search radar smacks of a military surveillance system. I'd say they are expecting a fight."

An hour later, Slater's guess was confirmed.

"We have detected a launch, Captain," Bela Marston reported from the Combat Control Center. "Correction, we have detected several launches!"

"How many and where from?"

"I make it six ships from Sandarson's World, sir. Doppler analysis says that they are headed this way at five standard gravities."

Drake whistled. "Someone is really straining himself to get here."

"Yes, sir. We estimate seventy hours to rendezvous if they make turnover and decelerate—fifty hours if they come straight on."

"Suggestions?"

"It might not be a bad idea to get on the horn and tell them we're friendlies, Captain."

Drake thought about it for a moment, then shook his head. "We've plenty of time for that later, Number One. I want to learn a bit more about our cousins before we identify ourselves."

"You're the boss. Combat Control, out."

"Mr. Cristobal."

"Yes, Captain?"

"Change in plans. Plot a course to bring us to a halt in the center of the foldpoint. Give us one-quarter gravity spin and prepare the ship to transition back to Napier if required."

"Dead stop in the foldpoint. Spin orientation, and prepare to jump. Aye aye, sir."

Forty-eight hours after their entry into the Hellsgate system, Bethany Lindquist knocked on the door of Richard Drake's cabin. When the muffled order to enter came, she touched the control that caused the door to slide back into its recess and then stepped over the raised coaming into the cabin beyond.

"You wanted to see me, Richard?"

Drake, who was viewing the workscreen on his desk, nodded. "Please come in. Make yourself comfortable."

"Thank you." Bethany moved to the leather couch beneath the oil painting of the square-rigged sailing ship and sat down.

"I understand that you have spent most of the last two days going over Mr. Slater's intercepts."

"I have."

"What do you think of our cousins' form of government?"

"I'm frankly surprised. One doesn't expect to encounter royalty outside of storybooks."

Drake nodded. "How do you suppose a constitutional monarchy managed to displace a parliamentary democracy?"

"I have no idea, but one thing to keep in mind is that there have been far more kings throughout history than

presidents. We tend to be prejudiced against the monar-
chical form, but that doesn't mean it can't be effective."

"What else have you learned from the intercepts?"

Bethany leaned back in the couch, steepled her fingers
together in front of her, and regarded him with serious
eyes. "I've learned that our suspicions are largely correct.
Sandar . . . you did hear that they've shortened the name
of the planet, didn't you?—Sandar is at war with the Ryall.
Apparently, there have been quite a number of major bat-
tles fought during the hundred years since the evacuation
of New Providence."

"Any firm numbers on how many?"

"That's hard to say, Richard. The broadcasts are heavily censored. Virtually nothing is reported that concerns
military operations."

"Have they mentioned us?"

"Not a word. If it weren't for those six ships headed
this way, I'd say they hadn't noticed our arrival in their
fair system."

"Do you have any suggestion as to the best way to tell
them who we are?"

"I think a simple statement of the facts would be best.
They've probably deduced our identity from the mere fact
that we popped out where we did."

Drake nodded. "I agree." He leaned forward and
pressed a control. A moment later his workscreen was
alight once again. Bethany couldn't see the face on the
screen, but the voice emanating from it belonged to one
of *Discovery*'s junior communicators.

"Where is Slater?" Drake asked.

"He's in his cabin, Captain. Shall I ring him?"

"Do that. Apologize for interrupting his rest, but tell
him that I need him. We'll go with the contact message
we recorded last watch. I'll be up on the bridge in five
minutes. We broadcast within the hour."

"Yes, sir," the communicator said. He repeated Drake's
orders and then signed off.

"Would you like to observe the historic moment?" Drake asked as he walked around his desk.

Bethany gave him her hand and allowed him to pull her to her feet. She smiled. "I would like that very much, Richard."

Richard Drake, followed closely by Bethany Lindquist, strode onto the bridge through one of the gimbaled airlocks. He went directly to his command chair and began to strap himself in. Bethany took her place at her own console and did likewise. Karl Slater arrived moments later.

"Prepare to transmit contact message when you are ready, Communicator," Drake ordered.

"Yes, sir," Slater replied. His fingers raced over controls. A new view flashed on the main viewscreen. The screen showed the system primary to one side, while six tiny points of violet white blazed at the viewscreen's center.

Telescopes on *Discovery* and *City of Alexandria* had been locked on the Sandarian ships since they'd departed parking orbit. Initially, the interceptors' drive flares had been only tiny patches of nebulalike luminosity against the black backdrop of space. Thirty-five hours after launch, however, the images had undergone a radical transformation. The dim fog gave way to eye-searing points of radiance as the Sandarian ships turned end for end and began decelerating for rendezvous with Task Force 001.

A tiny crosshair appeared on the screen. It moved toward one of the points of radiance, overshot, then corrected. It was soon joined by an aiming circle as one of *Discovery*'s communications antennas locked on its target. Slater moved the sighting marker five more times, each time pausing to englobe a tiny star with a tight communications beam before moving on. Finally, he reported: "All targets locked in, Captain. We're ready to transmit."

"Go ahead," Drake ordered.

The scene changed again. Richard Drake watched as

the recording he'd made earlier that afternoon began to play: "Greetings to the government and people of Sandar..." The contact message quickly explained who and what the Altan expedition was, assured the Sandarians that the expedition's intentions were peaceful, and concluded by asking that the approaching Sandarians communicate with the Altan fleet. There was a five-second delay after the message concluded before it began again. After the third repetition, Drake ordered the screen switched back to the approaching Sandarian ships. For long minutes, nothing happened. Then, finally, one of the aiming circles began to blink rapidly, indicating that a communication was being received from the ship within it.

The screen changed to display a hard-looking man in a black uniform. He was totally bald, even to the lack of eyebrows. His expression was that of one who has endured long hours at high acceleration.

The man in black spoke: "I am Commodore Silsa Bardak, Ducal Heir of Romal Keep and Commanding Officer of Strike Force 7735. I order you to surrender your ships to my boarding parties. You have a single hour to comply."

"Confident bastard, isn't he?" Drake said over the command circuit. "He won't be in position to attack us for another twenty hours yet."

"They must think the contact message is a Ryall ruse," Bethany responded.

"Mr. Slater. Put me on the communications channel to the Sandarian ships."

"You're on, Captain."

"This is Fleet Captain Richard Drake, commanding Altan Space Navy Cruiser *Discovery*. We are a scientific expedition. We mean you no harm."

The Sandarian commander's features froze on the screen for the long seconds it took the message to reach him. Finally, he said, "If true, Fleet Captain, you will be released once we verify your identity. I again order you to surrender your ships to my boarding parties."

"Negative," Drake replied. "We will not allow armed ships to close on us. I suggest an initial meeting in deep space by auxiliary craft."

The Sandarian commander's expression remained unreadable. Finally, he spoke. "Agreed. I propose that we each send an unarmed scout to a point one hundred thousand kilometers from your current position along a direct line toward Hellsgate. The meeting will take place in twenty-four hours."

"Agreed," Drake replied.

"I must warn you, Fleet Captain, that I will fire on any ship that attempts to leave the foldpoint."

"Fair enough," Drake responded. "I will be forced to return the favor should any of your ships attempt to enter it."

"Understood."

CHAPTER 17

Lieutenant Phillip Hall lay strapped into the pilot's couch of Landing Craft *Sysiphon* and watched the great cylinder that was *City of Alexandria* dwindle in the rear viewscreen. When the liner had disappeared from view, he switched to the command channel that would put him in communication with Richard Drake aboard *Discovery*.

"We're away, sir."

"Very good, Lieutenant," Drake's voice said in Hall's earphones. "Report when you are in range of the Sandarian shuttle."

"Aye aye, sir." Hall switched off the comm unit and turned to his copilot. "Think you can fly this thing, Hulse?"

Junior Lieutenant Hulse Arker, *Sysiphon*'s regular pilot, made a face. "I used to think the old man had a pretty good head on his shoulders. Of course, that was before he put you in charge of this expedition."

"Now, now, Lieutenant!" Hall said with mock severity. "We mustn't be bitter about the decisions of our superiors. After all, who else in this fleet has my vast quantity of contact experience?"

Arker's answer was a rude noise. "Hell, all you did was rendezvous with the dead hulk of an old Earth blast-ship and then make a high-speed run past the remains of an even deader planet! I would hardly call that 'contact experience.'"

Hall grinned. "Well, the old man does, and that puts

me in charge. Seriously, will you watch the store while I check on our passenger?"

"Will do, Lieutenant."

Hall unfastened his straps and climbed out of the acceleration couch. He reached for the ladder leading aft, placed his boots outside the vertical risers, and allowed the boat's half a standard gravity of acceleration to pull him toward the open hatchway below/aft.

The passenger cabin was equipped with two dozen acceleration couches arrayed in double rows on each side of the fuselage. However, only one of the couches was occupied. Seated at midcabin, reading a computer printout, was Stanislaw Barrett.

"Excuse me, Mr. Ambassador. Is there anything I can get you?"

Barrett glanced up from his reading. "No thank you, Mr. Hall. How long to the rendezvous point?"

"A little over two hours, sir."

"Any sign of the Sandarian emissaries, yet?"

"Not yet, Mr. Ambassador."

"Is that unusual?"

"Not for this boat's one-lung detector rig, sir. I figure that we'll be in detection range in another hour. If it'll make you feel better, my last report from *Discovery* had the Sandarian contact boat en route. It left their fleet on schedule and is proceeding to the rendezvous point as planned."

"What are the rest of their ships doing?"

"Just sitting out there, sir. Don't worry. *Discovery* will give us a yell if they make any unexpected moves."

"What can we do about it if that happens?"

Hall glanced about the interior of the landing boat. It had been chosen for this particular mission because it was the least threatening of any of Task Force 001's auxiliary craft. "I'm afraid *Sissy* is well named, Mr. Ambassador. If they attack while we're in this boat, there won't be a damned thing we can do about it."

"That's what I thought," Barrett said, laying his paperwork aside. "I'm sorry my workload caused me to miss your final briefing, Lieutenant. Bring me up to date on what they told you about this mission."

"Only that we were going out to meet some Sandarian noble and that we were to allow them to look at anything they wanted to see."

"And what is your opinion of those orders, Lieutenant?"

Hall shrugged. "They're orders. I'll carry them out."

"They're important orders, Lieutenant. We need to quickly convince these people that we are what and who we say we are. If they ask questions, tell them the exact truth. Don't embellish, no matter what you think they may want to hear."

"What if they ask me about *Conqueror*?"

Barrett's face suddenly took on the blank expression of a trained politician asked to explain the financing of his last campaign. "*Conqueror*? What's that?"

"Open a comm circuit, Pilot."

"I can only give you voice, sir."

"That will be fine, Mr. Hall."

"Circuit open."

Barrett took a deep breath and licked dry lips before speaking. "Attention onboard the Sandarian ship. My name is Stanislaw Barrett. I am the senior Altan representative aboard this boat. I bring you greetings from my Parliament and from the people of Alta."

"Hello," a youthful voice replied. "I am Ensign Randall Kyle of His Majesty's Long Range Interceptor *Avenger*. I represent my captain and my king."

Barrett frowned. "You are an *ensign*, you say?"

There was a subtle change in the other's voice. An underlying hardness had crept into the characteristic Sandarian accent. "You have no need to fear that my rank disqualifies me for this assignment, milord. In addition to my naval commission, I am privileged to be the second son of the Earl of Kyle Township and, as such, nineteenth in line of succession for the throne."

"No offense intended, sir," Barrett said hastily.

"No offense taken. Much has happened since the Great Nova first burst upon an unsuspecting galaxy. You of the lost colony can hardly be expected to be familiar with such things as the pattern of fealties within the peerage."

"I thank you for your understanding, Ensign. How would you like to handle the initial contact?"

"As we discussed with your commander. I will suit up and come aboard your vessel. After I have inspected it for weapons and confirmed that all is as you claim, then you may do the same for my ship. Is such an arrangement aggreeable?"

"It is."

"Very well. I will be there in ten minutes standard."

"We'll be waiting."

Ten minutes later, they watched as a solitary figure exited the Sandarian ship's airlock and jetted across the void separating it from *Sysiphon*. Lieutenant Arker was on duty at the airlock as Ensign Kyle grounded on the hull. It was a matter of half a minute to cycle him through. Barrett was waiting when the spacesuited figure came aboard. The Sandarian reached up, undogged his helmet, and lifted it over his head. He let it float to the end of its tether as he reached out to steady himself with a nearby stanchion.

Ensign Kyle was even younger than Stan Barrett had prepared himself for, perhaps eighteen standard years. His hair was close-cropped and sandy in color, his complexion was pale, and his light-blue eyes darted from side to side as he took in the details of the landing boat's interior. Finally, he glanced at Hulse Arker and then at Stan Barrett.

"Welcome aboard," Barrett said, extending his hand. Kyle reached out and grasped it in one gauntleted fist.

"Thank you, milord. Honor requires me to tell you that I am broadcasting pictures of your vessel to my ship and that they are being relayed in realtime to our flagship, *Vindicator*."

Barrett nodded. "Fair enough. We too are transmitting pictures of this meeting to our fleet. Please, won't you remove that bulky suit?"

"I cannot, sir. My orders do not permit it."

Barrett shrugged. "As you wish. Shall we begin the tour now?"

"I would like to start with the cockpit, if possible."

Barrett led the way forward. In spite of the awkward spacesuit around him, Kyle had no trouble pulling himself hand over hand through the zero-gee cabin to the forward hatchway. Phillip Hall spent several minutes explaining the flight controls while Stan Barrett observed their guest in silence. The Sandarian's holocamera was mounted on the chest of his suit. Whenever Hall would point to something, Kyle would swing his upper torso to point the camera in that direction. After Hall's explanation, and several more minutes spent closely examining the instrument panel, Kyle straightened up and said, "I would like to see your engines now."

"Certainly."

Barrett signaled for Hulse Arker to lead the way toward the engine compartment. Ensign Kyle followed, with Barrett at the rear. Hall remained at his station. Once in the aft compartment, Arker explained the workings of each part of the photon drive as Kyle used his chest camera to pan the scene. Barrett watched the youth's eyes eagerly trace the machinery. Finally, he seemed satisfied and nodded.

"Do we pass inspection?" Barrett asked.

"I will report to my superiors that you appear to be genuine, milord. It will be up to them to decide. And, of course, we will wish to inspect your other ships before we allow you to leave the foldpoint."

"Of course," Barrett said. "We have brought along a short tape concerning the history of our planet since the nova. Would you like to see it?"

"Very much."

"Fine. Let's adjourn to the passenger cabin where we can watch in comfort."

Barrett helped Kyle strap himself into an acceleration couch and then did the same for himself in an adjacent seat. He pressed a control and the documentary began to play on the holoscreen.

The History of Alta had been a project of Dr. Wharton's sociologists and Bethany Lindquist, a ten-minute holo-record that had been hurriedly spliced together while the Sandarian fleet bore down on the foldpoint.

When the holoscreen went dark, Stan Barrett pressed the light control on the armrest of his acceleration couch and turned to Ensign Kyle.

"Well, what do you think?"

The Sandarian turned to face him across the aisle. His expression was serious. "Have you no experience with the Ryall at all, milord?"

Barrett shook his head. "If it hadn't been for the ruins we found on New Providence, we would still be blissfully unaware of their existence."

Kyle's scowl made him look even younger. "Then you should consider yourself extremely lucky, milord. I'm afraid our history o'er the past century has been considerably more bloody than your own. My captain has authorized me to tell you of our struggle, if that is your pleasure."

"By all means, Ensign!"

"Very well," Kyle replied. His gaze shifted to *Sysiphon*'s far bulkhead, his eyes took on a glazed look, and his voice suddenly developed the singsong quality of someone who is reciting a well-remembered tale.

"They call the last of the Ryall raids 'The Great Burning,' milord. It need not have happened.

"At the time, my ancestors were of the opinion that the centauroids were from some star that, like Napier, was being threatened by the Great Nova. They theorized that the first Ryall raid had been triggered by the two vessels that jumped into the Ryall system while exploring the newly formed foldpoint. They presumed that the Ryall were surprised by the appearance of human ships in their system, interpreted that presence as an attack, and responded by launching their initial strike against New Providence.

"That attack was beaten back, although it cost six cities. Later, the Ryall launched a second such, and it too was defeated—this time without loss. 'Twas sixteen Taurus 2527 when the last Ryall fleet broke free of the foldpoint, thirty-six vessels in all, and quickly brushed aside our pickets at the foldpoint before sweeping toward New Providence itself. At the time of the attack, the evacuation was very nearly completed. Many of the armed ships in the system were engaged in convoying evacuation vessels to and from Sandar. Still, the Navy managed to dispatch forty warcraft of all types to intercept the invaders.

"For a week the carnage was great. The Ryall gave as good as they got. Indeed, because our ships were forced to attack singly or in small groups, they destroyed more of us than we did of them. By the time the Ryall reached New Providence, they had lost twenty of their ships—and we had lost thirty-five.

"Five more spacecraft were destroyed before they could close the range, but the ten survivors loosed more than a thousand weapons of mass destruction against the planet. The attack killed thirty million people that day and maimed thirty million others. Had the evacuation not been nearly complete, it would have killed billions.

"The survivors flooded aboard the evacuation ships as quickly as they could be recalled from Sandar. Within a month, the planet was deserted. What was left of the Navy stood guard at the foldpoint until the nova wavefront swept through the system and ended the Ryall threat."

Barrett frowned. "The foldpoint that the Ryall used to attack New Providence disappeared when the wavefront reached the Napier system?"

"It did, milord."

"Then how is it that you are still fighting them?"

"Because, milord, the Ryall inhabit a vast interstellar hegemony. Their civilization may well be larger than our own. We have charted their stars for a century and have discovered that our two spheres overlap one another in many places."

"Yet we humans have known interstellar travel for centuries," Barrett replied. "How is it that we didn't run across the Ryall long ago?"

"Because, milord," Kyle said, "there were no fold-space interconnections between the two realms prior to the Great Nova. When Antares exploded, it disrupted established foldline links, while simultaneously creating many new ones. Among these new linkages are three that provide direct access between human and Ryall space. One such opens directly into the Aezer system, the stellar system just beyond our other foldpoint."

Following the first successful meeting between Altan and Sandarian, the two fleet commanders agreed to exchange inspection teams. Two shuttles laden with Altans were dispatched toward the Sandarian interceptors while a like number of Sandarian auxiliary craft closed on the Altan fleet. For his part, Commodore Bardak had made it clear that he wanted to inspect the Altan ships for signs of Ryall influence in design and construction. Were such influence to be found, it would brand as a lie the Altan claim that they had known nothing of the Ryall prior to the exploration of New Providence. On the other hand, Richard Drake was concerned that Alta's technological development had been retarded by its long isolation. His purpose in dispatching an inspection team was to get a closer and more detailed look at the Sandarian ships.

The dual inspections went off without difficulty. By the time the Sandarians finished touring *Discovery*, *Alexandria*, and *Sultana*, they were relaxed and joking with their guides. The Altan inspectors reported back to Drake that while some of the machinery onboard the Sandarian interceptors was definitely in advance of anything Alta had, on the whole, the technological levels of the two systems were equivalent.

When the inspections were over, Drake and Bardak hosted dual formal dinners for the teams. A dozen Sandarian officers sat interspersed among *Discovery*'s officers and *Alexandria*'s diplomats, scientists, and commercial people. At the same time, a wall-size holo-screen showed a similar scene aboard *Vindicator* that was attended by the Altan inspection team. The parties went on for several hours, with the initial stiffness quickly giving way to laughter.

The following morning, Drake received a call from Commodore Bardak. "Good morning, sir," Drake said when the Sandarian commander's features solidified in the workscreen in his cabin.

"And to you, Fleet Captain Drake," Bardak boomed. "How's your head?"

"About as you would expect after last night's round of toasts."

Bardak nodded. "I feel as though someone is trying to dig his way out of my skull."

"I am in somewhat better shape," Drake replied. "There is an Altan herb that goes a considerable way toward alleviating the worst symptoms of a hangover. It doesn't make you feel good, mind you; but at least you aren't miserable."

"Such a wonder would be one of the first things we would want to import when interstellar trade resumes." Bardak looked out of the screen and seemed to judge Drake's expression before continuing. "Which brings me to the reason for my call."

"Yes?"

"It seems to me, Fleet Captain Drake, that we have done all in our power to alleviate our mutual suspicions."

"I agree."

"Do you also agree that the next step will involve some unavoidable risk on both of our parts? I am speaking, of course, of moving your fleet to the inner system. The king has expressed a desire to meet you."

Drake nodded. He had been expecting some such offer. Karl Slater's communicators had been picking up nearly continuous coded broadcasts between the Sandarian interceptors and their home planet. "I agree in principle, although my risk would seem to me to be the greater."

"How so? We will be risking our whole planet by allowing *Discovery* to move within striking range."

"I hardly think one old battle cruiser is up to the task of fighting your whole planet, Commodore. Indeed, the moment I move within range of your planetary defense system, you will be able to vaporize my command without warning. Then who would carry the word of what happened back to Alta?"

"Certainly a problem, Fleet Captain. Do you have a solution?"

"I do. I propose to leave *Sultana* here to guard my rear."

Bardak thought about it for a moment, then nodded. "A watcher positioned at a safe distance, poised to race for home at the first sign of treachery. A sensible precaution when dealing with strangers."

"I'm sure that it is a precaution that will prove unnecessary, Commodore."

Bardak laughed. "*I'm* sure of it, Captain Drake. You merely *hope* it will prove to be so."

CHAPTER 18

Sandar was a cold world, a planet that orbited at the very edge of the zone in which liquid water could exist in the Hellsgate system. Because of its position, Sandar was in the grip of a perpetual ice age. For billions of years, snow had fallen on the vast polar ice caps, there to be compacted into an ever thicker layer of hard ice. Wherever that ice overlaid an area of sloping terrain, large sections had broken away to form glaciers. If anything ruled on Sandar, it was the glaciers. In some places, they were nearly a kilometer thick. Over the eons they had bulldozed down mountain ranges, scooped out wide valleys, and roofed over lakes and seas.

Richard Drake watched the Sandarian wilderness flow swiftly past on the bridge viewscreen. Here and there, isolated patches of black betrayed the presence of particularly stubborn outcroppings of bare rock. At other places, dark-blue stringers marked the location of a deep crevasse overlaying some invisible sea. Only in that narrow band of land and sea that lay within twenty degrees of Sandar's equator did the ice grudgingly give up its mastery of the planet. In this strip, daily temperatures averaged well above the freezing point of water. Where the great ice flows spilled over into this "tropic" region, they melted. The runoff formed small streams, which joined to form rivers, which in turn merged to form larger rivers, which eventually flowed into Sandar's two warm-water oceans.

As Drake watched, the image on the viewscreen passed from the endless vista of ice and snow to the lush greenery of the inhabited equatorial zone. Even with minimum magnification it was possible to see the signs of human presence among the vegetation.

The mass evacuation of New Providence had boosted Sandar's population to more than two-thousand times its normal size. Of necessity, three billion homeless refugees had had to settle on a strip of land with a habitable area only one-quarter that of New Providence. The inevitable result was a population density that rivaled that of even the Japanese islands on Earth.

Sandar's cities were like the ancient metropolises of Earth, haphazard collections of buildings that sprawled aimlessly across the countryside. And everywhere the cities were not, the land was filled with greenhouses surrounded by mirrors—greenhouses to keep the cold out and mirrors to concentrate Hellsgate's feeble rays onto plants that had evolved under a hotter star.

"It's amazing that they've been able to do so much under such difficult conditions," Bethany commented from the observer's position next to Drake as the viewscreen showed a sprawling metropolis and its surrounding greensward.

Drake nodded. "Especially when you consider that they've been at war for most of their history."

The fact that Sandar was at war had been brought forcefully home to them during their final approach to Sandarian parking orbit. As they neared the planet, *Discovery* and *City of Alexandria* had fallen in line astern behind *Vindicator*. The parade of ships had then swept into Sandar's inner traffic zone through a carefully controlled approach corridor before decelerating to take up position in a pole-to-pole parking orbit. As they slowed to orbital speed, they passed very close to a large cluster of objects in high Sandarian orbit.

The grouping turned out to be an orbital shipyard. Intermixed with the dock facilities and construction cradles were dozens of spacecraft. They ranged in size from blastships to boats no larger than armed scouts. Maximum magnification had revealed hundreds of tiny firefly sparks hovering around the two largest ships in the yard. In one case, workers appeared to be cutting away the bow of a vessel whose forward structure had been mangled almost beyond recognition. In the other, the flash of many welders could be seen reflected against the hull plates of a ship that appeared undamaged.

Nor were the blastships and scout boats the only warcraft in the yard. Drake spotted several intermediate types, including cruisers of approximately the same class as *Discovery* and a number of vessels that were the right size to be destroyers.

The sight of the shipyard and its covey of broken ships had affected *Discovery*'s bridge crew more profoundly than had the carnage on New Providence. To most Altans, the long-dead cities of New Providence had seemed an episode out of ancient history. The shipyard, on the other hand, was tangible evidence of an ongoing war that could easily spread to engulf the Val system.

Drake named the first delegation to go down to the Sandarian surface shortly after taking up a parking orbit around the planet. The composition of the ground party had been a source of intense speculation ever since they had left the Hellsgate–Napier foldpoint ten days earlier, and at times, it had seemed as though practically everyone onboard wanted to go. In the end, Drake chose himself, Bethany Lindquist, Stan Barrett, and Alicia Delevan. He also included the two ambassadors' assistants—Nathan Kellog and Carl Aster—and Argos Cristobal on the roster. The latter would be responsible for gathering background data on the Sandarians while the ambassadors and Drake were occupied with higher-level contacts. Bethany chose not to take an assistant.

Prior to leaving *Discovery*, Drake held a final briefing for the ground party and boat crews who would transport them to the surface. He began by reading from the expedition's orders.

"Paragraph seven. All data concerning the Earth Fleet Blastship *Conqueror* shall be considered an Altan state secret, and shall not be revealed to non-Altan personnel."

"I'd like to take exception to that, Captain," Alicia Delevan had said, interrupting him.

Drake laid aside the printout from which he'd been reading, raised an inquiring eyebrow, and asked, "Why, Madame Ambassador?"

"As you well remember, I was opposed to our coming to this system in the first place. However, now that we're here, I don't think it wise to hide the truth about *Conqueror* from the Sandarians."

"Care to explain that?"

"Certainly. Paragraph seven was included in our orders because the prime minister's staff thought we would find ourselves in the middle of a war with no idea of who was fighting whom. They didn't want us talking about *Conqueror* until we were sure that we weren't talking to *Conqueror*'s enemies. It seemed a wise precaution at the time.

"However, in light of recent events, it is obviously a precaution that isn't needed. It's pretty clear that *Conqueror* got into a scrap with the Ryall. Therefore, I see nothing to be gained by keeping the truth from the Sandarians. Worse, I think we have a great deal to lose by not being honest with them. If we follow Paragraph seven, they'll find out sooner or later that we lied to them. That will cause them to wonder what else we've lied about. Our relations will have been damaged for no good reason."

"How do we know the Sandarians are being completely honest with us?"

"We don't," Alicia said. "But isn't it better to give them the benefit of the doubt?"

"In my opinion," Drake replied, "it is best that neither party trusts the other too far until we know each other better. That, by the way, is the reason we left *Sultana* on rear guard in the foldpoint. I see no reason to change that policy at this time."

"But they trust us!"

"Do they?"

"They trust us enough to let us take up parking orbit about their planet," Alicia replied. "When you consider *Discovery*'s weaponry, they're taking quite a risk letting us get in this close."

"It isn't as much of a risk for them as you might think."

"I don't understand."

"We've had time to map the planet rather extensively over the last thirty hours. In the process, we have spotted numerous large installations built on the polar ice caps. Our experts have tentatively identified them as a network of planetary defense centers. To judge by their number, this may well be the best-defended planet in human space!"

"Are you saying that they have us in their sights this very minute?" Stan Barrett asked.

"You can bet on it, Mr. Ambassador. If the installations we've seen have the power we believe they do, the Sandarians can vaporize us in any millisecond they choose." Drake surveyed the faces turned in his direction. "As for Ambassador Delevan's concerns in regard to Paragraph seven, I must insist that we follow our orders. You are free to observe, to deduce, and to question. But you will give them no hint that we are in possession of a derelict Earth blastship. If they bring the subject up, you are to pretend ignorance. Is that understood?"

There were several murmured assents. When all was quiet once more, Drake retrieved the printout and continued reading. "Paragraph eight . . ."

The wind that blew across the vast open space of Sandar's Capitol Spaceport was a mere ten degrees above freezing. It bit at Richard Drake despite his cold-weather clothing. He stopped momentarily in *Moliere*'s open air-lock to turn up his jacket thermostat. Overhead, the sky was blue-purple in color, a result of Sandar's atmosphere being relatively thin compared to that of most terrestrial worlds. The low density was more than made up for by a 30 percent oxygen content.

Inside the terminal, Drake found a reception committee waiting for him. Commodore Bardak and Ensign Kyle stood at attention in the front rank, while several senior Altan military officers stood a few paces behind. Judging by the ornate insignia on their uniforms, Drake tentatively identified this latter group as the planetary brass. A military band and large numbers of onlookers were gathered behind a demarcation line.

The rest of the ground party crossed the loading bridge leading from the landing boat then entered the terminal. Drake signaled Stan Barrett, Alicia Delevan, and Bethany Lindquist forward to join him. They then moved to where Commodore Bardak was standing. Bardak snapped to attention and saluted. Drake returned the gesture. The band struck up a fairly good rendition of the Altan planetary anthem, then segued into a solemn and ponderous tune that Drake took to be the Sandarian counterpart.

When the band had finished, Duke Bardak stepped forward and intoned formally, "Fleet Captain Richard Drake. In the name of my king and queen, I welcome you and your party to Sandar."

"Thank you, Commodore. It is our pleasure to be here."

Bardak took Drake by the arm, pivoted, and led him toward the line of dignitaries. "I would like you to meet my superiors, sir. May I present Admiral Fernando Zeilerbach, the Count of Draga."

Drake saluted then stuck out his hand. "Admiral..."

They quickly worked their way down the length of the reception line. In addition to Zeilerbach, two vice admirals, a fleet admiral, a Marine general, and a Commander-in-Chief of War Operations were present. Drake noticed that in addition to their military ranks the officers also had titles, although their ranks didn't always correspond to their patents of nobility. For instance, Commodore Bardak was commonly addressed as Duke Bardak and the third man in line, Fleet Admiral Villiers, only a Knight of Sandar, First Class, was "Sir Anthony."

"Fleet Captain Richard Drake, I would like to introduce His Highness, Commander of War Operations Jonas Walkirk. His Highness is the king's half brother."

"Your Highness," Drake said, saluting. "I am honored that you have come to the spaceport to meet us."

"The honor is mine, Fleet Captain. Frankly, we had given up hope of ever seeing an Altan face again. When Commodore Bardak reported who you were, the news spread across Sandar faster than the sonic wake of an atmospheric raider. By all the Saints, we can use your help against those damned centaurs!"

"So I've been told, sir."

Beside Drake, Stan Barrett and Alicia Delevan stiffened at the Commander of War Operations' easy assumption that Alta would soon be fighting alongside Sandar. Nor was it the first time that a Sandarian had mentioned the possibility of an alliance between New Providence's two daughter cultures. Commodore Bardak had brought the subject up during a teleconference with Drake and the two ambassadors before leaving the Hellsgate–Napier foldpoint. Stan Barrett had listened to the proposal and then responded that the question of an alliance would be one for Alta's Parliament to decide. Although, as Barrett was quick to point out, the members of Task Force 001 were certainly willing to listen to proposals.

The Commander of War Operations kissed the hands of both women, then offered his arm to Bethany and led the way to the exit from the terminal. With Alicia Delevan on his arm, the Sandarian Marine general fell in behind his commander. Drake accompanied Commodore Bardak, and Stan Barrett was escorted by Fleet Admiral Villiers. Other Sandarians assisted Carl Aster, Nathan Kellog, and Argos Cristobal. The entire party made their way through a wide corridor flanked by ranks of soldiers.

The corridor led to a cavernous main terminal building

several hundred meters farther on. At a square kilometer of area, it was nearly five times the size of the Homeport Spaceport, the largest on Alta. The double rank of soldiers continued into and across the crowded terminal. Behind them, a crowd of Sandarians stood and watched the arrival ceremony. Drake commented on the large percentage of people wearing uniforms.

"Everyone must work in the war effort, Captain," Bardak responded. "The uniformed services require a great many people. Here on Sandar, virtually everyone is involved in some manner."

"What of the other planets of human space?" Drake asked. "Do they provide you with assistance in your fight against the Ryall?"

Drake detected the slightest hesitation in Bardak's voice before the Sandarian replied. "They do what they can. Unfortunately, many of them find that it is all they can manage to handle their own defense."

The conversation was cut off when they reached a row of groundcars parked inside the main spaceport concourse. They were long and low, with an aerodynamic sleekness that bespoke high speed.

CWO Walkirk gestured to the first two cars in line. "Captain Drake and Ambassador Delevan in the first car, Ambassador Barrett and Miss Lindquist in the second. The other cars will transport your remaining people."

"Where are we going?" Drake asked as he climbed into the indicated seat.

Commodore Bardak seated himself across from Drake. "To the palace. The king is anxious to meet you."

John-Phillip Walkirk VI—Defender of the Foldpoints, Admiral General of the Fleet and Marines, Scourge of the Ryall Hegemony, Supreme Vicar of the Church on Sandar, and, by the Grace of God, Sovereign King of the Hellsgate and Napier systems—glanced up from his workscreen at the sound of his office annunciator.

John-Phillip was a big man with broad shoulders, a

prominent nose, and powerful hands. His hair had once been the color of deep space, but twenty-five years on the throne had streaked it with more than a little silver. He reached out and keyed the intercom on his desk.

"Minister Haliver, Majesty," his secretary's voice said.

"Send him in," John-Phillip replied. Simultaneously his hand broke a light-beam, opening the door to his office.

First Minister Terence Haliver stepped across the threshold into the king's carefully cluttered office. Haliver was a small man with steel-gray hair and a grim expression.

"They're here, Your Majesty. The boat landed a few minutes ago."

"Is everything in readiness for the initial audience and subsequent conference?"

"It is, Majesty."

"Bring me up to date on the backgrounds of our guests."

"Yes, sir. Since last we talked, our suspicions have been largely confirmed. Several factions are competing onboard the two exploration ships. We have tentatively identified them as the Navy, the two major parties in the Altan Parliament, and the scientists onboard their large transport. There is another group of commercial people whom they refer to as 'chartered representatives.' I'm afraid we haven't quite figured out their role in all of this yet."

"And the delegation on its way here includes the Navy and the two political parties?"

"That is correct, Majesty. It also includes this Miss Lindquist."

"What is her function?"

"That, Majesty, is a difficult question to answer. They claim that she represents the hereditary terrestrial ambassador on Alta. Frankly, we can think of no reason why she is given a prominent place in their delegation if that is so."

"Can she represent a hidden power bloc?"

"It is possible. She may well be the real power on their ship, possibly even the true expedition commander."

John-Phillip nodded. "Whether she is or not, let us pretend that we believe her cover story."

"Of course, Majesty. It isn't polite to call one's guests liars to their faces."

"How much do they know about our situation?"

"Commodore Bardak informs me that he has stuck quite closely to the sanctioned script, Majesty. They know that we are at war with the Ryall and that there is an interconnection between our two spheres of influence in the Aezer system. Beyond that he has been purposely vague."

"What was their response to the suggestion of an alliance?"

"As expected, they were cool to the idea."

"Why expected?"

"This is an exploratory mission, Majesty. They lack the authority to negotiate an alliance, or so they claim."

"Do you believe the claim?"

"I have no reason not to."

"Is there *any* possibility that they know of our recent reverses? Say from communications intercepts?"

Haliver shook his head sharply. "We've run a computer search of all broadcast programming since they appeared in-system. There hasn't been a single reference to the fate of our armada, not even an indirect one. Censorship is still in full force.

"However, we do have one problem. Miss Lindquist will undoubtedly want to talk to *our* terrestrial ambassador."

"That shouldn't be a problem. Not if we are clever and give ourselves sufficient lead time."

For the first time since he'd entered the king's office, Haliver smiled. "I understand perfectly, Majesty."

CHAPTER 19

From Capitol Spaceport to Capitol itself was a drive of fifteen minutes. Richard Drake and Alicia Delevan sat side by side in the rear seat of the limousine while CWO Walkirk and Commodore Bardak faced them across the passenger compartment. Behind them, three other long black groundcars purred silently through the maze of concrete tunnels that led away from the spaceport terminal complex. They broke into sunlight after half a minute, crossed over a long sweeping overpass, and swooped down to enter the acceleration lane of a crowded freeway. Drake was pressed into his seat by a surge of acceleration as the car matched its velocity to that of the traffic stream, then slipped into a hole between two large transports.

The vehicle rolled on between agricultural fields while Bardak pointed out the sights of interest along the way. Long, slender greenhouses lined both sides of the highway. Between the greenhouses, ten-meter-square mirrors swiveled slowly to track Hellsgate across the sky. Drake noticed with interest that the mirrors consisted of reflective film stretched tight on a tubular framework.

The highway cut through a range of low hills and broke out into a bowllike valley beyond. Capitol filled the valley, climbed its sides, and overflowed into the foothills beyond. For the most part, the city was a collection of low buildings constructed of stone, brick, or concrete; wood was very little in evidence. The buildings were brightly painted and roofed in colored tile.

At the center of the city, towering over the tallest of the surrounding brick and stone buildings, was a geodesic dome constructed of glass and aluminum. The dome was outlined by its endlessly repeated framework of hexagonal braces.

"Our destination," Commodore Bardak said, noting the object of Drake's attention. "The palace weather dome."

Drake estimated the size of the dome by noting that the insect shapes flying around it had to be full-size air-cars. He emitted a low whistle. "It must be expensive to heat."

CWO Walkirk cleared his throat and said, "Please don't get the wrong impression, Fleet Captain. The weather dome is no whim of a spendthrift monarch. The palace grounds are an arboreum for terrestrial vegetation; a conservatory, if you will." When Drake's expression showed his lack of understanding, Walkirk explained further.

"You see, a number of terrestrial vitamins have no counterpart in Sandar's natural biosphere. To remain healthy on this world, we must supplement our diet with terrestrial plants unsuited to our cold weather. We grow these in the greenhouses you saw coming in from the spaceport. The arboreums, of which the palace is the largest, are our insurance against an outbreak of blight in the commercial greenhouses."

The weather dome continued to expand as the car sped toward the center of the city. By the time the car left the freeway, it was a towering wall that blocked half the sky. A dozen seconds later, the limousine entered the dome. As the car passed from the cold, dry Sandarian air into the warm, moist air of the palace grounds, Drake's window fogged up and cut off his view of the outside world. Drake felt a momentary pang of fear as he wondered whether the driver could see. Evidently he could, because the car braked to a smooth halt shortly afterward.

"We're here," Bardak said as he leaned forward to open the car door. Beyond the doorway, two Sandarian Space Marines stood rigidly at attention, their right hands lifted in salute. "After you, Captain Drake, Ambassador Delevan!"

The Royal Palace was a glass-and-steel building constructed in a style popular at the very dawn of the Space Age. A central cylinder rose nearly to the apex of the weather dome, while at its base four horizontal wings spread out to the cardinal points of the compass. Much of the structure was open to the outside, as befitted a building within a building. And everywhere he looked, Drake saw green, living things. The nearby species ranged from a small plant with purple flowers, to blue-green grass, to broad-leafed water plants that floated in a fountain. The middle distance was dominated by small plots of food grains in various stages of development, while a variegated line of trees formed a boundary at the periphery of the weather dome. Like frozen waterfalls, vines spilled from hanging planters, and the balconies and doorways of the main structure were bordered by splashes of flowery color.

While Drake waited, people began to climb from the three other groundcars in the convoy. He watched as Bethany Lindquist ducked her head, stepped out of the second car in line, and then gazed around wide-eyed. She took a deep breath and held it for long seconds before exhaling deeply. She seemed enraptured as she made her way to where he was standing.

"Have you taken a good, deep breath?" she asked.

He nodded. "The air is certainly fresher here than what we're used to aboard ship."

"That's not what I mean. Have you *smelled* it?"

"I've noticed that it has a strange odor," he said, nodding.

"A strange odor?" she replied. "Captain Drake, you have no poetry in your soul! That *odor*, as you call it, is the fragrance of Earth."

Drake was still considering a suitable reply when Alicia Delevan and Carl Aster joined them. Stan Barrett stood off to one side and conferred hurriedly with Nathan Kellog, his assistant, while Argos Cristobal stood a few paces back from the rest of the crowd. Commodore Bardak gestured toward a flower-bordered walk leading to a side entrance into the palace, and the Altans set off down the path. Once inside the palace, they were guided past offices where clerks and functionaries labored at computer workstations. After walking the length of a long hall, they found themselves before a bank of lift doors.

CWO Walkirk turned to Drake. "Your ambassadorial party will now be taken to the throne room to meet their Majesties, Captain Drake. With your permission, I will have my people show the rest of your party to their rooms."

"Permission granted, Your Highness. Mr. Cristobal! Go with these gentlemen. Assist Mr. Aster and Mr. Kellog."

"Aye aye, sir!"

With that, Drake, Bethany, and the two ambassadors entered a lift with CWO Walkirk and Commodore Bardak. When the doors opened again, they found themselves facing a wood-paneled anteroom and several palace functionaries. The oldest of these was a gray-haired man with a distinguished look and a chest full of ribbons. He walked up to Stan Barrett and bowed.

"Greetings, Ambassador Barrett. My name is Opteris. I am the palace majordomo. It is my responsibility to make your stay here a pleasant one. May I take your heavy coat? I assure you that you will have no need of it here under the dome."

"Thank you," Barrett said, slipping out of his jacket.

Bethany, Alicia Delevan, and Richard Drake followed his example.

Opteris signaled and two waiting grooms advanced to take the clothing, then ordered a woman servant forward with a large mirror. Opteris turned to Bethany and Alicia Delevan. "I thought the ladies might welcome the opportunity to check their appearance before the audience."

"You are the perfect host, sir," Alicia Delevan said as she reached into a pocket to extract a comb.

"I thank the ambassador," Opteris replied.

Two minutes were spent repairing the damage done by the wind at the spaceport while Opteris outlined Sandarian court etiquette. ". . . Remember to stop behind the blue line just in front of the steps leading to the throne. It is customary to bow at the line and to address the king as 'Your Majesty' or simply 'Sir.' The queen is always addressed as 'Your Majesty.' Any questions?"

"How long will this audience last?" Alicia Delevan asked.

"Not long," Opteris replied. "The audience in the throne room is a formality staged for the benefit of the holovision cameras. The king will greet you and make a general statement of friendship. We invite your spokesperson to do the same. His Majesty may choose to discuss some noncontroversial subject for a few moments before offering you the hospitality of the palace. He will then declare the public audience at an end. Afterward, I will conduct you to a private audience with His Majesty and the first minister. Now, if there are no more questions, please take your positions on the red line."

They moved to the mark that Opteris had indicated. The line stretched across the marble floor of the anteroom just in front of two oversize wooden doors. As soon as everyone was in position, the majordomo signaled an unseen watcher via an unobtrusive video camera. The sound of trumpets emanated from hidden speakers as the giant doors swung ponderously open.

The throne room was pie-shaped, with the double doors

at the apex and a raised dais for the throne at the broad end. The ceiling was six meters high. The floor was of the same marble as the anteroom, and the walls were paneled in a dark wood of strange grain. Battle pennants, suspended from the ceiling, waved gently.

A row of ceremonial guards bordered each side of a wide aisle that extended the full length of the throne room. Behind the guards, prosperous-looking men and women stood in small conversational groups and pretended to talk to each other. Servants circulated among them with trays of food and drink.

At the end of the room, the king and queen sat side by side atop the high dais. The king wore the black uniform of the Sandarian Space Navy, while the queen wore a gown of some iridescent material. John-Phillip looked to be in his early fifties, standard; his queen appeared ten years younger.

The trumpets gave way to a full military band as the Altans and their escorts started their march down the aisle. The music stopped just as they reached the blue line. They halted and bowed in unison. A moment later, CWO Walkirk stepped forward, bowed again, and said:

"Your Majesties, it is my great honor to present to you the representatives of the Government of Alta—Ambassador Stanislaw Barrett; Ambassador Alicia Delevan. I would also present Fleet Captain Richard Drake, the commander of the Battle Cruiser *Discovery,* and Miss Bethany Lindquist, the representative of the Hereditary Terrestrial Ambassador to Alta. Ladies and gentlemen, I have the honor to present my sovereigns, John-Phillip Walkirk VI and his queen, Felicia."

"Thank you, Brother," John-Phillip replied. "Welcome, honored guests! Please convey our greetings and warmest regards to your Parliament and to the people of Alta."

"We thank Your Majesty," Barrett replied. "My prime minister has asked me to convey his own best wishes to Your Majesty and to the Sandarian people."

"I understand that there are representatives of your scientific and commercial classes onboard your ships."

"There are, Your Majesty. All of whom are eager to see your glorious planet for themselves, I might add."

"They will be welcome, sir," Queen Felicia said in a clear, soprano voice.

"You are most kind, Your Majesty." Barrett bowed in the direction of the queen. "We would consider it a great favor if your people would arrange interviews with the Sandarian scientific and commercial communities."

"We welcome such discussions, Mr. Ambassador," the king responded. "You may begin disembarking your specialists immediately if that is your desire."

"I will have our people start preparations for disembarkation, sir."

John-Phillip shifted his gaze to Richard Drake. "What of your crews, Fleet Captain? I would imagine that they are getting anxious for shore leave."

"Yes, sir. Overanxious in some cases."

"If you wish to authorize such leave, we will welcome them. If we have learned nothing else in a hundred years of war, we know how to show our warriors a good time when they are on leave. We will do the same for your people."

Drake bowed and said, "You are most generous, Your Majesty."

"My generosity is motivated by self-interest, Captain. The sooner we get to know each other, the sooner we'll all be able to work together against our common foe."

"A sensible proposal, Your Majesty."

John-Phillip turned his attention to Bethany Lindquist. "And you, Miss Lindquist, what may I do for you?"

"Does Earth maintain an embassy here on Sandar, Your Majesty?"

"Indeed Earth does!"

"I would very much like the opportunity to meet with the terrestrial ambassador at his convenience."

"I will have my people contact him immediately. I will

also be most happy to provide transportation when he is ready to receive you."

"Is the embassy far?"

"Halfway around the planet, Miss Lindquist. It was established before the Great Migration and has never been moved. You know how conservative the Central Government of Earth can be at times."

"I wish I did," Bethany replied. "Unfortunately, we of Alta have had no contact with Earth in one hundred twenty-five years."

"We'll have to see what can be done to remedy that," the king said.

"I thank Your Majesty."

John-Phillip gave a careless wave of his hand. "Think nothing of it." His gaze swept over all four Altans. "Now then, you must be tired from your journey. I suggest that we put off further discussions until you have rested."

"As Your Majesty wishes," Barrett replied.

The king signaled a functionary standing to one side of the throne, who immediately stepped forward and struck the floor with a long staff. "This audience is at an end! All give homage to the king!"

The whole of the court bowed as music welled up again from the walls. The king left the throne room in the company of a small entourage. As soon as he had gone, the groups of courtiers began to buzz with conversation. Majordomo Opteris appeared from nowhere and said: "If you will come with me, I will escort you to the private audience."

Opteris led them back through the double doors and into the lift. This time they were carried to one of the upper floors of the tower. After a few minutes' wait, they were ushered into a room that appeared to be part of the royal living quarters. Four couches were arrayed around a low table. At one side of the room a glass door opened onto a balcony overlooking the palace grounds. When the four Altans and their two Sandarian escorts were admitted, they found one of the ministers from the throne room waiting for them.

"Ladies and gentlemen," CWO Walkirk said, "I would like to introduce Terence Haliver, First Minister of the Realm."

Haliver shook hands with each of the Altans, then gestured to the seats. "His Majesty is changing and will be out shortly. He asked that you make yourselves comfortable."

Stan Barrett and Alicia Delevan sat down on one couch while Richard Drake and Bethany Lindquist took another. CWO Walkirk and Commodore Bardak occupied a third. Minister Haliver sat down opposite the two Altan ambassadors.

"Drinks?" he asked.

"I'll have my usual!" the king called from the next room.

Haliver took each of their orders in turn, keying them into a pocket terminal. A minute later, a servant entered with a tray of drinks. He had just completed passing them out when the king entered the room.

"Welcome," John-Phillip boomed out. The monarch had changed from his uniform to a single loose-fitting garment that sacrificed style for comfort. He waved them down as he strode purposefully across the room. "No, don't get up. There's too much damned formality around this place as it it."

He took his seat next to Minister Haliver, sipped from a glass filled with amber liquid, then noticed that he was drinking alone. "No need to stand on ceremony. Drink up!" When his guests had each sipped from their drinks, he leaned back and said, "I hope you weren't too intimidated by our little show downstairs. We do it for the masses, you know. They need such diversions to take their minds off the war. God knows, we work them hard enough the rest of the time."

"It was an elegant ceremony, Your Majesty," Stan Barrett replied.

"A necessary one, I assure you, Mr. Ambassador. Tell me, are you really ready to start transferring your scientists down here?"

"Yes, sir."

"I'd appreciate it if you would hold up for a few days while we get things organized on our end."

"If that is your wish, Your Majesty."

"It is. Give Minister Haliver a list of your people and their specialities. He'll try to match them with comparable members of our own scientific establishment. We'll let the two groups interact for a few weeks and see what matters of interest pop up."

"What about our commercial people, Your Majesty?" Alicia Delevan asked.

"Oh, you can start shipping them down immediately. We'll pass them on to the Chamber of Commerce for preliminary trade talks. If we find items of mutual interest, we'll get the Royal Commission on Intersystem Trade involved. I suppose the tariff people will have to be brought onboard, too—wouldn't want a bunch of bureaucratic rate setters to strangle a budding friendship, now would we?"

"No, sir."

"Miss Lindquist and Ambassador Delevan."

"Yes, Your Majesty?" Alicia answered.

"My wife would consider it an honor if the two of you will favor her with your presence at tea tomorrow. She has been unable to contain herself at the thought of meeting two Altan women."

"We would be honored, Your Majesty."

The king took another sip from his drink, lifted his feet to rest on the low table before him, and leaned back in his seat. "Okay, let's get on with new business, shall we? I'm sure you have a lot of questions for us. Fire away, and don't be overly concerned about diplomacy at this stage. Our function here is to exchange information."

Alicia Delevan cleared her throat. "On Alta, sir, we

are a parliamentary democracy, as were most worlds in human space prior to the nova..."

John-Phillip held up a hand to interrupt her. "And you want to know what in God's name we are doing with something as archaic as a functioning monarchy."

"Something like that, sir."

"It's simple enough," the king replied. "My ancestor, the first John-Phillip Walkirk, was admiral of the fleet that fought the last rear-guard action against the Ryall. That was the fight we call The Great Burning—the one that effectively destroyed New Providence. After the Ryall broke through our lines and destroyed what was left of the planet's major cities, Admiral Walkirk aided in the rescue efforts. They rescued ten million people from the poor old planet's corpse before they left for Sandarson's World, as it was then called.

"When they arrived in the Hellsgate system, they discovered that civil order had broken down. The earliest settlers were arguing with the latest refugees, people were refusing to accept the land allocated to them, and claim jumping had grown into an epidemic. Basically, the uprooting of their entire civilization had proven too much for New Providence's civil authorities.

"Admiral Walkirk moved in with his fleet and restored order. He replaced the civil government with his own officers. The arrangement was intended to be temporary, but something always seemed to interfere with a return to civilian rule. Eventually, the military dictatorship turned into the monarchy and John-Phillip Walkirk was declared the first king of Sandar and New Providence."

CWO Walkirk leaned forward when the king ceased speaking. "Of course, the 'something' that always happened to interfere was the Ryall. Shortly after John-Phillip took control of the government, he began receiving reports of Ryall attacks in other regions of human space."

"It was the damned supernova," the king said. "It

messed up foldspace all through this end of the galaxy. Bardak can quote you the official figures."

"Yes, Majesty," Bardak replied. "The explosion destroyed eleven charted foldpoints. Of these, only the foldpoint in the Valeria system—*your* foldpoint, that is— and one other have ever reestablished themselves. Antares also created a number of new foldspace interconnections. Fifteen that we know of. Six of these were short-lived phenomena like the Napier–Ryall foldpoint. The other nine, however, appear to be permanent. Of these, three lead to star systems inhabited by the Ryall. It is our bad fortune to have one such in the Aezer system next door. Aezer is a Class III variable star and, prior to the nova, was uninhabited. Now, however, both we and the Ryall raid each other's territory through it."

"We've observed a large number of installations around the Hellsgate–Aezer foldpoint," Alicia Delevan said.

"That, Madame Ambassador, is our first line of defense," CWO Walkirk responded. "Should the Ryall ever try to attack us here, we hope to give them a warm welcome, both at the foldpoint and in near-Sandar space."

"You must have collected considerable data on the Ryall in the last hundred years," Drake said.

"More than we would have wished," the King affirmed.

"Would it be possible for us to review such data? We have only a few old records that we dug out of New Providence."

"We'll do better than that," John-Phillip replied. "How would you like to meet a Ryall in the flesh?"

"You have prisoners?"

He nodded. "A few."

"I would very much like to see them!"

"Then so you shall. Commodore Bardak, please arrange it!"

"Yes, Your Majesty."

CHAPTER 20

Sandarian Military Headquarters was a truncated pyramid that had been built on an island of bare rock in the middle of an ocean of ice. At first the structure was a tiny patch of brown on the horizon amid an endless panorama of white. Then, as the aircar carrying Commodore Bardak, Richard Drake, and Argos Cristobal closed the distance, the building's true size became increasingly apparent with each passing second.

"Big building," Drake said to Bardak.

"Big enough," the Sandarian nobleman replied. "It measures one kilometer to a side and rises half a kilometer above bedrock. The sides are armor plated to a depth of two meters, and screened by antirad fields."

"Wouldn't it have been more convenient to build it near Capitol?" Drake asked. It had taken the aircar three hours to fly from Capitol to Military Headquarters, and for virtually the whole of that time, the car had droned above a seemingly endless expanse of ice.

"More convenient, yes. Safer, no. Military Headquarters doubles as a planetary defense center. You no doubt saw many of our PDCs from orbit."

Drake nodded.

"An operational planetary defense center requires a lot of power and generates a considerable quantity of waste heat. In a prolonged engagement the waste heat from a single fixed-mount laser can raise the temperature of even a medium-size river by several degrees. Were we to build our PDCs in the temperate zone, we would trigger a massive fish kill every time we tested the weapons. The polar ice cap, on the other hand, has a heat-carrying capacity that is virtually infinite. You can't see it, but the ice fields around Military Headquarters are honeycombed with heat pipes. Theoretically, we could fire every fixed-mount laser in the battery continuously for days before we would have to worry about overheating problems.

"Then, of course, there are the strategic considerations. By spreading our installations evenly over Sandar's surface, we avoid blind spots while also dispersing our military assets. Lastly, should the Ryall ever get this far— highly unlikely considering the power of our foldpoint fortresses—we hope to draw their fire to the PDCs and away from the cities."

As Bardak talked, the aircar circled Military Headquarters to give the Altans a good look at the manmade mountain below. The sides of the pyramid were studded with phased-array radar elements as well as a variety of less identifiable sensors. Around the base, the business ends of several dozen fixed-mount lasers poked skyward.

The aircar transitioned to a shallow descent before landing on the roof of Military Headquarters. As soon as the car came to a stop, Bardak, Drake and Cristobal disembarked into a biting cold wind. Bardak led them to a nearby stairwell and down one level to a room filled with lockers. There he directed them to shed their heavy coats and outerwear.

He next led them to a transport station where several small cars hung from a single overhead rail. They climbed into the first car in line, Bardak tapped out a destination code on the vehicle's control board, and the car accelerated into a long tunnel.

A minute later they arrived in another station, outwardly identical to the one they had just left. Bardak ushered them through the station and into a corridor. After several turns their way was blocked by a steel barrier and

two Marine guards armed with riot guns. A third Marine
sat at a desk and checked Commodore Bardak's identification before pressing a hidden control. The vault door
swung ponderously back on its hinges, and Commodore
Bardak signaled for Drake and Cristobal to precede him
into the chamber beyond.

Drake did as directed and found himself standing on a
catwalk ten meters above an alien plain. Overhead, a
reddish star blazed down through a hazy pink sky. Below,
yellow vegetation extended to the far horizon, while close
by, a small grove of alien trees exuded a pungent odor.
A brook rambled through the trees and disappeared into
thick, purplish vegetation.

Nor were the strange star and stranger plants the only
indication of an alien presence. A large herd of animals
roamed the plain halfway to the horizon. They were too
distant for a good look. Even so, they had a distinct air
of alienness about them.

Drake turned to Bardak and frowned. "What is this?"

"This is the cage where we keep our prisoners," the
commodore replied. "The walls are hidden by the hologram projection, of course. We obtained the scene from
a wrecked Ryall warship. The prisoners assure us that it
reminds them of home."

"Where are they?" Argos Cristobal asked. "The Ryall,
I mean."

"Right below you, Lieutenant," Bardak replied, pointing to the small grove of treelike growths. Under the trees,
arrayed in a rough circle, were four aliens.

The Ryall lay with their bodies flat to the ground, their
tails coiled around them and their six legs tucked up
beneath two-meter-long torsos. The vertical portion of
the torso rose fifty centimeters above the arch of the
creatures' backs. Two long arms sprouted from a pair of
shoulders at the midpoint of the vertical torso and culminated in hands with six supple fingers. Above the shoulders, a long, flexible neck lifted the head another sixty
centimeters off the ground.

The head was reptilian, with a long, toothy snout; two coal-black eyes peered from beneath heavy ridges of protective bone; the ears were flaps of skin stretched taut on four long spikes at the top of the cranium.

"My God, I looked right past them!" Cristobal whispered.

"No need to whisper, Astrogator," Bardak replied in a normal conversational tone. "This whole area is enclosed in a sound-suppression field and roofed over by a one-way hologram. They can neither see us nor hear us."

"What are they doing?" Cristobal asked.

"Conversing. Would you care to listen?"

"Yes, indeed!"

Bardak pressed a control set in the catwalk guardrail and they were suddenly surrounded by the amplified voices of the aliens. It was quickly evident that the Ryall tongue included a considerably wider variation of sounds than any human language.

"Do they speak Standard?"

"The ones who have been here a few years do. Their vocal equipment is substantially more adaptable than our own. Believe me, they are highly articulate when they wish to be."

"Would it be possible for me to speak to one of them?" Drake asked.

Bardak smiled. "That is usually the first question visitors ask. All is in readiness for an interview. Follow me to interrogation."

The interrogation room was a bare cubicle with a table, a single chair, and a variety of surveillance mechanisms mounted in the ceiling behind panes of armor glass. Richard Drake sat in the chair and waited for the heavy steel door at the opposite end of the room to be opened. He didn't have to wait long. The door retracted into the wall and one of the Ryall was ushered in by two Marine guards.

As it moved to stand on the opposite side of the table, the creature reminded Drake of pictures he'd seen of early experiments with all-terrain walking machines. The gait was a sequence of motions that was difficult for the untrained eye to follow. Drake toyed with the idea of asking the Ryall to walk around the room, then decided against it. The two beings regarded each other in silence for long seconds. If the Ryall was capable of facial expression, it didn't bother—or else Drake wasn't watching for the proper signals.

After nearly a minute of silence, the snout opened and speech issued from between two rows of conical teeth. "I am told that you wish to converse with me, sir or madame." The Ryall's voice was full of sibilants, but otherwise completely understandable.

"How long have you been held captive here?" Drake asked.

"Five standard years," the Ryall replied.

"And you still can't tell the difference between the two human sexes?"

"The sex of any particular human is not a matter of concern to one of my kind. I would guess that you are a male, since the overwhelming preponderance of my visitors is."

"You are correct. And, if I am not being too personal, which are you?"

"Neither," the Ryall replied. "I am neuter, what your species calls a drone, I believe."

"Do you have a name?"

There was a brief sound that began with a sharp inhaling noise and ended with a sound like a sneeze cut short. "A none-too-close translation would be Loyal-Hand-of-the-Egg-Which-Bore-Us-All. However, you may call me 'John.' That is the name which my keepers have given me."

"Well, John, my name is Richard Drake. Have the Sandarians told you who I am?"

The Ryall made an unrecognizable gesture with its hands, and its tri-forked tongue flicked into sight. "A zoo animal is not offered explanations, Richard Drake; nor does he ask them."

"Zoo animal? Is that what you think this place is?"

This time, the gesture was more expansive. The arms extended to their full extent, and six long fingers spread wide. "Is that not your name for a place where humans observe the antics of species other than their own?"

"It is. However, a more correct term for this place would be 'prison.' You are a prisoner of war."

"That is another distinction which is lost on those of my kind, Richard Drake. We apparently do not view reality the same as you humans do."

"I'm afraid you've lost me, John. Are you saying that you don't understand what a prison is, or what it means to be a prisoner?"

The Ryall flapped its ears. A quick, fluttering noise accompanied the movement. "I laugh, Richard Drake. After five standard years, the dual concepts of prison and prisoner are ones that I understand very well. Indeed, I and my fellows speak of little else."

"Then what . . ."

"You called me a prisoner of *war*. I find it hard to rationalize the Ryall concept of war with the loose interpretation that you humans seem to place on the word."

"What is the Ryall concept, then?"

"War is a battle of honor between two adversaries, as when one male sends his drones to secure a nesting place or a particular female from another. War is the clash of clans to see who will win the place of honor for their eggs. War is the struggle for dominance between entire civilizations wherein one civilization establishes its right to lead the other."

"Is that not what is happening between your species and mine right now?" Drake asked.

"Not at all," the Ryall replied.

"Then what do you call it?"

"The closest I can come in your language, Richard Drake, is to compare it to a contest between rival pest exterminators, each trying to rid the cosmos of the other's presence."

Bethany Lindquist sat in the aft cabin of a royal aircar and watched the green flow swiftly past below. Beside her sat Princess Lara, the second daughter of the king and queen of Sandar. Lara was a dark-haired beauty approximately twenty standard years old. She had been Bethany's unofficial guide ever since the queen's tea party of a week earlier. They had toured Capitol, seen Crandall Falls, and explored the ice caves of Arda. Lara had told Bethany of the history of Sandar, and Bethany had reciprocated with stories of Alta and old Earth.

"Doesn't it ever rain here, Lara?" Bethany asked, scanning the purple, cloudless sky overhead.

"Not this decade," the princess replied. "It's just as well. We very nearly drown in the glacier-melt at perihelion. If water were to fall from the sky, too—no telling what problems we would have."

"It seems strange to have so much greenery without rain."

"Not to us," Lara said, laughing. She glanced down at the ground. "I believe we have arrived."

The aircar banked and circled a large white building set alone on a verdant estate. After two circuits, the car slowed to a hover, then lowered itself onto a landing pad surrounded by tall trees. As quickly as the wheels touched ground, Bethany gathered up the briefcase containing her uncle's dispatches and waited for Lara to open the personnel hatch.

They found a white-haired, dark-skinned man waiting for them at the edge of the landing pad. He was attired in a formal costume that Bethany guessed was electrically heated since it didn't look substantial enough to keep out the Sandarian cold.

"Hello, Miss Lindquist, Your Highness," the waiting dignitary said. He bowed and kissed Bethany's gloved hand. "My name is Ambrose Cartier. I am Earth's ambassador to Sandar. You must be the lady from the lost colony in the Valeria system."

Bethany admitted that she was. Cartier turned to Princess Lara and greeted her before suggesting that the three of them adjourn to the inside of his house. "I'm afraid even the balmiest of Sandarian days is much too cold for my Bahamian blood, Miss Lindquist."

As they walked, Bethany asked, "The Bahamas? That is near North America, is it not?"

Cartier nodded. "Off the coast of Florida in the Atlantic Ocean. The climate is distinctly tropical most of the year, although some of our winter storms do have a bit of a nip in them."

"Bit of a nip?"

"It means 'cold,'" Cartier replied with a laugh. "Not so cold as here, though. Right, Princess?"

"If you say so, Ambrose," Lara replied.

"I do indeed!"

Cartier led them to the large house that they had spotted from the air. The building had originally been a residence, but one wing had been turned into an office where staff members worked at computer terminals.

"Is this the embassy?" Bethany asked.

"Officially, it is the ambassador's residence," Cartier replied. "However, I find it more convenient to run Earth's affairs from here than from that big pile of stone in Gosslaw."

"Gosslaw?"

"Nearest large city," Lara replied, "and one of the original mining sites."

Cartier ushered the two women into a study lined with printed-and-bound books. He offered them refreshments. When he had served both of them steaming cups of tea, he took his own seat, leaned back, and said, "My spies tell me that you are a comparative historian, Miss Lindquist."

"Yes, sir."

"I've heard of all types of historians in my day, but

that one is a new one on me. What, pray tell, is a comparative historian?"

Bethany explained her profession and its place in Altan society. Cartier listened without interrupting. When she had finished, he nodded.

"So you are a specialist in Earth history! I have to admit that it is one of my own passions as well. When we've completed our business, perhaps we can talk a little shop. I'll bring you up to date on the events of the last century."

"I'd like that, Mr. Ambassador. I hope to be able to visit Earth one day."

"You must do so! See Rome and die, as the old expression goes. Now then, young lady, how may I help you?"

Bethany recited the story of Granville Whitlow and his lifelong fight to maintain a terrestrial presence on Alta. ". . . the position of terrestrial ambassador has been handed down in my family ever since. My uncle is the current holder of the title. When he heard that Parliament was sending out an expedition to reestablish contact with the rest of humanity, he arranged to have me come along. I have a century and a quarter of dispatches to send on to Earth."

Cartier clasped his hands together and laughed out loud. "How marvelous, my dear! The diplomatic service must be told of your family's history. Such dedication to duty should be honored, even at this late date."

"Thank you, sir," Bethany replied. "I have the dispatches with me if you would like to take them." She reached into her briefcase and pulled out a small case containing record titles and handed it to Cartier. "I would consider it a great favor if you could include them in your next report to Earth."

Cartier took the case and opened it. He studied the crystal tiles inside for long seconds, then reclosed the case, and handed it back to Bethany. "You keep this for the time being, my dear."

"You don't want it?" Bethany asked. Her confusion was evident in her expression.

"Oh, I want it all right! It's just that there's no real hurry about it. The Ryall have been raiding the starlanes between here and Earth, and the traffic has been a bit erratic of late. I'll send word to you in plenty of time for the next diplomatic pouch."

Bethany frowned. "Perhaps you have a unit of the Grand Fleet going back to Earth soon. They could carry my dispatches."

Cartier and Lara glanced at each other for an instant, then both turned their attention to Bethany. Cartier cleared his throat and said, "I'm afraid that there are no units of the Grand Fleet in the system at this time, Miss Lindquist. Tactical considerations require that they be elsewhere. No, we'll have to await a commercial liner to get your very important documents to their destination."

"Pardon me for being persistent, Mr. Ambassador," Bethany said. "Earth *is* fighting the Ryall, isn't it?"

"My dear, the whole of the human race is fighting the Ryall. They haven't left us much choice in the matter." The ambassador put his teacup on a side table and leaned forward. "As a historian, I think you will find the story extremely interesting. The underlying cause of our current difficulty, it seems, lies not in ourselves, but in our stars ... and in the opaque mists of Ryall history."

"What I am about to tell you is a Ryall legend. It has been pieced together from interviews with thousands of prisoners from dozens of different planets within the Ryall hegemony. All the prisoners have told the legend in the same way, no matter what interrogation techniques were used—and I'm forced to admit that we haven't always conformed to the spirit of the ancient Geneva Convention.

"Thirty thousand years ago, the Ryall were simple fisherpeople dwelling on the banks of rivers and near the shallows of their world's seas. They spent much of their time in the water where they harvested other forms of marine life. They had lived this way for as long as anyone could remember. Then one day, a star blazed forth in the sky until its brightness rivaled that of the system primary."

"Another nearby nova?" Bethany asked.

"It would seem so. Of course, with the nova-light came radiation storms. They weren't strong enough to sterilize the planet, but they wreaked havoc nonetheless. The mutation rate rose precipitously. Some species went extinct and other species took their place. "Nor were the Ryall immune to the radiation. With each new generation of hatchlings came grotesque new shapes and new abilities. Most of these were harmful, killing their owners while still in the egg. Others were of limited utility and were weeded out by either natural selection or by the elders of the tribe. Some mutations proved beneficial and were incorporated into the quickly evolving race.

"The Ryall weren't the only race subjected to forced evolution. Some twenty-five thousand years ago, there came into existence another intelligent species on the Ryall home world. The Ryall prisoners have various names for these beings, but the most common is the swift eaters— swifts for short.

"The swifts were amphibians descended from a non-sentient carnivore that inhabited the oceans of the Ryall world. They were intelligent, cunning and voracious. The swifts attacked the Ryall breeding grounds and gorged themselves on Ryall eggs. As a result, the Ryall population underwent a precipitous drop. There was even a time when it appeared as though the swifts would force the older species into extinction.

"The Ryall finally devised a successful defense against the depredations of the swifts. They withdrew completely from the water and became full-time land animals, living in groups far enough inland to avoid attack by the swifts. They began to hunt other land animals and to herd land beasts. They learned about fire and metallurgy. They learned to farm to provide fodder for their herds. Eventually, they developed cities and a true civilization.

"Sometime during their Bronze Age, they began hunting the swifts. It was a long hunt. The prisoners tell us that it lasted some fifteen thousand years. We are inclined to believe them."

"Why?" Bethany asked.

"Because, Miss Lindquist, of the deep scar that their competition with the swift eaters left on the Ryall psyche. It has been ten thousand years since they wiped out the last of the swifts—twice the span of time since the earliest civilization on Earth. Yet, when we show individual prisoners drawings of swifts that have been prepared from the descriptions of other prisoners, they undergo a strong fight-or-flight reaction. Tell me, Miss Lindquist, are you afraid of snakes or spiders?"

"I really don't know, sir. I've never seen either. Except, of course, as pictures in books."

"Well, it's a documented fact that a certain percentage of the human race has an irrational fear of these creatures. In that respect, we and the Ryall are alike. The difference is that *all* the Ryall fear the swift eaters. It is less a phobia with them than an instinct. And that is why this war between humanity and the Ryall may well be unto the death."

"I'm afraid I don't understand," Bethany said.

"Ryall history teaches them to beware of exploding stars in the sky. To them, the Antares Supernova was the worst omen that could possibly be. Worse, they saw their fears confirmed when a starship full of alien creatures materialized in the sky of one of their worlds shortly afterward.

"Unlike humanity, the Ryall have experience in dealing with a rival intelligent species, Miss Lindquist. Their approach to the problem is validated by fifteen thousand years of pain and suffering on the part of their ancestors. It is a system that is simple and effective. *And it works every, single time!*

"Simply put, history has taught the Ryall that the only possible response to a potential competitor species is to seek its extinction. They give no quarter and they ask none. It is an article of faith among the Ryall that the hatchlings will never be safe so long as a single human being is left alive anywhere in the galaxy!"

CHAPTER 21

Bethany Lindquist shivered as thousands of tiny jets of hot water sprayed over her body. She ducked her head beneath the stream and let the furious rush massage her face and scalp until she was forced to breathe again. Surfacing, she inhaled deeply of the hot wet fog and stood unmoving for long minutes, as though the shower could wash away her feelings of disappointment.

She'd awakened early that morning, confident that this would be the day that Alta regained its rightful place as one of Earth's children. Her excitement had built with each passing kilometer during the flight with Princess Lara. Toward the end of the journey it had been all she could do to keep from bouncing up and down in her seat.

Then had come the meeting with Ambrose Cartier, and her high spirits had been smashed by two quick, hammerlike blows. The first had come when Cartier refused to accept her uncle's dispatches; the second when he'd revealed the true nature of humanity's adversaries. Bethany let the water run down her flanks and thought of the hundreds of wars she had studied in her life. How many times had the leaders of one side or another pledged to fight on to the last man? Yet how often had that actually happened? Offhand, she could think of only two instances separated by more than two thousand years in time.

Yet if the Ryall meant what they said, then there would be no peace until humanity beat them back to their home worlds. At the least they would have to be barred from interstellar space, and perhaps from space altogether. And, of course, there was always the possibility that *Homo sapiens* would apply the Ryall's own solution to the problem. Bethany would have liked to think that the human race would never exterminate another intelligent race—no matter what the provocation—but she knew too much history to believe it.

Bethany turned off the water then dried herself and padded barefoot into the bedroom of her suite. After the heat of the shower, the room seemed almost frigid. She dropped the towel, caught sight of herself in a full-length mirror, and examined her image for evidence of bulges brought on by too many banquets. She was pleased to note that her recent lifestyle had yet to take its inevitable toll, and resolved to restart her diet at the first opportunity.

Shivering slightly, she wrapped her wet hair in the towel and moved to choose an outfit for dinner. The choice was a difficult one. The suite—a living/sitting room, bedroom, and bath—had come equipped with a wardrobe, including a dozen evening outfits, each in her size. She hesitated for a moment before selecting a pearl-gray evening gown from a hanger. Gray to match my mood, she thought to herself.

Ten minutes later, she had finished dressing and dried and arranged her hair. She was in the midst of putting the finishing touches on her makeup when the door annunciator chimed. She hurriedly finished applying eyeliner, checked her appearance in the mirror, then padded barefoot into the living room.

"Who is it?" she asked.

"A *very* weary traveler."

She opened the door to find Richard Drake standing in the hall. His dress uniform, visible beneath an opened weather jacket, was rumpled from long hours in an aircar. "Hello."

"Hello, yourself, Bethany. Where is everyone? The whole floor seems to be deserted except for servants."

"They're at the party."

"What party?"

"The one the king and court are giving for the scientists and chartered representatives tonight."

"Oh, yeah. That's tonight, isn't it?"

She nodded.

"Why aren't you there?"

"I just got back from the embassy a couple of hours ago myself. I told Carl that I would get cleaned up and meet him there later."

"It looks like you are about ready. Your evening gown is beautiful."

"Why, thank you, kind sir!" she said, curtsying. "How was your trip? Did you actually see a Ryall?"

"Four of them. I even spoke with one."

"What was it like?"

He grinned. "I have to admit that I experienced a few moments of discomfort at first. After a while, though, listening to a six-legged alien seemed the most natural thing in the world."

"Did you learn anything of interest?"

"We talked about the Ryall point of view regarding the war."

Bethany nodded. "Ambrose Cartier filled me in on Ryall history. He painted a fairly stark picture. I found it depressing."

Drake raised a single finger to his lips in caution, then went on in a normal tone of voice: "When do you have to be at this celebration?"

Bethany, a look of confusion on her face, said, "I didn't give any specific time."

"In that case, let's go for a walk in the garden. I understand that it's beautiful at night."

"All right. Just let me get my shoes on."

At night the palace grounds beneath the weather dome became a sea of colored lights. Pastel floodlamps lit practically every bush and tree, while overhead a soothing pattern of glowing colors was projected onto the underside of the dome. Even with the abundance of lighting, however, the palace architect had made sure that there would still be a few dark places where two people could sit quietly and talk.

Drake led Bethany down a flower-lined path toward a small arboreum that was roofed over and screened on three sides by vines. As they walked, he slipped his arm around her waist, acting as though it was the most natural thing in the world to do. After a momentary start of surprise, she leaned into his embrace and fitted her walk to his.

When they reached the arboreum, they found a bench of carved stone just large enough for two. When they were seated side by side, Drake reached into his jacket and came out with a small cube. He thumbed a control and a low-pitched humming noise filled the air. He glanced at the readout on the face of the instrument and nodded in satisfaction.

"Okay, it's safe to talk," he said in a low voice.

"What is that thing?" Bethany asked.

"Random-noise modulator. Makes it almost impossible to separate our voices from the background noise if we don't speak too loudly."

"Do you think the Sandarians have been eavesdropping on us?"

"Wouldn't you in their place?"

Bethany thought about it for a moment, then nodded. "I suppose I would."

"Now, before they get suspicious, tell me about this talk you had with the Earth ambassador."

She quickly summarized what Cartier had told her of the Ryall legends regarding a nova in the sky of their home world. Drake listened intently. When she finished, he nodded and said, "That's approximately the same story I got from the Ryall prisoner. It's funny, but that legend did more to convince me that I was dealing with an alien than six legs and lizard hide."

"I don't understand."

"It made me realize that the Ryall don't think the way we do; the Ryall never questioned the assumption that conflict between our species is inevitable."

"Do you suppose they really think like that, Richard?"

"They do unless we've been the victims of Sandarian propaganda. I can see how they could get a prisoner to say anything they wanted, but how could they have bribed the Earth ambassador?"

"If he *is* the ambassador!"

Drake gazed intently at her through the gloom. "What do you mean by that?"

Bethany bit her lip and hesitated. When she finally spoke, she chose her words with care. "I'm not sure. It's just a feeling I had."

"How so?"

"His comment that he finds it more convenient to run the embassy out of his residence struck me as wrong somehow."

"Go on."

"Well, Richard, you know the Admiralty in Homeport is housed in the old terrestrial embassy. Think of that building. It's six stories tall and once housed two hundred and fifty diplomats and staffers! Yet, prior to the nova, Alta was never more than a struggling second-stage colony on the edge of human space.

"Sandar is supposedly fighting an interstellar war on the side of Earth, for God's sake! Space war is the most logistics-intensive of all wars, and interstellar war must be ten times as complicated. If the Sandarians are fighting on the side of Earth, there should be thousands of people and hundreds of ships engaged in keeping the supply pipelines filled. The terrestrial embassy ought to be about the size of this palace."

"And you are saying that it isn't."

"I am," Bethany replied. "I discovered one old man and a dozen or so assistants all working out of the ambassador's residence. I found out that there are currently no Earth warships in the system and that the ambassador isn't even sure when the next commercial vessel will arrive. Something doesn't feel right."

Drake nodded. "I agree. We'll have to look into the matter." He glanced at his wrist chronometer, then at the random-noise modulator. "It's time we wrapped this up before some security agent comes out to check on why his bug's gone dead. Anything else?"

"That's about it."

He thumbed the box in his hand again and the low-pitched *hum* ceased. He returned the box to his pocket, winked at her, and spoke in a normal conversational tone for the first time in several minutes. "Well, enough communing with nature. Time we got you back to the palace and on your way to the king's party."

"Not yet," Bethany replied. "Would you mind if we strolled through the gardens for a bit longer?"

He stood, offered her his arm, and said, "My pleasure."

They walked another hundred meters along the flower-lined path in silence. Bethany found that having confided her suspicions to someone, she was content for the first time in hours. She forgot her troubles and concentrated on the light show overhead. After a few minutes, she found that she was unnaturally conscious of the sounds of insects—from the buzzing of bees to the disconcertingly loud chirping noise of something the Sandarians had called a cricket. Finally, she said, "These lights are pretty, but you know what would be really beautiful?"

"What?"

"It would be nice if they would turn off all the lights and make it pitch black in here, then project the image of a moon onto the underside of the dome."

"Sandar already has four real moons to look at. I grant

you that they aren't very impressive, but why would they want a fake?"

"I'm not talking about just *any* moon here," she said with an intensity that made him smile. "I mean Earth's moon—Luna..." She glanced around and pointed to a spot on the dome on the opposite side of the palace building. "I'd put it right up there."

"Why?" he asked.

"Because all the ancient poets spoke very highly of the effect a full moon had on lovers."

"I'm not sure that I've ever seen a picture of Earth's moon."

"Oh, you should! It's a big brute, fully one-quarter as large as Earth itself. The books say that you could read by its light."

"Something like Antares dawn at home?"

"Oh, far lovelier than that! Antares dawn is like a welder's torch. Real Luna-light is a soft, silvery radiance. On warm summer nights, lovers would lie in the grass and spend hours watching it cross the sky."

"I've always heard that a full moon drove people crazy."

"Don't be silly. I have it on good authority that a full moon was the most beautiful sight in the universe. The next thing you'll be telling me is that you believe in vampires and werewolves."

"Oh, I do!" he said, laughing. He opened his mouth to say something else and then closed it again with a snap.

"What is it?" Bethany asked.

"Nothing," he replied.

"Come on, you were going to say something."

He sighed. "I was about to say that I wouldn't mind biting your neck right now."

Bethany stopped and turned to face him. They suddenly found themselves standing very close to each other.

"Would you really?" she asked in a whisper.

His answer was to pull her close and kiss her. She returned the kiss hungrily. They crushed their bodies together for an eternity of heartbeats. Finally, Drake gulped and stepped away. His face was flushed and his breathing ragged.

"Look, I'm sorry about that!"

She regarded him with shining eyes. "I'm not. I've wanted to do that for the longest time."

"What about your fiancé?"

"Carl isn't my fiancé; he's asked me to marry him, but I haven't given him an answer yet. Besides, one little kiss won't hurt him." She melted back into his embrace once more. After a long time they parted. Bethany took both of his hands in her own and said, "I'm ready to go back now."

They walked along the same flower-lined path, saying nothing but savoring each other's presence. It wasn't until after they'd passed the arboreum that Drake halted and turned to face her.

"I have to tell you something. It's none of my business, and I should keep my big mouth shut, but I have to say it anyway."

"What is it, Richard?"

"You shouldn't marry Carl Aster! You're much too good for him."

"Why, Richard, you hardly know him!"

"The hell I don't," he growled. "I was legislative liaison for two years, remember? He and I tangled on numerous occasions."

She nodded. "He told me that you two had quarreled over Navy funding."

"That isn't the reason I don't like him. Look, I had a number of adversaries as Navy legislative liaison. I respected most of them. I don't respect Aster. The man's one of Carstairs' sycophants! He isn't looking for a wife. He wants a decoration to hang on his arm at political functions."

"You sound just like my uncle. He isn't very fond of Carl either."

"Your uncle's a wise man. You should listen to him.

Why would you consider marrying Aster for even a second?"

"Because he asked me."

"Not good enough," Drake replied. "There are a million better men for you on Alta."

Bethany felt her cheeks grow hot. "Are you volunteering yourself, Captain Drake?"

Drake frowned. "I'm not right for you either."

"Oh? And why not?" she asked.

"Because I'm a spacer on active duty. No spacer should marry until he's ready to give up the ships."

Bethany was quiet for a long moment, then carefully pronounced a monosyllable that has decorated the language since at least the time of Chaucer. She added two other words for good measure and said, "That's a coward talking, Richard. Spacers have been getting married since the dawn of the Space Age. So did wet Navy sailors before them. Besides, you seem to be forgetting something."

"What?"

"Didn't that Ryall tell you today that his kind is out to exterminate our kind?"

Drake nodded.

"Then may I politely suggest that that changes everything?"

"I don't understand."

"You've planned your life to the smallest detail," she said, anger tingeing her words. "You figure that you'll space for another five years, then be promoted to a job at the Admiralty. Then you will look around, bestow yourself on the prettiest girl you can find, and raise fat children. Isn't that pretty close to your plan?"

Drake didn't answer.

"Well, I hate to be the bearer of bad tidings, Richard, but the Ryall have permanently messed up your plans. We'll probably be fighting them for the rest of our lives, maybe for the rest of our childrens' lives. We're going to need trained spacers—lots of them! You'll be lucky to get off the ships by the time you're eighty."

"What are you trying to say?"

Tears welled up in Bethany's eyes. "I'm trying to say that I love you, you big, dumb *skinker*, and that you're a fool if you throw away our chance for happiness!"

He blinked in surprise.

She averted her eyes. "I've loved you ever since that night you bawled me out for getting caught by the nova on New Providence."

He smiled down at her. "I've loved you ever since the first night we met. Why else do you think I refused Carl Aster a berth onboard *Discovery*?"

She looked up at him. "Would you mind holding me for a while?"

He took her in his arms. After a few minutes spent standing with their arms intertwined, he leaned down and whispered her name in her ear.

"What is it?" she asked, her words muffled in his uniform jacket.

"Will you marry me?"

She looked up at him, wiped away her tears, and frowned. "No, I won't."

"What?"

"You heard me. I won't marry you. Not until after I've finished my work for my uncle. After that . . . maybe. Now shut up and hold me!"

Sometime later, the annunciator in Bethany's suite chimed for attention. Two heads rose as one to peer over the back of the couch in the suite's living room. Two pairs of eyes glanced at each other as an irritated male voice growled, "Now who the hell can that be?"

Bethany laughed quietly at Drake's irritation. She leaned close and whispered in his ear, "Maybe they'll go away if we keep quiet!" As if in response to her comment, the annunciator chimed again, this time more insistently. She sighed. "Then again, maybe they won't."

"You'd better answer it," Drake said. "If it's our hosts, they may override the entry code."

Bethany lifted herself to a sitting position and straightened various parts of the pearl-gray evening gown. She commanded the lights from dim to full brightness, crossed to the suite's entry door, and opened it. Standing in the hallway was Alicia Delevan. She looked worried. Behind her was Carl Aster.

"Good evening, Bethany," Alicia began. "Have you seen Captain Drake? We can't seem to find him anywhere..." Her voice strangled to a halt as she caught sight of Drake on the couch. Nor was she the only one to take notice of his presence. Carl Aster's face suddenly became wooden. Bethany locked eyes with Aster's for a single, agonizing moment before he turned and stalked off.

Alicia Delevan stared at the lovers in silence. Finally she asked, "Am I to draw the obvious conclusion from this scene, Bethany?"

"You can draw any conclusion you like!"

Alicia frowned. "Don't get me wrong. Your personal life is your own. But Carl is a friend as well as a subordinate. I don't want to see him hurt any more than he has to be. What shall I tell him?"

Bethany sighed. "Tell him that I'm sorry it has to end this way. Tell him that Richard has asked me to marry him and that I may accept his proposal when my obligation to my uncle is ended."

"I wish you both all happiness," she said. Then her manner changed abruptly. She shouldered her way past Bethany to where Drake was still hastily fastening the closures on his uniform tunic. "Captain Drake, I must speak with you. Something very curious happened tonight at the banquet. Halfway through dinner, all the highest-ranking Sandarians were called away!"

"I don't understand."

"Neither do I. We first knew of it when a messenger stopped to confer with Minister Haliver. The first minister then leaned over and whispered in the king's ear. John-Phillip said something to the queen, and all three of them left. By then, other messengers had entered the hall. They worked like *gransi* pickers back home, sweeping among the tables, stopping to harvest someone here and there. Wherever they whispered in someone's ear, that worthy made his excuses and left the hall. The whole process took no longer than five minutes, and you could feel the tension building the whole time."

"How long ago did this happen?"

"Twenty minutes. Carl and I slipped out a side door while everyone was preoccupied. We made our way here to tell you about it."

Drake strode to the suite's viewphone, activated the instrument, and asked for the palace operator. A pretty, young woman came on the line immediately.

"Yes, Fleet Captain Drake. How may I help you?"

"You may put me through to my ship."

"Sorry, sir, but all orbital transmission circuits are in use. I'll be happy to put you on the waiting list and call when a circuit frees up, if you like."

"I wouldn't like. I need that circuit now!"

"I'm sorry, sir, but all circuits are in use."

"What are you going to do now?" Bethany asked as Drake switched the phone off.

"I'm going to call the ship." He reached into his uniform tunic and pulled out a portable communicator marked with the insignia of the Altan Space Navy. Every member of the ground party carried a similar device, although the Sandarians had requested that they not use them. The reason given had been the possiblity that the communicator signals might interfere with the operation of various pieces of automated equipment.

Drake thumbed the emergency call button on the communicator and was rewarded by the appearance of Bela Marston's features on the instrument's screen. His executive officer looked grim

"Ah, Captain! I thought I was going to have to send the Marines down to find you."

"What's the situation up there, Commander?"

"Approximately half an hour ago, space-side sensors detected a large number of weapon discharges in the Hellsgate—Aezer foldpoint. I thought they were testing their ordnance until one of the fortresses exploded."

"A fortress was destroyed?"

"More than one, Captain. Whoever they were shooting at was well shielded and well armed. After a while, things quieted down. Over the last fifteen minutes or so, we've been tracking the drive flares of at least a dozen ships accelerating away from the foldpoint at high gravities. Whoever they are, they're scattering all over the place!"

"Any identification on the ship types from their flares?"

"They aren't Altan or Sandarian."

"Aliens?"

"I'd put my money on it, sir."

"What's *Discovery*'s current status, Mr. Marston?"

"We can be ready to leave orbit as soon as your ground party is aboard, sir. Captain Fallan says that *Alexandria* can do the same as quickly as he gets his own people back. I'm having all personnel run continuous maintenance tests on all equipment, with emphasis on engines and weapons. I've told the chief engineer that if he's got anything dismantled, I want it put back together on the double."

"Good man!"

"When can we expect you back onboard, Captain?"

"Give me some time to find out what's going on down here, Bela. I'll call you again in an hour."

"Very good, sir."

"In the meantime, keep buttoning up the ship. Drake out."

"Marston out."

Drake turned to Bethany and Alicia and was about to speak when the suite door opened and four burly Sandarian Marines rushed in. They were followed by the palace majordomo.

Opteris' gaze fastened on the communicator in Drake's hand. "Please turn that damned thing off, Captain Drake.

Your transmissions are giving the palace security system a nervous breakdown."

"What's going on, Opteris?"

The majordomo shrugged. "Nothing to become unduly concerned about, I assure you. The Ryall tried to force our foldpoint defenses a short while ago."

"My people tell me that they not only tried, they succeeded!"

Opteris sighed. "Early reports indicate that most of their ships were destroyed in the fortresses' crossfire. However, we did take some damage. Several of their ships managed to exploit a gap in our defenses to break out into open space. We are now mobilizing our fleet to deal with them. At this time, there is no cause for alarm."

CHAPTER 22

Richard Drake and Bethany Lindquist sat together and waited for the long night to end. Sometimes they spoke of their lives before that first fateful night at Mrs. Mortridge's house on Nob Hill. Other times they lapsed into silence, content merely to be together. Toward morning they moved onto the balcony and stretched out together on a lounger. Bethany, her head pillowed on Drake's chest, fell into a fitful sleep. Drake lay quietly and held her close as he savored the warmth of her beside him.

Bethany finally stirred as the cold gray light of dawn began to tinge the eastern side of the weather dome. She opened her eyes and smiled up at him. "How long did I sleep?"

"Couple of hours."

She struggled to sit erect. "Your arm must have gone to sleep ages ago!"

"No problem," he lied. "You are as light as a flower, and twice as beautiful."

She grinned. "I thank my husband-to-be for the lovely compliment, but I've been to too many banquets lately to believe that first part. Any word from Opteris yet?"

"Not yet."

"What if he doesn't call?"

"I'll give him another hour, then I'll have Bela Marston send the boats down to pick us up."

"That won't be necessary, Captain!" a voice said from

262

behind them. Drake glanced over his shoulder to see Opteris standing in the open doorway leading from the suite to the balcony. The majordomo continued: "I hope you don't mind my barging in, Miss Lindquist. I signaled, but no one answered."

"My fault," Drake said. "I ordered the computer to turn the annunciator off so it wouldn't disturb Bethany."

"I suspected something like that," Opteris replied smoothly.

"What about my audience with the king?" Drake asked impatiently.

"His Majesty will see you now, Fleet Captain. He regrets not being able to break away any earlier."

"What about Ambassadors Barrett and Delevan?" Bethany asked. "Shouldn't someone notify them?"

"I understand that they are asleep, Miss Lindquist," Opteris replied, "and, in any event, the invitation was for Captain Drake alone."

Drake bent over to kiss Bethany. "See you soon."

"I'll be waiting."

Opteris led Drake to the palace central core where half a dozen lift shafts carried passengers and freight between floors. He slipped his identification card into a slot. In a moment, a door opened and he ushered Drake into a lift car. Opteris punched a code into the control panel and the lift began to drop rapidly. Drake expected it to brake in a matter of seconds as it reached ground level. He was therefore surprised when it continued its descent for nearly a minute.

After gulping to equalize the pressure on his eardrums for the second time, he asked, "How far underground are we going, Opteris?"

"Approximately one kilometer, Fleet Captain. We'll be there in another few seconds."

As the majordomo had predicted, the car began braking to a halt almost immediately. The doors opened to reveal a long, concrete corridor. Two armed guards checked Opteris' identification, then waved them on. Opteris led the way through a maze of tunnels until he reached a door outwardly like a dozen others they had passed. He inserted his identification card into a lock mechanism. With a series of quiet clicks a heavy steel door retracted into the wall. Opteris ushered Drake through into a small anteroom and pressed a control. The first door closed and a second opened immediately, revealing the anteroom to be a short length of corridor that had been turned into a personnel lock.

Beyond the second door was a large cavern filled with men and women in the uniform of the Sandarian Space Navy. Most sat in front of computer consoles and worked quietly at various tasks. Over their heads, mounted high up the walls of the artificial cavern, large glassed-in galleries looked down on the floor below. Several figures stood silhouetted against the light and watched the controllers working at their tasks. Here and there, an operator stood impatiently by while service technicians worked furiously to return a console to operation.

"This way, Fleet Captain," Opteris said as he led Drake down a corridor between two large groups of consoles. Drake scanned the workstations as they passed and noted a considerable variety in the images displayed on the console screens. He picked up fragments of conversation as he passed each station.

"... When can you clear orbit, *Instigator*?... All personnel will be aboard in the next hour, Lieutenant... The munitions loaders will arrive shortly, sir. Make sure your starboard cargo portal is clear for them..."

Opteris led him to another nondescript door and inserted his identification card once more. Again the muted clicking noise was followed by the door sliding quietly out of their way. Inside, they found a small room in which a dozen Sandarians were clustered around a table. Their backs were to the door and their attention was focused on a large situation display on the far wall.

John-Phillip Walkirk swiveled in his chair and glanced at Drake as he and the majordomo entered the conference room. He got to his feet and crossed the distance between them in four long strides.

"Welcome, Fleet Captain," John-Phillip said, holding out his hand.

"Thank you, Your Majesty," Drake replied, taking the king's hand. It wasn't until he felt John-Phillip's strong grip that he became conscious of the departure from normal court etiquette which the gesture represented. He also noted how much John-Phillip seemed to have aged in the week since their first meeting. In addition to the king, Drake recognized Commander of War Operations Walkirk, First Minister Haliver, and Commodore Bardak among those present.

"What do you think of our little command center here, Fleet Captain?"

"I'm very impressed, Your Majesty. I had no idea that this existed."

John-Phillip smiled. "It isn't something that we advertise. Now then, you asked to see me. I imagine you are concerned about the recent visit of our centauroid antagonists."

"Yes, sir. *Very* concerned. I have two ships in orbit and people spread out all over Sandar. I'd hate to be attacked in parking orbit without some room to maneuver."

"No possiblity of that, Fleet Captain," John-Phillip replied. He gestured toward the wall-size screen. "The display should convince you of our situation."

The display was of a type not too different from those used by the Altan Navy. The Hellsgate–Aezer foldpoint was depicted as a red ellipsoid around which sixty golden sparks had been arrayed in a perfect globular formation; seven of the sparks were replaced by crimson crosses to mark their former positions. Soft green lettering beside other markers told of battle damage. Trailing from the foldpoint, radiating outward in all directions, were twelve red arrowheads. Attached to each arrowhead was a pair of lines showing velocity and acceleration vectors. Several green arrowheads could be seen chasing their red counterparts. One glance at the vectors involved told Drake that it was going to be a long chase.

"Approximately fifty Ryall ships materialized in the foldpoint last night," John-Phillip began. "They were automatically identified and immediately attacked by our guard fortresses. All in all, we did pretty well. We destroyed eighteen outright and forced another twenty to jump back to Aezer. However, the remaining twelve concentrated their fire on one section of our defensive globe and punched through. What you see are the surviving Ryall ships trying to outrun our pursuit craft. Of course, they have no hope. Once we get the Third Fleet out there, they'll face an overwhelming force."

"You are dispatching one of your fleets, Your Majesty?" Drake asked. "Is it that serious?"

"It's serious until the last of those marauders is destroyed! However, that is not the main reason for dispatching the fleet. We've been fighting the Ryall for a century, Captain. We are getting to know their habits quite well. They may attempt probing attacks on the foldpoint for the next several weeks to gauge how badly we've been hurt. Reinforcing our defense line with the Third Fleet will help convince them that their attack has failed."

"When does all of this happen?"

"The fleet launches in twelve hours. I leave for my flagship in six."

"*You* are going, Your Majesty? Is that wise?"

"It will be no more dangerous for me than for tens of thousands of naval ratings. You wouldn't have me hide in a hole while others took risks in my name, would you?"

"Uh, no, sir!"

"Good man. Now then, we should discuss the matter of what to do with you and your people during this emergency."

"I thank you for your hospitality, Your Majesty," Drake said, "but I think the time has come for me to return home."

"You can't, man! Discussions between your ambassadors and my political people are at a critical stage. Considerable work will be lost if you leave now."

Drake frowned. "I appreciate your concern, Your Majesty. However, I have my duty to perform. We've gained a lot of data on this trip, more than we expected. I can hardly afford to risk what we've learned should the Ryall break through your defenses."

"No, of course not," the king said. "But perhaps there is a middle ground. May I make a counterproposal?"

"Yes, sir."

"I agree that you should gather up your people and load them back aboard your ships," John-Phillip began. "That is only common sense. In fact, we will be asking our own nonessential personnel to spend their nights in the shelters until the last Ryall ship is destroyed.

"However, once you've readied your vessels for space, there is no risk in your remaining in parking orbit until the battle is finished. Should one of the raiders get past us, there will be plenty of time for you to get clear. In the meantime, you can gather information on our defensive techniques—we'll even give you tapes of last night's battle—and your two ambassadors can complete their discussions with my political staff via teleconference."

Drake considered his options, then nodded. "All right, we'll stay in orbit until the current battle is over. After that, we'll see."

John-Phillip smiled a tired smile. "That's all I ask!"

To Drake's surprise, the order for all Task Force 001 personnel to return to the ships caused surprisingly little grumbling from members of the ground party. Except for an occasional halfhearted comment about having just arrived and the normal grousing that goes with having one's plans upset, the group that gathered at Capitol Spaceport that afternoon was unnaturally quiet. News of the battle at the Hellsgate–Aezer foldpoint had sobered even the most extreme ivory-tower types among the scientists and had shocked the commercial people into the realization that war is far more than merely an opportunity for profit. The sight of *Discovery*'s ring-and-cylinder shape even elicited a spontaneous cheer from several of the passengers aboard Drake's landing boat as it made its final approach.

As John-Phillip had predicted, the Third Space Fleet departed Sandar within twelve hours of Drake's audience in the war room. Drake hurried from the boat bay to the bridge in order to watch the departure. It was an impressive sight in the cruiser's telescopes and on its radar screens. One by one, four separate flotillas boosted away from the planet. Each consisted of a blastship, twenty armed escorts, and three times that many support vessels. Drake identified heavy and light cruisers, destroyers, even relatively tiny long-range scout boats. The support craft included all manner of tankers, freighters, and ammunition ships. As he watched them go, he was reminded of something one of his professors at the Altan Space Academy had once said: "Never forget, young gentlemen, that space war is ten percent offense and ninety percent logistics!"

For a day and a half after departing orbit, the Sandarian ships' drive flares were visible in *Discovery*'s telescopes. They showed as a star cluster composed entirely of violet-white stars of varying intensity. The main body of the fleet accelerated at two standard gravities for forty hours before turning end for end and decelerating for a like time until they reached the Hellsgate–Aezer foldpoint to take up guard positions among the surviving orbital fortresses.

Not all ships of the Third Fleet headed for the foldpoint, however. Several small groups split off to intercept the Ryall raiders, two of which had already been destroyed by their pursuers. By the fifth day after the Third Fleet's departure it was clear that the Sandarians had the situation under control. Nearly fifty warships had joined an equal number of surviving fortresses at the foldpoint, and the

Ryall raiders were scattered across the sky in disarray, thirty Sandarian ships in pursuit.

Even so, Richard Drake found it difficult to shake his unease as he reviewed the Sandarian formations.

"What's the matter with you?" Bethany asked when she brought his lunch to the bridge. "You look like you just bit into something rancid!"

He grinned, leaned back in his chair, and stretched to relieve the ache of sitting too long in one position. The ship was at one-quarter spin-gravity, but that did nothing to relieve the aches and pains induced by tension. "I guess I worry too much."

"What do you mean?" Bethany handed him a tray. He placed it on his lapboard while she maneuvered into the observer's chair beside him. Eating lunch together had become a ritual with them since their return to the ship.

Drake pressed a control that slaved Bethany's screen to one of his own. "Here, I want you to see something!"

Two more commands to *Discovery*'s computer brought up the Sandarian record of the battle at the foldpoint. Drake had studied the record for five days, hoping to divine something from the tactics the Ryall had used. The more he learned, the more troubled he became.

The record began with a close-up of one of the foldpoint fortresses; the Sandarians had obviously tacked on library footage for Altan benefit. The screen showed a great sphere that bristled with the dark snouts of several hundred laser ports and a like number of missile launchers. Other features included thick layers of ablative shielding, power plant exhaust ports, and vast radiators to rid the fortresses of internal heat. A destroyer cruised past the fortress in the foreground of the picture, giving a sense of scale to the scene. The battle station was as large as a small asteroid, and brimming with destructive power.

"My God, what a behemoth!" Bethany said.

Drake nodded. "It's even more impressive when you realize how much ship volume is normally taken up by photon engines and foldspace generators. That monster

was designed to deliver its punch to the target without
worrying about maneuvering. I'd estimate its power at
about that of five blast ships, maybe more!"

"If one fortress is that powerful, how did the Ryall
manage to break out of a foldpoint guarded by sixty of
them?"

"Watch the next sequence and find out." Drake touched
a control and the scene changed to a view of a starfield.
The background stars danced enough to show that the
scene was from a long-range camera set at high magnification. As Bethany watched, a cylindrical ship materialized in the center of the screen. Immediately the dull
gray surface of the newly arrived starship turned brilliant
against the black backdrop. A filter snapped into operation and the stars dimmed until the ship's outline was
once more visible. Vivid points of violet light stabbed at
the hapless ship in dozens of places. With so much laser
energy being poured into its hull, the Ryall craft had no
hope.

Yet somehow it survived.

From each of the points of radiance came incandescent
plumes of vaporized material. For long seconds, the Ryall
craft looked like a multitailed comet. The ship fought back
hard; beams of its own pierced the sudden fog that was
softening its outlines. Violet-white specks marked the drive
flares of missiles on their way to their target. The spacecraft seemed to hover unmoving for perhaps ten seconds
before the ravening beams finally ate their way to something vital. Then the ship exploded in a blinding flash and
began to expand in a cooling cloud of plasma. The faraway
telescopic camera reduced its magnification in order to
keep the fireball in its field of view until it had dimmed
to darkness.

"That was one of the first raiders through the foldpoint."

"How could it have survived so long?" Bethany asked.

"The geysers spouting from its sides were antilaser
ablative shielding being vaporized. Ablative shielding has

billions of tiny glass prisms in every cubic centimeter. Laser beams scatter in the stuff, and it takes a long time to drill a hole through to the ship."

The screen changed to show another star field. This time fifty Ryall starships materialized within the fold-point. They were far enough away to be invisible, but their positions were marked by electronic symbols. Once again, the Ryall ships blazed bright as the Sandarian fortresses opened up on them. Most of the attackers' shields failed within seconds, but not before the craft had released swarms of missiles at one section of the defensive globe. The interior of the globe filled with the flashes of fusion weapons. Most were detonated harmlessly in space, but some got through in both directions. And antilaser ablatives did little to thwart the power of a nearby nuclear burst. Drake and Bethany watched as one of Sandar's fortresses exploded. It was followed quickly by several others.

"It took about twelve seconds for the fortresses to overcome the Ryall shielding on each ship," Drake said. "That gave many of the Ryall ships time to unload their missiles against one section of the defensive globe and then jump back to the safety of the Aezer system. They managed to tear a hole in the globe, and a dozen of the raiders slipped through the gap."

"It hasn't done them any good," Bethany said. "The Sandarian fleet has them outnumbered and outgunned. Mr. Cristobal says the last of them will be hunted down in another hundred hours."

"Still," Drake said, "I wonder if the fact that they were able to break out at all doesn't point out a weakness in the Sandarian defenses."

"What weakness?"

"Look at the way they hug the foldpoint," he said, gesturing toward the red ellipse with its covering of Sandarian ships. "They are getting in close in order to concentrate their firepower. But that formation doesn't give them much defense in depth. Once the Ryall broke through, there was nothing between them and Sandar except four hundred million kilometers of vacuum. That is why they had to scramble the Third Fleet.

"Now, if I were running this show, I'd station a blocking force right about here," he said, pointing to a spot halfway between the foldpoint and Sandar. "That would give a lot more depth to the defense while cutting down on the response time should the Ryall achieve a breakout. That way, the Sandarians could enfilade an attacker all the way to the planet and then let the planetary defense centers take care of any survivors."

"You are worrying too much, Richard," Bethany said around a sandwich that she had just bitten into. "The Sandarians have been fighting the Ryall for more than a century now. They must know what they're doing!"

"I hope you're right."

CHAPTER 23

The sound of the alarm brought Drake to instant wake-fulness. He sat up in bed and triggered the interphone screen on the nightstand beside him. The screen lit to show Karl Slater, who was serving as Officer of the Watch.

"What is it, Mr. Slater?" Drake asked gruffly, noting the digits 0328 in the screen's chronometer display.

"You'd better come to the bridge, sir. All hell has broken loose in the foldpoint!"

"I'll be right up."

Drake slipped into a jumpsuit and a pair of ship shoes then headed for the bridge at a run. He arrived to find the bridge crew settling into their stations. "Report!"

"Yes, sir," Karl Slater replied. "Pursuant to orders, we have been monitoring the Hellsgate–Aezer foldpoint for signs of activity. Save for normal Sandarian communications traffic, all was quiet until about three minutes ago, when we observed a massive explosion within the fold-point."

"How massive?"

"Several orders of magnitude larger than what we observed during the battle six days ago, sir. Since the explosion, we've also detected fusion weapon bursts and a large number of high-power laser flashes."

"Let's see a replay!"

"Yes, sir."

As Slater had reported, the second battle for the Hellsgate–Aezer foldpoint had begun with a titanic blast from within the foldpoint itself. Drake watched as the eternal night of space was turned suddenly into day. At first there was only a single point of light at the center of a small starfield. The point brightened and grew until it was a tiny disk the color of an arc welder's spark. The disk continued to expand, changing color as it did. The actinic blue-white shaded slowly to green, and then to yellow. Orange splotches appeared, and the sphere turned completely orange before shading to red, where it lingered for long seconds before disappearing completely. In the meantime, other lights had appeared. These were the familiar white flashes that accompanied the detonation of a nuclear missile and the pure violet sparks of high-power military lasers in action.

Drake tapped a control and watched the sequence again. When it was over, he turned to his chief communicator. "I'll bet that every Sandarian ship and fortress near the foldpoint just had half its sensors burned out! Creighton!"

"Yes, Captain?"

"What have you got?"

"I'm having trouble extrapolating the power of that first big bang, sir. The spectrum indicates that it was a matter–antimatter annihilation reaction, though where anyone would find that much antimatter is beyond me."

"They didn't have to find it, Mr. Creighton. They manufactured it."

"A couple of hundred kilograms, sir? That would take years!"

Drake nodded. "And be highly dangerous to all concerned. Gentlemen, I think our Sandarian cousins have just fallen headlong into a Ryall trap."

"I don't understand, Captain."

"Imagine that you are the Ryall commander, Slater. You've been assigned to attack this system. What is your greatest difficulty?"

"Breaking out of the foldpoint defenses."

"Not at all. You proved that you could do that six days

ago. No, the prime difficulty is knowing the disposition of the defenders in advance. Remember, you have no reconnaissance capability. Yet you need to know where the Sandarian fleet is if you are to have a chance.

"*That* was what the initial raid was about. The Ryall used their normal pattern during the attack. They led the Sandarians to expect additional raids against the defense globe. The Sandarians reacted as *they* normally would by massively reinforcing the foldpoint. In so doing, they concentrated a significant percentage of their forces in a single spot. And don't forget that some of the Ryall raiders broke out of the defense globe. What did they do? They immediately scattered across half the sky, forcing the Sandarians to give chase, thus drawing off another sizable chunk of Sandar's strength.

"Six days later, you—as commander of the forces of the Ryall hegemony—can now confidently predict where you will find a large percentage of the Sandarian fleet. At the proper time, you send your planet buster through the foldpoint and set it off. The explosion temporarily blinds the defenders and, being an antimatter reaction, produces only high-energy photons. In other words, it produces a hollow shell of radiation that expands at the speed of light *leaving no nasty fireball of electrically charged plasma behind*! One second after the explosion, your invasion fleet jumps into a foldpoint clear of residual energy and immediately breaks through the encircling globe of human warships and fortresses. It won't really matter how many human ships survive your attack. If you can get to Sandar half an hour before they do, your mission is a total success. In a way, it's ironic."

"What is, Captain?"

"We keep telling ourselves that a hundred years of war should have taught the Sandarians all there is to learn about the Ryall. It never occurred to us that the converse must also be true!"

Drake stared at the main screen where firefly sparkles continued to mark the death of a lot of good men. After long seconds of silence, he turned to Slater. "Get me someone in authority down below."

"Yes, sir!"

Within two minutes Drake was staring at a man with the collar insignia of a Senior Commander, Sandarian Space Navy.

"Sorry to bother you, Commander," Drake began, "but we've been watching events in the foldpoint and have some input for you."

"Go ahead."

Drake related his fears concerning the possibility that the Third Fleet had been tricked into reinforcing the foldpoint fortresses. When he finished, the Sandarian officer nodded ruefully.

"We are beginning to come to that same conclusion here."

"If I were you," Drake said, "I would get the First and Second Fleets ready for a fight."

"Thank you for your advice, Captain Drake. Now, if you will excuse me, I have preparations to make."

When the screen went dark, Drake turned to Slater. "We'll monitor until morning. We should know by then if my suspicions are right."

"Yes, sir."

Three hours later, the fight for the foldpoint appeared to be over. In its place, *Discovery*'s sensors detected the expanding plasma trails of many ships. All were accelerating toward the planet. It was impossible to sort out the contacts at the distances involved, but Drake doubted that he was seeing the victorious Third Fleet headed home in celebration—not at five gravities of acceleration!

"Have any suggestions, Exec?" Drake asked Bela Marston. The executive officer was at his duty station in the combat control center.

"Only one, sir. I suggest that we get the hell out of here!"

Drake nodded. "I agree. Sound General Quarters, Number One. All hands are to prepare for space."

"Yes, sir!"

The clanging of the alarm bell brought a sudden flurry of activity to *Discovery*. Drake noted with pride that his console reported READY FOR SPACE in less than one-quarter the normal time. Obviously, much of the cruiser's crew had heard of the battle and had moved to their duty stations in anticipation of the order.

"Notify Captain Fallan onboard *City of Alexandria*, Mr. Slater."

"Yes, sir."

Thirty seconds later, Fallan's features were on Drake's display screen. "We're ready for departure at any time, Captain. Hate to leave the Sandarians in a fix, though."

"They're big boys, Kenil. They've got the rest of their fleet to fight off the Ryall. Our data is too important to risk getting caught in the crossfire. Besides, one more cruiser and an unarmed passenger liner isn't going to do them a whole lot of good."

"Yes, sir. *Alexandria,* out."

"*Discovery* out." Drake cleared his screen and punched for Control Room No. 3. "Chief Engineer Arnam, please."

"Here, sir."

"You may begin despinning her anytime, Gavin."

"Will do, Captain. I'll have you in zero gravity in ten minutes."

"Mr. Cristobal. Lay in a course for the Hellsgate–Napier foldpoint."

"Locked in, Captain."

"Mr. Slater. Please tell Sandarian traffic control that we are ready to depart orbit. Recommend a departure time for "—Drake's gaze went to his chronometer— "say fifteen minutes from now."

"Aye aye, sir."

His orders given, Drake sat back and gazed at the information coming in from the long-range sensors. The number of ships definitely identified as heading for Sandar continued to grow. Drake hoped the Sandarians could get their blocking force into position in time. If not, the planet was going to take one hell of a beating.

Five minutes passed. Communicator Slater buzzed for Drake's attention.

"What is it, Lieutenant?"

"Sir, traffic control denies us permission to depart orbit."

"THEY WHAT?"

"They refuse to clear us for deep space, Captain."

"Did you tell them that our asking was merely a courtesy, and that we'll leave any time we're damned good and ready?"

"Yes, sir. The chief controller says that he understands perfectly and that permission is still refused. Wait a second, Captain. New message is coming in . . . It's for you. Commodore Bardak."

"Put him on."

Drake's screen cleared to show Commodore Bardak's features. "Your people have told me that I can't leave orbit, Commodore."

"They did so at my orders, Fleet Captain," Bardak replied. "I ask that you delay your departure for another four hours. You will be free to go at the end of that time."

"Why four hours?"

"Because that is how long it will take me to reach your ship. I must speak to you concerning a matter that cannot be handled on an open comm circuit."

Drake hesitated, then nodded. "Very well, Commodore. You have four hours. At the end of that time we're leaving for home whether we have your permission or not."

"You will not only have my permission, Captain Drake. You will have my blessing."

Drake was waiting when Bardak stepped from the hangar bay airlock. The Sandarian stepped forward and shook Drake's hand. His expression was grim. "Thank you for delaying your departure, Captain."

"You're welcome, I think. Any news from the fold-point?"

Bardak touched fingers to the breast pocket of his uniform tunic. "We received an updated report from the Third Fleet just before I left Capitol. Is there somewhere we can talk? I'll need a tile reader."

"We'll be meeting in the wardroom. Stan Barrett, Alicia Delevan, and Bethany Lindquist have all requested that they be allowed to sit in. Several of my officers will also be there. Any objection?"

"None, Fleet Captain. The time for political games is over. The more people who hear my story, the better."

"Political games?"

"I'll explain later. Now, may we please hurry? My time onboard your ship is strictly limited. There is a great deal to do and little time in which to do it."

"By all means. Follow me."

Drake guided Bardak to the wardroom, moving hand over hand via guidelines in the zero-gravity environment of the ship. In addition to those he'd mentioned, Bela Marston and Argos Cristobal were also present at the wardroom mess table. Bardak glided to a chair and belted himself in. He then reached into his pocket, withdrew a record tile, and handed it to Drake.

Drake slipped the tile into a reader that had been attached to the wardroom table for the occasion. The screen at the end of the compartment lit to show a schematic of the Hellsgate system similar to the one John-Phillip had shown Drake in the palace war room. Bardak used the reader's remote pointer to cause a small golden cursor to appear on the screen at the location of the fold-point.

"Some hours ago, Captain Drake, you told a duty officer at headquarters of your suspicion that we had fallen into a Ryall trap. I am chagrined to say that I agree with you. Apparently, the Ryall know us far better than we realized. For reasons that I will explain shortly, the timing of their attack and its method of execution were masterstrokes!

"The attack began with the detonation of a very large antimatter bomb. Two of our ships on patrol within the foldpoint at the time were destroyed outright. The rest of our fleet, including the orbital fortresses, were blinded by the explosion. Approximately half of our sensors and seventy percent of our communications were temporarily knocked out by the explosion shockwave.

"Six-tenths of a second following the antimatter blast, sixty-five Ryall warships materialized within the foldpoint. Our forces immediately began to enfilade them with laser, antimatter projector, and missile fire. We took a heavy toll, but not nearly as heavy as we would have if our defense had been better coordinated. The Ryall used the same tactic they did six days ago. They concentrated their fire on one section of the defensive globe and were able to clear a hole through which they could pass. The last Ryall ship extricated itself from the foldpoint eight minutes and seventeen seconds after the initial explosion."

"What of the king?" Stan Barrett asked. "Is he safe?"

"He is," Bardak replied. "By the grace of God, his flagship was on the opposite side of the defense globe from the breakout." Bardak turned to the screen and moved the cursor to point out the Ryall ships. "Of sixty-five hostiles, thirty-six survived to break out of the foldpoint. They formed up in good order and immediately began accelerating toward Sandar. The Third Fleet is giving chase and, in fact, has superior numbers and ship-to-ship firepower. Unfortunately, in the last couple of hours the Ryall fleet has begun to break into two distinct groups."

"Why 'unfortunately'?" Barrett asked. "I would think you would prefer to take them in small groups."

"Because, Mr. Ambassador, we think we are beginning to understand their strategy. A group of eight ships has pulled ahead of the main body. They are continuing to accelerate at five point two standard gravities. The remaining twenty-eight ships have reduced their acceleration to four point five standard gravities. The larger group is obviously acting as a blocking force to shield the smaller group from the Third Fleet. We will have to defeat each of the ships in the main force before we can close with the leaders. To do otherwise would place the Third Fleet in a murderous crossfire.

"How can they possibly maintain five gravs?" Bela Marston asked. "They'll run their tanks dry before they reach Sandar."

"Or shortly thereafter," Bardak agreed.

"But they won't be able to slow down. Once their fuel is gone, they are on a one-way trip to infinity."

"The Ryall are out to destroy a human planet, Commander Marston. By their standards, trading sixty-plus ships for Sandar is a bargain."

"Any idea what sort of ships are in that leading group?" Drake asked.

Bardak manipulated the remote control again, and the scene zoomed in on the lead group of Ryall ships. The markers for three ships in the center of the group began to blink rapidly. "These three are the ones that concern us the most. They are the main strike force. The other vessels are merely armed escorts."

"What type?"

"We believe them to be attack carriers!"

There was sudden silence in the room. Only the two ambassadors looked perplexed.

"What the hell is an attack carrier?" Alicia Delevan asked.

Richard Drake turned to her and said, "An attack carrier is a large converted freighter that has been jammed to the hull plates with nuclear missiles." Considering the number and power of Sandar's planetary defense centers, if the Ryall were to use a conventional attack on Sandar as they did at the foldpoint, they would be vaporized before they could get within striking distance.

"That is where attack carriers come into play. Because

a missile is small, its range is limited. On the other hand, it is possible to transport a lot of missiles in an attack carrier. The Ryall carriers will probably release their missiles just before they get within range of the PDCs. Each one of those missiles represents a dead Sandarian city, at least, so the defense centers won't be able to ignore them. Instead of having eight targets to fire at, they'll have three hundred thousand or so! The Ryall aim is to saturate the defense and cause the defense centers' computers to malfunction from overload."

Alicia Delevan turned to Duke Bardak and said, "If I were you, Commodore, I would be getting the First and Second Fleets on their way to intercepting those attack carriers!"

Bardak looked pained for an instant, then sighed deeply. "That is excellent advice, Madame Ambassador. I wish that I could do so. Unfortunately, we possess no other fleets. Except for my own squadron of interceptors and a few dozen craft of great age and dubious condition, there are no warships left in orbit about Sandar."

The wardroom was silent for long seconds. The Altans stared at Commodore Bardak.

"I don't understand," Drake said. "You sent your entire naval force to guard the foldpoint?"

"Unfortunately, Fleet Captain, that is exactly what we did."

"But how could this happen, man?" Stan Barrett asked. "We were told that you had a five-hundred-ship Navy!"

"I'm afraid we haven't been totally honest with you, Mr. Ambassador. We feared that if you found out the true condition of our forces, you would avoid entering into an alliance with us. When the Ryall attacked the foldpoint and we were forced to send our whole fleet to strengthen the defenses, we referred to it as the Third Fleet, hoping that you would draw the conclusion that there were others."

"But Ambassador Cartier confirmed your strength to me!" Bethany said.

"He isn't an ambassador, milady. Ambrose Cartier immigrated from Earth some thirty years ago. We selected him to play the part of the terrestrial ambassador when you sought an audience.

"The truth is that we have been cut off from Earth since the Ryall moved into the Aezer system in force fifteen years ago. Since that time, we have launched three efforts to fight our way through to the Aezer–Hermes foldpoint and break through to Earth. The last such effort was six months ago. It cost us eighty-three ships and twelve thousand good men. That is the reason we are so weak at the moment. It is undoubtedly a factor in why the Ryall have chosen this particular time to make *their* big push."

"And you don't think you can stop those attack carriers before they pull within range?" Drake asked.

"I do not," Bardak replied. "Realistically, our chance of getting all three is less than one in ten."

"That's a gloomy assessment," Barrett said.

"Not gloomy, Mr. Ambassador. Realistic. It is also the reason why I asked Captain Drake to delay his departure. We have a favor to ask of you."

"What favor?" Drake asked.

"Queen Felicia, Crown Prince Phillip, and both princesses are aboard my shuttle. I will be eternally in your debt if you will take them with you to Alta."

"Of course," Drake replied. "They can space in *City of Alexandria*."

Duke Bardak's expression betrayed his unhappiness. He chose his next words carefully. "I thank you, Fleet Captain, but I would be much happier if they traveled aboard *Discovery*. The cruiser is better able to defend itself in case of trouble."

Drake shook his head. "I'm afraid that won't be possible."

"But why? What possible difference can it make?"

"A large one," Drake replied. "*Discovery* isn't going home. When we leave orbit, it will be to engage the Ryall attack carriers at your side."

"WHAT?"

The explosion of sound came from both ambassadors simultaneously. Stan Barrett looked as though he was having a heart attack, and Alicia Delevan's eyes were threatening to bulge from her face.

"You can't do that, Richard!" Barrett said when he'd regained control over his speech. "You have a responsibility to Parliament to get this expedition home safely. We've learned far too much to risk our ships now."

"I have to agree, Captain Drake," Bardak replied. "As much as we need the help, there is very little one more ship will be able to do. It may well be hopeless."

"Damn it! Hopeless or not, we have to try," Drake growled. "Your planet is about to be pulverized, man! Hundreds of millions will die."

"At the risk of seeming callous," Barrett said, "they will die whether you make this gallant gesture or not. Our duty is to look after our own people. We need you to get us safely out of the system. Alta must be warned of the menace!"

"I *am* thinking of our people, Mr. Barrett. That Ryall fleet is going to detect two ships leaving Sandar for the Hellsgate–Napier foldpoint and three ships actually making the jump. Surely they know that Napier is a dead end. What if they decide to investigate where we've gone?"

"I say they won't. We are only three small ships and they have more important things to worry about."

"Then consider what happens if Sandar *is* destroyed! Much of the Sandarian fleet will survive, as will millions on the ground. Where do you think those refugees are going to go? How many ships do you think the Ryall are going to watch disappear into the Hellsgate–Napier foldpoint before they get suspicious?

"No, Mr. Barrett. If the Sandarians lose this battle,

the Ryall will find Alta soon enough. Our only choice to keep our secret is to defeat them here and now."

Drake watched as realization dawned on Barrett's features. The ambassador went from angry, to perplexed, to horrified in a matter of seconds. He looked at Drake. When he spoke, it was in a whisper so soft as to be barely discernible. "All right, you win! We must stop them now if we are to avoid having a Ryall fleet on our own necks."

Drake turned to stare at Alicia Delevan. "Madam Ambassador?"

She stared back with hard eyes. Finally, she said, "I'd say that you just threw our mission orders out the airlock, Richard."

He shrugged. "I don't see any other way out."

"Neither do I. However, I also say that it is time to forget Paragraph seven as well!"

Drake blinked, nodded, and turned to Bardak. "You said earlier that the time for political games was past, Commodore. That being the case, there is something we would like to ask you..." He then described in detail the events that had followed *Conqueror*'s arrival in the Val system. When he finished, it was Bardak's turn to wear a shocked expression on his face.

"And you thought this derelict blastship came from *this* system?"

"Where else? It certainly didn't come from New Providence."

"Captain Drake. There has not been an Earth starship in this system in more than fifteen years. Believe me, we would have noticed!"

CHAPTER 24

"Attention, all civilian personnel! Report to the hangar bay immediately! Repeat, all civilian personnel to the boats. You have ten minutes!"

Richard Drake glanced up as the last echoes of the evacuation announcement died away. As he did so, his eyes surveyed the furious activity around him. Everywhere he looked, console operators were checking and rechecking their systems. Maintenance technicians hovered over them, ready to replace any module that tested marginal. Other crewmen were doing the same thing all over the ship. For the first time in the 150 years since its commissioning, *Discovery* was preparing for battle.

"All right," Drake ordered the bridge crew. "Let's wrap up the maintenance checks and prepare for space!"

His order started a new flurry of activity as maintenance technicians began replacing access panels and console operators began to bring their systems back online.

"Mr. Slater," Drake ordered.

"Yes, Captain."

"Give the order to cease maintenance checks and begin preparations for space."

"Aye aye, sir."

Bethany Lindquist was seated in her customary place in the observer's chair beside Drake. He listened to the communicator's announcement with half an ear as he resumed his efforts to convince her to join the other civilians onboard *City of Alexandria.*

"You haven't much time," he said.

Bethany shook her head petulantly and spoke through clenched teeth. "I'm sorry, Richard, but I'm not going. I'm a member of this crew, and when *Discovery* engages the Ryall fleet, I will be at my duty station."

"We don't need you at your duty station. We aren't going anywhere near a foldpoint. You're classified as nonessential personnel this trip."

"Oh?" she asked. "Then why don't I see you ordering the other nonessential personnel to *Alexandria*?"

"Would you go if I did?"

"No, Richard, I would not."

"I could have a couple of Marines escort you to the boat, you know."

"You could, but you won't!" She hesitated, then softened her tone and continued. "Look, darling, after we're married I'll be a good wife. I'll love, honor, and generally obey you. As of this moment, however, I'm a free citizen and I make my own choices. I am also a member of this crew, and I won't be discriminated against just because *Discovery* is going into danger. I appreciate your concern for my welfare. I really do. But I would think the captain of a ship about to do battle would have something better to do with his time than argue with me."

Drake threw up his hands. "Report to your duty station," he growled.

"Aye aye, sir!"

Drake watched as Bethany unbuckled her harness, lifted herself from the observer's chair, and lithely swam through the air to her console. He glanced down at his status screens to hide the sudden smile that came unbidden to his face. In spite of the emptiness that gripped his stomach at the thought of Bethany in danger, part of him was glad she was coming along.

"Captain," the chief communicator said in his ear.

"What is it, Mr. Slater?"

"Carl Aster wants to speak to you."

"Put him on."

Aster's face appeared on Drake's screen.

"Yes, Mr. Aster?"

"I just heard from Ambassador Delevan that Bethany plans to stay onboard, Captain."

Drake nodded. "I've tried to talk her out of it, but she won't listen."

"I'm not surprised," Aster replied. "I'd like to stay, too."

Drake's eyebrows lifted in an unspoken question.

"It isn't what you think. I'm not doing this to prove anything. At least, that isn't my main reason. I'm tired of being a mere manipulator of people, Captain. I want to do something important for a change. Destroying those attack carriers is important."

"I'm afraid there aren't any jobs onboard that you're trained for."

"I'll help with damage control or act as a message runner or assist in sick bay. Anything, Captain!"

"We're programmed for high gees all the way."

"I'll survive."

"All right. Ask the doctor if he needs help. If he says yes, report to the quartermaster for a billet assignment."

"Thank you. And, Captain..."

"Yes?"

"I hope you and Bethany are very happy together. I mean that sincerely."

Drake hesitated for a moment, not knowing quite how to respond. Finally, he said, "Why, thank you, Carl. I hope there are no hard feelings."

Aster shrugged. "I'll get over them."

"Report to the hospital. You've got"—Drake glanced at the chronometer— "less than four minutes to make the boat if Dr. Parsil doesn't want you."

"Aye aye, sir."

Drake sat in his command chair and listened to the quiet conversations on the ship's intercom. He was struck by the change he detected in the voices of individual crew-members. When he had first announced that they would be going out to fight the Ryall, there had been a spate of nervousness and graveyard humor. As the time for launch approached, however, anticipation and excitement seemed to be taking over.

He watched via *Discovery*'s internal video system as the landing boats were loaded. He saw Stan Barrett and Alicia Delevan board *Moliere* along with the Sandarian royal family and their retainers. He watched as a number of scientists were loaded onto a second boat. Then it came time for the boats to launch. The hangar bay was depressurized, the main hatch opened, and the boats disappeared out into space.

Fifteen minutes later, he received a signal from Captain Fallan that all passengers were aboard and *Alexandria* was ready to leave orbit.

"Got your clearances from Sandarian traffic control?"

"All clear, sir."

"Then you may boost when ready. Good luck. When you get to the foldpoint, tell Captain Lee that I commend him and his crew for their diligence."

"Aye aye, sir. Good luck to you as well."

"Thank you, Kenil."

Drake ordered a long-range view of the liner put on the main screen. He watched as the sparks of attitude control jets winked on and off and the liner's massive cylindrical hull began to turn slowly to line up with its launch vector. After a long wait, the liner's photon drive came alive at minimum power and *City of Alexandria* began to move away. Two minutes later, the dwindling star that was *Alexandria* brightened as Fallan brought the drive to full power. Shortly after that, Alexandria was little more than a bright star that hovered low over the limb of the ice-bound planet below.

Drake keyed for his executive officer. "Is combat control ready for launch, Mr. Marston?"

"Ready for launch, Captain."

"Chief Engineer?"

"Ready for launch, sir."

"Mr. Cristobal?"

"Course locked in, Captain. I'm updating every two minutes for a direct launch to join Commodore Bardak's squadron."

"Stand by. Mr. Slater, All Hands circuit, please."

"Yes, sir."

"Your attention, please! This is the captain speaking. We are about to launch to join up with Commodore Bardak's squadron. Immediately thereafter, the squadron will head for deep space at high boost to intercept the Ryall attack force as far from Sandar as possible.

"This will not be an easy voyage. We will be heavily outgunned. But our cause is far from hopeless. The battle will involve a single, high-speed pass in deep space. It will be the type of battle that gives a small, disciplined force a good opportunity to defeat a larger opponent if every man does his job and his duty. I know that each of you will do both. Now then, prepare for space and high gees. And good luck!"

Twenty-three hours out of Sandar, Bardak's Bastards dropped from three gravities' acceleration to one, to give the crews an hour's rest before engaging the Ryall strike force.

Bardak's forces numbered twenty: six long-range interceptors; one battle cruiser, *Discovery*; and a ragtag collection of ancient destroyers, long-range scouts, and two freighters. The freighters had been hastily converted to warships through the addition of jury-rigged fire-control systems and cargo holds filled with space-to-space missiles. In addition to the long-range craft, *Discovery* and Bardak's interceptors carried enough armed auxiliaries between them to nearly double the size of the fleet. Sandar had superior numbers—if not firepower.

Long-range observation had confirmed that the attack carriers were being escorted by two blastships, two heavy cruisers, and a single light cruiser. In theory, each of the blastships carried more firepower than all of Bardak's Bastards put together. In practice—and as Drake had told his crew—the contest would be much more even than the vast disparity in the megatons-per-second statistics of the two fleets would suggest.

In a classic battle, opposing space fleets intercept one another on similar (but slightly skewed) paths. Each side opens up with its long-range weapons as soon as the opponents are within range and continues to fire until their respective trajectories have taken the antagonists out of range once again.

In such a set-piece battle, the Ryall heavies would have made short work of the weaker Sandarian ships. Even *Discovery* could not survive long in the withering fire from a blastship. Luckily, the coming battle was not developing along anything approaching classical lines.

When they finally met midway between Sandar and the foldpoint, the two fleets would be traveling in diametrically opposite directions at a relative velocity of more than eight thousand kilometers per second. With a closing rate that was equivalent to 2.6 percent of the speed of light, the normal problems of fire control would be multiplied a thousandfold for both sides. From maximum range to closest approach would take but twenty-five seconds. Once the fleets interpenetrated, there would be a like period in which directed energy weapons could still be brought to bear on the swiftly receding enemy. Then the surviving ships of both fleets would pass out of range, and the battle would be done.

The Sandarian high command was hoping that Bardak's motley fleet of defenders could destroy all three attack carriers in a single pass. If the fleet failed, Sandar's planetary defense system would be overwhelmed and billions would die.

Recognizing the problems inherent in such a high closing speed, Commodore Bardak had split his forces into three groups and stationed each a quarter-million kilometers apart to maximize time on target. Each wave would come in range of the Ryall precisely six and a quarter seconds after the previous wave had penetrated the enemy formation (and while it still had nearly twenty seconds in which to harry them with laser fire and antimatter projectors).

The first wave consisted of half the interceptors, both converted freighters, and the interceptors' armed auxiliaries. The second wave included the three remaining interceptors, three overage destroyers, and, again, the interceptors' various armed auxiliary craft. Bardak had assigned *Discovery* to command the third, and final, wave of the attack. Her flock of escorts consisted of two destroyers, all the Sandarian long-range scouts, and the Altan cruiser's four armed scout boats.

"All Hands circuit, Mr. Slater."

"Aye aye, sir."

Drake keyed his intercom to life.

"Attention! This is the captain speaking. All hands, don your vacuum suits! Do so by turns. Leave no station unmanned."

Ten minutes after giving the order to suit up, Drake lifted a pressure helmet over his own head and snapped it into place. He tested his communications and listened to the hollow sound his voice made inside the helmet, before turning his attention briefly to events beyond the Ryall attack carriers.

Another battle was raging 40 million kilometers behind the main Ryall attack force. The Sandarian Third Fleet was fighting a running battle with Ryall blocking force, and had been doing so ever since both sides departed the Hellsgate–Aezer foldpoint. It had been a costly business for all concerned. After thirty hours of nonstop battle, the Ryall blocking force had been reduced from twenty-eight vessels to sixteen. The pursuing Third Fleet had lost eight. However, no Sandarian ship had yet succeeded in breaking through the blockers to engage the Ryall attack carriers.

"Everyone pressure-tight?" Drake asked the bridge crew. He waited for the chorus of acknowledgments to end, then said, "Get me the scouts, Mr. Slater."

"Aye aye, sir."

Lieutenant Hall's face appeared on his screen.

"Here we go again, Phillip."

"Yes, sir," the scout leader replied. "We're armed, fueled, and ready for fried lizard!"

"Very well, Lieutenant. Proceed to your place in the formation. You may launch when ready."

"Launching now, Captain."

Drake watched the scout boats lift from the hangar deck and, one by one, drop through the open hatch into the blackness beyond.

"Scouts report that they are away, Captain!"

"Very well. Are you there, Number One?"

"Here, Captain," Commander Marston reported from the Combat Control Center.

"Are you ready for battle?"

"Ready, sir."

"Very well. Seal all pressure-tight doors, arm all weapons, bring the computer to tactical mode. We're going in!"

"Two minutes to first contact!"

Commodore Bardak's announcement seemed as relaxed as if he were on a training cruise. Yet Bardak's flagship, *Vindicator*, was at the center of the first wave. On the main viewscreen, *Vindicator*'s green star was surrounded by icons representing the other ships of the first group. The green symbols moved inexorably toward a similar group of red symbols.

"First wave. Pre-position missiles, now!"

The boxlike symbols that represented the two converted freighters were suddenly surrounded by a cloud of yellow sparks. The Ryall fleet was still almost one million kilometers ahead of the first wave, far beyond effective missile range. Bardak's order involved dispersing all of the first wave's nuclear-tipped ordnance into space where they would wait for the Ryall attack force to come within range. It was essentially the same tactic that the Ryall planned for Sandar with their attack carriers. Even if the missiles found no targets, they would force the Ryall gunners to waste ordnance that might otherwise be directed against Sandarian ships.

The eight red symbols on *Discovery*'s main screen were quickly surrounded by missile markers of their own. Drake queried the computer and was not surprised to see that all of the Ryall missiles had come from the two blastships. It had been too much to hope that the enemy would waste the attack carrier's ordnance on Bardak's Bastards.

"Thirty seconds," Bardak said over the fleet circuit. "All crews, stand by. Twenty seconds ... ten ... five, four, three, two, one. Commence firing!"

One of Drake's auxiliary screens was suddenly alight with the violet flash of Ryall lasers and the white bursts of fusion warheads. He ignored the distraction. If he lived, he would watch the pyrotechnics on playback. A space battle is best comprehended in schematic form. The unleashed lightnings are pretty, but largely irrelevant. If the image has time to pass from eyes to brain, then the weapon has missed its target.

The main bridge viewscreen was alive with lines representing the contending forces. As Drake watched, a symbol representing a Sandarian interceptor winked out. Almost as quickly, one of the missile freighters was destroyed. An instant later, the second freighter followed it into oblivion. Suddenly, one of the Ryall icons disappeared from the screen; an enemy heavy cruiser had been destroyed.

Another Sandarian interceptor disappeared. Two armed scouts followed their parent a few seconds later. Then the first wave was in among the Ryall and the impossible happened. The attack carrier on the Ryall right flank exploded.

"My God!" an unidentified voice yelled over the intercom. "One of the scouts rammed the damned thing!"

"Stop that chatter!" Drake ordered.

As Drake watched, a single interceptor and two scouts began pouring ineffective laser and antimatter plasma fire into the Ryall fleet. The surviving interceptor was *Vindicator*.

The voice of the second-wave commander erupted from his helmet phones: "Second wave, launch missiles."

Once again the deadly swarm of tiny furies rushed forth from Bardak's Bastards, and once again an answering swarm jumped away from the Ryall escorts. The same symbols of battle and death appeared on the screen. The three interceptors of the second wave fixed themselves on one of the attack carriers and fired with every weapon at their disposal. Their escorts chose the second carrier and did the same.

This time the smaller ships began winking out of existence first. Apparently the loss of the attack carrier had taught the Ryall respect for their tiny opponents. One, two, then three were gone in an instant. One of the destroyers exploded. Another's marker began flashing to indicate that the ship had been disabled. Two seconds later, the damaged craft disappeared from the screen.

The interceptors continued to bore in. Their lasers flashed bright violet, while invisible beams of antimatter arced across space at nearly the speed of light. Millions of bits of metal were launched from electromagnetic cannons and sprayed wholesale into the paths of the oncoming Ryall. Their efforts were to no avail. When it came time for the second wave of Sandarian ships to penetrate the Ryall formation, there were no survivors left to do so. Fourteen ships and auxiliaries, and more than five hundred men and women, had been turned into expanding clouds of plasma.

As the last of the second wave was being beamed into vapor, Drake keyed the ship-to-ship circuit. "Third wave. All captains, report status!"

There was a quick flurry of voices as the fleet around

Discovery reported its willingness to engage in battle. The last to report in was Lieutenant Hall's *Catherine*.

"Watch yourself out there, Phillip."

"Will do, Captain. Give 'em hell!"

Drake licked dry lips inside his pressure helmet as he watched the Ryall close on his own wave of defenders. Just before the Ryall entered lethal range, he gave the order to launch missiles. *Discovery* bucked as salvo after salvo rushed away toward the Ryall fleet. A few seconds later, Bela Marston said over the intercom:

"All missiles launched, Captain."

"You have the conn, Mr. Marston," Drake replied. "Give them hell!"

"Aye aye, sir."

In truth, it was *Discovery*'s computer that was flying and fighting the ship. No human being could react even one-thousandth as quickly as was needed. But humans could observe trends and redirect strategy, which is what Marston's experts in the Combat Control Center were doing.

Drake watched the screen as the battle passed out of his control. For him, it was as though time had slowed down. Where before it had been a conflict of lightninglike thrust and parry, now the battle seemed suspended in syrup. *Discovery* fought on automatically while red and green icons moved toward each other on the screen. A third-wave defender disappeared. Drake noted with a pang that it had been one of *Discovery*'s armed scouts. The next ship to die was a Sandarian long-range scout. A fusion burst went off close enough abeam that light filled the outside screens and the radiation detector's chatter became a roar. Then Drake's pressure suit went rigid around him.

"We've been holed at Bulkhead Sixteen. Damage control responding. Emergency medical teams to Compartment Alpha-Twelve immediately," an emotionless voice said on the interphone. Drake glanced down at his status board. Red lights flashed across its face. As he did so, another voice screamed in his ears:

"We got one! We got one!"

Drake looked back at the screen. One of the attack carrier markers was fading swiftly from the screen. Drake suppressed a surge of joy and ordered all fire concentrated on the sole remaining attack carrier.

Even as the words left his mouth, he knew that he was too late. The opposing lines of ships were drawing too close together on the screen. The formations were about to interpenetrate and the third attack carrier was still unscathed!

Then, unbelievably, just as *Discovery* came abreast of the Ryall fleet, the last of the attack carriers exploded in a cloud of plasma. Two surviving Ryall blastships and two cruisers flashed past and were gone as though they had never been.

CHAPTER 25

"Accurs'd be he that first invented war."

—*Christopher Marlowe, from his play* Tamburlaine the Great, *1590.*

"Fondly do we hope, fervently do we pray, that this mighty scourge of war may speedily pass away."

—*Abraham Lincoln, Nineteenth-Century United States President, 1865.*

"In a war, whichever side may call itself victor, there are no winners, but all are losers."

—*Neville Chamberlain, Twentieth-Century British Prime Minister, 1938.*

"If everyone hates war so much, how come we have so damned many of them?"

—*John Semper Fife, Twenty-first-Century Philosopher, 2016.*

As he watched the symbols denoting the surviving Ryall blastships and cruisers pull away from those of *Discovery* and her escorts, Richard Drake felt that, for the first time, he truly understood the attraction that battle held for members of his species. Those thirty seconds in which *Discovery* had traded blows with the Ryall invaders had been the most frightening—and the most exciting—of his life.

The adrenaline that coursed through his veins had

sharpened his senses and slowed the apparent passage of time. The colors of the warning lights and viewscreen were suddenly brighter and more distinct; the reports issuing from his earphones, louder and more frenzied. His heart had beat a staccato rhythm from his temples to his toes, and the smell of old socks inside his vacuum suit had been displaced by the stink of his own fear.

As quickly as it had come, that fear had been turned into euphoria as he realized that he, his ship, and his crew had survived the battle. He suppressed an urge to yell for joy, and as he did so, he remembered something one of his academy professors had said regarding the aftermath of battle: "Young gentlemen, as a great and wise statesman once observed, 'Nothing in life is so exhilarating as to be shot at without result!'"

Drake placed a clamp on his emotions and let his eyes scan the bridge. His gaze sought out Bethany first, then the other crewmembers. He keyed the BRIDGE ONLY intercom circuit. "Everyone all right?"

He got back a chorus of acknowledgments. Then he turned to the intercom and his executive officer. "Are you still there, Number One?"

"Here, sir," Commander Marston reported from Combat Control.

"How did your people come through?"

"All safe, Captain. I'm afraid we lost *Drunkard* and *Gossamer Gnat*, though."

"I know," Drake replied. He'd seen both scouts disappear from the screen at the height of the battle. Eight good men had crewed those ships, including Scout Pilots Marman and Garth. They would be missed. "That was good shooting, Mr. Marston. Pass my compliments on to your people."

"Thank you, sir."

Drake keyed for Control Room No. 3. "Engineering."

"Here, sir," the reedy voice of the chief engineer responded.

"We're open to vacuum here on the bridge, Mr. Arnam. What can you do about it?"

"We've got a large gash in our hull near the bridge, Captain. I've got damage-control parties out patching it. We should have you pressurized in a few minutes."

"What other damage have we suffered?"

"Our cryogen tanks have been cut to ribbons, sir. I've ordered all ruptured tanks pumped into four and six."

"How much fuel have we lost?"

"About half so far. We'll lose another five percent before the transfer is complete."

"Any problems with the engines?"

"Negative, sir. We've got full power if you need it."

"Right. Have your people hurry on the damage survey. We may have to go to high gees at any time."

"Aye aye, sir."

"Mr. Slater."

"Yes, Captain."

"Get me Commodore Bardak."

"Will do, Captain."

Drake's screen lit to show the features of the Sandarian nobleman. Bardak's face was enclosed by a vacuum helmet just as Drake's was. Bardak's stiffened suit indicated that he too was in vacuum.

"We did it, Commodore!" Drake reported.

"Tell me about it, Captain," Bardak replied. "One of those blastships raked us as we interpenetrated. All my aft sensors are gone. I'm blind back there."

Drake quickly reported the results of the second and third wave attacks against the Ryall, including the destruction of the attack carriers and the loss of 80 percent of Bardak's Bastards. The commodore took the news without emotion.

When Drake finished, Bardak gave a sharp nod and said, "Any suggestions before we are intercepted by the Ryall blocking force?"

Drake looked at the situation screen. On it, the Ryall attack force continued to distance itself from *Discovery* and *Vindicator*, but the second group of Ryall ships was coming up fast on a collision course. The two clusters of ships would close the 40-million-kilometer gap between them in less than an hour.

"*Discovery* is in no shape to conduct another attack, Commodore. I'm low on missiles and have been holed in more places that I can count."

"*Vindicator* isn't any better," Bardak replied. "What say we dodge them?"

"Yes, sir."

"Very well, turn your ship due galactic north and accelerate at"—Bardak turned away from the camera pickup, performed a rough calculation, and said— "two gravities for forty minutes. That should get us out of their path."

"Yes, sir."

"*Vindicator* out."

"*Discovery* out," Drake replied before turning to the astrogator. "Do we have enough fuel to sidestep the Ryall and then get back to Sandar under our own power, Argos?"

"No, sir," Cristobal replied. "We've lost too much."

"What's the best you can do?"

Cristobal turned to his console and keyed in several figures. After a moment, he swiveled in his seat and said, "We've enough fuel to return to Sandar if we use a Hohmann transfer orbit."

"How long a coast period are you talking about?"

"Six months, Captain."

"Too long," Drake replied.

"There's another alternative, sir. We're headed directly for the foldpoint. Why don't we rendezvous with the orbital fortresses there?"

"It's a good idea, Astrogator. I should have thought of it myself. Now then, turn the ship due galactic north and increase thrust to two gravities."

"Galactic north, and two gravs. Aye aye, sir."

Sixty minutes later, Drake watched the Ryall blocking force slip past *Discovery* at a safe distance. The Ryall ships were still closely pursued by the Third Fleet. When

they had passed, Drake ordered Cristobal to turn the ship
and begin decelerating along the orbit that would end in
their rendezvous with the foldpoint fortresses.

Two hours after that, he once again found himself seated
in his command chair with all his attention focused on
the main viewscreen. Instead of a tactical display, however, the screen showed a long-range telescopic view of
Sandar, which looked like a white billiard ball with a green
stripe around its middle. Drake alternated between watching the planet and checking the chronometer as the now-
familiar tension built within him.

The four surviving ships of the Ryall attack force had
continued their approach to Sandar, taking only three hours
to cross the same distance that had taken the small Sandarian fleet twenty-four hours to transit outbound.

"What are their chances?" Drake asked, his question
apparently addressed to thin air.

"Not good," his executive officer's voice replied in his
ear. "The PDCs should be able to stop anything they have
left. Of course, the Ryall could get lucky the way we did."

Drake nodded but did not speak. The countdown clock
showed thirty seconds until the centaurs' ships drew within
range of the planet. He licked dry lips and waited.

After an interminable time, Sandar exploded in a fire-
storm of violet-white light.

Richard Drake sat in his cabin, gazed at the orbital
fortress centered on his workscreen, and pondered the
events of the last few weeks. The great sphere was vastly
more powerful than the largest spaceship ever built, easily
the equal of ten blastships. Within its depths dwelt engines
of destruction undreamed of by earlier generations. Yet,
as powerful as it was, the fortress and its fifty-odd brethren had been unable to halt the Ryall thrust by themselves.
They had done their part, as had many strong ships and
brave men. But it had still taken the power of an entire
planet to finally bring the danger to an end.

The surviving Ryall ships had attacked bravely, but

without their attack carriers to saturate the defense, they had been hopelessly outgunned. One by one, the Ryall warships had glowed red and then slumped into boiling slag as the planetary defense centers burned through their antilaser armor and into the steel decks beneath. The battle between planet and warships had been a lopsided contest that was over thirty seconds after it began.

One hour later, the surviving vessels of the Ryall blocking force had arrived on the scene. They numbered only ten as they entered the planetary defense zone. Once again Sandar seemed to explode in violet-white light as the planetary defense centers opened up with their heavy fixed-mount lasers. Once again orbital defense satellites and fortresses on Sandar's moons joined the battle with beams of antimatter plasma. Once again the Ryall fleet was overpowered and destroyed in less than a minute.

After the battle, John-Phillip had signaled all ships his congratulations and had sent a message thanking Drake personally for *Discovery*'s efforts. Along with the message had come an invitation for the Altans to return to Sandar to continue diplomatic discussions. Drake had declined as politely as he could and informed the king that his ship would be leaving for home as soon as the worst of its battle damage was repaired.

Ten days later, Chief Engineer Arnam informed Drake that *Discovery* was ready for space. Drake wasted no time in requesting permission to leave the foldpoint defense globe and proceed to the waiting *City of Alexandria* and *Sultana* at the Hellsgate–Napier foldpoint. As he had done once before, Bardak asked Drake to delay his departure for a few hours in order that the two of them could meet aboard the cruiser for discussions of "important matters."

Drake's reverie was interrupted by the buzz of the door annunciator. He yelled his permission to enter. The cabin door opened and Bethany Lindquist stepped over the high coaming.

"Duke Bardak's ship is on final approach, Richard. You wanted to be notified."

"I wonder what the holdup is this time," he mused.

"I'm sure he'll tell us," she replied.

When they arrived at the boat bay, the boat from *Vindicator* was already in the docking cradle and the bay was being repressurized. A double row of Marines stood to attention.

"Welcome, Admiral," Drake said, noting the shiny new comets on his Sandarian visitor's collar.

Bardak reached out and grasped Drake's hand. A broad grin crossed his face as his naked pate reflected the glow of the overhead polyarcs. "I always seem to be delaying your departure for home, Richard."

"I hope this delay won't be as exciting as the last one."

"I assure you that it will not." Bardak turned to Bethany. "Have you two set a date for your marriage yet, milady?"

Bethany reddened slightly as she shook her head. "I still have my obligation to my uncle. Marriage will have to wait."

"Don't delay too long," Bardak warned. "If we Sandarians have learned anything from this war, it is to take our happiness while we can."

Bethany slipped her arm under Drake's and snuggled close. "Thanks for the advice, Admiral. We'll try to follow it."

"Good for you!" Bardak turned his attention to Drake and said formally, "I come as an offical emissary of my government, Fleet Captain. Where can we meet?"

"The wardroom?" Drake asked.

"Excellent."

When the three of them were strapped into seats in the wardroom, Bardak opened the briefcase he carried and took out a series of official-looking papers. "These are telecopies, of course. The originals will be sent out to *Alexandria* on the ship that has been dispatched to retrieve the royal family. You will find a draft treaty of cooperation between our two systems, several trade protocols, and a personal message from my king to your Parliament.

"Also included in this packet is a comprehensive record of everything we have learned of the Ryall in a century of war. You may also inform your Parliament that they can expect a diplomatic delegation to arrive in the Valeria system sometime within one hundred days of your return. We will send a ship as soon as we have repaired some of the damage to our defenses caused by this latest attack."

Drake took the papers and the record tiles. "We'll be watching for you."

"Good luck on your homeward journey. I only wish I could have helped you with your mission as well as you helped me with mine."

"Beg your pardon?" Drake asked.

"The matter of this derelict Earth blastship," Bardak replied. "I only wish we could have told you how it came to be in your system."

"Don't worry about it," Drake replied. "*Conqueror* had to come from somewhere. We merely need to figure out from where..." The words gurgled to a halt as Drake's mouth fell open.

"What's the matter, Richard?" Bethany asked.

"I just had the strangest thought," he said. "I think I may have just solved the mystery of *Conqueror*'s origin!"

"Where did it come from, then?"

"Wait a minute," Drake said, getting up from the table. He moved to the holoscreen on the far bulkhead and called up a foldspace diagram. After a dozen seconds of leafing through various frames, he found the one he was looking for. It was a three-dimensional map showing the foldspace interconnections among the Val, Napier, Hellsgate, and Antares star systems.

The Val system was readily identified because it was the only system with a single foldpoint (Val–Napier). Hellsgate was next, with two (Hellsgate–Aezer, Hellsgate–Napier); followed by Napier with its three foldpoints (Napier–Antares, Napier–Hellsgate, and Napier–Valeria). Finally, there was Antares with its six prenova foldpoints. Drake stared at the diagram for long seconds before continuing.

"I just realized that we overlooked something back at New Providence. We know that *Conqueror* entered the Val system from the Napier system. So, when we found New Providence deserted, we naturally concluded that *Conqueror* had to enter the Napier system from Hellsgate. Yet you say it isn't so, Admiral Bardak."

"It isn't," Bardak responded.

"I believe you," Drake said, gesturing toward the hologram on the screen. "Can you see our mistake?"

"Frankly, no," Bardak replied.

"Neither can I," Bethany replied. "We've eliminated all of the foldpoints in the Napier system as candidates."

"Not *all*," Drake said. He pointed at the foldpoint on the screen labeled NAPIER–ANTARES.

"But that's impossible!" Bethany exclaimed.

"Why?"

"Because that foldpoint leads directly into the heart of the Antares Nebula!"

"Yes, it does."

"I remember someone chastising me for getting caught by nebula-rise on New Providence, Richard. Do you?"

He grinned. "I seem to remember something about that."

"If the radiation was so dangerous on New Providence, fifteen light-years from the nebula, *what must it be like in the nebula itself*?"

"It's fierce," Drake replied. "Nevertheless, *Conqueror* successfully passed through the Antares Nebula on its way to our system. I can prove it."

"How?"

"First by the condition of the bodies we found. Several were in pressurized compartments that still contained oxygen, yet there was no evidence of physical decay. The ship had been sterilized by radiation. Furthermore, we found the computers had all been radiation wiped, all except those designed specifically to be radiation resistant. Even those were suffering. We thought at the time that we were seeing evidence that *Conqueror* had taken a nuclear burst close-in. We were wrong. What we saw was the result of the blastship having penetrated the Antares Nebula."

Bardak frowned. "If you are right, Captain, then knowing *Conqueror*'s route to the Val system is totally useless. It's a pathway that can only be traveled by a damaged ship and a dead crew!"

"Not necessarily. We have antiradiation fields. In theory, they could be improved to the point where they would protect a ship and crew inside the nebula."

"I wouldn't want to bet my life on it," Bardak replied.

"How many times have you Sandarians tried to run the Ryall blockade in the Aezer system?" Drake asked.

"Three."

"And how successful have you been?"

"You know damned well how successful we've been," Bardak growled.

"Sandar and Alta are cut off from the rest of human space," Drake said. "How long do you think two backwater colonies can hold off the might of the Ryall hegemony alone?"

"Unless we get some help, we'll be overrun in another fifty years," Bardak replied. "Make your point."

"That is my point. We *have* to get help from Earth. Obviously, either we break out through the Aezer system, or else we brave the nebula. If there is a third choice, I fail to see it."

Discovery rode through the Napier system on a jet of pure light. She was followed closely by *City of Alexandria* and *Sultana* as the fleet transited from one foldpoint to another. Napier–Hellsgate was two days astern while Napier–Valeria was still eight days in the future. As the three ships sliced across the system in a flat hyperbolic orbit, the scientists and naval personnel occupied themselves in gathering all the data they could on the Antares Nebula.

Drake sat in his command chair on *Discovery*'s bridge and gazed at the image of the nebula on the main viewscreen. It was night watch and the overhead lights had been turned down to a dim blue. His eyes scanned the great ball of light, moving impatiently from the hellishly bright star at the center to the milky-white ring of gas at the rim. At first glance the nebula seemed featureless, save for the general shading of colors from ring to central star. But hours spent in careful observation revealed swirls and currents of gossamer gas. With practice it was possible to perceive the nebula as a three-dimensional phantom hovering in the eternal night of space.

"Beautiful, isn't it?"

Drake turned at the sound of the voice to find Bethany standing beside him. "What are you doing up at this time of night?"

"I couldn't sleep," she said. "I thought I'd watch the nebula. What's your excuse?"

"The same," he replied. He turned and looked at the viewscreen again. After a moment, he shivered. "I've been having second thoughts."

"About what?" she asked.

"About diving into that damned thing! I'd forgotten just how *big* it is! I must have been suffering from an attack of megalomania to even suggest it."

"More likely an attack of inspiration," she replied.

"Then you believe we can do it?" he asked.

"I *have* to believe it," she replied. "Earth is beyond Antares and I promised my uncle that I'd take his dispatches to Earth."

He reached up and stroked her cheek. "Are you always so stubborn, woman?"

"Always!"

"I can tell I'm going to have my hands full when we're married."

She laughed. "Not if you always let me have my own way, you won't."

Drake smiled. "I've been thinking what Parliament will do when I tell them that the only way to save ourselves from the Ryall is to build a fleet of ships to dive into the remains of an exploded star!"

"They'll do what they always do in a crisis," Bethany replied. "First they'll scream, evade the question, and think up a thousand reasons why they should just ignore the problem until it goes away. Then they'll settle down, accept the challenge, and do what has to be done. That's the human way."

"I hope you're right."

"Of course, I'm right," she said, sliding into the observer's chair beside him. The two of them watched the screen without speaking for a long time. Finally, Drake broke the silence. "Do you remember how excited you were when you first learned that the foldpoint was open again?"

She nodded. "I heard it on the news coming home from work one day. I remember thinking about how great it would be to get out among the stars again."

"Would you have thought that if you had known about the Ryall? What I mean is, if you had a choice, would you want the foldpoint open or closed?"

"I'd want it open, of course."

"Why?"

"Because I believe that human beings weren't meant to be cooped up in a single star system. If the opening of the foldpoint has given us the Ryall, it has also given us the freedom of the stars once again. We'll beat the Ryall, Richard. Either that or our children will. We'll beat them because we're tougher than they are, and smarter, and more determined. We're human beings. We're winners. It's built into us. We haven't any choice in the matter."

"In other words," Drake said with a smile, "I should

stop worrying and start planning on how I'm going to get a fleet through the Antares Nebula."

"Damned right! Since when did *Homo sapiens* ever let a little thing like a supernova stand in its way?"

ABOUT THE AUTHOR

Michael McCollum was born in Phoenix, Arizona, in 1946 and is a graduate of Arizona State University, where he majored in aerospace propulsion and minored in nuclear engineering. He has been employed as an aerospace engineer since graduation and has worked on nearly every military and civilian aircraft in production today. At various times in his career, Mr. McCollum has also worked on the precursor to the Space Shuttle Main Engine, a nuclear valve to replace the one that failed at Three Mile Island, and a variety of guided missiles.

He began writing in 1974 and has been a regular contributor to *Analog Science Fiction*. He has also appeared in *Isaac Asimov's* and *Amazing*. *Antares Dawn* is his fourth novel for Del Rey.

He is married to a lovely lady by the name of Catherine and is the father of three children: Robert, Michael, and Elizabeth.